FROM A CASINO
IN LISBON

where a beautiful woman gambled for her lover against the most infamous agent of the Third Reich

TO A THIEVES' DEN
IN MARSEILLES

where sex, gold and violence conspired to carve out a vast underworld empire

TO A LUXURY HOTEL
IN PARIS

where a man wearing the most prestigious uniform of Hitler's Germany issued an order that turned the war around

TO A GREAT MODERN
SWISS BANK

where a mysterious international financier made a huge deposit, and began collecting his interest in the most diabolical vengeance that hate ever hatched

MONTE CRISTO COVER-UP

All the masks come off in a powerful, pounding thriller guaranteed to stretch you taut and leave you limp!

Also by Johannes Mario Simmel and available from Popular Library:

THE CAESAR CODE
THE CAIN CONSPIRACY

THE MONTE CRISTO COVER-UP

SIMMEL

The fabulously daring adventures and exquisite cooking recipes of the involuntary secret agent Thomas Lieven. . . .

Told by Johannes Mario Simmel

Translated from the German by James Cleugh

(Original Title: IT CAN'T ALWAYS BE CAVIAR)

POPULAR LIBRARY • NEW YORK

POPULAR LIBRARY EDITION
February, 1977

Original edition in German language was published by Schwéizer Verlagshaus, Zurich
Library of Congress Catalog Card Number: 65-10626

Published by arrangement with Schweizer Verlagshaus A.G.

ISBN: 0-445-08563-0

This novel is based on first-hand information. Names and characters are wholly imaginary. Any similarity of the names to those of living or dead persons can only be accidental.

Original Title: IT CAN'T ALWAYS BE CAVIAR

PRINTED IN THE UNITED STATES OF AMERICA

PROLOGUE

[1]

"We Germans, my dear Kitty, can produce an economic miracle but not a salad," said Thomas Lieven to the black-haired girl with the attractive figure.

"Yes, sir," said Kitty. She spoke rather breathlessly, for she was terribly in love with her fascinating employer. She gazed with loving eyes at Thomas Lieven as he stood beside her in the kitchen.

Thomas Lieven wore a cook's apron over his dinner jacket, which was midnight blue, with narrow lapels. He was holding a napkin. The napkin contained the delicate leaves from two most beautiful lettuces.

What a man, thought Kitty. Her eyes were shining. One of the chief reasons why the girl so adored her employer, the master of this many-roomed villa, was that he clearly felt quite at home in her own realm, the kitchen.

"The correct preparation of salads is almost a lost art," said Thomas Lieven. "In central Germany they're sweet and taste like stale pastry, in the south they're sour, like rabbits' food, and in the north the women actually use salad oil. Shades of Lucullus!"

"Yes, sir," said Kitty, still breathless. Church bells began to ring in the distance. It was seven o'clock in the evening of April 11, 1957.

April 11, 1957, seemed a day like any other. But it was not so for Thomas Lieven. That day he meant to be done forever with a wild and lawless past.

On that April day in 1957, Thomas Lieven, just forty-eight years old, was occupying a rented villa in the best part of the Cecilien Allee at Düsseldorf. He possessed a substantial balance at the Rhine Main Bank and a German sports car de luxe which had cost thirty-two thousand marks.

He was extraordinarily well-preserved for his age, of slim

build, tall and bronzed, with shrewd, rather melancholy eyes and a sensitive mouth in his lean face; he had close-cropped black hair, going a little gray at the temples.

Thomas Lieven was unmarried. His neighbors thought him a quiet, well-behaved fellow and a good, patriotic businessman. But they found it a bit disappointing that so little was really known about him.

"My dear Kitty," said Thomas Lieven. "You're young and pretty and I'm sure you've still a lot to learn. Would you like me to teach you?"

"Oh yes, please," she whispered, more breathlessly than ever.

"Good. Then I'll give you a recipe for making lettuces appetizing. What have we done so far?"

She curtsied. "Two hours ago, sir, we washed two middle-sized lettuces. Then we took out the tenderest stems and leaves only . . ."

"And what did you do with those leaves?" he went on, in a searching tone.

"We wrapped them in a napkin and tied the four ends of the napkin together. Then you shook it, sir—"

"Swung it, my dear Kitty, not shook it. That was to get rid of the last drops of liquid. It's extremely important for the leaves to be absolutely dry. Well, now we'll see about the sauce. I want a glass bowl, please, and a salad fork and spoon."

Kitty accidentally touched the long, slender hand of her employer, shuddering delightedly as she did so.

What a man, she thought.

Innumerable other people who had met Thomas Lieven in the past had also thought, What a man! The sort of people they were may be guessed from considering what Thomas Lieven loved and what he hated.

Thomas Lieven loved beautiful women, smart clothes, antique furniture, fast cars, good books, civilized meals and common sense.

Thomas Lieven hated uniforms, politicians, war, unreasonableness, force of arms, lies, bad manners and insensitivity.

Once upon a time Thomas Lieven had been the pattern of a respectable citizen, detesting intrigue and devoted to a life of security, peace and comfort.

But a strange fate, the details of which will be narrated later, uprooted this placid personage from the even tenor of his career.

That orderly citizen Thomas Lieven found himself obliged to take steps as violent as they were grotesque in order to hoodwink the German Intelligence Service and Gestapo, the British secret service, the French Deuxième Bureau, the American Federal Bureau of Investigation and the Soviet state security service.

That orderly citizen Thomas Lieven found himself obliged to use sixteen forged passports of nine countries during five years of war and twelve of the postwar period.

During the war he caused endless confusion in both German and Allied headquarters, though he hated doing it.

After the war he had thought for a short time, as probably we all did, that the madness in which and on which he had lived was over.

What a mistake!

The gentlemen behind the scenes kept on after Thomas Lieven. But he revenged himself on his tormentors. He fleeced the Occupation profiteers, the currency reform hyenas and the new rich of the Economic Miracle.

The Iron Curtain did not exist for Thomas Lieven. He schemed and traveled in both East and West. Officials trembled before him.

Deputies of several provincial Governments and members of the Bonn Parliament are still trembling. For Thomas Lieven is alive today and he knows a lot about speculative finance, housing deals and the new German federal army contracts.

His name is not, of course, Thomas Lieven.

We shall be forgiven, in the circumstances, for changing both his name and his address. But the story of this once peaceful citizen, who still loves cooking and who involuntarily became one of the most daring adventurers of his day, is true.

We begin it on the evening of April 11, 1957, at the historic moment when Thomas Lieven was lecturing on the preparation of lettuces.

Let us go back, then, to the kitchen in his villa.

"Never let a salad come in contact with metal," said Thomas Lieven.

Kitty gazed as though hypnotized at her employer's slender hands and listened to his instructions with continually renewed excitement.

"For the sauce," said Thomas Lieven, "we need a pinch of pepper, a pinch of salt and a teaspoonful of strong mustard. We add a hard-boiled egg, sliced small. Then plenty of parsley and even more chives. Four tablespoonfuls of genuine Italian olive oil. The oil please, Kitty!"

With a blush, Kitty handed him the desired article.

"Four spoonfuls of that, as I said. And now a cup of cream, sweet or sour according to taste. I'll settle for sour—"

At that moment the kitchen door opened and a giant entered. He wore pin-striped trousers, a jacket striped blue and white, a white shirt and a white tie. Without his upright thatch of hair he would have resembled a second, excessively large, edition of Yul Brynner.

"What is it, Bastian?" asked Thomas Lieven.

The manservant answered in a slightly drawling French accent: "Herr Direktor Schallenberg has arrived."

"On the dot, eh?" Thomas commented. "That's the kind of man I can work with."

He slipped off his apron. "Then we eat in ten minutes. Bastian will serve. You, my dear, can have the evening off."

While Thomas Lieven washed his hands in the black-tiled bathroom, Bastian gave his master's dinner jacket another brushing.

MENU

Lady Curzon Soup
Paprika Chicken
Clara Salad
Rice
Apple Hedgehog with Wine Custard
Toast and Cheese
11 APRIL 1957

This dinner brought in 717,850 Swiss francs.

Lady Curzon Soup

Lady Curzon, wife of the former Viceroy of India and an excellent cook prepared her turtle soup with the forepaws of the animal, which are its most delicate parts. Her seasoning comprised tarragon, thyme, ginger, nutmeg, cloves, and curry. A glass of sherry is added if possible also turtles' eggs and giblets. A less complicated proceeding would be to buy turtle soup ready-made in a tin. But in that case a good mouthful of sherry and a cupful of cream are also essential.

Paprika Chicken

A tender fowl is fried in the usual way with butter but not allowed to get too brown. Four or six portions, according to the size of the bird, are kept warm. Meanwhile an onion chopped very fine and a teaspoonful of paprika are braised in the butter used, and the mixture is then brought to a boil with a little water or stock. Plenty of thick sour cream is next added, mixed with a little corn flour and seasoned to taste with salt and more paprika if desired. Tomato purée may be added for further reddening of the sauce, but not enough to give it a strong tomato flavor. The portions of chicken are then laid in the sauce and allowed to steep for a few minutes before serving.

Rice

Rice has a constant tendency to get sticky. The remedy is quite simple. After being well washed it should be boiled in any quantity of water for ten to fifteen minutes. It is then transferred to a strainer and rinsed under the cold-water tap. This gets rid of the starch. Shortly before serving, the rice is warmed, still in the strainer, over steam, and then placed in a dish where butter, salt and if desired curry, saffron and pepper to taste are added prior to serving.

Apple Hedgehog with Wine Custard

Ripe apples of equal size are peeled, slowly simmered in vanilla-flavored syrup and before they disintegrate removed to a strainer to drain. Meanwhile almonds are blanched, cut into strips, put on a baking sheet and well roasted. As soon as the apples are properly drained they are drenched with a liqueur, rum or cognac, speared with the cut almonds and placed on a dish. For the custard the yolks of two eggs are mixed till foamy with half a cup of sugar, two tablespoons of cornstarch, half a cup of water and a cup of white wine. The mixture is then stirred over a small flame until thick. The whites of the eggs are beaten until stiff and folded into the mixture, being flavored if desired with rum, arrack, cognac or similar spirits.

Toast and Cheese

Slices of white bread are thickly buttered in the middle. Gruyère or Dutch cheese is spread on the butter. The slices are then dried for five minutes on a baking tin in a section of the stove well warmed beforehand, till they are golden-yellow, and served quite hot.

"Well, what's the Herr Direktor look like?" asked Thomas Lieven.

"Usual sort," answered the giant. "Plenty of flesh on him. Bull neck and beer belly. Regular provincial type."

"Doesn't sound too repulsive."

"Couple of dueling scars too."

"All right. I take it back." Thomas slipped on his dinner jacket. Then he noticed something. He said in a disapproving tone: "Bastian, you've been at my cognac again."

"Just a snifter. I was a bit excited."

"You cut that out. If one of those awkward things happens, I shall need you wide-awake. You won't be able to handle the Herr Direktor if you're stewed."

"I could handle that fat slug if I were seeing pink elephants!"

"Shut up. You're quite clear about the bell signals?"

"Sure."

"Repeat what I told you."

"One ring, next course. Two rings, photostats. Three rings, sandbag."

"I'd be grateful," said Thomas Lieven, filing away at his nails, "if you could possibly avoid getting then mixed up."

[2]

"That soup was excellent," said Schallenberg, the Director, leaning back and dabbing his thin lips with a damask napkin.

"Lady Curzon," said Thomas. He pressed a button under the table top, once.

"Lady how much?"

"Curzon. That's what the soup's called. It's turtle, with sherry and cream."

"Ah yes, of course."

The flames of the candles standing on the table suddenly flickered. Bastian had entered noiselessly with the paprika chicken.

The candle flames steadied. Their warm yellow light fell on the dark blue carpet, the wide Old Flemish table, the comfortable wooden chairs with their cane backs and the big Old Flemish sideboard.

The chicken also delighted Herr Schallenberg. "Delicate, there's no other word for it. Really charming of you to invite me, Herr Lieven, when after all you only wanted to speak to me on business . . ."

"One can always talk business better over a good meal, Herr Direktor. Take some more rice, it's right there in front of you."

"No, thanks. May I ask what it was you wished to discuss with me, Herr Lieven?"

"A little more salad?"

"No, thanks, really. Please go ahead."

"Right," said Thomas. "Herr Direktor, you have a big paper mill."

"That's correct, yes. Two hundred employees. Whole thing built up again out of rack and ruin."

"Congratulations. Your health—" Thomas Lieven raised his glass.

"And your next point?"

"Herr Direktor, I'm told that you manufacture a particularly fine type of watermarked paper?"

"I do."

"You supply it for, among other purposes, the new share certificates which the German Steel Union is now putting on the market?"

"Correct. And I can tell you, they give us a lot of trouble, those G.S.U. people with their perpetual inspections to make sure that none of my staff get around to printing a few certificates for their own benefit, ha, ha!"

"Ha, ha! Herr Direktor, I should like to order from you fifty full-sized sheets of that watermarked paper."

"You'd like to—*what*?"

"Order fifty full-sized sheets. As head of the firm it ought not to be very difficult for you to dodge those inspections."

"But what on earth do you want the sheets for?"

"To print G.S.U. certificates of course. Why did you think I wanted them?"

The Director folded his napkin. He glanced, not without regret, at his still half-full plate. Then he announced: "I fear I must be going."

"Oh, I can't allow that! There's still the apple hedgehog and the toast and cheese to come!"

The Director rose. "Sir, I shall forget I was ever here."

"I doubt if you ever will," said Thomas, helping himself generously to more rice. "What are you standing up for, my dear Director of Organization for Total War? Do please sit down."

Schallenberg's face turned dark red. He said in a low tone: "What was that?"

"Sit down, please. Your chicken's getting cold."

"Did you say Director of Organization for Total War?"

"Yes. That was your job, you know, even if you forgot all about it in 1945, when you filled in your questionnaire for instance. There was no point in reminding people of it then, when you had fixed yourself up with brand-new papers and a new name. When you were in the Total War Organization you were known as Mack."

"You're crazy."

"Not at all. You were Director of Organization for Total War in the Warthegau district. You're still on one of the Polish Governments extradition lists. As Mack of course, not Schallenberg."

The Director dropped into his Old Flemish chair with the cane back. He dabbed his forehead with the damask napkin and murmured feebly: "I really don't know why I should listen to all this."

Thomas Lieven sighed. "My dear Herr Direktor, I too have had a rather troubled past which I should like to get rid of. That's why I need your paper. It would take too long to counterfeit it. On the other hand I have reliable printers at my disposal. . . . But aren't you feeling well? Take a sip of champagne, that'll cheer you up. . . . Now, as I was going to say, in those days, just after the war, I had access to all sorts of secret files. You had just gone underground at Miesbach . . ."

"Liar!"

"Oh, excuse me, I meant Rosenheim. At the Lindenhof there."

This time the Director only lifted his hand weakly.

"I knew you were in hiding there. I was in a position to have had you arrested. But I thought to myself, What's the use of that? He'll simply be locked up and then extradited. But—" Thomas chewed, with relish, a portion of chicken leg. "But, I said to myself, if you just leave him quietly in peace, then in a few years he'll come floating to the top again. That sort never goes under. It always comes up again."

"Impudence!" croaked the voice from the cane chair.

"Then he'll be much more use to you, I said to myself. I acted accordingly. And look how well it's turned out."

Schallenberg, with an effort, stood up again. "I'm going straight to the police to report you."

"There's a telephone in the next room." Thomas pressed the bell push under the table, twice.

Once more the candle flames flickered as the manservant Bastian silently entered. He was carrying a silver tray with a number of photostats on it.

"I think you'd be interested to glance through those, Herr Direktor," said Thomas. "They include photographs of you in uniform, Herr Direktor, and a number of decrees you signed between 1941 and 1944. There's also a receipt by the so-called National Socialist Treasury Comptroller for a contribution of one hundred thousand marks for SA and SS expenses."

Schallenberg sat down again.

"You can clear away, Bastian. The Herr Direktor has finished."

"Very good, sir."

After Bastian had gone Thomas said: "Apart from that you cleared a cool fifty thousand on the job. Proof enough?"

"I'm not standing for blackmail!"

"Didn't you also spend an awful lot during the last election, Herr Direktor? Let me see. What's the name of that German news magazine that takes such an interest in such things?"

"You must be mad! Wanting to print false certificates! You'll be locked up! And so shall I, with you! I'll be ruined if I give you that paper!"

"I shan't be locked up. And you'll only be ruined if you *don't* give me that paper, Herr Direktor." Thomas pressed the bell push once. "Wait and see how good that apple hedgehog is going to taste."

"I'm not going to swallow another mouthful in this house, you blackmailer!"

"How soon can I count on receiving the paper, then, Herr Direktor?"

"Never!" yelled Schallenberg, beside himself with fury. "You'll never get one single sheet out of me!"

[3]

It was almost midnight. Thomas Lieven sat with his servant Bastian before a flickering open fire in the big library. The red, gold, blue, white, yellow and green backs of hundreds of books glimmered in the half-dark. The strains of the Second Piano Concerto of Rachmaninoff sounded softly from a record player.

Thomas Lieven still wore his immaculate dinner suit. Bastian had unbuttoned his shirt collar and put his feet up on a chair, though he had first, with a side glance at his master, placed a newspaper on it.

"Schallenberg will be delivering the paper in a week's time," said Thomas Lieven. "How long will your friends be over the printing?"

"About ten days," Bastian answered. He lifted a balloon-shaped glass of brandy to his lips.

"Then on the first of May—an admirable date, that of Labor Day—I'll be off to Zurich," said Thomas. He handed Bastian a share certificate and a list. "This is a pattern for the printers and here's a list of the current numbers I want printed on the certificates."

"Wish I knew what you were up to," mumbled the man with the bristling hair in a bewildered tone.

It was only when Bastian felt sure he was absolutely alone with his master that he spoke so familiarly to him. He had known Thomas for seventeen years and had been anything but a domestic servant at one time.

Bastian had been devoted to Thomas ever since he had first met him at the headquarters of a Marseilles lady gangster. At times, too, he had shared a prison cell with him. That sort of experience promotes loyalty.

"Tommy, why don't you tell me what the idea is?"

"At bottom, my dear Bastian, the scheme's perfectly legal and respectable. Its purpose is to create confidence. My certificate swindle will be an elegant certificate swindle. No one will ever guess—touch wood—that it ever was a swindle. All concerned will make a bit and be quite satisfied."

Thomas Lieven smiled dreamily and took out a gold repeater. It had belonged to his father. That flat watch with its spring lid had accompanied Thomas in all the dangers of his career. It had been with him on all his daring flights and pursuits. Again and again he had succeeded in hiding it, preserving it or getting it back again. He pressed the spring and the lid flew open. The striking mechanism within chimed the hour in silvery tones.

Bastian said gloomily: "I can't get it into my skull. A share certificate signifies participation in an important undertaking. The certificate coupons entitle one to receive at certain intervals a certain dividend representing a share of the profit made by the undertaking."

"So what, dear boy?"

"Well, damn it all, no bank in the world is going to accept coupons from your forged certificates! Their numbers will also be printed on the genuine certificates held by someone or other. The swindle's bound to be spotted right away."

Thomas stood up. "Well, of course I'm not going to hand in coupons."

"How are you going to get away with it then?"

"I've got a surprise for you," said Thomas. He crossed to a wall safe and spun the combination. A heavy steel door swung open. In the safe lay bundles of notes, a few "gold" ingots with lead centers (and an amusing history) and three jewel boxes containing set and unset stones. In the foreground lay a little pile of passports.

Thomas murmured, as if to himself: "It'll be safer to travel to Switzerland under another name. Now I wonder what German passports we still have left?" Smiling, he read out some names. "Lord, what a lot of memories! Jakob Hauser . . . Peter Scheuner . . . Baron Ludwig von Trendelenburg . . . Wilfried Ott . . ."

You were supposed to be Trendelenburg when you shunted those Cadillacs to Rio. I'd give the baron a bit of a rest if I were you. Hauser too. They're still looking for him in France," Bastian murmured, also as if to himself.

[4]

"Sit down, Herr Ott. What can we do for you?" asked the chief clerk of the Stocks Department, laying down the caller's modest visiting card, which read: "Wilfried Ott, Industrialist, Düsseldorf." The chief clerk's name was Jules Vermont. His office was situated on the first floor of the Swiss Central Bank in Zurich.

Thomas Lieven, who had just mentioned his own name as Wilfried Ott, asked: "You are French, monsieur?"

"On the mother's side."

"Then let us speak French," proposed Thomas, alias Wilfried, using that language with a faultless accent. Jules Vermont beamed like a rising sun.

"Could I by any chance have a deposit number here?"

"By all means, monsieur."

"I've just acquired a few of the new German Steel Union share certificates. I'd like to keep them here in Switzerland, under a deposit number, as I've just suggested, not under my own name . . ."

"Of course. Those awful German taxes, eh?" Vermont blinked one eye.

He was quite used to foreigners depositing securities at the bank. Some 150 milliards of Swiss francs belonging to foreigners reposed in Switzerland in 1957.

"Before I forget," said Thomas Lieven. "Would you mind having the coupons for 1958 and 1959 detached? I'm not sure when I shall be in Zurich again, so I'd prefer to keep those coupons by me and redeem them myself when the time comes. That'll save you trouble, won't it?" And it'll also save me going to prison, he added mentally.

A little later everything had been arranged. Thomas Lieven's inside pocket contained a formal statement by the Swiss Central Bank to the effect that a certain Herr Wilfried Ott, an industrialist from Düsseldorf, in West Germany, had deposited new G.S.U. certificates to the nominal value of one million German marks.

He drove his sports car, which even in Zurich attracted a lot of attention, back to his hotel, the Baur au Lac, where he was very popular with all the staff. Wherever he stayed, in hotels all over the world, all the staff adored him. His sunny disposition, his democratic views and his lavish tips were responsible.

He took the elevator up to his suite. On arrival he went first to the bathroom and washed the coupons for 1958 and 1959 down the drain, to prevent any trouble ever arising from that direction. His sitting room had a balcony. Thomas sat down there under a bright awning and gazed contentedly at the little vessels floating on the glittering waters of the Züricher See, while he meditated for a time. Then with a gold pencil he composed the following advertisement on a sheet of the hotel notepaper.

GERMAN INDUSTRIALIST

requires Swiss capital loan repayable in two
years. High interest and first-class security

offered. Serious investors only. Banker's reference essential.

This advertisement appeared two days later in a prominent position among the advertisements in the *Neue Züricher Zeitung*, followed by a box number. After another three days Thomas collected forty-six replies.

Seated on his balcony in gloriously sunny weather Thomas made a careful classfication of the offers.

They could be divided into four groups.

Seventeen of the letters offered the advertiser real estate, antique furniture, jewelry and car retail businesses but did not mention money in commending their offers.

Ten letters came from gentlemen who, though they had no money, offered introductions to other gentlemen who allegedly disposed of this commodity.

Eleven letters, some with and some without photographs, came from ladies who, though they had no money, nevertheless offered, some with and some without charm, their own persons.

Finally, eight letters came from people who offered money.

Thomas Lieven tore the thirty-eight letters of the first three groups into small pieces. Of the remaining offers two attracted Thomas Lieven's special attention on account of their complete contrast.

One was typed with a rather poor machine on rather poor paper in rather poor German. The writer offered "In return for interest what I can accept amounts up to one million Swiss francs." The offer was signed: "Pierre Muerrli, House Agent."

The other letter was handwritten in small, delicate script. The yellowish handmade paper of the best quality bore at the center of the top of the page a small gold crown with five points.

The text read:

Château Montenac
8 May 1957

Dear Sir,

With reference to your advertisement in the *Neue Züricher Zeitung* I should be glad if you would telephone for an appointment here. H. de Couville.

Thoughtfully Thomas laid the two letters side by side. Thoughtfully he examined them. Thoughtfully he drew his gold repeater from his waistcoat pocket and listened to the silvery chimes striking the hour. One, two, three and then two more strokes. It was half-past three.

Pierre Muerrli, Thomas reflected, was undoubtedly a very rich man, though also a very mean one. He bought poor-quality paper and typed on an old machine.

Now H. de Couville, though he used a pen, also used the best paper. Could he be a count? Or a baron?

We'll go and see . . .

The Château Montenac stood in an immense park on the southern slope of the Zurichberg. A broad, winding gravel path led up to the small palais, painted an imperial yellow, with green shutters. Thomas parked his car opposite the great porch.

An uncommonly haughty-looking manservant appeared suddenly before him. "Monsieur Ott? Please follow me." He led him into the house, through several splendid rooms and finally into a splendid study.

Behind an elegant writing desk a slender, fashionably dressed young woman of about twenty-eight rose to receive him. The soft waves of her chestnut hair fell almost to her shoulders. Her wide mouth was a brilliant pink, her brown eyes slanting and her cheekbones high. The lady also possessed long silky lashes and a gold-tinted skin of velvety softness.

Thomas remembered with a slight pang that ladies with slanting eyes and high cheekbones had caused him trouble in the past.

That type, he thought, always behaves in the same way. Dismissively, coldly, haughtily. But when you get to know them better there's no holding them!

The young lady gave him a steady look. "How do you do, Herr Ott? It was I who answered your telephone call. Please sit down."

She resumed her seat and crossed her legs, the skirt slipping back a little.

Good long legs into the bargain, thought Thomas.

"Herr Ott, you require capital and you mentioned first-class security. May I ask what its nature is?"

That's going a bit too far, Thomas thought. He answered calmly: "I don't think I really ought to trouble you with that. If you would be so kind as to tell Herr de Couville that I have called? It was he who wrote to me."

"It was I who wrote to you. My name is Hélène de Couville. I manage all my uncle's financial affairs," explained the young lady with extreme deliberation. "So I should like to know, Herr Ott, what you call first-class security."

Thomas bent his head, smiling. "Newly issued G.S.U. share certificates deposited at the Swiss Central Bank. Nominal value, one million. Previous shares quoted at two-seventeen . . ."

"What interest are you offering?"

"Eight per cent."

"And what amount of capital do you require?"

Good God, what a cold stare, he thought. He answered: "Seven hundred and fifty thousand Swiss francs."

"I beg your pardon?"

Thomas Lieven perceived to his astonishment that Hélène de Couville had suddenly lost her equanimity. She moistened her bright red lips with the tip of her tongue. Her lashes quivered a little. "Is not that a—well, rather a high figure, Herr Ott?"

"Oh, I hardly think so, considering the value of the shares as quoted."

"Of course . . . yes . . . but . . ." She stood up. "I'm sorry, but I think I really must fetch my uncle. Excuse me, please, for a moment."

He rose. She disappeared. He sat down again. He waited for eight minutes by his old gold repeater. Instinct acquired in many years of a lawless career told him that something was wrong. But what was it?

The door opened. Hélène returned. She was accompanied by a tall thin man with tanned features and a heavy jowl. He had close-cropped iron-gray hair and wore a white nylon shirt under a single-breasted jacket. Hélène introduced him. "Baron Jacques de Couville, my uncle."

The gentlemen shook hands. Thomas thought, with growing suspicion, He's got a paw like a cowboy's and the kind of jaws that are always chewing gum. As for his accent . . . if that man's a born French aristocrat I'll eat my hat.

He was now determined to cut the interview short. "Baron, I fear I have shocked your charming niece. Let us forget the whole matter, shall we? It has been a privilege to meet you both."

"One moment, M. Ott. Please don't be in such a frightful hurry. Let's all sit down." The baron also seemed nervous. He pressed a bell. "Let's talk this business over quietly. With a few drinks."

When the haughty-looking manservant brought in the drinks the whisky turned out to be bourbon, not scotch. I'm getting to dislike that fellow Couville more and more, thought Thomas.

The baron raised the question again. He observed that he had actually been thinking of a considerably smaller amount. "... perhaps a hundred thousand would ...?"

"Baron, please let us drop the subject," said Thomas.

"Or, say, a hundred and fifty thousand?"

"Really, Baron, really ..."

"I might go to two hundred ..." His tone sounded almost plaintive.

At that moment the haughty-looking manservant entered to announce a long distance telephone call. The baron and his niece immediately left the room.

Thomas was gradually beginning to be amused by this aristocratic household. When the baron returned alone after an absence of nearly ten minutes, pale under his tan and in a dreadful state of perspiration, Thomas felt almost sorry for the poor fellow. But he took his leave abruptly.

In the hall he met Hélène. "Leaving already, M. Ott?"

"I've been worrying you for far too long," said Thomas. He kissed her hand. He became aware of her perfume and the odor of her skin as he did so. He added: "You would make me very happy if you would dine with me this evening at the Baur au Lac or wherever else you would like. Do please come."

"Herr Ott," said Hélène—she sounded like a marble statue talking—"I don't know how much you've been drinking but I assume that accounts for your behavior. Good day."

[5]

The transaction with the house agent Pierre Muerrli went though as smoothly, immediately afterward, as the discussion with Baron de Couville had proved unproductive. As soon as Thomas got back to his hotel he called up Muerrli and briefly told him what he wanted, viz., a sum of 750,000 francs against the security of the G.S.U. certificates on deposit.

" 'S that all?" Pierre Muerrli inquired in his throaty German-Swiss dialect.

"Yes, that'll do me," Thomas replied, thinking, Moderation in all things!

The house agent paid a visit to the hotel. Red-faced and stocky, he struck Thomas as a fast worker.

Next day the following agreement was drawn up in the presence of a solicitor.

> Herr Wilfried Ott, Düsseldorf industrialist, hereby agrees to pay interest at eight per cent on a loan of three quarters of a million francs, to be repaid at latest by midnight on the 9th May 1959.
>
> Until that date Herr Pierre Muerrli, Zurich house agent hereby agrees to leave undisturbed the deposit of share certificates assigned to him by Herr Ott as security.
>
> If however the loan should not be repaid by the agreed date Herr Muerrli will be entitled to dispose of the securities in any way he desires.

Armed with this agreement Thomas and Muerrli drove to the Central Bank. There the authenticity of the receipt for the deposit was confirmed.

Pierre Muerrli then handed over to Thomas at the former's agency a check for 717,850 Swiss francs, being the sum required less all expenses and eight per cent interest for two years.

Thus Thomas had in a twinkling, so to speak, secured a sum of 717,850 Swiss francs, with which capital he would be able and in fact intended to work for two years. In May 1959, as stipulated, he would pay the whole amount back, then retrieve the forged certificates from deposit, tear them up and wash them down the bathroom sink. Everyone would then have made a profit, no one would have suffered any loss. Better still, no one would ever guess the kind of trick that had been played. And there you are! That sort of thing works simply enough if it works at all . . .

When, some hours later, Thomas Lieven, alias Wilfried Ott, entered the hall of his hotel, he saw Hélène de Couville sitting in a chair.

"Hallo! How nice to see you!"

Hélène looked up, in infinitely slow motion, from her fashion magazine. In an infinitely bored tone she murmured: "Oh, good evening."

She wore a brown shepherd's plaid costume, the day having been rather chilly, and a jacket of Canadian mink. No man in the lounge could have helped repeatedly looking at her.

Thomas said: "You're just a little bit late. But I'm so delighted that after all you were able to make it."

"Herr Ott, please note that I am not here to meet you, but a woman friend who lives in this hotel."

Thomas said: "If this evening won't do, then perhaps tomorrow morning for an appetizer?"

"I leave for the Riviera tomorrow."

Thomas struck his palms together. "Why, what a coincidence! It so happens that I'm also going to the Riviera tomorrow. I'll call for you. Shall we say about eleven o'clock?"

"Obviously I'm not going to drive down with you. Ah, there's my friend." She stood up. "Good-bye, have a good time—if you can."

Next morning at seven minutes past eleven Hélène de Couville drove out of the park gates of the Château Montenac in a small sports car—past Thomas. He bowed. She looked away. He got into his car and drove after her.

Nothing special happened until they had passed Grenoble.

Just beyond the town Hélène's car came to a stop. She alighted. He pulled up beside her.

"Engine trouble," she said.

He checked the engine but could find nothing wrong with it.

Hélène had already entered a nearby house in order to telephone for a mechanic. The latter soon arrived and declared that the petrol pump was "absolutely down the drain." He added that the car would have to be towed away and that repairs would take at least two days.

Thomas felt certain that the mechanic was lying, so as to be able to present a big bill. But he was only too pleased to have a liar to deal with. He invited Hélène to continue her journey in his own vehicle.

"Very kind of you, Herr Ott," she answered after prolonged hesitation.

Her luggage was transferred to the other car. Thomas surreptitiously slipped the liar a princely tip.

Hélène only spoke once during the next sixty miles or so. It was to say *"Gesundheit!"* when Thomas sneezed.

After another sixty miles she announced that she had arranged to meet her fiancé in Monte Carlo.

"Poor fellow," said Thomas. "He won't be able to see much of you."

At Monte Carlo he drove her at her request to the Hôtel de

Paris. There a note awaited her. Her fiancé had been detained in Paris and could not keep the appointment.

"I'll take his accommodation," Thomas announced.

"Very good, sir," said the reception clerk, pocketing the five-thousand-franc note Thomas passed him.

"But suppose my fiancé turns up after all?"

"Then he'll have to see what he can do," said Thomas. He drew Hélène aside and whispered: "He's obviously the wrong man for you. Don't you see the hand of Providence in all this?"

At that she was obliged to burst out laughing.

They stayed for two days at Monte Carlo, then drove to Cannes, where they booked in at the Carlton. Thomas thoroughly enjoyed himself for a few days. He drove with Hélène to Nice, St. Raphael, St. Maximin and St. Tropez. They went swimming together. He hired a speedboat. They water-skied and lay side by side on the beach.

Hélène laughed at the same things as he did and liked the same kinds of food, books and pictures.

When, after a glorious week, she became his mistress, he realized that they understood each other in every respect. Then, during the first hour of their eighth day together—

Hélène de Couville was lying on her bed, her eyes moist and shining. Thomas sat beside her. They were both smoking. He was stroking her hair. Soft music sounded in the room, where only a single small lamp was burning.

Hélène sighed, stirring languidly. "Oh, Will, I'm so happy . . ." She called him Will because Wilfried, she said, reminded her too much of Richard Wagner.

"I too, my dearest, I too."

"Really?"

There it was again, that strange, brooding look in her slanting eyes. He still couldn't account for it.

"Really, *chérie*."

Hélène suddenly flung away from him, so that he could only see her exquisite, golden-brown back. She sobbed into the pillows, so wildly as to alarm him: "I've lied to you! I'm wicked—oh, I'm so wicked!"

He let her go on sobbing for a while, then said primly: "If you mean your fiancé . . ."

She threw herself round on her back again and exclaimed: "Oh, that's rubbish about my fiancé! I haven't one! Oh Thomas, Thomas!"

An icy chill seemed to run down his spine. "What was that you said just now?"

"I said I hadn't got a fiancé."

"No, that's not what I meant." He gulped slightly. "Did you say 'Thomas' just now?"

"Yes," she sobbed. Big tears began to roll down her cheeks and throat onto her breast. "Yes, of course I said Thomas. That's your name, my poor darling Thomas Lieven . . . Oh, why did I ever have to meet you? I never loved anyone so much before . . ." Again her shoulders rose and fresh tears fell. "And it was you of all people I had to do that to—"

"Do? Do what?"

"I work for the American secret service," moaned Hélène in a tone of despair.

Thomas did not notice that the glow of his cigarette was getting nearer and nearer to his fingertips. He remained silent for a long time.

At last he gave a deep sigh. "Oh God, is all that business starting up again?"

Hélène blurted out tragically: "I didn't want to tell you . . . I was forbidden to tell you . . . They warned me not to—but I had to tell you the truth after tonight . . . It would have choked me otherwise . . ."

"Take your time and start at the beginning," said Thomas, who was gradually regaining control of himself. "I suppose then that you're an American agent?"

"Yes."

"And your uncle?"

"He's my chief, Colonel Herrick."

"And the Château Montenac?"

"Rented. Our people in Germany reported that you were planning something big. Then you came to Zurich. When your advertisement appeared we were authorized to offer you a loan of up to a hundred thousand francs."

"Why?"

"We were sure your advertisement was a cover for some kind of trick but we didn't know what it was. We would have found out in the end and then we would have had you at our mercy. The FBI want to get hold of you at all costs. They're quite mad about you!"

She burst out crying again. Thomas dried her tears.

"Then when you asked for seven hundred fifty thousand we put through an urgent call to Washington. And do you know what they told us? That seven hundred fifty thousand was crazy. They wouldn't chance it. They put me on the job instead . . ."

"Put you on," he repeated idiotically.

"That was why I started on this journey. It was all a put-up show. That mechanic from Grenoble . . ."

"Oh God, he was in it too! And I, like a fool, tipped him for his trouble!"

"The fiancé story and everything else was phony, too, Tommy. And now—now I've fallen in love with you and I know that if you won't work with us they'll have you arrested!"

Thomas got up.

"Stay with me!"

"I'll be back later, darling," he replied, lost in thought. "I've just got to think something over quite by myself if you don't mind. It's not the first time, you know, that this sort of thing's happened to me . . ."

He left her sobbing and went through the sitting room into his own bedroom. There he sat down by the window. For a long time he gazed out into the night.

Then he picked up the telephone. When the switchboard answered he said: "I want the chef, please. . . . Never mind that, wake him up . . ."

Five minutes later the telephone rang. Thomas lifted the receiver. "Gaston? Ott here. I've just had a pretty bad shock. I need something light and stimulating. Make me a tomato cocktail and a few anchovy sandwiches . . . thank you."

He replaced the receiver.

Well, there's no escape then, he was thinking. They've got me by the short hairs in 1957 just as they had in 1939.

Thomas Lieven stared out through the open door of the balcony at the deserted Corniche d'Or and up to the remote, indifferent stars glittering above the Mediterranean. Out of the velvety darkness the men and women of his past seemed suddenly to take shape, approach and descend upon him. There were fascinating beauties among them, icily relentless women agents, mighty tycoons, wily petty traders, unscrupulous killers, gang leaders and top racketeers who stopped at nothing.

His whole previous life came back to him, the wild, adventurous life which had now come full circle since the warm day in May 1939 when it all started . . .

BOOK I

CHAPTER 1

[1]

On May 24, 1939, two minutes before ten in the morning, a black Bentley saloon stopped at No. 122 Lombard Street in the heart of London.

An elegant young gentleman alighted. His tanned features, nonchalant movements and somewhat unruly dark hair contrasted curiously with his conventional attire. He wore trousers striped black and gray, with a knifelike crease, a short, double-breasted black jacket, a black waistcoat adorned with a gold watch chain, a white shirt with a high stiff collar and a pearl-gray tie.

Before closing the door of the car the young gentleman reached into its interior and extracted a black bowler, an umbrella and two newspapers, the *Times* and the pink *Financial Times.*

The thirty-year-old Thomas Lieven stepped into the entrance hall of the building, where a black marble plate bore the following legend in gold lettering:

MARLOCK AND LIEVEN
DOMINION AGENCY

Thomas Lieven was the youngest private banker in London, but a successful man. He owed his lightning rise to his intelligence, his ability to inspire confidence and his talent for leading two entirely different lives alternately.

Nothing could have been more fastidiously correct than his behavior on 'Change. But when away from those hallowed precincts he became one of the most charming of lady-killers. No one, least of all those most directly concerned, ever guessed for a moment that in his spare time he kept no less than four mistresses going simultaneously, for his vigor matched his discretion.

Thomas Lieven could be more formal than the most formal of City gentlemen. But once a week he danced energetically, incognito, in the noisiest club in Soho, and twice a week he took judo lessons in equal secrecy.

Thomas Lieven loved life and life seemed to love him. He succeeded in everything so long as he carefully refrained from disclosing how young he really was . . .

Robert E. Marlock, the senior partner, was standing in the counter hall of the bank when Thomas Lieven entered, doffing his bowler with solemnity.

Marlock was fifteen years older than Thomas. Tall and lean, he had the rather disagreeable habit of never fixing his watery blue eyes on those of any person he happened to be talking to.

"Hallo," he said, looking past Thomas as usual.

"Good morning, Marlock," said Thomas gravely. "Good morning, gentlemen!"

The six employees at their desks returned his greeting with equal gravity.

Marlock was standing near a metal pillar with a glass top within which a little brass teleprinter was tapping out the latest stock market prices on endless ribbons of ticker tape.

Thomas joined his partner. They watched the quotations together. Marlock's hands were trembling a little. A more suspicious observer than Thomas then was might have thought them typical swindler's hands. But in those days Thomas Lieven's optimistic spirit was anything but suspicious.

Marlock asked him nervously: "When do you fly to Brussels?"

"Tonight."

"And about time too. Just look how those prices are falling! That's because of that damned Steel Pact of the Nazis. You seen the papers, Lieven?"

"Of course," said Thomas. He was fond of saying "Of course." It sounded more dignified than "Yes."

That morning, May 24, 1939, the newspapers had announced the conclusion of a treaty of alliance between Germany and Italy. The treaty was called the Steel Pact.

Thomas walked through the dark, old-fashioned counter hall into his dark, old-fashioned private office. The cadaverous-looking Marlock followed him and dropped into one of the leather armchairs in front of the high desk.

The two gentlemen began by discussing what securities Thomas was to buy up on the Continent and what he was to get rid of. Marlock and Lieven had a branch office in Brussels. Thomas Lieven, in addition, had shares in a private bank in Paris.

After the gentlemen had settled this business, Robert E. Marlock broke a lifelong habit. He looked his junior partner straight in the eye. "Ahem! Lieven, I've also got quite a private favor to ask of you. I expect you remember Lucie . . ."

Thomas remembered Lucie quite well. The girl, a pretty blonde from Cologne, had lived in London for years as Marlock's mistress. Then something rather serious must have happened. No one knew exactly what it was. But one day Lucie Brenner suddenly returned to Germany.

"I'm a swine to bother you with it, Lieven," Marlock went on in a gloomy tone, managing with a considerable effort to continue looking his junior partner straight in the eye. "But I thought that while you're in Brussels you might perhaps make a quick dash to Cologne and have a talk with Lucie."

"To Cologne? But why don't you go yourself? You're also a German, after all . . ."

"I'd be very glad to go to Germany," Marlock replied. "But the international situation . . . And then, I treated Lucie very badly, I'll be quite honest with you about it—" Marlock was fond of saying he'd be "quite honest" with people. The phrase was always on his lips. "To be quite honest, there was another woman. Lucie had every right to leave me. Tell her that I want her to forgive me. I'll make it all up to her if only she'll come back . . ."

His voice had taken on the pathetic accents which the voices of politicians take on when they talk of their longing for peace.

[2]

Thomas Lieven reached Cologne on the morning of May 26, 1939. Huge swastikas were flying from the Cathedral Hotel. Swastikas were flying all over the town. The Steel Pact was being celebrated. Thomas saw many uniforms. The stamping of jackboots in the lounge of the hotel clattered like gunfire.

On the desk in his room stood a photograph of the *Führer*. Thomas leaned his return-flight ticket against it. He took a hot bath. Then he dressed and called up Lucie Brenner.

As the receiver was lifted at the other end of the wire a suspicious click sounded. But Thomas Lieven did not notice it. In

1939 the super-agent of 1940 had never heard of such a thing as telephone-tapping.

"Brenner."

There was the seductively hoarse voice, that of a heavy smoker, which he remembered so well.

"Fräulein Brenner, this is Lieven. Thomas Lieven. I've just arrived in Cologne and . . ." He broke off. It was not the second click along the wire that he had noticed, but a suppressed shriek from the girl.

He inquired with a pleasant smile: "Was that a cry of joy?"

"Oh God," he heard her exclaim. A third click sounded.

"Fräulein Brenner, Marlock asked me to look you up . . ."

"That blackguard!"

"No, no . . ."

"That miserable wretch!"

"Fräulein Brenner, do please listen! I'm to tell you that Marlock begs you to forgive him. May I call on you?"

"No!"

"But I promised him . . ."

"Go away, please, Herr Lieven. Catch the first train you can. You don't know what's going on here."

A fourth click sounded. But Thomas Lieven still did not notice it.

"No, no, Fräulein Brenner. It's you who don't know what . . ."

"Herr Lieven . . ."

"Just stay where you are. I'll be with you in ten minutes."

He rang off and pulled his tie straight, with the zeal of a sportsman ready to go all out.

A taxi took Thomas, naturally complete with bowler and carefully rolled umbrella, to the suburb of Lindenthal, where Lucie Brenner lived on the second floor of a villa in Beethoven Park.

He rang the doorbell of the flat. On the other side of the door he could hear muffled whispers in female and male voices. Thomas was a bit surprised, but only very slightly. For in those days Thomas's optimistic spirit was anything but suspicious.

The door opened. Lucie Brenner appeared. She wore a dressing gown and apparently little else. She seemed in a great state of excitement. At the sight of Thomas she gasped:

"Madman!"

After that things happened fast.

Two men appeared behind Lucie. They wore leather jackets

and looked like butchers. One of the butchers pushed Lucie roughly aside. The other butcher seized Thomas by the lapels of his coat.

The banker's self-control, calm and modesty vanished. Thomas caught the butcher's fist in both hands and executed a graceful turning movement, like a dancer's. Suddenly the butcher, to his extreme astonishment, found himself hanging over Thomas's right hip.

Our hero bent slightly backward. A joint cracked. The butcher, with a piercing scream, went whizzing through the air and landed with a crash on the floor of the little hall. He went on lying there in a painfully cramped posture. My judo training, thought Thomas, was well worth while.

"And now for you," he said, approaching the second butcher.

The blond Lucie started screaming. The second butcher stepped back, stuttering: "N—no, p—please, sir. Don't try that again . . ." He drew a revolver from his shoulder holster. "I warn you. Be reasonable."

Thomas stood still. Only an idiot fights unarmed against a butcher with a revolver.

"In the name of the law," said the butcher nervously. "You're under arrest."

"Arrest by whom?"

"By the Gestapo."

"Oh boy," said Thomas Lieven. "What a story for the club!"

Thomas Lieven loved his London club and the club loved him. The members, sitting around the open fire on the hearth with glasses of whisky in their hands and pipes in their mouths, were in the habit, every Thursday evening, of listening to the wild stories that were going the rounds.

When I get back this time, thought Thomas, I'll have a story to tell that's not too bad either.

The story was certainly not a bad one and it was destined to get better and better. But it was doubtful when Thomas would be able to tell it in his club and indeed whether he would ever see his club again.

He was still in a perfectly cheerful mood on that day in May 1939 as he sat in an office of the Special Department D at the Gestapo headquarters in Cologne. Naturally the whole thing's nothing but a misunderstanding, he was thinking. I shall be out of here in half an hour.

Haffner was the name of the inspector who received

Thomas. A stout man with cunning pig's eyes, he was also careful about his toilet. He never stopped cleaning his fingernails with an endless collection of toothpicks.

"I hear you've been assaulting one of my colleagues," said Haffner angrily. "That's going to be a damned awkward business for you, Lieven."

"I'm still *Herr* Lieven to you. What do you want with me? Why have I been arrested?"

"Breach of the currency regulations," said Haffner. "I've been waiting for you quite long enough."

"For me?"

"Or your partner Marlock. Ever since that girl Lucie Brenner came back from London I've had her watched. I thought to myself, One of these days one of you two impudent scoundrels is going to pop up again and then—whoops!" Haffner pushed a file across the desk. "I'd better show you what evidence we've already got against you. Then perhaps you'll sing a bit smaller."

Well, that really makes me curious, thought Thomas. He started turning the leaves of the thick file. After a while he couldn't help laughing.

"What's so funny about it?" Haffner asked.

"Well, look here, this is the most comic affair!"

It appeared from the file that the London private bank of Marlock and Lieven had pulled a fast one on the Third Reich a few years ago. They had exploited the fact that owing to the political situation German mortgage bonds had for a considerable time been worth only a fifth of their nominal value.

Marlock and Lieven, or whoever had been operating in the name of that firm, had acquired such bonds in Zurich in January, February and March 1936 with illegally transferred German currency. Then they had put up a Swiss citizen to buy certain paintings of the kind called "decadent art" which had no value in Germany but commanded high prices abroad. The Nazi authorities were delighted to export the paintings in question. For in the first place they could thus get rid of these "undesirable" works and secondly they would be paid for in the currency so necessary for German rearmament, since the Swiss figurehead had agreed to pay thirty per cent of the purchase price in Swiss francs.

But they did not find out until much later that he had paid the other seventy per cent with German bonds which on arrival in their native land commanded their normal value, in other words one fifth of what Marlock and Lieven had paid for them in Zurich.

Thomas Lieven thought, as he studied the relevant documents, Well, it wasn't I who put through this comic transaction. So it can only have been Marlock. He must have known that the Germans were after him, that Lucie Brenner was being watched, that I would be arrested and that nobody would believe a word I said. He must have realized that in that way he could get rid of me, and have the bank all to himself. Good God, good God in heaven . . .

"Aha," said Inspector Haffner complacently. "So now the old babblebox shuts up at last, does it?" He took a fresh toothpick and turned his attention for a while to using it in the normal way.

Damn it, what on earth am I to do now, thought Thomas. An idea struck him. Not a very good one. But he couldn't think of a better. "May I use the telephone, please?"

Haffner screwed up his pig's eyes. "To whom do you want to speak then?"

All I can do is to go ahead, thought Thomas. It's my only chance.

"Baron von Wiedel."

"Never heard of him."

Thomas suddenly roared: "His Excellency Baron Bodo von Wiedel, ambassador seconded for special duty in the Foreign Office! Do you mean to say you've never heard of him?"

"I—I—"

"I should be glad if you'd take that toothpick out of your mouth when you talk to me."

"But—but what do you want to speak to the baron about?" stammered Haffner. His usual diet was one of scared middle-class citizens. He had not yet got accustomed to prisoners who roared at him and knew the top brass.

Thomas continued to fume. "The baron is my best friend."

Thomas had met Wiedel, a much older man, at a non-dueling student's club in 1929. Wiedel had introduced Thomas into aristocratic circles. Thomas had sometimes covered the baron's checks when they bounced. Their intimacy continued to flourish until one day Wiedel joined the Party. Thomas had then, after a violent quarrel, dropped him.

Our friend was now wondering, as he went on raging at Haffner, whether Wiedel had a good memory. "If you don't get the connection for me this instant, you can start looking for another job tomorrow morning!"

The switchboard girl had to bear the brunt of Haffner's ill temper. Snatching up the receiver, he began roaring in his turn. "AA Berlin! And jump to it, you clumsy bitch!"

It's fantastic, it's positively fantastic, Thomas was thinking, when almost immediately afterward he heard the voice of his former fellow member. "Von Wiedel here . . ."

"Bodo, it's Lieven. Thomas Lieven. Do you still remember me?"

A jovial bellow answered him. "Thomas! Man alive! Well, what a surprise! Last time we met you gave me such a dressing-down for my political views and now you're in the Gestapo yourself!"

The enormity of this mistake made Thomas screw up his eyes for an instant. The baron's voice roared cheerfully on. "Too funny! Why, only the other day either Ribbentrop or Schacht told me you were running a bank in England!"

"So I am. Look here, Bodo—"

"Ah, service abroad, eh? I understand. Camouflage, what? God, what a joke! Come around to my way of thinking at last, have you?"

"Bodo—"

"And how are you getting on in your new job? Ought I to call you Inspector now?"

"Bodo—"

"Or Superintendent, is it?"

"For goodness' sake listen to me, man! I'm not working for the Gestapo! I've been arrested by them!"

A short silence ensued at the Berlin end.

Haffner smacked his lips complacently. He kept the other receiver glued to his ear with his shoulder and carried on with the cleaning of his left thumbnail.

"Bodo! Did you understand what I said?"

"Yes, I did, unfortunately. What—what are you charged with, then?"

Thomas told him.

"H'm, well, that certainly is a nuisance, old boy. It's absolutely impossible for me to interfere. The law of the land has to be respected. If you're really innocent, it's bound to come out. All the best. Heil Hitler!"

"Your best friend, eh?" grunted Inspector Haffner.

[3]

They took away his suspenders, tie, shoelaces, brief case and beloved repeater. They locked him up in solitary confinement. He remained there for the rest of the day and all that night. His brain worked feverishly. There must, there simply must be some way out. But he couldn't think of one. . . .

On the morning of the twenty-seventh Thomas Lieven was again brought up for examination. As soon as he entered Haffner's office, he saw an army major standing next to the inspector. The officer looked pale and worried, Haffner furious. They seemed to have had a quarrel.

"There's your man, Major. As instructed, I'll leave you alone with him," the Gestapo inspector growled ill-temperedly and went out.

The officer shook hands with Thomas. "Major Loos of the Cologne Recruiting Office. Baron von Wiedel called me up to say I was to look after you."

"Look after me?"

"Well, you're entirely innocent, of course. Your partner let you in for this. That's quite clear to me."

Thomas uttered a sigh of relief. "I'm so glad you've arrived at that decision, Major. I suppose I can go now, then?"

"Go? No. You'll be going to prison."

Thomas sat down. "But if I'm innocent?"

"You'll have to explain that to the Gestapo, Herr Lieven. Your partner's scheme was pretty watertight, I'm afraid."

"H'm." Thomas stared hard at the major, thinking. He's got something else to say.

He had. It came out at once. "Look here, Herr Lieven. There is, of course, one way for you to get out of this mess. You're a German citizen. You know the world. You're an enlightened man. You speak fluent English and French. Such people are in demand these days."

"In demand by whom?"

"By us. By me. I'm an Intelligence officer, Herr Lieven. I can only dig you out of here if you undertake to work for Military Intelligence. Incidentally, the pay's quite good . . ."

Major Fritz Loos was the first secret service officer Thomas Lieven had ever met. He was to meet countless others, British, French, Polish, Spanish, American and Russian.

Eighteen years after this first encounter Thomas Lieven was thinking, on May 18, 1957, in the nocturnal silence of a luxury suite in a hotel at Cannes, that at bottom all those people were monotonously alike. They all seemed melancholy, embittered, disappointed. Probably they had all been expelled from their chosen careers. They all looked ill. They were all rather shy and consequently put up an endless show of the absurd attributes of their power, their secret activities and the terror they could inspire. They were all perpetually on the stage and they all suffered from a deep inferiority complex. . . .

On that beautiful night of May 1957 Thomas Lieven was well aware of all that. But on May 27, 1939, he still did not know it. So he was simply delighted with Major Loos's suggestion that he might work for German Military Intelligence. In that way I can at last free myself from this ghastly muck heap, he thought. He had no idea how deep he was already stuck in it. . . .

[4]

As the Lufthansa machine dropped down through the low-lying clouds over London, the passenger in Seat 17 uttered a peculiar sound.

The stewardess hurried along to him. "Not feeling so well, sir?" she asked him sympathetically. Then she noticed that he was laughing.

"I'm feeling first-rate, thanks," said Thomas Lieven. "Sorry, I must just have been thinking of something funny."

He hadn't been able to help remembering the disappointed expression of the warder at the Gestapo headquarters in Cologne when the man returned him his property. The fellow could hardly bear to part with that gold repeater.

Thomas extracted his beloved possession and fondly stroked its decorative lid. In so doing he noticed that there were still traces of printers' ink under the nail of his forefinger. He couldn't help laughing again as he remembered that his fingerprints were now preserved in a secret card index and his photograph in a file of other particulars about him.

A gentleman named John Smythe (*y* and *the* essential) would call upon him the day after tomorrow to inspect the gas meter in the bathroom. Herr Smythe's orders were to be obeyed to the letter, Major Loos had been most careful to emphasize.

Herr Smythe was in for a surprise, thought Thomas. If he really does turn up, I shall soon send him packing. The aircraft was losing height. It was heading southwest of the Thames for the airport at Croydon.

Thomas pocketed his watch and rubbed his hands together for a moment. He stretched himself contentedly. Aha, England again! Freedom! Security! The Bentley and a hot bath, then a whisky, a pipe, friends at the club and the great yarn he was going to tell them . . .

Ah, yes, and then of course there would be Marlock.

But Thomas Lieven was so intensely happy over his return home that half his anger at Marlock's treachery had already subsided. Would he really have to part from Marlock? There might be some explanation which one could reasonably accept. Marlock might have been in a jam. Anyway, one would first have to hear what he had to say . . .

Seven minutes after these reflections our friend was speeding gaily down the gangway from the aircraft to the rain-wet tarmac in front of the four-storied airport building. He strode whistling, under his umbrella, up to the entrance hall. Here two avenues, cordoned off by ropes, were marked, to the right, BRITISH SUBJECTS and to the left, FOREIGNERS.

Still whistling, Thomas took the left-hand direction and marched up to the high desk where the immigration officer stood.

The latter, an elderly man with a walrus mustache stained by nicotine, took the German passport which Thomas handed to him with a friendly smile. After glancing through it, he looked up. "I'm sorry, sir. But you won't be permitted to return to this country."

"What on earth do you mean?"

"You were sentenced to deportation today, Mr. Lieven. Please follow me. There are two gentlemen waiting to see you." He was already walking away . . .

The two gentlemen rose as Thomas entered the small office to which the immigration officer had led him. They both looked like overworked civil servants suffering from ulcers and lack of sleep.

"Morris," announced one of them.

"Lovejoy," announced the other.

Now just whom do those two remind me of, Thomas wondered. But he couldn't think who it could be. He was now in a really towering passion. But he managed to control himself so far as to inquire, with the bare minimum of courtesy: "Gentlemen, what does all this mean? I've been living in this country for seven years now. And I've never done anything wrong."

The man called Lovejoy showed him a newspaper, pointing to a headline that covered three columns.

LONDON BANKER ARRESTED IN COLOGNE

"So what? That was the day before yesterday. Today I'm here. The German police discharged me!"

"And I wonder why," Morris remarked. "Why did the Gestapo discharge a man they had only just arrested?"

"Because my innocence was proved."

"Aha," said Lovejoy.

"Aha," said Morris. They exchanged significant glances. Then Morris announced with characteristic pomposity: "We are from the secret service, Mr. Lieven. We have information from Cologne. There is no point whatever in your trying to mislead us."

Now I know whom you two remind me of, Thomas thought suddenly. That sickly-looking Major Loos! They've all three got the same melodramatic way of talking and behaving! Aloud he said wrathfully: "It's all the better if you are from the secret service, gentlemen. For in that case you'll certainly be interested when I tell you that the Gestapo only let me go because I undertook to work for German Intelligence."

"Mr. Lieven, just how simple-minded do you really think we are?"

Thomas grew impatient. "I'm telling you the plain truth. The German Intelligence people blackmailed me. I feel no obligation whatever to keep my promise to them. I want to live here in peace and quiet."

"Surely you can't believe yourself that we shall let you enter this country after such a confession? You are officially under sentence of deportation, simply because every foreigner who comes into conflict with the law is deported."

"But, damn it, I'm absolutely innocent! My partner cheated me! You might at least put me in touch with him! Then you'd soon see I'm telling the truth."

Morris and Lovejoy again exchanged significant glances.

"Why are you exchanging significant glances, gentlemen?"

Lovejoy said: "I'm afraid you can't talk to your partner, Mr. Lieven."

"And why not?"

"Because your partner has left London for six weeks," Morris said.

"Lo—London?" Thomas turned pale. "Lo—left?"

"Yes. He's said to have gone to Scotland. But nobody knows exactly where he's gone."

"Confound it! Well, what am I to do then?"

"You better go back to your own country."

"And be locked up there? Haven't I told you that I was only released in order to go spying in England?"

The two gentlemen again exchanged glances. Thomas knew they had something else to say. They had. It came out at once.

Morris observed in a cool, impartial tone: "So far as I can see, there is positively only one chance for you now, Mr. Lieven. Work for us!"

Good God in heaven, thought Thomas Lieven, what a story for the club! But nobody will believe it.

"Play for our side against the Germans and we'll let you into England and help you to run down Marlock. We'll protect you."

"Who will protect me?"

"The secret service."

Thomas was shaken by a slight spasm of laughter. Then he grew serious. He pulled down his waistcoat, set his tie straight and drew himself up to his full height.

His momentary mood of perplexity and depression had passed. He knew now that he had mistaken something for a terrific spree which was probably nothing of the kind. He realized that he was in for a fight now. And he was fond of fighting. No man just lets himself be ruined without a struggle.

Said Thomas Lieven: "I decline your offer, gentlemen. I am going to Paris. There I shall engage the best lawyer in France to bring a suit against my partner and against the British Government."

"I shouldn't do that, Mr. Lieven."

"But I'm going to do it just the same."

"You'll get into trouble."

"We'll see about that. I refuse to believe that the whole world's a madhouse!" said Thomas Lieven.

A year later he had changed his mind.

And eighteen years later, as he sat in a luxury hotel at Cannes and thought over his past he was absolutely convinced that he had been wrong the first time.

That the whole world was a madhouse seemed to him the only profound truth a man could and ought to be sure of in this crazy century.

[5]

On May 28, 1939, shortly after midnight, an elegant young gentleman was ordering a meal in a restaurant well know to connoisseurs, Chez Pierre of the Place Graillon, Paris. "We'll take a little hors d'oeuvre, Emile, then crayfish soup, followed by loin fillets with mushrooms. And for dessert, what about a Coupe Jacques?"

The old white-haired headwaiter Emile smiled with great cordiality at his customer. He had known Thomas Lieven for many years.

Next to the young gentleman sat a pretty girl with glossy black hair, gay, rather prominent eyes and an oval face like a doll's. Her name was Mimi Chambert.

"We're hungry, Emile! We've been to the theater to see Jean-Louis Barrault in Shakespeare."

"Then instead of cold hors d'oeuvre I'd recommend hot salmon canapés, monsieur. Shakespeare takes it out of one."

They all laughed. The old maître d'hôtel disappeared into the kitchen.

The restaurant was a long dark room of old-fashioned aspect, but extremely comfortable. The young lady was very much less on the old-fashioned side.

She wore a very low-cut gown of white silk, tightly gathered up on one side. The young actress with the dainty little figure always looked well, even in the morning, directly after waking up.

Thomas had known her for two years. He smiled at Mimi, heaving a deep sigh. "Ah, Paris! The only city in which one can still live, *mon petit chou*. We're going to have a few glorious weeks together . . ."

"I'm so glad you're enjoying yourself again, *chéri!* You were so restless last night . . . You were chattering away in three languages, but I could only understand the French . . . Was there something wrong with your passport?"

"Why do you say that?"

"You kept talking about deportation orders and residential permits . . . and there are so many Germans in Paris just now who have trouble with their passports . . ."

He kissed the tips of her fingers tenderly. "Don't worry. A stupid thing just happened, that's all. Nothing really disagreeable." He spoke with calm conviction, really believing what he said. "Someone played a dirty trick on me, you know, my dear. I was cheated. Sometimes an injury like that lasts a long time. But it's never permanent. I've got a first-rate lawyer now. It'll only be a short time before they come and apologize. And I'm going to spend the interval of waiting with you. . . ."

The waiter returned. "M. Lieven, two gentlemen would like to speak to you."

Thomas looked up unsuspectingly. Two men in not overclean trench coats were standing at the entrance to the restaurant, bowing to him in some embarrassment.

Thomas stood up. "I'll be back in a moment, *ma petite*."

He walked to the entrance. "Gentlemen what can I do for you?"

The two men in crumpled mackintoshes bent their heads obsequiously. Then one of them said: "Monsieur, we have just paid a visit to Mlle. Chambert's flat. We are detectives. I'm sorry, but we have to arrest you."

"What have I done?" asked Thomas quietly. He really felt more like laughing.

"You'll hear all about that later."

So the nightmare continues, thought Thomas. He said amiably: "Gentlemen, you are French. You know what a sin it is to interrupt a good meal. May I ask you to postpone my arrest until after I have eaten?"

The two detectives hesitated.

"Can we ring up our chief first?" one of them asked.

Thomas gave him permission to do so. The man disappeared into a telephone booth and returned almost immediately afterward. "That's all right, monsieur. The boss had only one request to make."

"What was that?"

"He wondered whether he might come along and join you. He said that things are always more easily discussed over a good meal."

"Very good, that's all right with me. But who, may I ask, is your boss?"

The two detectives told him.

Thomas went back to his table and beckoned to the old waiter. "Emile, I'm expecting another guest. Please lay a third place."

"Who's coming then?" asked Mimi with a smile.

"A certain Colonel Siméon."

"Oh," said Mimi. And quite contrary to her usual custom that was all she did say.

MENU

Crayfish Soup
Hot Salmon Canapés
Loin Fillets with Mushrooms
Pommes Frites
Coupe Jacques

28 May 1939

During this meal Thomas Lieven became a secret agent.

Crayfish Soup

For four persons cook a dozen crayfish in boiling water for fifteen minutes. Next detach the meat from pincers and tails, pound all the shells to a not too fine powder and stir with a quarter of a pound of butter over a fire till the mixture begins to rise and turn red. A tablespoon of flour is then added, together with a quart of stock, and the mixture strained through a muslin-covered hair-sieve. Shortly before dishing up the soup bring it to a boil again and add the crayfish meat. The soup must not be too thick, a fault always to be avoided in soups served at banquets.

Hot Salmon Canapés

Dip thin slices of white bread in milk, place smoked salmon slices of the same size already soaked in milk between them. Sprinkle the top slices with grated cheese and little dabs of butter and bake on a greased baking sheet in the oven.

Loin Fillets with Mushrooms

The fillets are quickly fried on both sides in hot fat, placed on a dish and kept hot. The following mushroom garnish is served with this course: One onion, sliced, is braised in butter and a cup of white wine is added and brought to a boil: three yolks, lightly beaten with one tablespoonful of butter, the juice of half a lemon and salt and pepper are stirred into it; more wine is added and the mixture is whisked over steam until thick. The mushrooms are braised separately, with chopped shallots, in butter and half a cup of white wine. Meanwhile a *roux* is prepared from one tablespoonful of butter, one of flour and two cups stock. The mushrooms and sauce are then added and the whole mixture is brought to a boil again.

Coupe Jacques

One portion of vanilla ice cream is covered with whipped cream. On top of it is placed a fruit salad (fresh or tinned) which has already been soaked for half an hour in maraschino. On top of the fruit salad a portion of strawberry ice is laid, covered with whipped cream and decorated with crystallized cherries.

Colonel Jules Siméon proved to be an agreeable gentleman. With his neatly groomed mustache, Roman nose and shrewdly ironical eyes, he recalled the actor Adolphe Menjou, though the colonel was rather taller. He greeted Thomas with great respect and Mimi as an old friend—an attitude which caused our hero some uneasiness.

Siméon's dark blue suit had undoubtedly been made by a first-class tailor. But it was already a bit shiny at the elbows and on the back. The colonel wore a gold tie pin, set with a pearl, and small gold cufflinks. But the heels of his shoes needed repairing.

Over the soup and canapés the talk was of Paris. Over the loin fillets Colonel Siméon became more confidential. "M. Lieven, I must apologize, not only for disturbing you in the middle of the night, but over a meal too. Beautifully crisp, these *pommes frites,* don't you think so? I had an order from a highly placed authority. We've been looking for you all day."

Thomas suddenly thought he could hear in the distance the voice of Jean-Louis Barrault, who had been playing in Shakespeare's *Richard III* that evening. A few lines rang vaguely in his ears. But he couldn't quite catch their sense.

"Really," he said. "Yes, the *pommes frites* are excellent, Colonel. They know the secret at this place. It's dipping them twice in the oil, you know. Nothing like French cooking . . ."

Thomas laid a hand on Mimi's arm. The colonel smiled. I'm getting more and more fond of this colonel, thought Thomas.

The colonel said: "But it wasn't only for French cooking that you came to Paris. We too have our people in Cologne and London. We know all about your dealings with the worthy Major Loos. Is he as liverish as ever, I wonder . . ."

Thomas again fancied he could hear the voice of Jean-Louis Barrault. Again the lines of the immortal dramatist echoed in his head. But he still could not make out their meaning.

And why was Mimi smiling so very sweetly?

"M. Lieven," said the colonel. "I really do sympathize with you. You love France. You love its cookery. But I have my orders. I shall have to deport you, M. Lieven. You are too dangerous for my poor, threatened country. We shall be taking you to the frontier this very night. And you must never return to France again . . ."

Thomas burst out laughing.

Mimi glanced at him. And for the first time since he had known her she did not immediately join in his laughter. Thereupon he too stopped laughing.

". . . unless," the colonel was saying, as he helped himself generously to more mushrooms, "unless, M. Lieven, you make a right about turn and work for us, for the Deuxième Bureau."

Thomas sat up straight. I'm not quite so drunk as that yet, he thought. He said quietly: "Are you offering me work in the French secret service in the presence of Mlle. Chambert?"

"But why shouldn't he, chéri?" Mimi asked affectionately, giving Thomas a kiss on the cheek. "After all, I'm in the combine too."

"You're . . ." Thomas choked.

"Oh, only in a small way. But I'm in it. I earn a little on the side from the job. Are you cross?"

"Mlle. Chambert is the most delightful patriot I know," the colonel declared.

Suddenly the voice which had been worrying Thomas Lieven for so long, the voice of the actor Jean-Louis Barrault, came clearly to his ears. Now Thomas understood at last the meaning of the words spoken by King Richard III.

> And therefore, since I cannot prove a lover
> to entertain these fair, well spoken days,
> I am determined to prove a villain—

"M. Lieven," the colonel demanded, a glass of red wine in his hand. "Are you prepared to work for us?"

Thomas looked pensively at the sweet-natured, affectionate Mimi, at the colonel, that man of breeding, and at the well-stocked table.

So there's nothing else I can do, thought Thomas Lieven. I've got this world all wrong. I'll have to change my mode of life and pretty quick too if I don't want to go under in this flood of folly.

Mimi's voice sounded at his ear. "*Chéri,* do be nice and join us. We'll have such a wonderful time!"

The colonel's voice sounded at his other ear. "Monsieur, have you made up your mind?"

The voice of the actor Jean-Louis Barrault rumbled. "I am determined to prove a villain . . ."

"I am determined," Thomas Lieven murmured.

[6]

First it was German Intelligence. Then it was the British secret service. Now it was the Deuxième Bureau. And all within ninety-six hours. Only days ago, thought Thomas, I was still living in London as a respected citizen and a successful private banker. Who would ever take my work for it? Who would ever believe my story at the club?

Thomas Lieven ran his lean, delicately formed fingers through his close-cropped black hair and said: "My situation looks hopeless but not serious. I am seated, pleasantly satiated, on the ruins of my existence as a plain citizen. This is a historic moment. Emile!" The old headwaiter hurried forward. "We have grounds for a celebration. Champagne, please!"

Mimi kissed him tenderly. "Isn't he sweet?" she asked the colonel.

"Monsieur, I deeply appreciate your attitude," said Siméon. "I am delighted to hear you say you are ready to work for us."

"I don't say I am ready to do so. I simply have no choice."

"Comes to the same thing."

"Of course, you can only count on me so long as my lawsuit lasts. As soon as I have won my case I intend to live in London again. Is that clear?"

"Quite clear, monsieur," said Colonel Siméon. He smiled as though he were a clairvoyant and already knew that Thomas Lieven would still not have won his case even after another world war and that he would never live in London again.

"For the rest," said Thomas, "I haven't the slightest idea in what way I could be useful to you."

"You're a banker."

"So what?"

Siméon winked. "The lady has told me how capable you are."

"But Mimi," said Thomas to the little actress with the glossy black hair and merry eyes. "That was very indiscreet of you."

"She did it out of patriotism. She's such a charmer!"

"I should think you were in a good position to know that, Colonel!"

Mimi and Siméon both spoke at once. "I give you my word of honor as an officer . . ." "But *chéri,* that was long before your time, you know."

Then they both stopped speaking and laughed. Mimi snuggled up to Thomas. She was really in love with this man, who could appear to be so serious and yet be no such thing, who looked like the prototype of every English gentleman and banker and was at the same time more lovable and brainy than any of the gentlemen Mimi knew. And she knew quite a crowd.

"Long before my time," said Thomas Lieven. "Aha. I see. Right . . . well, Colonel, do I understand from you then that I must consider myself financial adviser to the French secret service?"

"Exactly, monsieur. You will be entrusted with special duties."

"Allow me," said Thomas, "before the champagne comes, to put in a few rapid remarks of an entirely honest nature. In spite of my relative youth I've already acquired certain moral principles. If you should ever find them imcompatible with my new duties I would ask you to be so good as to resort to the alternative of deportation."

"Well, monsieur, and what are these principles of yours?"

"I decline to wear uniform, Colonel. You may find it incomprehensible, but I am not in the habit of shooting human beings. Nor will I ever consent to terrorize, arrest or torture anyone."

"But my dear sir, we think far too highly of you to employ you in such trifles."

"I shall also refuse to injure or rob anyone, except within the recognized sphere of my profession. But even then I would only do so after being convinced that the victim had deserved such treatment."

"Monsieur, have no fear. You will be able to remain true to your principles. It's only your brains we have in view."

Emile arrived with the champagne.

After they had each taken a sip the colonel said: "I must insist however on your attending a training course for secret agents. That is necessary under our regulations. You will be taught many ingenious tricks you don't know anything about yet. I'll take care to see that you are transferred as soon as possible to one of our special camps."

"But not tonight, Jules, please," said Mimi, stroking Thomas Lieven's hand affectionately. "Tonight he's already learned enough. . . ."

On the early morning of May 30, 1939, two gentlemen called for Thomas Lieven at his girl friend's flat. The gentlemen wore cheap ready-made suits and baggy trousers. They were underpaid subordinate agents.

Thomas wore a single-breasted pepper-and-salt suit (black on gray) with a white shirt, a black tie, a black hat, black shoes and of course his beloved repeater. He carried a small suitcase.

The gentlemen, with serious expressions, packed Thomas into a truck. He found, on trying to look out, that the blinds drawn over the windows had been tightly clamped down so as to exclude all light.

After five hours every bone in his body ached. When the truck at last pulled up and the gentlemen permitted him to alight, Thomas found himself in extraordinarily depressing surroundings. High barbed-wire fencing enclosed a stony tract of hilly country. In the background Thomas perceived a gray building of dilapidated aspect with a gloomy little wood behind it. A heavily armed guard stood at the entrance to the building.

The two shabbily dressed gentlemen went over to the stern-faced sentry and produced a mass of credentials for his inspection. He studied the papers with deep attention.

Meanwhile an old peasant driving a little cart loaded with timber came past.

"Got a long way to go still, grandpa?" Thomas asked.

"Yes, damn it, a good two miles yet to St. Nicolas."

"Where's that, then?"

"Why, down there of course. Just before you get to Nancy."

"Aha," said Thomas Lieven.

His two companions returned. One of them explained: "We must apologize for having locked you up in that truck. We had strict orders to do it, as otherwise you might have found out where you are. And it's absolutely essential for you not to know that."

"Aha," said Thomas.

The old building was furnished like a third-class hotel. A bit on the squalid side, thought Thomas Lieven. The people who run it don't seem to have much money. Let's hope there aren't any bugs. One certainly gets into queer situations.

The new course was attended by twenty-seven other agents besides Thomas. They were mostly French. But there were also two Austrians, five Germans, a Pole and a Japanese.

The trainer in charge was a lean, pale fellow with an unhealthy complexion, every bit as secretive and depressed-looking, overbearing and nervous, as his German colleague, Major Loos, whom Thomas had met at Cologne.

"Gentlemen," said this being to the assembled agents, "I am Jupiter. For the duration of the course every one of you will adopt a false name. You have half an hour to think out a suitable imaginary career to go with it. From now on you will have to stick to the identity thus assumed under all circumstances. I and my colleagues will do everything in our power to prove to you that you are not the persons you pretend to be. So you must try to invent a personality which you can maintain against all our attempts to discredit it."

Thomas decided to adopt the prosaic name of Adolf Meier. He was not in the habit of indulging his fancy in pointless enterprises.

In the afternoon he received a suit of gray overalls, with his false name stitched on the front. The other trainees were issued similar clothing.

The food was bad. The room assigned to Thomas was hideous and the bedding scanty. Before going to sleep our friend ruefully made his beloved repeater strike the hour again and again. Thereupon he closed his eyes and tried to imagine he was lying in his comfortable bed in London. At three o'clock in the morning he was roused from sleep by a coarse yelling in his ear.

"Lieven! Lieven! How many more times? Answer me, Lieven!"

Thomas sat up, sweating, and groaned "Here!"

The next moment he felt a couple of resounding boxes on the ear. Jupiter was standing by his bed, grinning fiendishly and saying: "I thought your name was Meier, Herr Lieven. If you'd behaved like that on active service you'd have been a dead man. Good night. Have a good sleep now."

Thomas didn't have a good sleep. He kept thinking how he could evade any further boxes on the ear. He soon discovered the method. During the following nights Jupiter could yell as brutally as he liked. Thomas always woke up slowly, pulled himself together and then at once insisted upon his false identity. "What are you shouting at me for? My name's Adolf Meier."

Jupiter was delighted. "Fantastic self-control, eh?"

He didn't know that all Thomas had done was to put a sufficient amount of cotton wool in his ears.

The trainees learned all about drugs, explosives, tommy-guns and revolvers. Thomas found to his astonishment that eight out of the ten shots he fired scored bull's-eyes. He murmured in amazement: "Pure chance. I don't know anything about shooting."

Jupiter chuckled. "No, Meier? Why, man, you've got a natural talent for it!"

Of the next ten shots nine, actually, scored bulls. Thomas was quite shocked. "What puzzling creatures human beings are," he muttered.

That night he couldn't sleep for thinking of it. What's wrong with me, he thought. Anyone so abruptly switched from his normal routine as myself ought really to be in despair, take to the bottle, curse God and commit suicide. But, good heavens, I'm neither desperate, nor drunken, nor demoralized, nor blasphemous, nor planning to kill myself!

Far from it.

To myself I can confess the frightful truth. The whole thing's beginning to amuse me. I'm finding it great fun. I'm still young. I've no family ties. Who ever had such a crazy experience?

I'm in the French secret service. That means I'm working against my own country, against Germany. But just a minute. Is it against Germany or against the Gestapo?

Well, then.

But I simply can't understand how it is I can shoot. I can see of course why I find it all more amusing than shocking. It's because so far I've been engaged in such a serious profession. There I had to keep up a permanent pretense. But apparently my present position is much more congenial to my true nature. The devil! A nice sort of character I must have!

He learned Morse signaling. He learned to write in code and decipher codes. For the latter purpose Jupiter distributed tattered copies of *The Count of Monte Cristo.*

He explained: "The system is simplicity itself. On active service you'll keep a book like this handy. Suppose you receive a message in code that begins with three figures that afterward continually change. The first figure indicates the page of the novel you are to use, the second figure indicates the line on that page and the third number is that of the letter in the line, which is your starting point. Then you can begin calculating, according to the other code numbers in the message, what the rest of the letters must be . . ."

He distributed slips of paper which contained messages in code.

Half the class deciphered them correctly. The other half, including Thomas Lieven, failed to do so. His efforts to achieve a text in clear read as follows: "Twmxdtrrre illd m ionteff . . ."

"Try again," said Jupiter.

They all tried it again, with the same fifty-fifty result.

"Well, we'll just have to go on all night," said Jupiter.

They went on all night.

By dawn it had been discovered that two different editions of the novel had inadvertently been distributed to the pupils, viz., the second and the fourth. The editions differed because certain cuts had been made in the fourth. The cuts had entailed a slight disarrangement of the pages.

"Of course," said Jupiter, pale, but determined as ever, "that couldn't possibly happen on active service."

"Of course not," said Thomas Lieven.

[7]

Then Jupiter organized a big celebration at which a very great deal of liquor was provided. One of the trainees, a lad named Hänschen Nolle, with burning eyes, long eyelashes and a complexion like a mixture of milk and blood, got excessively drunk. Next day he was dismissed from the course. The only Englishman and one of the Austrians went with him. During the night it had been discovered that they did not deserve to be secret agents. . . .

In the fourth week the class was taken to a dreary wood. They stayed there for eight days with their teacher.

They slept on the bare ground, were exposed to all the rigors of the weather and learned, when their provisions ran out at the end of three days, as had been planned, to feed on berries, bark, leaves and disgusting little animals. Thomas Lieven did not learn this last lesson, for he had foreseen something of the kind and smuggled some tinned foods into the school. On the fourth day he was still enjoying Belgian goose liver. Accordingly, while the other pupils were already coming to blows over the carcass of a field mouse, he remained stoically calm, for which demeanor he was praised by Jupiter. "You should follow Herr Meier's example, gentlemen. There's a real man for you!"

In the sixth week Jupiter took the class to the edge of a towering cliff, where they stood and looked into a terrifying abyss, the bottom of which was covered by a flimsy-looking cloth.

"Jump!" shouted Jupiter. The pupils, all except Thomas, drew back, shuddering. But he thrust his colleagues aside, dashed at full speed to the brink and with a cheerful shout sprang into the void. It had only taken him a second or two to realize that the French authorities would hardly be paying out so much for his physical and mental training merely in order to drive him to suicide. As he had anticipated, the flimsy cloth covered several layers of rubber, which broke his fall quite comfortably. Jupiter proclaimed estatically: "You're my best man, Meier! One of these days you'll be famous!"

The prophecy was destined to come true.

Thomas only fell foul of his teacher on one occasion, when Jupiter was instructing the class in writing with invisible ink. The only materials required were a pen, some onion juice and a raw egg. Thomas demanded, in his innocent zeal for knowledge: "Please, sir, to whom would it be best to apply in a Gestapo prison when one needs onions, pens and raw eggs?"

The course ended with a final examination, for which the pupils were tumbled out of their beds at midnight and brought before a German Intelligence court, composed of the instructional staff, with Jupiter in the chair. The instructors, by this time all well known to the trainees, sat in German uniforms behind a long table. Jupiter turned dazzling spotlights on them and kept them without food and drink all night, though this was not a serious deprivation, as they had all partaken of an ample evening meal.

Jupiter treated Thomas with special severity. He boxed his ears several times, stood him with his face to the wall for long periods and pushed the cold barrel of a revolver into the back of his neck.

"Confess!" he bawled. "You are a German spy!"

"I'm not saying anything," Thomas retorted heroically. Then they fitted thumbscrews on him and began tightening them. As soon as Thomas felt the first slight pain he ejaculated "Ow!" whereupon the screws were immediately loosened. About six in the morning he was sentenced to death for espionage.

Jupiter called on him for the last time to reveal military secrets in order to save his life.

Thomas spat on the floor at the chairman's feet and shouted: "I'd rather die!"

They complied with his wishes by taking him out into a dirty courtyard, where they stuck him up against a cold wall in the gray dawn and shot him without military honors, though they compensated for this omission by using blank cartridge.

Then they all went in to breakfast.

It is almost unnecessary to record with any special emphasis that Thomas Lieven came through the course with flying colors. Jupiter had tears in his eyes as he handed him a diploma corresponding with the distinction he had gained, together with a forged French passport in the name of Jean Leblanc. "Good luck, comrade! I'm proud of you!"

"But Jupiter, aren't you afraid, if you let me go like this, that one of these days I might be captured by the Germans and tell them everything I have learned here?"

Jupiter answered with a smile: "There wouldn't be much to tell, old boy. Secret service training methods are the same all over the world. They all run neck and neck. They all take advantage of the latest medical, psychological and technological inventions."

On July 16, 1939, Thomas Lieven returned to Paris. Mimi received him with as much affection as if she had really been faithful to him for the last six weeks.

On August 1, Thomas Lieven acquired through Colonel Siméon comfortable quarters in the Bois de Boulogne, fifteen minutes by car from his bank in the Champs Elysées.

On August 20, Thomas Lieven obtained permission from the colonel, despite the tense European situation, to take a holiday with Mimi at Chantilly, the popular racing and excursion center for Parisians, after all his recent hardships.

On August 30, Poland declared general mobilization.

That afternoon Thomas and Mimi set out on foot to visit the lakes at Commelle and Queen Blanche's castle.

A blood-red sun was sinking as they returned to the town toward evening. Arm in arm they strolled past sleepy villas erected at the turn of the century, making their way over the worn cobbles to the Hôtel du Parc in the Avenue du Maréchal Joffre, where they were staying.

When they entered the lounge the porter signaled to them. "A call for you from Belfort, M. Lieven."

A few minutes later Thomas heard the voice of Colonel Siméon. "Ah, at last, Lieven!" The colonel was speaking German and immediately explained why he was doing so. "I can't take the risk of anyone in your hotel understanding me. Listen, Lieven. The balloon's gone up."

"War?"

"Yes."

"When?"

"Within the next forty-eight hours. You must catch the first train to Belfort tomorrow morning. Report to the Hôtel du Tonneau d'Or. The porter will be expecting you. We have to . . ."

At that moment the connection was cut.

Thomas rattled the key. "Hallo, hallo!"

A severe feminine voice announced: "M. Lieven, you have been cut off. You were speaking in a foreign language."

"Is that forbidden?"

"Yes, since six o'clock this evening. Long-distance calls can now only be made in French."

The line went dead.

As Thomas Lieven left the telephone booth the porter gave him a strange look. Thomas took no particular notice of it. He did not remember it again until five o'clock in the morning, when someone knocked at the door of his room.

Mimi was asleep, bunched up like a kitten. He had not been able to bring himself to tell her, the evening before, what he had heard from Siméon.

Outside, it was already light. A lot of birds were twittering in the old trees.

The knocking was repeated, very much more loudly. Surely that can't be the Germans already, thought Thomas. He decided not to answer.

A voice sounded behind the door. "M. Lieven, open up. If you don't we'll break the door down."

"Who's there?"

"Police."

Thomas sat up with a sigh. Mimi woke, with a little shriek. "What's happening, *chéri?*"

"I think I'm probably being arrested again," he said. His suspicions proved to be correct. A French police officer with two of his men was standing in the doorway. "Dress and come with us."

"Why?"

"You are a German spy."

"Why do you suppose that?"

"You had a suspected conversation on the telephone yesterday. The supervisor reported it to us. The porter saw you. So it's no use lying."

Thomas said: "Send your people away for a minute. I've something to tell you."

The two gendarmes disappeared.

Thomas produced his identification papers and the passport Jupiter had given him. He explained: "I'm employed by the French secret service."

"Can't you think of anything better than that? And with such clumsily forged papers into the bargain! They're a joke! Come along, dress!"

[8]

Thomas Lieven arrived late in the afternoon of August 31, 1939, at the formerly fortified town of Belfort on the River Savoureuse. He took a taxi through the little Old Town, passing the Place de la République and the monument commemorating the three sieges, straight to the Hôtel du Tonneau d'Or. He was as immaculately dressed as ever. His waistcoat displayed the gold chain of his old repeater.

Colonel Siméon was waiting for him in the hotel lounge. Although in uniform, he looked just as friendly as he had in mufti.

"My dear Lieven, I'm so awfully sorry for the idiotic behavior of those policemen! As soon as Mimi at last got me on the telephone, I gave the whole lot of them a good dressing down. Well, come along now, General Effel is already waiting for us. There's no time to lose. You'll soon have your baptism of fire, my friend."

A quarter of an hour later Thomas Lieven was seated in the general's office at the headquarters of the French General Staff.

Military ordnance maps of France and Germany covered all four walls of the plainly furnished room.

The tall, slim, white-haired Louis Effel paced to and fro, his hands behind his back, in front of Thomas Lieven, who sat at a card table with Siméon beside him.

The general's deep voice announced:
"Mr. Lieven, Colonel Siméon has told me all about you. I know you are one of our best men."
The general halted by the window and looked down into the pleasant valley between the Vosges and the Jura mountains. "This is no time for pretense. The facts are that Herr Hitler has initiated hostilities and in a few hours he will be receiving our own declaration of war. But . . ." The general faced round. "France, Herr Lieven, is not prepared for this war. Nor are we of the secret service in any sense prepared for it . . . The problem pertains to your sphere of operations. Will you please state it, Colonel."
Siméon gulped. Then he said to Thomas: "The fact is we're pretty well broke, old boy."
"Broke?"
The general nodded emphatically. "Yes, sir. We're practically without funds. We're reduced to ridiculously small subsidies from the War Office. We should be incapable of operating on the large scale now required. We're tied hand and foot. We can't move."
"Well, that's a bad show," said Thomas Lieven, though it was all he could do to not burst out laughing. "You'll excuse me for saying so, but if a nation has no money, then it seems to me it would be better not to have a secret service at all."
"We might have had enough money to prepare ourselves for an attack by Germany. Unfortunately, monsieur, there are people in France who are selfish and egotistical enough to evade supplementary taxes and concentrate entirely on enriching themselves at the expense of their country." The general drew himself up to his full height. "I know that it's almost too late to apply to you, Herr Lieven. I know that I may be demanding the impossible. Yet I ask you whether you can think of any conceivable way in which we can acquire really substantial—and I mean substantial—funds in double-quick time—and I mean double-quick—so that we can set to work?"
"Well, I shall have to think that over, General. But I can't do it here." Thomas glanced at the military ordnance maps. "I shan't get any useful ideas here." His face cleared. "If you gentlemen have no objection, I'd like to take my leave now, go back to the hotel and prepare a little dinner, over which we could discuss everything in more detail."
Louis Effel looked flabbergasted. He said: "You mean you want to go and do some cooking? Now, at this moment?"

"If you will permit me, General. I always get my best ideas in the kitchen."

Accordingly, a memorable meal took place on the evening of August 31, 1939, in a special private room at the best hotel in the place.

MENU

Snail Soup
Pheasant and Oysters with Sauerkraut
Lemon Meringue Cream with Cerises Flambées

31 AUGUST 1939

This meal revolutionized French monetary policy.

Snail Soup

To clean snails boil them in salt water for one hour, then extract them from their shells with a fork, skin them, salt them to get rid of the mucus, then thoroughly wash them three or four times, drain and dry. Some forty are then boiled in broth till tender. Two thirds of them are then removed, chopped very fine and braised in butter. Add as much broth as is needed for the quantity of soup required and bring to a boil several times with a little nutmeg. The yolks of three eggs are then whisked in a soup tureen and the soup poured over them. It can then be served with fried croutons and the rest of the snails.

Pheasant and Oysters with Sauerkraut

After preparation of the bird as though for roasting, two pounds of lightly squeezed sauerkraut are placed in a casserole and covered with equal measures of white wine and water. A piece of bacon and a grated onion are added. The mixture is boiled for one hour. The pheasant is then laid in it and braised for another hour. It is removed when tender and the sauerkraut is thickened with a little béchamel. The oysters are cleaned, and dried. They are then sprinkled with salt and pepper, rolled in flour, egg and bread crumbs and fried in clear butter till light brown. The pheasant is then jointed and served in a double ring of sauerkraut and oysters.

Lemon Meringue Cream with Cerises Flambées

For four persons four lemons are cut into thick slices and boiled with sugar. The extract is thickened with a little almond flour and, after cooling, passed through a sieve. The whites of five eggs, beaten up hard, are added and champagne glasses are filled with the mixture. Preserved cherries are then heated, drenched in cherry brandy or cognac and set alight. As soon as the flame dies down they are placed on top of the lemon cream.

"Exceptional!" remarked the general after the main dish, dabbing his mouth with his napkin.

"Fantastic," remarked the colonel.

"The best of all was the snail soup. I never tasted any so good," the general added.

"I'll give you a little tip," Thomas said. "The snails must always be big ones in gray shells, General. But the shells must be unbroken."

Waiters brought in the last course. Thomas rose. "Thank you. I'll attend to that." He lit a small spirit lamp, announcing: "This is a lemon meringue cream with a delicious supplement which we set on fire."

He took preserved cherries from a plate, laid them in a small copper pan and heated them over the flame of the spirit lamp. He next sprinkled the cherries with French cognac and a pellucid liquid. Everyone watched him with fascination. Colonel Siméon half rose to his feet.

"What's that stuff?" asked the general, pointing to the clear, colorless liquid.

"Practically pure alcohol, chemically tested. It's needed to set the whole dish alight." With a dexterous gesture Thomas brought the flame into contact with the cherries. A hissing, spluttering blue flame shot up, quivered, flared and went out. Our friend distributed the hot fruits over the cream with grace and precision.

"Now," said he, "let us consider our problem. I believe I have found a solution to it."

The general nearly dropped the little spoon he held. "For heaven's sake tell us!"

"Well, General, this afternoon—really good these cherries, aren't they?—and you were complaining of the behavior of certain people who were still trying to enrich themselves at the country's expense. I can set your mind at rest. There are gangs like that in every country. All they want is to make a profit and they don't care how. If anything goes wrong they take their money and clear out. Humbler citizens remain behind." Thomas ate a spoonful of cream. "Perhaps it's a bit sour. No? Well, it's probably a question of taste. Now, gentlemen, I believe we can put the French secret service on its legs at the expense of that selfish, unpatriotic lot."

"But how would you set about it? By what means?"

"All I need is an American diplomatic passport, an ordinary Belgian passport and fast work by the Secretary of the Treasury," said Thomas Lieven modestly. It was on August 31, 1939, that he made this announcement.

On September 10, 1939, the following order was reported by the French press and radio.

COUNCIL OF STATE

> An Order prohibiting or regulating in time of war the export of capital, exchange transactions and monetary trading . . .
>
> *Article 1*
>
> The export of capital in any form without Treasury authority is prohibited.
>
> *Article 2*
>
> All approved exchange transactions without exception must be carried out through the Bank of France or such other Bank as may be duly authorized by the Treasury for the purpose . . .

Further regulations concerning specie and currency followed. Very severe penalties for infringement were notified.

The decree was signed by:

Albert Lebrun, President.
Edouard Daladier, President of the Council.
Paul Marchendeau, Chancellor.
Georges Bonnet, Foreign Secretary.
Albert Sarraut, Home Secretary.
Paul Reynard, Secretary of the Treasury.
Fernand Gentin, President of the Board of Trade.
Raymond Patenôtre, Economics Minister.
Georges Mandel, Colonial Secretary.
Jules Julien, Postmaster-General.

[9]

On September 12, 1939, a young American diplomat traveled by the regular 8:35 A.M. express from Paris to Brussels. He was dressed like an English banker and carried a big black pigskin suitcase.

Officials on the Franco-Belgian frontier were very strict. The immaculate young gentleman's diplomatic passport, which opened out like an accordion, enabled the representatives of both nations to identify him as William S. Murphy, offical courier to the American Embassy in Paris. His baggage was not investigated.

In Brussels the American courier, who was really a German named Thomas Lieven, checked in at the Hôtel Royal, producing a Belgian passport in the name of Armand Deeken.

During the following day Deeken, alias Murphy, alias Lieven, spent three million French francs in Brussels, buying up dollars. The francs came out of the black pigskin bag and the dollars went into it.

Thomas's original stock of three million francs had been supplied by his own little bank. There had been nothing for it but to advance them to the Deuxième Bureau. . . .

Political events had caused the international value of the French francs to fall by twenty per cent. Private citizens in France, in their panic fear of a further devaluation of the franc, were intent on buying up dollars. Consequently, dollar quotations had risen in a few hours to astronomical heights.

But this was not the case in Brussels. There dollars could be acquired at a substantially lower price, since the Belgians had not been infected by the French terror of war. They expressed their firm convictions by the statement: "We shall remain neutral. Under no circumstances whatever will the Germans attack us for the second time."

In consequence of the swift decision taken by the French Government to forbid the export of capital no foreign countries were being flooded with French francs. The franc, therefore, in spite of the unfavorable circumstances, was remaining fairly stable, just as Thomas had anticipated. Its relative stability constituted, so to speak, the axis of the whole operation.

Thomas Lieven, as William S. Murphy, traveled back to Paris with a suitcase full of dollars. Within a few hours this valuable currency was eagerly snapped up by the same rich people who intended to leave their country in the lurch as soon as possible and carry off their capital into safety.

Thomas Lieven made them pay double and triple prices for the realization of their despicable plans.

His first journey brought him in 600,000 francs personal profit. Next, again as William S. Murphy, he returned to Brussels with five million francs in his courier's luggage. He repeated his procedure. The margin of profit rose. One week later four gentlemen with diplomatic passports were traveling back and forth between Paris and Brussels, as well as between Paris and Zurich. They were taking francs out of the country and dollars into it. Two weeks later there were eight of them.

Thomas Lieven was in charge of the entire transaction. He took care, through his connections in Brussels and Zurich, that enough reserves remained available to meet his requirements. The enterprise already showed a profit of millions of francs.

The melancholy eyes of the French secret service officers began to show faint gleams of hope, an expression of still incredulous gratitude, as Thomas Lieven transferred larger and larger sums to their accounts.

Between September 12, 1939, and May 10, 1940, the date of the German attack on Belgium, Thomas Lieven's turnover reached the amount of eighty million francs. By reckoning his expenses and commission at ten per cent in all and investing the money thus earned in dollars he found himself in possession of 27,730 of those units of currency. Everything had gone quite smoothly except for one little accident. . . .

Thomas Lieven, traveling on the evening train from Brussels on January 2, 1940, could not himself remember how many times he had made the journey before. The train stopped at Feignies, on the frontier, longer than usual. Thomas, feeling slightly uneasy about the cause of the delay, was about to inquire the reason for it, when the door of his compartment was opened. The chief of the French frontier police, a tall man whom Thomas had often seen before put his head into the compartment.

He spoke in a calm, official tone of voice. "Monsieur, I would advise you to alight, drink a bottle of wine with me and go on by the next train."

"And why would you so advise me?"

"This train is waiting for the American ambassador to France. His Excellency has had a slight automobile accident near here, in which his car was damaged. The next compartment to yours has been reserved for him. Three of his embassy staff are with him. . . . So you see, monsieur, you really ought to take the next train. Let me help you with that big bag of yours . . ."

Five minutes later Thomas was asking him: "Who told you about me?"

The tall police officer raised his hand in a warning gesture. "Colonel Siméon notifies us every time you travel this way and asks us to take special care of you."

Thomas took out his wallet. "What ought I to offer you?"

"No, no, monsieur! I'm only too glad to be of service. You owe me nothing in return. But perhaps . . . There are sixteen of us on duty here and recently we've been running very short of coffee and cigarettes . . ."

"Well, next time I'm traveling to Brussels . . ."

"Just a minute, monsieur. It's not so simple. We shall have to take care that those customs toughs don't spot the game. Next time you travel, but only if you come by the night express, please stand on the forward platform of the first-class coach and have the parcel ready. One of my boys will jump on to take it . . ."

Thenceforward this trick was played two or three times a week. The Feignies frontier police station was better supplied than any other in France. "Humdrum jobs breed kind hearts," said Thomas Lieven.

[10]

General Effel offered him a decoration. But Thomas declined the honor. "I'm a convinced civilian, General. I don't care for those things."

"Then is there anything else you would like, M. Lieven?"

"I wonder if I might have a certain number of French passport forms, General? With the right rubber stamps. There are a whole lot of Germans in Paris today who will have to go to ground when the Nazis come. They can't afford to run away. I'd very much like to help the poor devils."

For a moment the general made no reply. Then he answered: "It goes rather against the grain, monsieur. But I respect your wishes and will grant them."

Thenceforth Thomas received many visitors at his luxury flat in the Bois de Boulogne. He didn't charge them anything. They got their forged passports for nothing. The only condition he made was the production of proof that they could only expect imprisonment or death at the hands of the Nazis.

Thomas called his new business "playing consul." He enjoyed the game of helping the poor a little after he had lifted so much money from the rich.

For the rest, the Germans seemed in no hurry. The French called this strange war a *drôle de guerre*.

Thomas Lieven kept up his journeys to Brussels and Zurich. In March 1940 he returned home a day earlier than he was expected.

By that time Mimi had long been living with him. She always knew exactly when to expect him home. But on this occasion he had forgotten to let her know that he was coming back sooner than usual.

I'll give the darling a surprise, Thomas said to himself. And he really did surprise her—in the arms of the fascinating Colonel Jules Siméon.

"Monsieur," said the colonel, busy with the many buttons of his uniform, "I take all the blame for this situation. I have seduced Mimi. I have betrayed her trust, monsieur. There can be no excuse for my conduct. You have the right to choose weapons."

"Just you get out of this flat and don't let me ever see you here again!"

Siméon's face turned a deep strawberry color. He bit his underlip and left the apartment.

Mime said timidly: "Oh, you *were* rude!"

"You love him, I suppose?"

"I love both of you. He's so gallant and romantic, and you're so clever and cheerful!"

"Oh Mimi, what on earth am I to do with you?" said Thomas in a dejected tone. He sat down on the edge of the bed. He had suddenly realized that he was very fond of Mimi . . .

On May 10, the German offensive started. The Belgians had been mistaken. They *were* attacked for the second time.

The Germans had 190 divisions in the field. Against them were ranged 12 Dutch divisions, 23 Belgian, 10 British, 78 French and 1 Polish. Allied aircraft totaled 850, some of obsolete design. They were opposed by 4500 German machines.

The collapse followed at breath-taking speed. Panic broke out. Ten million French citizens took to the roads in a piteous plight.

Thomas Lieven, in Paris, quietly dismissed his domestic staff. He was handing out the last few forged passports for his countrymen when he first heard the distant rumbling of the guns. He made neat bundles of his franc, dollar and pound notes, tied them up separately and hid them in the double lining of a suitcase. Mimi helped him. She wasn't looking well these days. Thomas was friendly but cool. He hadn't yet recovered from the affair with the colonel.

Outwardly he appeared to be cheerful. "According to the latest reports the Germans are moving from the north to the east. So we'll just put a few more things together and then leave Paris in a southwesterly direction. We've enough petrol. We'll go by way of Le Mans. Then on down to Bordeaux and . . ." He broke off. "Are you crying?"

Mimi sobbed: "Are you going to take me?"

"Yes, of course. I can't very well leave you here, can I?"

"But you know I've been unfaithful to you . . . ."

"My dear child," he retorted with dignity. "To be unfaithful to me you'd have had to start on Winston Churchill!"

"Oh, Thomas—you're so wonderful! And—and are you going to forgive him too?"

"That'll be easier than forgiving you. He loves you and I can understand that."

"Thomas . . ."

"Yes?"

"He's in the garden."

Thomas gave a start. "What on earth's he doing there?"

"He's feeling so desperate. He doesn't know what to do. He's just back from a service trip. He can't find any of his people. He's all alone, no car, no petrol . . ."

"How do you know all this?"

"He—he told me. He was here an hour ago. I told him I would speak to you . . ."

"Well, that beats everything," Thomas said. Then he suddenly started laughing so heartily that the tears came into his eyes.

[11]

On the afternoon of June 13, 1940, a heavy black Chrysler was moving in a southwesterly direction through the Paris suburb of St. Cloud. Progress was slow. For innumerable other vehicles were rattling and bumping along in the same direction, carrying crowds of refugees from Paris.

The near-side fender of the black Chrysler displayed the flag of the United States. A similar but larger banner covered the entire roof of the vehicle. Badges glittered on the front bumpers bearing the brightly polished letters CD: *Corps Diplomatique*.

Thomas Lieven sat at the wheel. Mimi Chambert sat next to him. At the back, half buried among hat boxes and suitcases, sat Colonel Jules Siméon. He was now again wearing his once smart but now somewhat threadbare blue suit, his gold cufflinks and gold tie pin. Siméon was watching Thomas with an expression of mingled gratitude, shame and extreme embarrassment.

Thomas was doing his best to relieve the tense atmosphere with optimistic conversation. "Our lucky star will see us through." He glanced at the flag on the radiator. "Our forty-eight lucky stars, I should say!"

The colonel grunted gloomily from behind him: "Running away like cowards! We ought to stand and fight!"

"Jules," said Mimi soothingly, "we lost the war long ago. If you're captured now you'll only be put up against the wall."

"That would be more honorable," said the colonel.

"And stupider," said Thomas. "Personally I'm very keen to see how all this nonsense is going to end. Honestly I am!"

"If the Germans catch you, they'll stick you up against the wall too," the colonel told him.

Thomas turned the car off into a side road which was less crowded, and drove on into a little wood. "The Germans," he explained, "have surrounded Paris on three sides. The open side runs roughly from Versailles to Corbeil. And that's where we are."

"And suppose some German troops have already reached this zone?"

"Believe me, there won't be any Germans in this insignificant side road or in this part of the country at all. Not one."

They had now emerged from the wood and could see some way ahead. Along the "insignificant side road" a long column of German reconnaissance tanks marked with the black cross was moving toward them.

Mimi screamed.

Colonel Siméon groaned.

Thomas Lieven said: "I wonder what they're doing here? They must have lost their way."

"We're done for," said the colonel, who had turned as white as a sheet.

"Oh, don't start all that again! You make me quite nervous!"

Jules Siméon explained in a choking voice: "I've got secret

files in my brief case with the names and addresses of all French agents."

Thomas caught his breath. "Have you gone absolutely crazy? What on earth are you carrying that stuff for?"

The colonel shouted back at him: "I've orders from General Effel to get those lists to Toulouse without fail and hand them over there to a certain person, cost what it may!"

"I wish you'd told me that before!" Thomas snarled.

"Well, if I had, I wonder if you'd have taken me along?"

Thomas had to laugh. "You're right there!"

A minute later they had met the head of the column.

"I have a pistol," whispered the colonel. "So long as I live no one is going to touch my brief case."

"I don't suppose they'll mind waiting those few minutes," Thomas observed, switching off the engine.

German soldiers in dusty uniforms approached the car, staring inquisitively. A slim, blond first lieutenant alighted from a jeep. He walked up to the Chrysler, saluted and said:

"Good afternoon. May I see your papers, please?"

Mimi sat silent, as though paralyzed. The soldiers had now surrounded the Chrysler on all sides.

"It's okay," said Thomas haughtily, in English. "We are Americans, see?"

"I can see the flags," said the blond lieutenant in excellent English. "And now I want to see your papers."

"Here you are," said Thomas Lieven, handing over his passport.

First Lieutenant Fritz Egmont Zumbusch opened out the American diplomat's pass as if handling an accordion. After examining it with wrinkled brows, he scrutinized the smartly dressed young gentleman sitting with an expression of the most utter boredom behind the steering wheel of the heavy black car.

Zumbusch demanded: "Your name is William S. Murphy?"

"Yes," replied the young gentleman, yawning but politely raising his hand to cover his mouth.

If one's name is not William S. Murphy but Thomas Lieven, if one is on the blacklist of the German secret service as an agent of the French secret service and apart from that happens to have landed right in the middle of a column of German military reconnaissance tanks, and if in addition one has a little French mistress and a high-ranking officer of the Deuxième Bureau in mufti sitting in the car, and if, finally, one knows that this officer is carrying in a black leather case secret files and lists of all the French agents and their addresses, well, it isn't at all a bad idea to appear most frightfully and utterly bored.

First Lieutenant Zumbusch, with tight-lipped courtesy, handed back the diplomatic pass. For on that scorching day, June 13, 1940, the United States was of course still neutral. And of course Zumbusch, with Paris only thirteen miles away, didn't want any trouble. But, having made an unfortunate marriage, he happened to be a keen soldier. Accordingly he demanded, with conscientious attention to duty: "The lady's passport, please."

Pretty little black-haired Mimi didn't understand his words. But she guessed what he meant, opened her handbag and produced the document required. As she did so she smiled at the soldiers thronging round the car, who responded at once with a unanimous murmur of appreciation.

"My secretary," Thomas explained to the lieutenant, thinking, Well, everything's going fine. There's only Siméon now and we shall be through. But the very next moment came the catastrophe.

First Lieutenant Zumbusch had stuck his head through the window of the car in order to give Mimi back her passport. He then turned to Siméon, who was sitting at the back among hatboxes and suitcases, with his black leather case on his knees.

Zumbusch may have made rather a rapid movement in stretching out his hand. Anyhow Colonel Siméon drew back from the approaching fingers of the Teuton and clutched the black leather case tightly to his chest with the fanatical expression of an early Christian martyr.

"Hallo," said Zumbusch. "What have you got there? Let's have a look at it."

"Non, non, non!" cried the colonel.

Thomas, who had turned his head to intervene, suddenly found Zumbusch's elbow in his mouth. After all, a Chrysler isn't exactly a playground.

Mimi began screaming, Zumbusch banged his head against the roof of the car and began cursing. And the gear lever caught Thomas, as he turned, on a sensitive spot, his kneecap.

That imbecile of a hero, thought Thomas grimly. Then, to his indescribable disgust, he saw a French army revolver in Siméon's hand and heard him gasp in broken German: "Hands off or I fire!"

"You idiot!" yelled Thomas. He nearly dislocated his arm

as he knocked up Siméon's hand. The revolver went off with a deafening explosion, the bullet lodging in the roof of the car.

Thomas tore the weapon out of Siméon's hand, growling at him in French: "You give people nothing but trouble, don't you?"

First Lieutenant Zumbusch snatched open the door of the car and bawled at Thomas: "Out you get!"

Thomas alighted with a polite smile. The lieutenant was also now holding a revolver. The tankmen stood round them in a circle, their weapons at the ready. Everything had suddenly grown very quiet.

Thomas hurled Siméon's pistol into a cornfield. Then he gazed with raised eyebrows into the barrels of fifteen others.

There's nothing for it now, he thought, but to make an appeal to our national respect for authority. Accordingly, he drew a deep breath and roared at Zumbusch: "This gentleman and the lady are under my protection! My car carries the United States flag!"

"Out you get or we'll let you have it!" bawled Zumbusch at the apparent civilian, Colonel Siméon, still sitting, white-faced, in the back of the car.

"Stay where you are!" yelled Thomas. He couldn't think of anything better to say. "This car is neutral territory! The people in it are on American soil!"

"I don't give a damn for that . . ."

"Okay, okay, if you want to provoke an international incident. It was just that sort of thing that brought us into the First World War."

"I'm not provoking anything. I'm simply doing my duty. That man might well be a French agent."

"Do you think that, if he were, he'd behave so crazily?"

"Give me that brief case! Come on! I intend to know what's in it!"

"It contains diplomatic material under international protection. I shall complain to your superiors."

"You can do that right away."

"What do you mean?"

"You're coming along with us."

"Where to?"

"Operational Headquarters. A blind man can see that there's something fishy going on here. Get back behind the steering wheel and turn your car round. Try to get away and we shoot. And not at your tires," said First Lieutenant Zumbusch in a very quiet tone.

CHAPTER 2

[1]

With a melancholy sigh Thomas Lieven surveyed the bedroom, decorated in red, white and gold, to which he had been taken. It belonged to Suite 107, one of the four most luxurious in the Hôtel George V, itself one of the four most luxurious hotels in Paris. For some hours the swastika had been flying from its roof. For some hours heavy tanks had been thundering past the front entrance. A black Chrysler stood in the courtyard. And in the bedroom of Suite 107 sat Thomas Lieven, Mimi Chambert and Colonel Jules Siméon.

Twenty-four completely crazy hours had passed. The black Chrysler, preceded by one reconnaissance tank and followed by another, had tried for a long time to catch up with Operational Headquarters. First Lieutenant Zumbusch had attempted to contact his general by radio. But the German advance had been so rapid that the staff could no longer be found, apparently, at any fixed point. It was only after Paris had been occupied without fighting that even the general himself, it seemed, had come to a halt, viz., at the Hôtel George V.

Heavy jackboots were tramping up and down in the corridor. In the hotel lounge military store-chests, tommy-guns and telephone wires were lying about. A tremendous rumpus was going on.

A quarter of an hour ago First Lieutenant Zumbusch had taken his three prisoners to the bedroom of Suite 107. After that he had disappeared. Doubtless he was reporting to his general. The black leather brief case was now lying on Thomas Lieven's knees. He had taken charge of it after locking the car. He considered that the case would be safer with him in the future.

Suddenly angry shouting became audible through the lofty elaborately decorated door leading to the sitting room of the suite. Then the door flew open. An immensely tall officer stood on the threshold. "General von Felseneck wishes to see you, Mr. Murphy," said he.

So I'm still considered to be an American diplomat, thought Thomas Lieven. So far so good . . .

He rose without haste, the brief case under his arm. Passing the adjutant with dignity, he entered the sitting room.

General Erich von Felseneck was a short man with close-cropped, iron-gray hair and gold-rimmed spectacles.

Thomas beheld a small table bearing two dish covers, flanked by the hotel cutlery and plates. The general had evidently been interrupted while taking a hasty meal. Thomas took advantage of this circumstance to prove his familiarity with international courtesy. "General, I deeply regret interrupting you over your meal."

General von Felseneck shook hands with him. "It is I who owe you an apology, Mr. Murphy."

Thomas almost fainted when the general handed him back his forged diplomatic pass and the forged passports of Mimi and Siméon. "Your papers are in order. I hope you will pardon the first lieutenant's action. The behavior of your male traveling companion had understandably aroused his suspicions. But he unquestionably exceeded his authority."

"Well, General, these things do happen," Thomas murmured.

"But such things ought not to happen, Mr. Murphy. The German Army knows how to behave. We respect diplomatic usage. We're not robber knights!"

"Certainly not," said Thomas in English.

"Mr. Murphy, I'll be quite frank with you. Only last week we got into a frightful row. I very nearly went to the Führer about it. Near Amiens some overzealous lads of mine arrested and searched two gentlemen from the Swedish Military Mission. All hell to pay. I had to offer them my personal apologies. Might have been a warning for me. Anyhow, I don't intend to let it happen again. Have you had lunch, Mr. Murphy?"

"Er—no—"

"May I ask you to join me before you leave? Plain soldiers' fare. The hotel kitchen hasn't got going yet. And Prunier's is probably shut today, ha, ha!"

"Ha, ha!"

"Well then, could you take a bombardment of German goulash?"

"You're sure I'm not intruding?"

"No, no. It'll be a pleasure. Kogge, have another place laid. And let the people next door have something too, will you?"

"Very good, Sir."

Five minutes later . . .

"Bit monotonous this grub, Mr. Murphy, eh?"

"Oh, no. Considering the circumstances it's quite nice," said Thomas Lieven, who was gradually recovering his equanimity.

"I don't know why it is, but my boys can't do a decent hot pot," the general complained.

"General," said Thomas Lieven quietly. "I'd very much like to return your kindness by giving you a little tip."

"My word, Mr. Murphy! You speak the most marvelous German!"

That's a compliment which might cost me my life, thought Thomas. He at once reduced his command of the language. "Thank you, General," he said in English. Then in German: "My nursery governess was a Mecklenburg. Her specialty was Mecklenburg hot pots . . ."

"Interesting, eh, Kogge?" said the general to his adjutant.

"It certainly is, sir."

"Hot pots have been most unjustly condemned," Thomas Lieven proceeded, taking care to give his authoritative tone an American accent and to distort German syntax, "and I should be glad to explain how an original Mecklenburg hot pot is prepared. But a delicate touch can be given to the cooking of even a potato goulash." Thomas lowered his voice. "One thing, though, has been worrying me for a long time, General. Is it really true that German military rations are actually concocted with—ahem—*soda?*"

"That's a rumor that's always being repeated. I can't judge of the truth of it. I simply don't know. But of course the boys are often on active service for months, far away from their wives and—well, I need say no more."

"Naturally not, General. But whatever the truth may be, onions are always a great help."

"Onions?"

"They are the alpha and omega of potato goulash, General. And in France, God knows, there are enough of them about. The trick is quite simple. You take the same weight of onions as you have of beef, add marjoram and gherkins cut small . . ."

"Just a moment, Mr. Murphy. Kogge, write it all down. I must pass this on to my quartermaster general."

"Very good sir."
Thomas proceeded to dictate the recipe to the adjutant.

MENU

Varieties of Hot Pot

14 JUNE 1940

At this meal Thomas made a conquest of a German general.

Potato Goulash

Fry the onions until lightly browned, season well with salt and paprika and add beef cut into small cubes. Just before the beef is tender add small diced potatoes and last of all a little marjoram and chopped, pickled gherkins.

Risi-Bisi

Boiled rice is mixed with tinned or freshly cooked peas and lightly stirred over a small flame in butter or lard. Diced cold meat or sausages are added, the mixture is seasoned to taste, preferably with curry, and after serving sprinkled with grated Parmesan cheese.

Irish Stew

There are various recipes for cooking mutton or lamb with white cabbage for this form of hot pot. One of the best comes from Mecklenburg. The meat is diced, salted and boiled for from one to one and a half hours. Pick off the outside leaves of the cabbages, quarter them if large and remove as much of the stalk as possible. Boil fast for fifteen minutes and then press to remove moisture. A casserole is then lined with slices of bacon, a layer of cabbage, round sides up, is next placed on top of the bacon, and the diced meat and chopped onions, with seasoning including a pinch of ground cloves, is laid on top of the cabbage. More layers of this kind are superimposed, the last of all being of cabbage. Finally the casserole is filled to the brim with the stock in which the mutton was boiled, and left to simmer for about an hour.

Thomas was still at work on his dictation when a knock sounded at the door. An orderly appeared. A whispered conversation between the orderly and the general ensued. Then both left the room.

Thomas went on dictating to the adjutant.

Two minutes later the general returned.

He said in a quiet, ice-cold tone: "After I had reprimanded First Lieutenant Zumbusch he became very worried and telephoned the American Embassy. No one there had ever heard of any Mr. Murphy. Can you explain that, Mr. Murphy?"

[2]

Heavy tanks and army trucks were still trundling past the hotel entrance. The rattling of their tracks and the roaring of their engines sounded excessively loud in Thomas Lieven's ears.

Out of sheer habit he took out his repeater and pressed the spring to set the chiming mechanism in motion. Fourteen silvery strokes indicated the hour of two P.M. The general did not move a muscle. Thomas's brain was working at lightning speed. There's nothing for it, he thought. I'll have to play my last card.

"Well," he said. "I see I've no choice but to disobey my strictest orders. I would ask you, General, to accord me an interview between ourselves alone." He was now speaking faultless German.

"Now look here, Mr. Murphy, or whatever you call yourself, I warn you that a court martial in a case like this can be called pretty quickly."

"I only want five minutes alone with you, General." Thomas Lieven made an effort to appear portentous.

The general took some time to think it over. Then he dismissed his adjutant with a jerk of the head.

The officer had scarcely left the room before Thomas started chattering like a machine gun. "General, I am now going to entrust you with a great secret. After I have gone you will immediately forget that you ever met me . . ."

"Are you out of your senses?"

". . . I am about to reveal to you a top secret matter and I must have your word as an officer that you keep it entirely to yourself . . ."

"I never hear such impudence in my life before . . ."

". . . I had strict orders from Admiral Canaris . . ."

"Ca—Canaris?"

". . . Canaris personally, to insist in all circumstances upon my identity as an American diplomat. But now circumstances compel me to tell you the truth. Please examine this document." Thomas Lieven unbuttoned his waistcoat with a vigorous gesture and produced a paper from its inside pocket. "Read it, please, General."

Felseneck read the paper. It was a genuine German Intelligence pass, made out by a certain Major Fritz Loos, Intelligence officer at the Cologne Army Recruiting Office. Thomas had preserved the pass, feeling certain that it might one day be useful to him.

The general demanded, thunderstruck: "You—you're in the Intelligence Service?"

"As you see." Thomas was now getting into his stride. "If you still have the slightest doubt about my credentials, I beg you to put through an immediate priority long-distance call to Cologne." If he does, I'm done, he was thinking. If he doesn't, I shall get away with it.

"But surely you must realize . . ."

It looks as though I *am* going to get away with it, Thomas thought. He began to shout. "Do you know who those two people next door are? They're top-ranking French secret agents who've agreed to work for us!" He pummeled the black brief case. "This contains the files and the names of all the members of the Deuxième Bureau. Now do you understand what's at stake?"

General von Felseneck, impressed, drummed nervously with his fingertips on the table. Thomas Lieven was thinking: Files, lists and names of agents. If my German compatriots get hold of these lists, they'll kill the French agents. They'll be a regular blood bath. But if they don't get their hands on them, then the French agents will do all they can to take German lives. I don't want either of those two things to happen. I hate violence and war. So I'll have to consider very carefully what I'm going to do with this black brief case. But that will be for later on. For the moment all I've got to do is to get out of here . . .

The general stammered: "All the same—all the same, I don't understand it. If those people are really willing to work for us, what's all the secrecy about?"

"General, don't you really see even now? The French Intelligence service is on our heels! They may strike at any moment! That is why the admiral conceived the plan of moving those two people out of Paris under the diplomatic protection of a neutral power and hiding them in a castle near Bordeaux until an armistice is concluded." Thomas laughed bitterly. "Unfortunately we didn't bargain for a conscientious German first lieutenant throwing a wrench in the works!" He shook his head solemnly. "Time has been lost, most valuable time! General, if those two people fall into French hands, the consequences—the international consequences—cannot be predicted. . . . Well, aren't you going to call Cologne?"

"Why should I, if I believe you?"

"Oh, you believe me? Thank you very much. Then may I ask you to let *me* at least ring up Cologne and report the breakdown of our arrangements?"

"I'd rather you didn't, in view of the similar trouble I've had quite recently. I hope you won't insist."

"What else can I do? How can I get on with the scheme now? If I am now finally allowed to leave here after all this delay, how can I ensure that we're not all three of us arrested again, at the next street corner, by another of those overzealous lads of yours?"

The general groaned. "I'll give you a pass . . . you won't be held up any more . . . never again . . ."

"Ah, that's better," said Thomas. "Just one thing more, General. Don't start bawling out First Lieutenant Zumbusch again, will you? He only did his duty. Suppose I really had been a French agent and he'd let me through . . ."

[3]

As the black Chrysler carrying the Stars and Stripes on its roof drove out of the courtyard of the Hôtel George V two German sentries saluted. Thomas Lieven, alias William S. Murphy, laid a hand to the brim of his Homburg in courteous acknowledgment of their attentions.

After this he was less polite. He gave Jules Siméon a terrific dessing-down. The colonel received it without a word of protest.

Nearly forty-six hours after their arrest they found themselves once more on the road to Bordeaux. Thomas demanded: "Who is supposed to take charge of that brief case?"

"Major Débras."

"Who's he?"

"Second in command of the Deuxième Bureau. He is to take the papers to England or Africa."

And then what will happen, Thomas wondered apprehensively. Oh, what a glorious place this world would be if there were no secret services!

"Is the major at Toulouse?"

"I've no idea where he is just now," replied the colonel. "It is not yet certain when he will arrive or in what circumstances. I've orders to look up our mailbox in Toulouse."

"What do you mean by your 'mailbox'?" asked Mimi.

"That's what we call a person who receives or passes on news."

"I see."

"The man's completely reliable. He's a garage proprietor named Gérard Perrier."

The roads were so crammed with refugees and troops that it took them several days to reach the outskirts of Toulouse. The pass which General von Felseneck had given Thomas worked wonders. The German check-points treated them with exemplary courtesy. Toward the end Thomas was actually driving on army petrol. A captain at Tours had put five cans at his disposal.

Just before Toulouse, Thomas stopped and made a few alterations to the appearance of his car. He screwed off the CD badges and removed both the large and the small American flags. He stored this equipment in the trunk for possible later employment and extracted from that receptacle a couple of French number plates.

"I want you to remember that henceforward my name is no longer Murphy but Jean Leblanc," he said to Mimi and Siméon. The forged passport given him by his instructor Jupiter at the espionage school near Nancy had been made out in that name.

Toulouse was a city of 250,000 inhabitants—in peacetime. Now over a million people were living there, as in the hectic atmosphere of a fairground, with tragic overtones. Crowds of refugees camped in the open air under the ancient trees of the squares of the rue des Changes and Saint Sernin. Thomas saw cars with number plates from all over France and half Europe. He noticed a Paris omnibus still marked as bound for the Arc de Triomphe and a delivery van inscribed: "Alois Schildhammer and Sons, Soda and Mineral Water Manufacturers, Vienna XIX, Krottenbach St. 32."

While the colonel went to look for his "mailbox," Mimi and Thomas went to look for rooms.

They tried hotels, boardinghouses and hostels for foreigners. They went everywhere. There wasn't a single vacant room in the whole of Toulouse. At the hotels families were sleeping in the lounges, dining rooms, bars and lavatories. Bedrooms were occupied by twice or three times the number of persons normally accommodated.

After hours of searching Mimi and Thomas returned with aching legs to the parked Chrysler. They found the colonel sitting on the footboard. He looked worried and still held the black brief case under his arm.

"What's been happening?" Thomas asked. "Didn't you find the garage?"

"Oh yes," Siméon replied wearily. "But I didn't find M. Perrier. He's dead. His only surviving relative is a half-sister, Jeanne Perrier. She lives at Number sixteen in the rue des Bergères."

"Well, let's drive there," said Thomas. "Perhaps Major Débras has left his address with her."

The rue des Bergères was situated in the Old Town, a maze of narrow, cobbled streets and picturesque houses which had scarcely changed since the eighteenth century. It was full of shrieking children, blaring radios and gaudily colored clothing hung out to dry across the lanes.

The rue des Bergères contained drinking shops, tiny restaurants and small bars. There were a great many pretty girls about. They were a little too loudly made up and a little too provocatively dressed. They were tripping hither and thither as if they expected something special to happen.

No. 16 proved to be a small, old-fashioned hotel with a shabby eating place on the ground floor. A brass plate engraved with a female figure and the words CHEZ JEANNE hung over the entrance.

In a dark, cramped office by the door they found a porter with heavily brilliantined hair. A steep staircase led to the first floor. The porter said that Madame would come at once. Meanwhile perhaps the visitors would like to take a seat in the drawing room.

Chandeliers, plush upholstery, dusty potted plants, bead curtains, a gramophone and a vast mirror covering the whole of one wall decorated this apartment. It smelt of scent, powder and stale cigarette smoke.

Mimi murmured with some distaste: "Good heavens, it looks like a—"

"Hm, hm," said Thomas.

With a puritanical grimace the colonel exclaimed: "Come on, let's go—"

At that moment a good-looking woman about thirty-five entered the room. She wore her sandy hair cut short and her make-up had been subtly applied. She gave the impression of an energetic woman who not only understood life but also found it most amusing. Her figure immediately aroused Thomas Lieven's interest.

She exclaimed in a rather husky tone: "Glad to see you all. Three of you, eh? Well, isn't that delightful! I'm Jeanne Perrier. May I introduce you to some of my little girl friends?"

She clapped her hands.

Behind a red silk curtain a door opened. Three girls, one of them a mulatto, came in. All three were attractive and all three were naked. They walked smiling to the big mirror and turned round in front of it. The interesting lady with sand-colored hair remarked: "Allow me to introduce, from left to right, Sonia, Bébé, Jeannette . . ."

The colonel interrupted her in a low voice. "Madame—"

". . . Jeannette comes from Zanzibar and she has . . ."

The colonel interposed more loudly: "Madame . . ."

"Monsieur?"

"There's been a misunderstanding. We wished to speak to you alone, madame." The colonel stood up and walked over to Jeanne Perrier. He asked softly: "What did the ant say to the grasshopper?"

Jeanne Perrier's eyes narrowed. She answered in an equally low tone: "Dance away, dance away. In winter you'll be starving." She clapped her hands again and said to the girls: "You can go."

They left the room giggling.

"Sorry, I had no idea . . ." Jeanne laughed and glanced at Thomas, who seemed to attract her. Mimi suddenly started frowning irritably. Jeanne went on: "It was only two days before his death that my brother put me wise and told me your password and what to answer." She turned to Siméon. "So you are the gentlemen who is to receive it."

"Then I shall have to wait for him. It may be some time before he turns up. He's in an extremely dangerous position."

Thomas thought, and he'll be in a still worse one when he does turn up. For he's not going to keep it. I'll see to that. I intend to stop things getting any worse and more blood being shed . . . They ought to have let me alone, the lot of them. But now it's too late. I'm in the game too. But I'm going to play it my way.

He said to Jeanne: "Madame, as you know, Toulouse is chock-a-block. Couldn't you possibly let us two rooms?"

Mimi jumped "Here?"

"It's the only chance I can see, my dear . . ." Thomas gave Jeanne a winning smile. "Do please be so good, madame!"

"Well, really I only let rooms by the hour . . ."

"Madame, might I be permitted to give your heart the discreetest possible patriotic nudge?"

Jeanne's eyes softened dreamily. "A charming tenant," she murmured. "Well, all right then."

[4]

Major Débras kept them waiting. One week went by, then two. He still hadn't arrived. Well, thought Thomas, alias Jean, it would suit me splendidly if he never arrived at all.

He began to make himself at home "Chez Jeanne." Whenever he had time he went to look for his attractive landlady with the lion-colored hair.

"My cook's bolted, Jean," she complained to her German tenant, whom she took for a dyed-in-the-wool Parisian and had begun on the second day of his stay to address him by his pleasant-sounding first name. "And provisions get shorter and shorter. If I could only make that restaurant of mine pay . . ."

"Jeanne," replied Thomas who had himself begun on the second day of his stay to address his hostess by her pleasant-sounding first name, "let me make you an offer for our mutual benefit. Suppose I do the cooking and arrange for the supply of provisions and we go fifty-fifty on our earnings? How about that?"

"Are you always so quick off the mark?"

"Does that worry you?"

"On the contrary, Jean, on the contrary. I can hardly wait to find out more about your hidden talents . . ."

While Thomas busied himself with the attempt to get Jeanne's restaurant going again, Colonel Siméon again showed his aptitude for secret service work. After an absence of two days he proudly reported to Thomas and Mimi: "Neither of the mechanics would tell me anything. But I rummaged around in the garage and found all sorts of useful things. A key, a map and some directions. It seems that old Perrier had a secret petrol dump."

"Good Lord! Where?"

"In a wood near Villefranche de Largais, about thirty miles from here. The stuff's in a dugout. There are at least a hundred cans. I've just come from there."

Mimi jumped up and gave Siméon a long, ostentatious kiss.

That's her revenge for Jeanne, thought Thomas. "Congratulations, Colonel," he said appreciatively.

"Ah, my dear friend," replied Siméon, assuming a modest and benign expression as soon as he could get his breath, "I'm only too glad that at last I've been able to do some useful work." And I only wish, thought Thomas, that all secret agents could show as much sense occasionally.

So they went and fetched the petrol. Thomas laid up the black Chrysler in the garage and bought a little Peugeot with a few of his 27,730 dollars. Such a car would need less fuel.

Thomas soon became a familiar figure on the rough country roads around Toulouse. All the farmers waved to him, grinning, and kept their own counsel. Some of them regularly received good prices for their produce from Thomas, whilc he supplied others with what they needed from the city.

He thoroughly enjoyed himself baking, roasting and boiling. Jeanne helped him. It was hot in the kitchen. So far as clothes were concerned, Jeanne kept herself cool to the utmost limit of decency. The partnership was a happy one. She admired him and he admired her. Mimi went for long walks with Siméon.

The restaurant was soon packed every day. The customers were nearly all male refugees, coming from all the countries Hitler had hitherto taken over. Consequently, there had to be plenty of variety in Thomas Lieven's cooking. The refugees were delighted with it. They particularly appreciated, too, the very reasonable prices.

The resident girls were even more delighted. The charming young cook fascinated them all with his elegance and audacity, his amiability and shrewdness. They found that he treated them all like real ladies, never becoming too intimate with any of them.

Consequently, it was not long before he was acting as their father confessor, moneylender, adviser in legal and medical problems and unwearying listener whenever they revealed the innermost secrets of the feminine heart.

Jeannette had a baby farmed out in the country. The peasants who were looking after the child made more and more shameless demands. Thomas persuaded them to be more reasonable.

Sonia had a legacy due to her which a rascally lawyer was withholding. Thomas made him shell out.

Bébé had a brute of a boy friend who was always having affairs with other women and knocking her about. By dropping discreet hints about certain police regulations and putting a painful judo hold on the fellow, Thomas forced him to behave decently.

The man's name was Alphonse. He was destined to cause Thomas a very great deal of trouble in the future.

Among the regular customers at the restaurant was a banker named Walter Lindner who had first left Vienna and then Paris in order to escape Hitler.

Lindner had become separated from his wife during their flight and was now waiting for her to join him in Toulouse.

Walter Lindner was much attracted by Thomas and on hearing that the latter was also a banker made him the following proposal. "Come with me to South America. As soon as my wife gets here I'm going over there. I've capital in that part of the world. You could be my partner . . ." He showed Thomas a recent passbook of the Rio de la Plata Bank crediting him with a balance figure of over a million dollars.

At that moment it seemed to Thomas Lieven that in spite of all his recent experiences he could take courage and believe in human reason and a bright future.

But he still wished to settle the matter of that black leather brief case as satisfactorily as possible. Neither German Intelligence nor the French secret service would get hold of those files if he could help it.

Then nothing would stop him from saying good-bye to war-mad, corrupt old Europe and plunging into a new world, where he would again be a banker, a solid citizen and a civilian. He could hardly bear to wait for that glorious day.

But his longing was never to be appeased. He was soon to be freed from his conscientious scruples about having worked for the French against the Germans. He would soon be working for the Germans against the French. And then again for the French. And against the British. And for the British. And for all three. And against all three. The madness had only just begun. That basically decent fellow Thomas Lieven, who loved peace and loathed violence, had no idea yet what was in store for him. . . .

June passed, and then July. By that time they had been

nearly two months in Toulouse. One hot morning Siméon, Jeanne and Thomas held a little council of war.

Siméon seemed rather excited. But Thomas did not remember that until later. Said the colonel: "We shall have to broaden our field of action, my friend. Madame has a new address for you." He bent over the map. "Look. It's about a hundred miles northwest of Toulouse, in the valley of the Dordogne, near Sarlat."

"There's a little castle there," Jeanne explained. She was smoking nervously. But Thomas did not remember that either until later. "It overlooks the village of Castelnau-Fayrac. The name is Les Milandes. The residents are themselves farmers, with lots of pigs, cattle and all sorts of livestock . . ."

Three hours later the little Peugeot was bumping over the dusty roads, further and further to the west. By the banks of the Dordogne the landscape grew romantic and the castle called Les Milandes also looked romantic. It was a tall white fifteenth-century building, with two big and two smaller watchtowers, commanding the whole of the main road. The place was surrounded by an ancient park containing meadows and fields.

Thomas stopped his car at the open entrance to the park and sounded his horn a few times. No one answered.

He drove in onto a large graveled forecourt. A massive old oak door stood ajar. A flight of steps led up to the threshold.

"Hallo, there!" shouted Thomas.

Then he heard a shrill giggle, which gave him quite a shock. For the sound could not have been made by a human being.

Next moment a tiny brown monkey darted through the chink in the doorway, hopped down the steps, still squealing eerily, and turned a somersault at Thomas Lieven's feet. Before he had recovered from his amazement the creature was already sitting on his left shoulder, giggling incessantly, and kissing his face.

He heard a woman call out: "Glou-glou, Glou-glou! Where are you? What are you up to now?"

The oak door opened. A dazzlingly beautiful, dark-skinned woman stood on the threshold. She wore tight-fitting white trousers and over them a loose white blouse. Golden bracelets tinkled on her slender wrists. Her perfectly smooth black hair was parted in the middle.

Thomas caught his breath. He knew who she was and had adored her for years. But he couldn't utter a word. He had been prepared for anything, but not suddenly to see, in the midst of this crazy period of war and the ruin of France, an idol of the whole world, the faultless incarnation of exotic beauty, the famous Negro dancer, Josephine Baker.

With a charmingly gentle smile she murmured: "Good morning, monsieur. I'm sorry you had such a noisy welcome. Glou-glou seems to like you."

"Madame—you are—you have—you live here?"

"As a tenant, yes. What can I do for you?"

"My name is Jean Leblanc, I believe I originally came here to buy provisions . . . But now that I have seen you, madame, I can't quite remember," said Thomas. He walked up the steps, the little monkey still on his shoulder, bowed deeply and kissed Josephine Baker's hand. "Anyhow, it doesn't matter in the least why I came. I am only happy to find myself in the presence of one of the greatest artists of our time."

"You're very kind, M. Leblanc."

"I have all your recordings. I have three copies of *J'ai deux amours*. I have seen you on the stage I don't know how many times . . ." He gazed at the "Black Venus" with deep admiration. He knew that she had been born at St. Louis in the United States and was the daughter of a Spanish businessman and a Negress. He knew that she had been desperately poor when she started her fabulous career and that she had achieved fame throughout the world after being rapturously received in Paris, where she had danced in ecstatic style, clad only in a wreath of banana leaves.

"Are you from Paris by any chance, monsieur?"

"Yes, as a refugee . . ."

"You must tell me all about it. I'm so fond of Paris. Is that your car at the gate?"

"Yes."

"You're alone?"

"Certainly. Why do you ask?"

"I only just wondered. Please come with me, M. Leblanc."

The castle was full of antique furniture and pet animals. Apart from the little female monkey, Glou-glou, he made the acquaintance of the extremely dignified baboon, Mica, the tiny Gugusse, which moved like a flash of lightning and had a bristling mustache, an enormous Great Dane named Bonzo, a lazy python called Agathe, which lay coiled in front of the empty fireplace in the hall, Hannibal the parrot and two little mice, introduced to him by Josephine Baker as Miss Curl-paper and Miss Question-mark.

All these animals lived in the greatest harmony with one another. Bonzo lay on the carpet and allowed Miss Questionmark literally to dance about on his great muzzle. Mica and Hannibal played football with a screwed up piece of silver paper.

"You've a happy world here," said Thomas.

"Animals understand how to live together in peace," said Josephine Baker.

"Unfortunately human beings don't."

"But even they will one day," said the dancer. "But now do tell me about Paris."

Thomas Lieven complied. He was so fascinated by this meeting that he lost all count of time. At last he glanced guiltily at his golden repeater. "Good heavens, it's six o'clock!"

"I've so enjoyed this afternoon. Won't you stay a little longer and dine with me? I'm afraid there's not much in the house, as I wasn't expecting visitors. Even my maid is away . . ."

Thomas beamed boyishly. "I should be only too pleased. But then you must let me do the cooking. One can prepare something appetizing even with very little."

"That's right," Josephine said. "It can't always be caviar."

In the big old-fashioned kitchen Thomas, in his shirt sleeves, worked with furious energy. Outside, the sun went down behind the range of hills beyond the river. The shadows lengthened. Evening came on.

Josephine Baker watched Thomas with a smile. The highly seasoned eggs he was preparing interested her most.

"My own invention, madame. I am going to call the dish *Oeufs à la Joséphine* in your honor."

"Isn't that nice of you! Well, I'll leave you now while I go and change. I shan't be long." She left the kitchen. Thomas, in high spirits, went on cooking. What a splendid woman, he thought.

As soon as he had finished his work he washed his hands in the bathroom and went into the dining room. It was lit by two chandeliers which each held twelve candles. Josephine Baker was wearing a close-fitting green gown. Beside her stood a tall, powerfully built man in a dark suit. His features were bronzed and his close-cropped hair graying at the temples. His eyes and mouth made a favorable impression. Josephine Baker was holding his hand as she addressed Thomas. "Forgive me for surprising you, M. Leblanc. I have to be very careful, you know." She gave the man with the graying temples a loving glance. "Maurice, may I introduce a friend?"

The man in the dark suit shook hands with Thomas. "I'm extraordinarily pleased to have met you at last, Thomas Lieven. I've already heard so much about you."

Thomas stiffened at this unexpected mention of his real name. What an ass I am, he thought, walking straight into such an obvious trap.

"Oh," cried Josephine Baker. "But how stupid of me! Of course, you haven't met Maurice yet. This is Maurice Débras, Herr Lieven. Major Débras of the Deuxième Bureau."

[5]

Confound it all again, thought Thomas Lieven. Am I never to get out of this devil's circle? Good-bye to our delightful dinner for two!

"Major Débras is a great friend of mine," Josephine told him.

"Then he's a happy man," said Thomas rather crossly. He looked hard at the major. "Colonel Siméon has been waiting for you for weeks at Toulouse."

"I only reached here yesterday. I had a difficult job getting away, M. Lieven."

Josephine said: "Maurice can't afford to be seen in Toulouse. He's too well known there. The town is swarming with German agents and French detectives."

"Madame," said Thomas, "you are overwhelming me with joyful tidings."

The major said gravely: "I know what you mean, M. Lieven. Few people have faced greater perils than you have for the sake of France. When I reach London I shall take care to inform General de Gaulle with what daring you rescued that black brief case from the clutches of a German general."

That black brief case! For days Thomas Lieven had been losing sleep over it.

"Colonel Siméon has it in Toulouse."

"No," said Débras amiably. "It's under the tools in the trunk of your car."

"My—"

"That little Peugeot of yours at the park gates. Come, Herr Lieven, let's go and pick it up right away, shall we, before dinner . . ."

They've trapped me, thought Thomas Lieven in a fury.

Siméon and Mimi and Jeanne have put me on the spot. What am I going to do now? It's true enough that I didn't want German Intelligence to get hold of the brief case. But I don't want the French to get hold of it either. That would only mean bloodshed, French blood or German . . . I'm absolutely determined to stop that . . . I was a peaceable man once. You people have made me a secret agent. If only you'd left me alone . . . Now look at the mess you've made of things!

Thomas Lieven was still thinking along these lines while he sat at the table with Josephine Baker on his right and the major opposite. He poked listlessly at the savory sausage course ("nests") he had himself prepared.

The black brief case now lay on an antique sideboard under the window. It really had been in the trunk of his car.

Débras, as he ate away with relish, explained how it had got there. "I was on the telephone yesterday with Siméon, M. Lieven. I asked him how I was to get hold of that brief case. He said: 'You can't come to Toulouse or you'll be recognized. But that amazing fellow, Lieven, quite an extraordinary man, has been driving for weeks all round the country here, buying provisions. No one will be surprised to see him. He can bring you the brief case.' " Débras sniffed. "This stuffing is magnificent. What's it made of?"

"Braised onions, tomatoes and various herbs. What was the point of all that secrecy, Major? Siméon might just as well have told me."

"I arranged for it to be done that way. I didn't know you then . . ."

"Do have some more of these nests, M. Lieven." Josephine smiled brilliantly at Thomas. "It was really the best way. As you see, the brief case has reached its destination safe and sound."

"Yes, I can see that," said Thomas, staring at the silly thing, with its silly lists, that might still cost hundreds of people their lives. There it lay. After all the trouble taken to rescue it from the Germans it had finished up in French hands.

Pity, thought Thomas. If it hadn't been for politics, secret services, violence and death, this might have turned out such a delightful evening!

A quatrain from *The Threepenny Opera* came into his mind.

"For on this earth—I wish there were another—
Victuals are scarce and men are brutes, you know,

We'd like to live in peace and love each other,
But circumstances just won't have it so."

No, thought Thomas. That's true. They just won't. And from then on, for that reason, every sentence he spoke was accompanied by thoughts that had nothing whatever to do with it.

He said: "Now I'm going to serve a special dish which I have called, in honor of Madame, *Oeufs à la Joséphine*." At the same time he thought, That brief case must not remain in Débras's possession. I like him and I like Josephine. I don't want to do them any injury. On the other hand I'm not going to be of any use to them if I can help it.

The major evidently found Thomas Lieven's eggs much to his taste. "A delicacy, monsieur. You're really a great man."

Josephine asked: "You used nutmeg, didn't you?"

"Just a trace, madame," he answered. "The most important thing to remember is to melt the butter first and then beat up the yolks, but in such a way that they both stay bright."

At the same time he thought, I understand Josephine and I understand Débras. Their country is in danger. We have attacked them and they naturally want to defend themselves and make a stand against Hitler. But personally I don't intend to have blood on my hands.

Thomas Lieven said: "The milk should only be added after poaching the eggs, the mixture being continually stirred until the sauce is thick."

At the same time he thought, I remember that when they put that book into my hands at that idiotic spy school near Nancy in order to learn decoding it seemed to me that the hero of that novel had practically the same experiences as myself. What was his name again? Ah, yes. The Count of Monte Cristo . . .

MENU
(An Improvisation)

Sausage Nests
Oeufs à la Joséphine
Swedish Fruit Salad

19 AUGUST 1940

The "Black Venus" was enchanted by Thomas Lieven's *Oeufs à la Joséphine.*

Sausage Nests

German or Polish *wurst* (sausage) is cut into large round slices a quarter of an inch thick, without removing the skin. Lard is heated in a saucepan, the slices placed in it and rapidly heated until they form "nests" Then they are immediately taken out of the saucepan and put on a plate, where some of the nests are filled with apple-cream (grated apples and horseradish with a dash of vinegar and salt). Other "nests" are stuffed with braised onions, tomatoes and such herbs as parsley and chives, together with olive oil. To be eaten with plenty of coarse brown bread.

Oeufs à la Joséphine

A béchamel sauce is prepared and, when cool, two yolks and a little grated nutmeg are added. The sauce, which can also be used for other dishes, is in this case brought to perfection by chopped ham and grated Parmesan cheese. Poached eggs are then introduced so as to be well covered by the sauce. Parmesan cheese and flakes of butter are sprinkled over it and the dish is left to bake in the oven for five minutes.

Swedish Fruit Salad

A tin of fruit salad is well chilled in the refrigerator. The fruit is then sprinkled with a little rum and covered with plenty of cream, which may be tinned if fresh cream is not available.

Thomas Lieven inquired in honeyed accents: "Which way will you be traveling to England, Major Débras?"

"Madrid and Lisbon."

"Isn't that a very dangerous route?"

"I have another forged passport."

"All the same, as Madame was saying, there are spies all over this part of the country. If the brief case is found in your possession . . ."

"I shall have to risk it. Siméon is needed in Paris and has to return there. I shall have no one with me."

"You could have."

"Whom?"

"Me."

"You!"

The devil take all the secret services in the world, thought Thomas. He answered eagerly: "Yes, me. I just can't bear to think that the Germans might get hold of the thing!" Nor can I bear to think of you having it, he added inwardly. "Now that we have met you can see that I'm reliable." If only you knew how unreliable I am, he was thinking. "Besides, the idea amuses me. I should feel like a sportsman competing for a prize." Oh, how I wish I could be a peaceful citizen again, he thought ruefully.

Josephine looked up from her eggs and said: "M. Lieven is right, Maurice. You are like a red rag to a bull for the Germans and their spies."

"Of course, my dear. But how can we save that brief case from falling into the hands of German Intelligence?"

And of all the other secret services, thought Thomas. He said: "I met a banker named Lindner in Toulouse. He's only waiting for his wife to join him and then he's off to South America. He's offered to make me his partner. We shall be emigrating by way of Lisbon."

Josephine said to Débras: "You could meet them in Lisbon."

Débras asked: "And why do you want to do all this?"

Because of my convictions, thought Thomas Lieven. He answered: "Because of my convictions."

Débras said slowly: "I should be infinitely obliged to you . . ." Patience, thought Thomas. "And apart from that the double journey would offer us further special opportunities." If certainly would to me, thought Thomas. "I could attract the attention of our pursuers to myself. That would ensure safety for you and the brief case." No doubt of that, thought

Thomas. "Very well then. I shall travel by rail via Madrid. You, M. Lieven, since you will hold a transit visa, will still be able to go by air from Marseilles."

Thomas thought: You two are so likable with your pluck and your enterprise. I hope you won't be angry with me later on. But what else can a decent human being in my position do? I really don't want French agents to die. But nor do I want German soldiers to die. My country is not populated *entirely* by Nazis.

Thomas said: "It's simply a question of common sense, M. Débras. All the hunting dogs of this world are after you. I am still a blank sheet of paper so far as German Intelligence is concerned . . ."

[6]

By a strange turn of inscrutable fate it happened that about the same time on this very same evening General Otto von Stülpnagel, commander in chief of the German Army in France, was raising his glass of champagne in the Hôtel Majestic, his staff headquarters in Paris, to drink a toast with two other gentlemen. One was the head of German Intelligence, Admiral Wilhelm Canaris. The other was the short, gray-haired tank general, Erich von Felseneck.

With a silvery clinking of cut-glass goblets the gentlemen drank to one another under an enormous portrait of Napoleon I. Uniforms of all the branches of the services gleamed brightly. Medals blazed.

General von Stülpnagel said: "To the unknown, invisible heroes of your outfit, Admiral!"

"To the incomparably greater services of your soldiers, gentlemen!"

General von Felseneck had already drunk a little too much. He sniggered slyly. "Don't be so modest, Admiral. Your fellows can be pretty cunning." He was evidently enjoying himself. "I'm afraid I can't tell you the story, Stülpnagel. I've been sworn to secrecy. But I can tell you that our friend Canaris has got quite a head on him."

They drank.

Generals von Kleist and Reichenau joined the group and carried off their colleague von Stülpnagel.

Canaris suddenly began to take an interest in General von Felseneck, offering his cigar case and inquiring in a casual tone: "What were you referring to just now, my dear sir?"

Felseneck giggled. "Sworn to secrecy, Herr Canaris. You won't get a word out of me!"

"Who was it, then, who insisted on your keeping such absolute silence?" the admiral wanted to know.

"One of your lads. And a daring young devil, too, I can tell you. Take my hat off to him!"

Canaris smiled, but with his lips only. "Come on, let's hear about it. I'd really like to know which of our little stratagems made such an impression on you."

"Well, well! It really would be a bit too absurd if one couldn't mention it to you of all people. But I think all I need say is 'the black brief case'!"

"Ah, yes!" Canaris nodded amiably. "Of course! The black brief case!"

"What a lad, eh, Herr Canaris? You ought to have seen him posing to me as an American diplomat! The confidence? The quiet self-possession after one of my people had arrested him!" Von Felseneck laughed heartily. "He carries off two French spies and the entire Deuxième Bureau staff list into safekeeping for our benefit and still take time off to give me a recipe for potato goulash! I can't get the chap out of my mind. He's the sort I could well do with on my own staff!"

"Yes," said Canaris. "We have a few smart boys like that in the department. I remember your story now . . ." Of course he didn't really remember it at all. But his instinct told him that something pretty awful must have happened in this case. He said with assumed indifference, as though thinking aloud: "Let's see, what was that fellow's name again?"

"Lieven. Thomas Lieven, Intelligence Department, Cologne Recruiting Office. He showed me his pass. Thomas Lieven! I shan't forget that name in a hurry!"

"Lieven, of course. Yes, that's certainly a name I'll have to take a note of." Canaris beckoned to an orderly and took two full glasses of champagne from a heavy silver tray. "Come, General, let's have another drink together, over in that alcove. I'd like to hear more about your meeting with our friend Lieven. I always enjoy feeling proud of my boys."

[7]

The telephone bell rang relentlessly.

Major Fritz Loos sat up in bed, bathed in sweat. More trouble, I suppose, he thought sleepily. What a stinking job this is!

It was some time before he could find the switch of the

lamp on the bed table and pick up the receiver. "Loos speaking," he croaked.

Crackling and crashing noises sounded over the wire. "Urgent priority call from Paris. I'm connecting you with Admiral Canaris."

At the last word a stabbing pain shot through the major's interior organs. My liver again, he thought testily. That just about puts the lid on it.

Then he heard a familiar voice. "Major Loos?"

"Yes, Admiral."

"Look here, there's been an appalling mess-up . . ."

"Mess-up, Herr Admiral?"

"Do you know a certain Thomas Lieven?"

The receiver slipped from the major's hand and dropped to the counterpane. He heard quacking sounds on the wire, snatched up the receiver again in a great state of excitement and stammered: "Yes, certainly, Herr Admiral, I do know the—the name—"

"Ah, so you know him, do you? Did you ever give him an Intelligence pass?"

"Yes, Herr Admiral."

"Why?"

"I—I engaged him, Herr Admiral. But it—well, it didn't work. The man disappeared. I've been worrying about the matter for some time—"

"You've got every reason to do so, Major Loos! Get on the next plane right away. I want you here at the Hôtel Lutetia at the earliest possible moment. Is that clear?"

The Hôtel Lutetia in the Avenue de l'Opéra was the headquarters of German Intelligence in Paris.

"Very good, Herr Admiral," said Major Loos submissively. "I'll come as soon as I can. What, if I may ask, has the fellow been up to?"

Canaris told him what the fellow had been up to. Major Loos turned paler and paler. At last he shut his eyes tight. No, no, no, surely, surely not! And all my fault . . .

The voice in Paris blared like a trumpet at the walls of Jericho. "The man has lists of the names, addresses and recognition signals of every French agent! Do you realize what that means? The man carries our lives in his hands! We must get hold of him at all costs!"

"Very well, Herr Admiral, I'll put my best men on the job . . ." Major Loos drew himself up in bed in martial fashion. Unfortunately his nightshirt rather spoiled the effect.

"We'll get those lists and draw the fellow's teeth, if I have to shoot him down myself . . ."

"You seem to have taken leave of your senses, Major Loos," said the voice from Paris in silken tones. "I want that man alive. He's much too good to shoot."

[8]

20 August 1940 0215 hours

calling all stations—urgency roman figure one—chief intelligence to all service posts of secret police active duty france—german citizen thomas lieven wanted—30 years old—slim build—narrow face—dark eyes—close cropped black hair—smart civilian clothes—speaks fluent german, english, french—in possession of german intelligence pass issued by major fritz loos army recruiting centre cologne—genuine german passport number 543231 series 1 c—forged american diplomatic pass in the name of william s. murphy—left paris 15 june 1940 in black chrysler with corps diplomatique badges and american flag on roof—in possession of pass issued by general erich von felseneck—travelled in company of young french woman and french man—in possession of most important enemy documents—immediate research ordered—all information including negative reports to major loos head of special group z secret police headquarters paris—in arrest of lieven weapons to be used only if absolutely necessary—message ends—

While this order was startling secret police and many military personnel, including the captain who had put five cans of German army petrol at the disposal of a certain Murphy on June 16, at Tours, that urgently wanted man, Thomas Lieven, was alighting in high spirits from his little Peugeot in the rue des Bergères at Toulouse. Contentedly clasping a black brief case under his arm, he banged the door of the car.

The gay girls Chez Jeanne were already asleep. The little restaurant was closed. The only light came from the old-fashioned drawing room with the gigantic mirror and the red plush upholstery. Mimi, Siméon and the seductive sandy-haired owner of the establishment were sitting there waiting for Thomas.

Sighs of relief resounded as he entered. Jeanne announced: "We were getting quite worried about you!"

"Is that so?" Thomas retorted. "And were you worried, too, when you sent me away?"

"We were obeying orders," Siméon told him. "But I must say I don't understand why *you've* got that brief case still."

Thomas helped himself to a generous measure of Remy Martin from a bottle on a side table.

"Here's to all our futures," he said. "The hour of parting is at hand, dear friends. I managed to convince Major Débras that it would be better if *I* took the documents to Lisbon. You, Colonel, are to return to Paris and report to Lotus Flower Four whoever she may be."

"That's the code name for underground resistance," replied the colonel in a solemn tone.

"Well, I hope you'll enjoy it," said Thomas. He looked at his handsome landlady. "And the best of luck to you too, Jeanne. All prosperity to your establishment!"

"I'll miss you a lot," said Jeanne sadly. Thomas kissed her hand. "It's always painful to part," he said.

Mimi, who usually took everything so lightly, suddenly burst into a tempest of tears. She choked and sobbed and moaned, exclaiming in high-pitched, forlorn tones: "Oh, I am stupid—forgive me—I don't really want to cry—"

Some hours later, as she lay beside Thomas—it was already light outside and raining—he heard her voice through the sound of the downpour. "I've been thinking about it for such a long time, torturing myself . . ."

"I understand," he said sympathetically. "You're worrying about Siméon, aren't you?"

She suddenly flung herself against his chest. Her tears trickled over his lips, hot and salty. "Darling, I love you. I'm really frightfully in love with you. But the last few weeks in this house have shown me clearly that you're not the marrying kind . . ."

"If you're talking about Jeanne," he began. But she interrupted him. "Oh, it's not only Jeanne, specially. You're a man who likes women. But you like them all, not just one. You could never be faithful . . ."

"I could try, Mimi."

"You could never be so faithful as Jules. He's not nearly so clever as you are. But he's much more romantic, much more idealistic."

"My dearest, you really don't have to apologize for feeling that way about him. I've been expecting it for some time. You are both French and love your native land. But for me just now there isn't such a thing. So I want to get away and you want to stay . . ."

"And you can forgive me?"

"I've nothing to forgive."

She snuggled up to him. "Oh, please, please, don't be so kind, darling. Otherwise I shall start crying again . . . Oh, isn't it awful not to be allowed to marry two husbands!"

Thomas smiled. Then he moved his head to avoid the pressure of the black brief case lying under his pillow. Thomas had determined never to part from it until he was ready to board the plane for South America. He couldn't do anything about the case while he was in Toulouse. There wouldn't be time. But in Lisbon he would take care that it could never do any harm.

"Thank you, *chéri*," he heard Mimi whisper sleepily. "Oh, thank you."

"What for?"

"Oh, for everything . . ." She felt an overwhelming sense of gratitude to him for his gaiety and generosity, for the short hours of their happiness together amid bright lights, in luxurious hotels and railway sleepers, in bars listening to soft music and in expensive restaurants, enjoying marvelous meals.

That was how Mimi thanked Thomas once more, while the rain of that dreary morning drummed on the black cobbles of the rue des Bergère and the couple ended their affair as they had begun it and as all lovers should end their affairs—in love.

[9]

Thomas Lieven did not know that the German Army and German Intelligence were looking for him as if he were a pin. Consequently he was ready to rejoice with anyone when the prospective emigrant, Walter Lindner, crimson in the face and completely out of breath, burst into the kitchen of Jeanne's restaurant. Thomas was just making some onion soup.

Lindner dropped onto a stool, knocking over a bowl of cucumber salad, and blurted out: "My wife, my wife—I've found my wife!"

"Where? How?"

"Here in Toulouse!" Lindner was laughing and crying at the same time. It looked as though he were happily married. "I went into that little café on the Place du Capitole and was about to sit down and play chess with those fellows from

Brünn when I heard a woman's voice behind me say: 'Excuse me, do you by any chance know a Herr Lindner?' Next moment she called out, 'Walter!' and rushed into my arms!"

Lindner and Thomas executed a little dance of joy, during which, sad to say, they completely ruined the spilled salad.

"Forward, quick march to the consulate!" cried Lindner. "Now we can get a move on, Herr Lieven! Heavens, how I'm looking forward to our new life together!"

And I even more, thought Thomas.

Then the future partners in a South American bank still to be founded started their preparations, at breakneck speed, for emigration. No country with a French frontier issued entry permits at this date. The very best one could hope for was a transit visa. But this in its turn needed a preliminary overseas entry permit.

After Walter Lindner had proved to the Argentinian consul in Marseilles that he had a balance of over a million dollars at the Rio de la Plata Bank, he immediately obtained an entry permit for himself and his wife. Lindner than explained that he wished to take M. Jean Leblanc to Buenos Aires as his partner. Thereupon M. Jean Leblanc also had a genuine entry permit stamped on the forged passport with which he had formerly been issued at the spy school near Nancy by the man who called himself Jupiter. On August 26, accordingly, the three of them also obtained Portuguese transit visas. The way to emigration was then clear.

Thomas Lieven next drew up a precise time chart for the plan he had in mind. Quite a lot, including his own life, depended on this plan being adhered to. After a further telephone conversation with Major Débras at Les Milandes the chart read as follows:

August 28: Departure of Thomas Lieven and the Lindners to Marseilles.

August 29: Departure of Major Débras by train via Perpignan, Barcelona and Madrid to Lisbon.

August 30: Thomas Lieven and the Lindners leave Marseilles by air for Lisbon.

September 10: Thomas Lieven and the Lindners leave Lisbon aboard the Portuguese steamer *General Carmona* for Buenos Aires.

From September 3 onwards Major Débras was to await Thomas Lieven every evening at 10 P.M. in the Estoril casino to take delivery of that ominous black brief case. Between August 30 and September 3 Thomas hoped to find time to make certain alterations in the contents of the brief case.

With a winning smile an elegantly dressed young gentleman, during the morning of August 29, entered the office of Rainbow Airways, a private American charter company in the rue de Rome at Marseilles. Lifting his Homburg, he approached the ticket counter and addressed the clerk in fluent French. "Good morning, monsieur. My name is Leblanc. I have come to fetch the air tickets to Lisbon for M. and Mme. Lindner and myself."

"One moment, please." The clerk searched his lists. "Yes, here we are. Tomorrow at 1545 hours." He began to write out the tickets.

A small omnibus pulled up outside the office. Two pilots and a stewardess came to the counter. Thomas learned from their talk that they had just landed and would fly tomorrow at 1545 hours to Lisbon. It was then that he had the brain wave.

The stewardess, who could not have been more than twenty-five, began to make up her face. She was built on the lines of a racing yacht, had slanting eyes, high cheekbones, a golden-brown complexion and wonderful chestnut-colored hair falling in a soft wave across her finely molded forehead. She looked a cool, evasive sort, reminding Thomas of a fawn.

He knew that type. He understood exactly what she was like. Once a walking icicle like that began to melt there would be no holding her.

Thomas Lieven dedicated thirty seconds to the affectionate recollection of his parting from Mimi, Siméon, Jeanne and her ladies in the rue des Bergères. They had all kissed him, even the colonel. "Freedom forever, comrade!" the latter had cried. And when the taxi drove up Jeanne had burst into unrestrained sobbing. Oh, it had been a most touching scene, as if they were all one family.

The thirty seconds were over. Ah well, thought Thomas. Circumstances just won't have it so!

The fawn was still making up her face. The fawn dropped her lipstick.

I am impelled by noble motives, Thomas assured himself, with a view to providing a moral foundation for what he meant to do. Then he picked up the lipstick and handed it to the evasive fawn with the brown eyes in which golden gleams came and went.

"Many thanks," said the fawn.

"Let's go, then, shall we?" Thomas suggested.

"What on earth do you mean?"

"Or have you got anything else to do here? I don't mind waiting. I suggest we go first to the Grand Hôtel, where I am staying and have an aperitif. After that probably the best place to lunch would be at Guido's in the rue de la Paix. Then we might go swimming."

"I *beg* your pardon—"

"You don't care to swim? Well then, I propose we stay in the hotel and rest."

"I've never had such an experience as this in all my life!"

"My dear young lady, I'll do my very best to arrange for you to say that again tomorrow morning." Thomas drew his beloved repeater from his waistcoat pocket and made it chime the hour. Eleven strokes and then two sounded clear and soft as a bell. "Half-past eleven. I see I'm making you nervous. I'm aware that I have a most disturbing effect on women. Well, I'll expect you in the bar of the Grand Hôtel at—about twelve, shall we say?"

The fawn threw her head back and stalked away, indignation in every tap of her high heels on the stone floor.

Thomas went off to the Grand Hôtel, sat down in the bar and ordered whisky. The fawn entered the bar at three minutes past twelve, carrying a swimsuit.

[10]

Thomas Lieven, wearing a gray flannel suit, a white shirt, a blue tie, black shoes, his Homburg and his umbrella, strolled beside the two corpulent Lindners in a group of other passengers making their way across the tarmac to the waiting plane. He looked happy, though also a bit heavy-eyed.

Mabel Hastings, the stewardess, stood at the top of the gangway, beside the entrance. She looked happy, though also a bit heavy-eyed.

"Hallo," said Thomas, as he came up the gangway.

"Hallo," said Mabel, the golden gleams in her fine eyes sparkling. She had really never come across anything like Thomas Lieven in all her life. They hadn't after all gone swimming after the lunch at Guido's, but had rested in the hotel, where they both happened to be staying.

As he was helping Mabel Hastings to pack her bag on the morning of August 30, she had quite unconsciously done him yet another favor, not unconnected with a certain black brief case . . .

The machine taxied past the airport building preparatory to taking off. Thomas, glancing out of the window of the airplane over the smooth turf and a big flock of sheep peacefully grazing beyond it, remembered that sheep were supposed to be lucky. Then he saw a car stop outside the airport building. A man jumped out. He wore a blue, crumpled suit and a crumpled yellow mackintosh. His face was glistening with sweat. He was waving both his arms about.

Thomas felt sorry for him. Bad luck! The plane would be taking off in a moment and that poor chap would have to watch it disappear.

Actually the pilot had just given both engines full throttle, as is always done immediately before taking off.

An icy chill ran down Thomas Lieven's spine. That waving man over there by the airport building . . . his face . . . he knew that face . . . seen it before somewhere . . .

Suddenly Thomas Lieven realized where he had seen that face before. The Gestapo headquarters at Cologne! The man over there was Major Loos of German Intelligence!

Keep your head, thought Thomas Lieven. They're after me. But it looks as though Providence is on my side. Major Loos is going to miss me in a minute, for the second time. Only five more seconds now before we take off and then . . .

The plane didn't take off. The roar of the engines at full throttle ceased. The door of the pilot's cabin flew open. Mabel Hastings, cool as ever, appeared on the threshold. She announced in velvety tones: "Ladies and gentlemen, there is no cause for alarm. We have just been informed by radio that a belated passenger has arrived whom it is essential to take aboard at all costs. So we shall pick him up and then make a fresh start in a few minutes' time."

Shortly afterward Major Loos entered the plane. He apologized to the passengers in English for having delayed their departure and bowed formally to Thomas Lieven. The latter stared straight through him, as if the major had been transparent.

[11]

Lisbon! A narrow ledge of freedom and peace in a Europe being progressively torn to pieces by war and barbarism.

Lisbon!

A fantastic paradise of wealth, plenty, beauty and elegance in the midst of a world of distress and misery.

Lisbon!

The happy hunting ground of the secret services, the arena of monstrous and monstrously absurd intrigues.

Thomas Lieven was already deeply involved in them from the moment he landed. Dogged at every step by the weary but indefatigable Major Loos, who had fallen asleep during the flight, snoring gently with his mouth wide open, Thomas Lieven was immediately subjected to a particularly rigorous customs examination. He was stripped to the skin, his luggage was ransacked, his pockets all turned inside out. Someone seemed to have dropped quite a hint to the Portuguese Security Police.

But oddly enough they found neither his substantial fortune in dollars nor that special black brief case in his possession. The customs men dismissed him with ceremonious courtesy. The Lindners had long since driven off to their hotel.

Thomas marched to the passport barrier. Major Loos marched close behind him. Thomas marched to the airport taxi line. Major Loos marched close behind him. They still had not exchanged a single word.

Well, now I'm going to give you a bit of exercise, my lad, thought Thomas, jumping into a taxi. Loos jumped into another. Both vehicles whizzed off toward the center of the city on the seven hills. Thomas had once spent six glorious weeks on holiday in the imposing Portuguese capital and knew his way about it quite well.

He paid the taxi off in the Praça Dom Pedro. The major's taxi stopped just behind his own. The cafés behind their gardens bordering on the pavement swarmed with Portuguese citizens and refugees, all engaged in vociferous debate. Thomas Lieven, as he passed them, could hear every language of Europe.

He plunged into the milling crowds, followed closely by the major, who made desperate efforts not to lose sight of him.

Now, said Thomas mentally to the major, we'll start using our legs a bit, my lad. Exercise is good for the health.

Accordingly, Thomas marched rapidly downhill to the narrow little streets leading to the sea and then uphill again to the steeply rising main arteries of traffic. He made use of short cuts and arcades, darted unexpectedly around corners, but always took care not to overstrain the major to an intolerable extent. He wanted his pursuer to curse him—but not to lose him.

Thomas Lieven continued his game of catch-me-if-you-can for over an hour. Then he hailed another taxi and drove, followed by the major, to the fishing village of Cascais, near the fashionable seaside resort of Estoril. He knew a smart open-air restaurant in the village.

The sun went down, blood-red, into the sea. A warm wind rose as the evening came on. The small fishing village in a bay of the Tagus estuary was the most picturesque spot anywhere near Lisbon. Thomas Lieven was looking forward to watching a drama which took place there every evening, when the fishing fleet came in.

He alighted from his taxi in front of the restaurant. The major's old rattletrap pulled up behind him. The German Intelligence officer, gasping for breath, tottered into the open air. He looked wretched.

Thomas decided to stop the cruel game he was playing. He went up to Loos, raised his Homburg and spoke to him kindly, as if to a lost child. "Well, we might as well take a bit of a rest here now. I'm sure the last few days have been a great strain on you."

"You can say that again." The major did his best to maintain the prestige of his profession. He snarled: "You can go to the end of the world, Lieven. But you won't escape me a second time!"

"Don't be too sure, dear boy, don't be too sure. We're not in Cologne now, you know. A German major doesn't amount to so very much in this part of the world, Loos, my friend."

The Major in mufti swallowed hard. "I should be obliged if you'd call me Lehmann, M. Leblanc."

"That's better! I much prefer your present tone of voice, Herr Lehmann. Be seated, pray. Look down there. Isn't that marvelous?"

Out at sea the fishing fleet, a swarm of lateen-sailed vessels, resembling so many butterflies, was coming into harbor in the Tagus estuary. Just as they had a thousand years ago, the fishermen dragged their boats on wooden rollers up the beach, shouting and singing. Women and children came to help them. Fires kindled in small kilns all along the darkening shore.

Thomas, as he gazed down at the beach, inquired: "How did you come to trace me?"

"We had no difficulty as far as Toulouse, despite all your precautions. The ladies at Mme. Jeanne's behaved very nobly. Neither our threats nor our promises could get a word out of them."

"Who gave the game away, then?"

"A tough called Alphonse. He had it in for you, for some reason."

"Ah, yes, poor Bébé's boy friend. I had to touch him up a bit." Thomas half closed his eyes at the recollection. Then he opened them to stare hard at the major. "Portugal is a neutral country, Herr Lehmann. I may as well warn you that I shall defend myself."

"But my dear Herr Liev—sorry, I mean M. Leblanc, you have quite a wrong idea of the situation. I have orders from Admiral Canaris to ensure your complete immunity if you return to Germany. And I also have orders to purchase from you the black brief case you know of."

"Oh."

"How much do you want?" The major bent across the table. "I know perfectly well that you still have the lists."

Thomas dropped his eyes. Then he stood up, murmuring a brief apology. "Sorry, I have to telephone now."

But he did not go to the telephone booth in the restaurant. In the circumstances he thought that would be hardly safe enough. He walked a few yards along the street to a public kiosk, where he called up the Hotel Palacio do Estoril-Parque, and asked to speak to Miss Hastings. The American stewardess answered immediately. "Oh, Jean, where on earth have you been? I've been longing to see you!"

"I'm afraid I'll be a bit late. Held up by a—ahem—a business conference. Mabel, this morning, while I was helping you to pack in Marseilles, I inadvertently put a black leather brief case into your bag. Do be an angel and take it down to the porter, so that he can put it in the hotel safe."

"Of course I will, darling . . . and please, please, don't make it too late, will you? You know I shall be flying to Dakar tomorrow."

As he listened to the girl's voice, Thomas suddenly felt quite certain that someone was eavesdropping outside the telephone box. He pushed open the door abruptly. A cadaverous-looking man staggered back with a cry of pain, clutching at his forehead.

"Oh, pardon," said Thomas Lieven. Then he raised his eyebrows, smiling resignedly. He knew the fellow, who looked like a close relative of Major Loos. Thomas had met the man at the London airport in May 1939, when he had been deported. It was this fellow who had deported him.

CHAPTER 3

[1]

Well, that's done it, thought Thomas Lieven. I must really have gone off my head this time. I could swear that this fellow, whose skull I have just cracked with the door of a Portuguese telephone kiosk, is Mr. Lovejoy of the British secret service. But of course that can only mean that I've gone absolutely and perfectly balmy. It can't be Lovejoy. How could he possibly have come down here from London to the outskirts of Lisbon? He can't conceivably have any business here.

Thomas decided to try an extremely bizarre experiment. He said to himself, I'll address this phantom, this outcome of my unbalanced imagination, as Lovejoy. Then I shall immediately know for certain whether I'm really mad or not.

Thomas Lieven, raising his eyebrows, inquired: "How are you, Mr. Lovejoy?"

"Not so well as you, Mr. Lieven," replied the cadaverous one promptly. "Do you suppose I enjoyed chasing you all over Lisbon? And then that bang with the door too!" Lovejoy dabbed the back of his sweating neck with a pocket handkerchief. A bruise was slowly but persistently forming on his forehead.

So it's not I who have gone crazy, but the world I'm living in! And it's getting worse and worse! And now apparently there's a sort of method in its madness, Thomas thought. He took a deep breath, leaned back against the telephone box and said: "What brings you to Lisbon, Mr. Lovejoy?"

The representative of the interests of Great Britain made a face. "I should be obliged if you'd call me Ellington. That's my name in Portugal."

"One good turn deserves another. So you can call me Leblanc. That's *my* name in Portugal, Meanwhile, you still haven't answered my question."

The man who had just called himself Ellington demanded

furiously: "I suppose you still think that we of the secret service are idiots, don't you?"

The man who had just called himself Leblanc replied politely: "I beg you not to press me for an answer to that leading question."

The British agent came up quite close to him. "Do you suppose we don't know that Admiral Canaris himself wants to get hold of you? Do you suppose that we don't tap German transmissions in London?"

"I thought they went out in code."

"We can crack their code."

"And the Germans can crack yours," said Thomas, suddenly beginning to feel extraordinarily cheerful. "Why don't both your teams get together and play Kiss-in-the-Ring?"

The Englishman retorted sternly: "I know you're a heartless cynic. I know nothing is sacred to you. I saw through you right from the start, at the airport in London. You are the sort of man who has no sense of honor, no morals, no patriotism, no decency . . ."

"Flatterer!"

"That was why I said straight away, Let me tackle the fellow, he only understands one kind of language—" Lovejoy rubbed his forefinger and thumb together.

"Just a moment. One thing at a time, please. I ask you again what brings you here . . ."

Lovejoy told him. According to his account of the matter—and one had to believe him—the British secret service had really tapped all the transmissions which had anything to do with the search of Major Loos for Thomas Lieven. The last of them had revealed the good news that Loos would be following the wanted man to Lisbon.

"To Lisbon," said Lovejoy finally. "I flew out at once by courier aircraft, arriving two hours ahead of you. I followed you here from the airport. You and the other gentleman sitting over there on the restaurant terrace. I assume that's Major Loos."

"I say, you're a sharp fellow! You don't yet know the major personally?"

"No."

"Good Lord! Well then, you must come along to the restaurant and I'll introduce you to each other. We'll dine together, on mussels of course, in Cascais you just have to eat mussels . . ."

"Stop talking rot, will you? We know you're playing a double game—"

"Oho?"

"You're in possession of a brief case containing lists of the most important French agents in France and Germany. I shan't permit you to auction off those lists to that precious Major Loos, though naturally he'll offer you plenty of money for them—"

"Hush, hush—"

"But I'll offer you just as much, more!" Lovejoy laughed scornfully. "I know that money's all you care about. For you there are no such things as honor, faith, conscience, remorse, idealism, decency—"

"That'll do," Thomas Lieven interrupted in measured tones. "I've heard quite enough now and you'd better shut your trap double-quick. Who stopped me returning to England and continuing my life as a peaceable citizen? Who helped to upset my whole existence? You and your infernal, accursed secret service. You don't suppose, do you, sir, that I have any special fondness for you?"

He was thinking: I'll give you something to chew over before long, you devils, the whole lot of you!

"Sorry I had to leave you for a while," said Thomas Lieven as he returned to Major Loos three minutes later, the officer who might really have been taken for a close relative of his Anglo-Saxon colleague.

"Met a friend, didn't you? I saw you standing over there by the telephone box."

"Oh, yes, an old friend. And incidentally one of your rivals, Herr Lehmann."

Dozens of storm lanterns had by this time been lit on the terrace of the restaurant. The solemn, deep-throated singing of the fishermen could still be heard down below. A gentle southwester was blowing up from the Tagus estuary, where the waters had taken on the hue of smoky mother-of-pearl in the twilight.

Loos repeated nervously: "Rivals?"

"The gentleman works for the British secret service."

Loos thumped the table with his fist. "You damned scoundrel!" he cried, beside himself with rage.

"Steady, Lehmann," Thomas reprimanded him. "If you can't behave decently I shall leave you to yourself."

The major pulled himself together with a tremendous effort. "You are a German. I appeal to your sense of patriotism . . ."

"Lehmann, for the last time I must ask you to behave yourself!"

"Come back with me to our own country. You have my word as an Intelligence officer that nothing will happen to you. An Intelligence officer's word of honor is not to be trifled with . . ."

"No," said Thomas quietly. "The best thing is not to trust it from the start."

The major swallowed hard. "Then sell me that black brief case. I offer you three thousand dollars."

"The gentleman from London offered me double that just now."

"Well, how much do you want, then?"

"That's a silly question. As much as I can get."

"What a depraved rascal you are!"

"Yes, that's what your colleague was saying just now."

The major's expression changed with startling suddenness. He murmured admiringly: "Man alive, I wish we had you on our side . . ."

"Come on, Lehmann. How much?"

"I—I must ask Berlin again—request fresh instructions . . ."

"Go ahead then, Lehmann. Request them. And hurry up about it. My boat will be leaving in a few days' time."

"Just tell me one thing. How did you get that brief case into this country? I know the Portuguese customs men stripped you to the skin!"

"I got a foreigner to help me." Thomas Lieven thought with gratitude of his evasive fawn. "Tricks of that kind, you know, Lehmann, require a certain little quality which is quite out of the reach of people like you."

"And what is that, may I ask?"

"Just charm."

"You hate me, don't you?"

"Herr Lehmann, I have led a happy life. I used to be a peaceful citizen. You and your colleagues in Britain and France are responsible for my sitting here at this moment. Do you expect me to be grateful to you for that? I didn't want to have anything to do with any of you. So you'd better be careful how you deal with me. Where are you staying?"

"In the Casa Senhora de Fatima."

"I'm in the Hotel Palacio do Estoril-Parque. So is the gentleman from London, incidentally. Ask your chief how much that black brief case is worth to him. Your colleague was asking *his* chief this evening . . . Well, that's that. And now I really must eat!"

[2]

The night was still warm.

Thomas Lieven drove back to Lisbon in an open taxi. He could see the moonlit foam of waves breaking along the shore, the luxurious villas bordering the wide highway, the dark pinewoods, the palms and the picturesque night clubs perched on low hills, from which echoes of feminine laughter and dance music floated to his ears.

He drove on past the fashionable bathing resort of Estoril, with its casino sparkling with lights and its two great hotels.

Elsewhere Europe was sinking further and further into ashes and ruin. But here people were still living in an earthly paradise.

It was a poisoned paradise, thought Thomas Lieven, a deadly Garden of Eden, filled with the reptiles of many nations spying on and threatening one another. It was here in the Portuguese capital that they met, grew powerful and played their monstrous devils' harlequinade in whole battalions of the so-called Fifth Column.

In the heart of Lisbon, the splendid Praça Dom Pedro, with its pavements in black and white mosaic, Thomas Lieven alighted. The gardens in front of the great cafés that surrounded the vast square were still crowded with native citizens and foreigners.

Church clocks in all directions were resonantly striking eleven. While the strokes were still echoing around the square Thomas was surprised to see the people in the cafés, both the Portuguese and the refugees from Austria, Germany, Poland, France, Belgium, Czechoslovakia, Holland and Denmark, jumping up from their seats and pouring across to the lower end of the Praça Dom Pedro. Thomas allowed himself to be swept along in the tide of humanity.

At the end of the square stood a massive newspaper office. High across the façade of its top floor ran a neon-lit band recording a stream of the latest news. Thousands of eyes stared upward in fascination at the procession of illuminated letters, which might mean life or death to so many of them.

Thomas read:

DNB The German Foreign Minister von Ribbentrop and the Italian Foreign Minister Ciano, at an arbitration meeting in the Belvedere Castle, Vienna, have finally reached a decision on the question of the new frontiers to be drawn between Hungary and Rumania . . .

UNITED PRESS Heavy German air raids on Britain continue, causing serious damage and loss of life in Liverpool, London, Weybridge and Felixstowe . . .

INTERNATIONAL NEWS SERVICE Italian heavy bombers have attacked Malta in great force. Concentrated air raids are also being directed against British military establishments in North Africa . . .

Thomas Lieven turned to watch the faces of the crowd. Few of them bore indifferent expressions. Nearly all appeared shocked, anxious, dismayed or actually despairing.

On the way back to his hotel Thomas Lieven was four times accosted by good-looking women. One was from Vienna, one from Prague and one from Paris. The youngest of the four, almost a child, had a face like a madonna. Thomas gave her some money and wished her luck. She told him she had fled from Spain after Franco's victory.

In the garden of the six-storied Parque Hotel the scent of the flowers was overpowering. Even the lounge resembled a sea of exotic flowers. As Thomas walked through it dozens of attentive glances, suspicious, menacing or alarmed, followed him.

Here too he heard nearly all the languages of Europe.

But none of the people seated in the lounge looked shocked, anxious or despairing. They were for the most part secret agents of both sexes, living in luxury as they plied their base and stupid trade under the cloak of patriotism.

The moment Thomas entered his suite soft arms were flung around his neck and he smelled the perfume used by Mabel Hastings. The young stewardess was wearing a white pearl necklace and high-heeled shoes. Nothing else.

"Oh, Jean—at last, at last! What a time you've been!"

She kissed him tenderly. He inquired in a businesslike tone: "Where's that black brief case?"

"In the hotel safe—just as you told me—"

"That's fine," said Thomas Lieven. "Then we needn't talk of anything but love now—"

Next morning about half-past eight a tired but happy Mabel Hastings flew off to Dakar. Next morning about ten o'clock a happy and not in the least tired Thomas Lieven, after partaking of a copious breakfast, set about his plans for a thorough revenge, before he left Europe, on his tormentors of the German, British and French secret services.

That morning, August 31, 1940, a smartly dressed gentleman entered the biggest bookshop in the city, on the Avenida da India. He asked for plans of some German and French towns. He found what he wanted, among other sources, in a 1935 Baedeker. Then he went to the General Post Office. His charm and persuasive eloquence succeeded in persuading an elderly female clerk to put the telephone books of five German and fourteen French towns at his disposal for an hour. The General Post Office of the cosmopolitan city of Lisbon possessed a complete library of all the telephone registers of Europe.

Thomas copied 120 names and addresses out of the books. In the Rua Augusta he bought a typewriter and some paper. Then he returned to his hotel, fetched the black brief case from the safe and went upstairs to his pleasantly cool suite on the first floor. The windows overlooked a park full of strange shrubs and trees, fountains and brightly colored parakeets.

In order to get into the best possible frame of mind for his task he ordered a second tomato cocktail from the floor waiter. Then he sat down to work.

He opened the black brief case, which contained his whole fortune in cash. It also contained six closely written lists and some blueprints of new types of heavy tanks, flame throwers and fighter aircraft.

I wish I could drop all this accursed muck down the pan right away, thought Thomas. But Major Débras is sure to know of them and would miss them. Lovejoy and Loos, however, don't know anything about them. They only want the lists.

Well, they'll get lists.

He examined the six sheets of typewritten paper. They gave the names of the service and civil members of the Deuxième Bureau, the names of French agents in Germany and of trusted persons in Germany and France. There were 117 altogether.

The names were accompanied by addresses, followed by a couple of sentences, the first to be used in speaking to the agent and the second to be used by the agent in replying. Only then could one be sure that one was dealing with him and no one else.

For example, Thomas Lieven read: "Willibald Lohr, Düsseldorf, Sedanstrasse 34. (1) Have you by any chance seen a gray miniature poodle with a red collar? (2) No, but they're still selling honey over in Lichtenbroich.

"Adolf Meier-Wilke, Berlin-Grünewald, Bismarckallee 145. (1) Are those your pigeons on the summer-house roof? (2) Don't turn around. Your buttons are undone."

And so on.

Thomas shook his head and sighed. Then he inserted a clean sheet in his new typewriter and unfolded a street plan of Frankfurt-am-Main. One of the names he had copied from the Munich telephone book was of Friedrich Kesselhuth.

He typed that name, then bent over the Frankfurt street plan.

Suppose we take Erlenstrasse, he thought. He found that it adjoined the road leading into the town and was short. The scale of the map, he noted, was 1:16,000

How many houses could there be in Erlenstrasse? Thirty or forty, definitely under sixty. All the same, we may as well make sure.

He typed: "Friedrich Kesselhuth, Frankfurt-am-Main, Erlenstrasse 77. (1) Is that girl at Fechenheims's dark or fair? (2) Eat that bird of yours quick, it's tainting the air."

Now for the next!

Thomas transported a certain Paul Giggenheimer from Hamburg-Altona to Düsseldorf, No. 51 of the extremely short Rubensstrasse. "(1) John Galsworthy is 66. (2) We must get our colonies back."

Well, that's Number Two, thought Thomas Lieven. I need another 115. And I'll have to type the whole blasted rubbish out three times. One for Lovejoy, one for Loos and one for Débras. Quite a job. Never mind, it'll pay off well.

He went on typing. After half an hour he suddenly felt he really couldn't carry on. He went to the window and looked down into the park.

Confound it all, he thought. This will never do. Let's think again.

The idea was to get rid of the genuine lists because they could only cause more harm whoever got hold of them, Germans, British or French. I've made up my mind that no one else is to die on account of those lists.

On the other hand I've also made up my mind to take vengeance on all the idiots who have ruined my life. But am I really taking vengeance on them by doing this? Am I really preventing fresh harm from being done?

If the French and British start working with my bogus lists they'll find out that they're all wrong. And that'll be fine.

But what about the Germans?

Let's suppose that Friedrich Kesselhuth of Munich has a namesake in Frankfurt who hasn't got a telephone. Or let's suppose that they've lengthened Erlenstrasse in Frankfurt lately and there really is a No. 77 there now. The Gestapo will arrest all men of the name of Kesselhuth. They'll be tortured, imprisoned, executed . . .

And that's only one of the names and addresses. There will be 116 others!

Perhaps the gentlemen of the three secret services will find out how they've been had and throw the lists away. They might have at least enough intelligence for that. All the same, after all my recent experiences, I'd better not rely on it.

But, damn it. Débras will be coming for that brief case on September 3. What the devil am I to do?

How easy it is to betray and kill people. And how laborious and troublesome it is to rescue and protect them from torment, persecution and death . . .

[3]

The telephone bell rang.

Thomas Lieven, startled out of his reflections, picked up the receiver. He shut his eyes when he heard a well-known voice say: "Lehmann speaking. I've been talking to the party in question. He offers six thousand dollars."

"No sale," said Thomas.

"What do you mean by that?" The voice of the major from Cologne sounded panic-stricken. "Have you sold it already?"

"No."

"What's the position, then?"

Thomas stared glumly at the sheet inserted in his typewriter. "I'm still negotiating. I'll take your offer into consideration. Call me up again tomorrow." He hung up without another word.

I'll have to call one of the fellows on my lists Fritz Loos, he thought angrily. Then he put all the papers back into the black brief case and carried it downstairs to the head porter, who locked it away in the hotel safe. Thomas resolved to take a little walk and think things over. There must be some solution to this problem. There must, there *must* . . .

The agent Lovejoy was sitting in the lounge, still with an enormous bruise on his forehead.

Lovejoy sprang up and dashed across to Thomas, his eyes alight with cupidity "What about that brief case? I saw it in your hand quite clearly. What's going on?"

"I'm still negotiating. Ask me again tomorrow."

"Look here, I'll give you more than that Nazi of yours, I don't care how much it is!"

"All right, all right," said Thomas Lieven, hurrying away. Deep in thought he went out into the sunny street. Deep in thought he wandered off through the city. In the Avenida da Liberdade he had to stop. A funeral procession was going by under the palms. Police were holding up the traffic. Apparently the funeral was that of an important Portuguese citizen, for hundreds of men and women in black were following the coffin with solemn expressions. Many were in tears. Passersby raised their hats. Prayers resounded. The air smelled of incense.

Suddenly a hoarse chuckle was heard amidst the murmuring of the mourners. It was an elegant young gentleman, who had interrupted the proceedings with such appalling tactlessness.

"Dirty foreigner!" exclaimed an old woman, spitting on the pavement at his feet.

"Yes, ma'am," said Thomas Lieven. Then he raced off, shouldering his umbrella, to the Central Station close by.

In the main hall newspapers and magazines from every country in the world were on sale at a big bookstall. Pictures of Churchill and Hitler, Goering and Roosevelt, hung peacefully side by side, surrounded by photographs of pin-up girls, nude athletes and martial headlines in many languages.

"I want some newspapers, please," said Thomas Lieven breathlessly to the wrinkled old salesman. "All the French and all the German papers."

"They're all two days old."

"Doesn't matter. Give me all you have. Last week's too. And any from the week before last."

"Drunk, aren't you?"

"No, perfectly sober. Come on, dad!"

The old man shrugged his shoulders. Then he sold out his entire stock of old numbers of the *Reich*, the *Völkischer Beobachter*, the *Berliner Zeitung*, the *Deutsche Allgemeinen Zei-*

tung, the *Müncher Neuesten Nachrichten, Le Matin, L'Oeuvre, Le Petit Parisien, Paris Soir* and nine French provincial newspapers.

Thomas took the whole lot back to his hotel and locked himself into his suite. Then he began to examine the dusty old pages, but only those at the back, where the columns of obituary notices were printed. Plenty of people died daily in Paris and Cologne, Toulouse and Berlin, Le Havre and Munich. The dead were safe from the clutches of the Gestapo.

Thomas Lieven started typing. He worked fast. For he could now put down genuine addresses with a clear conscience.

On September 2, 1940, our friend bought certain leather goods, two black brief cases, in the Avenida Duarte Pacheco. Early that afternoon he took one of them to the ultra-smart establishment of Senhor Gomes dos Santos.

Senhor dos Santos, one of the best tailors in Lisbon, personally welcomed Thomas, laughing jovially as he shook his hand. Laughter gave Senhor Santos a very prosperous appearance, since he had a great deal of gold in his mouth.

In one of the dressing rooms, curtained with a delicate shade of pink, Thomas Lieven met Major Loos, who was wearing a new, well-cut suit of dark gray flannel.

"Thank God," exclaimed Loos with great relief, as soon as he caught sight of Lieven.

For the last three days he had been continuously kept on tenterhooks by Thomas. He had repeatedly met him in bars and hotel lounges and on the beach. But the man had repeatedly put him off. "I can't make up my mind yet. I must speak to the Englishman again first."

Lovejoy had been given exactly the same treatment by Thomas, who had kept him guessing whenever they met, telling him that his rival was always increasing his offers. In this way an offer of ten thousand dollars had by this time been made by both gentlemen. Thomas decided to let the matter rest at that figure.

He told both gentlemen in a serious tone: "Until you leave you must keep it absolutely secret that it is to you that I have sold the brief case. Otherwise your life will be in danger. Consequently the transfer must take place where no one is likely to see us."

Loos had suggested a dressing room in the stately establishment of Senhor dos Santos. He told Thomas: "That tailor's a miracle-worker. He can make you a faultless suit, to measure, of the best English cloth, in three days." He tapped his sleeve. "Just feel the stuff."

"Yes, really excellent."

"We all deal here."

"Who is 'all'?"

"All the agents who live in Lisbon."

"And you call this a place where no one is likely to see us?"

"Of course I do! Don't you understand? Not one of my respected colleagues would ever dream that I'm employed here!"

"I see."

"Besides, I gave José a hundred escudos."

"Who's José?"

"The cutter. We shan't be disturbed here."

"Have you got the money?"

"Naturally. In this envelope. What about the lists?"

"They're in this brief case."

The major proceeded to examine six lists of altogether 117 addresses and Thomas Lieven an envelope containing two hundred fifty-dollar notes. They both seemed to like what they were looking at.

The major shook hands with Thomas. "I'm flying out in an hour's time. Wish you luck, you old rascal. I was really beginning to get quite fond of you. Hope we'll meet again."

"God forbid!"

"Very well then. Heil Schicki!"

"What was that?"

"Our mission staff here always put it that way. You see, it seems the fellow was once called Schicklgruber. The boys down here are a grand bunch, really. You ought to get to know them better."

"I'd rather not, if you don't mind."

"But I can assure you they're not Nazis!"

"Oh, of course not," said Thomas Lieven. "A pleasant journey, Herr Lehmann. And don't forget to give the Herr Admiral my kind regards, thought we don't know each other."

[4]

"In view of the special political position of Portugal no newsreel will be shown," announced a placard in the vestibule of the Odeon Cinema in Lisbon.

All the same, the Odeon showed the German film *Baptism of Fire*.

During the four-hour program Thomas Lieven met the British agent Lovejoy in a box. While the screen presented German Stukas swooping on Warsaw, a black brief case and ten thousand dollars once more changed owners. While bombs exploded, houses flew into the air and imposing martial music blared, Lovejoy bawled into Thomas Lieven's ear through the noise of battle: "It was my own idea to choose this cinema. We can talk undisturbed here. No one's going to understand a word we say. Good scheme, eh?"

"Oh, very good."

"That Nazi of yours will blow up!"

"When are you flying to London?"

"This evening."

"Well, a pleasant journey to you, then."

"What did you say?"

"A pleasant journey, I said!" Thomas yelled back into his ear.

He had of course long before torn the genuine lists into tiny pieces and washed them down the pan in the bathroom of his suite. In the original black brief case, which lay in the safe of the Parque Hotel, the third edition of the concocted lists, containing the names of 117 beloved but deceased persons, awaited the arrival of Major Maurice Débras.

Débras was in Madrid. He had arranged to be in Lisbon on September 3. He had told Thomas, "From September third on we shall wait for each other every evening after ten P.M in the casino at Estoril."

Now the only one left to settle with is the major, thought Thomas Lieven as he sat in the Estoril express on the evening of September 3. Then I'll go to ground in a little boarding-house until the tenth.

His boat, the *General Carmona,* was due to leave on that date. It would be better, Thomas considered, to keep as invisible as possible until then. For it could be assumed that the gentlemen in Berlin at any rate would have found out before then the sort of trick he had played on them.

As for Débras, it was rather unlikely that he would notice anything. He intended to go straight on to Dakar. Thomas thought: Some time in the near future he too, of course, will be very disappointed in me. Poor chap! I'm sure that he would have done the same if he had been in my place. Josephine is a woman. She'll understand me . . .

[5]

"Mesdames, messieurs, faites vos jeux."

The croupier threw his little white ball with graceful precision into the slowly rotating wheel. It darted off in a confusing counter-movement.

A lady in a red dinner dress watched the ball as though hypnotized. She was sitting next to the croupier. Her hands hovered uncertainly over the piles of counters in front of her. Very pale and very beautiful, she looked about thirty. Her black hair, parted in the middle, lay close to her head like a cap. The provocative bow of her mouth, her brilliant black eyes, her air of self-control and aristocratic refinement, contrasted oddly with her intense concentration on the roulette wheel.

Thomas Lieven had been watching her for an hour. He was sitting at the glittering bar of the vast hall and drinking whisky. The light of the chandeliers illuminated the splendid pictures on the walls, the great mirrors framed in white and gold, the thick carpets, the waiter in pumps, the male visitors in dinner jackets, the bare shoulders of the women, the spinning wheel and the running ball . . .

Click!

"Zero!" called the croupier next to the lady in red. She had lost. She had been losing for an hour, ever since Thomas had been watching her. She was not only losing a fortune. She was also slowly losing her self-possession. She lit a cigarette with trembling fingers. Her eyelids fluttered. She opened her gold-embroidered evening bag, took out some notes and handed them to the croupier, who gave her counters in exchange. She began staking again.

Play was going on at many other tables, including *chemin de fer*. Many of the women present were beautiful. But Thomas Lieven had eyes only for the lady in red. The mingling of self-control and agitation, good manners and the passion for gambling in her fascinated him, as it always did.

"Vingt-sept, rouge, impair et passe!" called the croupier.

The lady in red had lost again. Thomas saw the bartender shake his head. "Terrible luck," he murmured sympathetically.

He too was looking at the lady.

"Who is she?"

"A crazy gambler. You wouldn't believe how much she's lost."

"What is her name?"

"Estrella Rodrigues."

"Is she married?"

"Widow of a lawyer. We call her the Consul."

"Why?"

"Well, because she is one. She acts as consul to one of those banana republics."

"I see."

"Cinq, rouge, impair et manque!"

The Consul had lost again. She only had seven counters left now.

Thomas suddenly heard someone address him in a quiet tone.

"Mr. Leblanc?"

He turned slowly to face the speaker. It was a short, fat man with a red face, perspiring and evidently much excited. He went on in French: "It is M. Leblanc, is it not?"

"Yes."

"Follow me to the washroom, please."

"Why?"

"Because I want to tell you something."

Damn it, my lists . . . one of those secret service bloodhounds has smelled a rat. But which of them is it? Lovejoy or Loos? Thomas shook his head. "Tell me here, then."

The little man whispered into Thomas's ear: "Major Débras has run into trouble in Madrid. His passport has been taken away. He can't leave Spain. He wants you to send him a forged passport as soon as possible."

"What sort of passport?"

"You had a whole lot of them in Paris."

"I've already disposed of all those."

The little man didn't seem to have heard that. He whispered hurriedly: "I've just put an envelope into your brief case. It contains photographs of Débras and my address in Lisbon. Bring me the passport there."

"I'll have to find one first!"

The little man glanced nervously over his shoulder. "I must go now . . . do whatever you can. Ring me up." He hurried away.

"Look here—" Thomas called after him. But the little man had vanished. Good Lord, nothing but trouble!

What do I do now? Débras is such a decent fellow. I had to play him up on account of my principles. But I'm hanged if I'm going to leave him in the lurch. How am I going to get him out of Spain? Where am I going to find a bogus passport for him with so little time available?

Thomas Lieven glanced again at the lady in red. She was just rising from her chair and looked pale with consternation. Apparently she had lost all her money.

It was then that Thomas had his brain wave . . .

Ten minutes later he was sitting with Estrella Rodrigues, the Consul, at the best table in the splendid casino restaurant. A small ladies' orchestra was working its way through Verdi. Three waiters were performing an expert ballet around Thomas Lieven's table. They had just served the main course, liver à la portugaise.

"The paprika sauce is excellent," Thomas commented enthusiastically. "Really quite excellent. Don't you think so, madame?"

"It taste very nice."

"It's the tomato juice that gives it the flavor, madame . . . but is there anything wrong?"

"Why do you ask?"

"You gave me such a strange look just now—it—it seemed so severe!"

The Consul answered with great dignity: "Monsieur, I should not like to think that you have made a mistake of any kind. I am not in the habit of accepting invitations to supper from strangers."

"Madame, there is no need for you to tell me that. A gentleman knows when he is in the company of a lady. Let us not forget that it was I who entreated, even obliged you to share this little snack with me."

The Consul sighed and suddenly glanced at him in a very far from severe, even an extraordinarily sentimental manner. Thomas wondered how long ago her husband had died. Meanwhile he said: "At times of great nervous tension and psychological distress one should always eat something rich in calories. Have you—ahem—lost a great deal of money?"

"Yes. A very great deal."

"Then you shouldn't gamble, madame. A few more olives? Women with your looks are bound to lose. It's only right and proper."

"Alas . . ." The Consul's beautiful bosom heaved in her anguish. "Don't you play at all, M. Leblanc?"

"I don't play roulette."

"You're lucky."

"I'm a banker. Games on which I can't bring intelligence to bear bore me."

The black-haired Estrella, suddenly resuming her formerly harsh and agitated expression exclaimed: "I hate roulette! I hate it and I hate myself when I play it!"

Thomas Lieven began to feel excited. People who change without notice from lamblike to tigerish behavior . . . good Lord, what fun that might be, what tremendous fun . . .

"There are two things in this world I hate, monsieur."

"And what are they?"

"Roulette and Germans," hissed Estrella.

"Aha."

"Monsieur, as a Frenchman you will I am sure understand that second feeling of mine at any rate."

"Entirely, madame, entirely. Ahem—but why, in particular, do you hate the Germans so?"

"My first husband was a German."

"Ah, I understand."

"And the manager of a gambling establishment into the bargain! I need say no more, I think!"

This conversation is getting off the point, thought Thomas Lieven. He said, accordingly: "Naturally not. But there's one thing I should much enjoy doing . . ."

"May I ask what?"

"I should like to finance your play for the whole of one evening."

"Sir!"

"If you win, we can go fifty-fifty."

"Impossible—out of the question—you're a perfect stranger—" the Consul began.

But after another ten minutes she was saying: "Well, all right then—but only on condition that we really share out if I win."

"Of course."

Estrella's eyes began to shine. She breathed fast. Her cheeks reddened. "What's happened to our dessert—oh, I'm so excited, I feel quite certain I'm going to win now, win anything I like . . ."

An hour later the temperamental lady who hated Germans and roulette had lost twenty thousand escudos. She looked quite unnerved, resembling a repentant Mary Magdalene, when she returned to Thomas, who was sitting at the bar. "Oh God, I'm so ashamed of myself."

"Whatever for?"

"I don't know where to find the money to repay you. I—I'm absolutely broke now . . ."

"Oh, consider it a gift."

"That's impossible!" Now she once more looked like an avenging angel carved in marble. "For whom do you take me? It's my opinion that you've made a very great mistake about me, sir!"

MENU

Sardines on Toast
Liver à la Portugaise
Melons in Champagne

This meal made a conquest of a beautiful female consul.

Sardines on Toast

Skin and bone selected good-sized sardines and fry on both sides for a short time in their own oil. Then place them on slices of hot toast fresh from the grill, add slices of lemon and serve. At the table drops of lemon juice and a little pepper should be sprinkled over them.

No more than two such slices of toast are required for each person, this dish being merely an appetizer.

Liver à la Portugaise

One slice of calf's liver per person is rolled in flour. Do not salt before cooking. Chop two large onions. Clean one pound of green peppers by removing pips and stem and cut into thin, short strips. The onions are braised in half a cup of oil till they are pale yellow. Then add the peppers. As soon as the peppers are soft add one pound of skinned ripe tomatoes. The mixture is left to braise for five minutes. It is then passed through a sieve, cream is added and the whole reheated. Season with salt and hot pepper. When the sauce is ready the liver is quickly fried, placed on a dish and the hot sauce is poured over it. It is garnished with olives and served with plain boiled rice.

Melons in Champagne

After cutting off the top end of a ripe cantaloupe scrape out the contents as far down as possible. Remove the pips, cut the flesh into medium-sized cubes and replace it in the rind. Pour enough dry champagne onto the cubes to cover them well. Replace the top end and serve iced.

For variety one may add liqueur cherries or other fruits. But a refined taste prefers the recipe given above, which best brings out the natural aroma of the melon.

[6]

The boudoir, in semi-darkness, was illuminated by small red-shaded lamps. On a side table stood the photograph of a serious-looking gentleman with pince-nez and a large nose. A reduced version of Pedro Rodrigues, solicitor, deceased a year ago, gazed from a silver frame upon his widow Estrella.

"Oh, Jean—Jean, I am so happy—"

"I too, Estrella. I too. Cigarette?"

"Let me share yours . . ."

He handed it to her and studied her beauty with appreciation. Midnight was long past. Everything was quiet in the Consul's big villa. The staff were asleep.

She snuggled up to him, stroking his cheek.

"Estrella, darling . . ."

"Yes, my sweet?"

"Are you very much in debt?"

"Madly . . . the house is mortgaged . . . I've been pawning my jewelry. But I'm still hoping that one day I shall win it all back . . ."

Thomas glanced at the photograph. "Did he leave you much?"

"A small fortune . . . that wretched, devilish roulette! How I hate it!"

"And Germans too."

"Yes. And Germans."

"Tell me, darling. Which country do you represent as consul?"

"Costa Rica. Why do you ask?"

"Did you ever issue a Costa Rican passport?"

"No, never."

"But I expect your husband did, eh?"

"Yes, he did . . . but no one has been here since the beginning of the war. I don't believe there are any Costa Ricans left in Portugal."

"But all the same, darling—ahem—I suppose there are still a few passport forms left in the villa?"

"I don't know . . . when Pedro died I packed all the forms and stamps away in a trunk and took it up into the attic . . . why are you so interested?"

"Because I should rather like to issue a passport myself, Estrella darling."

"A passport?"

In reliance on the low state of her finances he added quietly: "Or even several."

"Jean!" She sounded horrified. "Are you trying to be funny?"

"No, I'm quite serious."

"What an extraordinary person you are!"

"I'm all right really."

"But—what are we going to do with those passports?"

"We can sell them, my dear. There must be plenty of people here who would buy them. And they'd pay high prices. And the money would enable you to—well, need I say more?"

"Oh!" Estrella drew a long breath. She looked ravishing when she drew a long breath. Then she remained silent for a long time, thinking it over. Finally she jumped up and ran into the bathroom. She returned with a dressing gown.

"Put that on!"

"Why, where are we off to, darling?"

"To the attic of course!" she retorted, tottering off in front of him in her high-heeled silk slippers, to the door.

The attic was big and bare. It smelt of wood shavings and naphthalene. Estrella held a pocket torch while Thomas, puffing and blowing, hauled an old wooden box from underneath an enormous rolled-up carpet. He banged his head on a beam and cursed. Estrella knelt down beside him. By their united efforts they managed to lift the creaking lid of the box. Inside lay blank forms, registers, rubber stamps and passports, passports by the dozen!

Estrella, with flying fingers, picked them up and riffled through one after the other till she had examined fourteen. They were all old and spotty, with photographs of unknown people in them and innumerable stamped entries on the pages. All out of date now!

Out of date . . . out of date . . . invalid . . .

Deeply disappointed, Estrella rose to her feet. "Not a single new one, all expired . . . we can't do anything with those . . ."

"Oh, can't we," said Thomas Lieven quietly. He gave her a kiss. "Old out-of-date passports are the best!"

"I don't understand that . . ."

"You soon will," Thomas Lieven, alias Jean Leblanc, promised her, beaming. He did not feel the icy breath of fate rising behind him like the bottle-imp in the oriental fairy tale, ready to strike him yet another blow and fling him into a vortex of fresh adventures and perils.

[7]

With measured tread, a Homburg on his head and a big leather brief case in his hand, an elegant young gentleman of most prepossessing appearance advanced, about midday on September 4, 1940, into the maze of the Alfama, the old quarter of Lisbon.

The narrow, crooked lanes between the decaying rococo palaces and the gaudily tiled houses of the less wealthy were full of barefooted children at play, dark-skinned men arguing and women hurrying to market with baskets of fruit or fish on their heads.

Snow-white garments hung on countless clotheslines. Black iron lattices glistened in front of high Moorish windows. Weirdly shaped trees grew from broken stairways. And again and again a break in the walls revealed a glimpse of the river close by.

The elegant young gentleman entered a butcher's shop. He bought a promising cut of veal. In the shop next door he acquired a bottle of madeira, some bottles of red-wine, olive oil, flour, eggs, sugar and plenty of herbs of various kinds. At last, in the market place, glowing with a thousand hues, he finished up with a pound of onions and a couple of fine heads of lettuce.

He lifted his hat to the market woman and took his departure with a bow and a winning smile.

Turning into the dark, narrow Rua do Poco des Negros he entered the courtyard of a house half in ruins.

He was immediately greeted by the sanitary arrangements of this dilapidated structure in the form of numbers of weather-beaten wooden sheds standing on narrow balconies. A network of the pipes serving these places spread out on the walls behind. Thomas Lieven thought it looked like the pedigree of a proof of Aryan descent.

In a sunny corner of the courtyard sat a blind old man, plucking at the strings of a guitar and singing in a weak, high-pitched voice:

Fate is even as my shadow.
Never leaves me be.
Still to me she brings but sorrow,
One for the other born were we.

Thomas put some money in the singer's hat and spoke to him in Portuguese.

"Could you tell me, please, where Reynaldo, the painter, lives?"

"Second entrance. Reynaldo lives right at the top, under the roof."

"Much obliged," said Thomas Lieven, again courteously raising his Homburg, though the blind man, of course, could not see him do it.

Inside the second entrance the stairs were dark. But the higher Thomas climbed the lighter it grew. He heard many voices. The place smelled of olive oil and poverty. On the top floor he found only two doors. One led up to the attic. On the other the name REYNALDO PEREIRA was daubed in huge red letters.

Thomas knocked. No answer. He knocked louder. Still nothing stirred. He turned the handle of the door. It opened, creaking.

Thomas Lieven walked through a dark antechamber into a large studio. The room was full of light. Through a vast window dazzling sunshine fell upon dozens of somewhat indecipherable pictures, upon a table overloaded with tins and tubes of paint, brushes and bottles, upon full ash trays and upon a man of about fifty lying on a couch, fully dressed and fast asleep.

His hair was thick and black. Dark stubble covered his pale, sunken cheeks. He snored loudly and rhythmically. On the floor near the couch lay an empty bottle of brandy.

"Pereira!" The unshaven man snored still louder and threw himself on his side. "All right then," Thomas Lieven muttered to himself. "Then we might just as well start getting lunch ready . . ."

An hour later the painter Reynaldo Pereira awoke. There

were three reasons why he did so. For one, the sun was shining right in his face. For another, there were clattering noises in the kitchen. And thirdly a strong smell of onion soup was invading the room.

He called huskily: "That you, Juanita?" Still half stupefied, he scrambled to his feet, hitched up his belt, pushed in his shirt and staggered to the kitchen door. "Juanita, my darling, my dearest, have you come back?"

He opened the door. A man he had never seen before was standing at the stove cooking, with an old apron around his waist.

"Good morning," said the stranger with a pleasant smile. "Glad to see you up at last."

The painter suddenly began to quiver all over. He groped to a chair and let himself fall heavily on it. He groaned: "That accursed brandy! It's got me at last . . ."

Thomas Lieven filled a glass with red wine. He handed it to the trembling man on the chair and laid a fatherly hand on his shoulder.

"Don't worry, Reynaldo, you haven't got D.T.s yet. I'm quite real. My name is Jean Leblanc. Here, take a sip of this. It'll do your hangover good. Then we can have a decent meal."

The painter drank, wiped his lips and demanded hoarsely: "What are you doing in my kitchen?"

"Onion soup, veal in madeira sauce . . ."

"Have you gone crazy?"

". . . and for the last course I thought we might have pancakes. I know you're hungry. And you're going to need a steady hand."

"What for?"

"To forge a passport for me after lunch," replied Thomas amiably.

Reynaldo jumped up. He seized a heavy frying pan. "Get out of here, you spy, or I'll smash your skull for you!"

"No, no," said Thomas. "Wait a minute. I have a letter for you here." He wiped his hands on the apron, fumbled in the breast pocket of his jacket and produced an envelope which he handed to Reynaldo. The other tore it open, drew out a sheet of paper and glared at it. After a while he glanced up. "Where did you meet Luis Tamiro?"

"Our paths crossed last night in the Casino at Estoril. Fat little Luis told me than an old friend of mine was in a jam at Madrid. They'd taken his passport away. So he needed a new one. And fast. Luis Tamiro said you were the right man for the job, a real artist, top-notcher, with years of experience."

Reynaldo shook his head. "Sorry. Can't possibly do it. I told Juanita so too. She's my wife, you know . . ."

". . . and she's left you because you're up against it. Luis told me all that. Don't give her another thought. A woman who leaves a man in the lurch when he's up against it isn't worth a damn. You'll soon see how she'll come rushing back the moment she hears you've got money again."

"Money from whom?"

"From me, among others."

Reynaldo scratched the stubble on his cheeks and shook his head. He spoke in the tone of a teacher addressing an idiotic child. "Listen. This is wartime. A passport can only be imitated if you have the right watermarked paper. And in each case you can only get hold of that in the country supposed to be issuing the passport . . ."

"I know all that."

"Then I suppose you also know that in wartime that sort of paper is no longer imported. Consequently, one can no longer imitate passports. One has to forge them. And how do we do that?"

Thomas tasted the madeira sauce. "Probably as a rule," he said, "by making people drunk or knocking them on the head and then pinching their passports and altering them."

"Exactly! And I just don't do that sort of thing, you know. I haven't got it in me. If I no longer have the materials to do a straightforward forgery job I don't do one at all. I'm a pacifist, I might tell you!"

"So am I. Look over there on your windowsill. I've brought a present for you."

Reynaldo rose and reeled heavily over to the window. "What's this?"

"Four out-of-date Costa Rica passports, full up with entries. You can have three if you'll alter one for me."

The forger picked up one of the passports, drew a long breath and gave Thomas an awestruck, admiring glance. "How did you get hold of these?"

"I found them. Last night."

"You found four Costa Rica passports last night?"

"No."

"What then?"

"I didn't find four Costa Rica passports last night. I found forty-seven," said Thomas Lieven, taking the hot onion soup off the stove. "Luncheon is served, Reynaldo."

He was thinking, what a bit of luck that my lovely young consul happened to have kept so many lovely old passports!

He was also thinking. So here I am in Senhor Pereira's studio in the Rua do Poco des Negros, where I shall be able to learn how to forge passports like an expert. And only a short time ago I was the youngest private banker in London. Good God Almighty! And I shall never, never, never be able to tell the story in the club!

MENU

Fried Onion Soup
Veal Fillets in Madeira Sauce
Pancakes Flambées

4 SEPTEMBER 1940

This mean inspired a passport forger to his best job.

Fried Onion Soup

Plenty of onions are cut into thin rings and fried in butter or oil till golden brown. Slightly more boiling water than the quantity of soup required is added and let on the boil for fifteen minutes. Season to taste. Stock may be used instead of water. While boiling cut thin slices of bread and place them in the soup after removing it from the stove. Cover thickly with grated cheese. Place in hot oven until cheese is lightly browned. Portions for each person should be prepared in separate casseroles.

Veal Fillets in Madeira Sauce

Cut good thick slices of filleted veal, beat lightly and fry quickly on each side. The interior should remain pink. Salt only after cooking. Chop half an onion with five almonds and handful of mushrooms and toss lightly in butter. Add a large glass of madeira and simmer slowly for fifteen minutes. Season with salt and pepper. Pour this sauce over the veal, which should be served with fried potatoes and a green salad.

Pancakes Flambées

The pancakes are fried in the normal way, but they must not be too thin. They should be the same size as the plate on which they are served. The pancakes are left open and covered thickly with sugar. At table plenty of good quality rum is poured over them and kindled. While still alight the pancakes are rolled up and sprinkled with lemon juice.

[8]

The four passports lay open on the big worktable under the window. They contained photographs of four different citizens of Costa Rica. One was fat and old, one young and slim, one had spectacles and one had a mustache.

Next to the four passports lay four photographs of Major Débras of the French secret service, who was impatiently awaiting help in Madrid, Little Luis Tamiro had slipped the photographs into Thomas Lieven's brief case in the casino at Estoril.

Lunch was over.

Reynaldo Pereira, in his white working smock, resembled a renowned surgeon, a Harley Street specialist in passport forgery, concentrating soberly on the preparations for a difficult operation.

He said quietly: "You know the man in Madrid personally. awaiting help in Madrid. Little Luis Tamiro had slipped the four passports. Read the descriptions of the bearers. Tell me which of them most nearly resembles your friend. For I shall naturally choose the passport I have to alter least."

"Well, I should think this is the one most like him." Thomas pointed to the second from the left. The name of the bearer of that passport had been Rafaelo Puntareras.

The passport had been issued on February 8, 1934. Its validity had expired on February 7, 1939. It contained many stamped visas and frontier entries. Only a few pages remained blank. It was probably for this reason that Puntareras, who was a commercial traveler, had preferred to have a new passport issued by his consul, Pedro Rodrigues, since deceased, instead of continuing to use the old one.

Thomas said: "The description of the bearer suits my friend, except that he has brown hair and blue eyes."

"Then we shall have to alter those two details, exchange the photographs, continue the mark of the stamp over the photograph of your friend, change the dates of issue and expiry and also those on the various visa and frontier stamps, which would otherwise be too early."

"What about the name Puntareras?"

"Will your friend be staying long in Lisbon?"

"No. He'll be flying on to Dakar almost at once."

"Then we needn't change the name."

"But he'll require a transit visa for Lisbon and an entry permit for Dakar."

"So what? I've got a whole drawerful of stamps. Probably the biggest collection in Europe. No, no, that won't be much bother."

"Well, what do you consider would be?"

"A passport in which everything had to be altered and the new photograph had been stamped. For a job like that I should need a good two days."

"And for Señor Puntareras?"

"You'll have to allow for my private worries, my mental instability and my unhappy marriage—but, damn it, in seven hours at most I'll have the job ready."

In a relaxed mood, humming softly to himself, Reynaldo Pereira began his work. He took up a conical metal prong with a wooden handle, a sort of shoemaker's awl, and inserted it gently between the first and second layers mounting Puntareras's passport photograph. Then he started cautiously rolling up the edge with a tiny penknife.

"We always take the photo off first," said the artist, "so as to avoid inadvertently damaging the rubber stamp." He belched slightly. "Really marvelous, that onion soup of yours!"

Thomas sat motionless by the window. He made no reply to the expert, in case it might disturb the necessary concentration.

Three quarters of an hour later Reynaldo had rolled up the edges of both mounts of the photograph. Then he cautiously removed the metal tubing with the awl.

Next he switched on an electric hot plate, put an old book cover on it and the passport on top of the cover.

"It has to be thoroughly warmed for ten minutes," said the expert. "We call that resuscitating the passport. The paper becomes softer and more elastic. It absorbs liquid more easily and is in every respect more amenable to treatment."

After taking time off for a cigarette Pereira set to work on the passport again. With a pair of tweezers he raised, about a millimeter, one corner of Puntareras' photograph which the stamp had not touched. Then he dipped an extremely fine-haired brush into a strong-smelling liquid contained in a small bottle.

"Only the finest badger or red marten fur, size zero, is any good," the maestro said.

He proceeded to dab the liquid delicately between the photograph and the passport page, holding the former away from the latter with the tweezers. Gradually the paste between them dissolved. After five minutes he had removed the photograph and taken it to the other side of the room, where he placed it on a book cover. "That's to make sure I don't inadvertently damage it."

He returned to the table, closed his eyes, loosened his fingers and obviously began to concentrate on the next step.

Then the maestro said: "My first contact will consist of quite an easy change. I am going to take out a dot."

He placed the document under a large, stationary microscope. He moistened a fresh fine-haired brush with a colorless liquid.

Then he simultaneously moistened a full stop in the printed list of personal details and pressed the knob of a stop watch.

He waited until the printed dot was almost entirely erased, then he soaked up the remainder of the liquid at lightning speed with a piece of blotting paper cut at an acute angle.

"Three seconds. Now we've got a basic figure. Calculating on that, we can tackle the upstroke of a letter."

He removed all the upstrokes on one page by dabbing them as a number of dots. Then he turned to the thicker downstrokes, eliminating them by applying the mysterious liquid from both sides to the middle. "In the trade we call that working in to the core."

After two hours of "working in to the core" and using the dot method, all the unusable data had disappeared, including the dates in the visa and frontier stamps which were too early and the dates of issue and expiry.

The maestro then relaxed for half an hour. He danced about a little, in order to loosen up his muscles.

Thomas made coffee. Before Pereira drank his he broke the shell of an egg and dropped the white on a flat plate. "So that the air can get at it over a good large area. In our jargon, it must have 'stood.' "

After ten minutes he filled in, with the viscous, quick-drying white of egg, the furrows and depressions left in the paper, despite the care he had taken, by the bleaching agent. He worked with close attention, so as to ensure that perfectly smooth surfaces would be restored. He then sprayed them with an invisible fixative.

Next he fetched the photograph of the commercial traveler Puntareras, which he had extracted, wrapped it in extremely thin tissue paper and gummed the paper to the back of the photograph to prevent it slipping. He then, with an agate pencil, drew on the paper the contours of that of the stamp which had touched the photograph.

Next, he cut one of the four photographs of Major Débras in such a way that it very slightly exceeded that of Puntareras in area. He laid a strip of carbon paper, almost the same color as the stamp-dye, over the photograph. He then removed the tissue paper from the old photograph, superimposed the tissue paper on the carbon paper he had placed over the photograph of Débras and gummed it again. Then once more he drew, with the agate pencil, the contours thus obtained.

He then carefully removed the coverings. The photograph of Débras now showed the stamp.

Rapidly, so as to prevent effacement of his work, the maestro applied fixative to it.

He proceeded to perforate the photograph of Débras with sharp tweezers at points which had already been precisely determined and fastened it with gum arabic and two shoelace eyelets to the passport, turning down their edges with another pair of tweezers.

Next, with India ink, he wrote fresh numbers in at all the points he had bleached, observing: "We always, if it's at all possible, substitute numbers resembling the old ones in shape, changing a three, for example, into an eight, or a one into a four."

After six and a half hours of strenuous labor Pereira stamped the passport with a Portuguese transit visa and a Dakar entry permit, filling in the necessary figures.

"Ready!"

Thomas clapped his hands delightedly. The maestro bowed with dignity. "Anything in this line. Always happy to oblige!"

Thomas shook his hand. "I shan't be here to profit from your unique gifts in the future. But keep your spirits up, Reynaldo. I'm going to send you an attractive customer. I'm sure you'll get on marvelously well together . . ."

[9]

High up across the top floor of the big newspaper office in the Praça Dom Pedro IV the latest illuminated tape was running. Thousands of pairs of eyes gazed upward, with tense anxiety, at the flickering letters. Portuguese citizens and emigrants crowded the splendid square with its pavement in black and white mosaic or sat in the gardens of the cafés surrounding it. They all stared up at the moving letters, reading:

> UNITED PRESS Madrid—Persistent rumors of secret negotiations between Germany and Spain. Germany allegedly demands free passage for troops in order to attack Gibraltar and close the Mediterranean. Franco determined to remain neutral. British ambassador's energetic warning to Spain. Anti-British demonstrations in Barcelona and Seville . . .

Two men were sitting at a café table close to the pavement, drinking Pernod. One of them, the stout little Luis Tamiro, was looking through the passport which had been forged that afternoon. He murmured admiringly: "First-rate work. Really first-rate!"

"When does your plane leave?"

"In two hours."

"Give Débras my regards. He must do his best to get here before my boat leaves in five days' time."

"I certainly hope he'll be able to manage it."

"What do you mean by that?" Thomas Lieven asked.

Luis Tamiro, looking worried, pulled at his little Brazilian cigar. "The Spaniards are supposed to be neutral. But they let German agents do pretty much as they please. Three German 'tourists' are closely shadowing the major in Madrid all day and all night. They relieve one another every eight hours. He's quite well aware of it. But he can't shake them off. Their names are Löffler, Weise and Hart. They are staying at the same hotel as he is, the Palace."

"What's the idea?"

"As the major's had his passport taken away, he can't leave Madrid. The three Germans know who he is but they can't prove it yet. They want to find out what he's doing in Madrid. Moreover, if he makes any attempt to leave the city, the Spanish police would have an excuse to arrest him immediately.

And once he's in the jug he could be spirited away to Germany without anyone being much the wiser."

"So he's got to shake off those three."

"Yes, but how can he? They're straining at the leash like pointers. The moment he tries to escape they'll pounce."

Thomas Lieven looked curiously at the little man. "Tell me, Tamiro, what's your profession actually?"

The stout little fellow sighed, then pursed his lips. "I supply girls for all prohibited purposes. I smuggle people and weapons. I deal in the black market. Anything I'm paid for. I used to be a jeweler in Madrid."

"And then what happened?"

"The Civil War ruined me. My shop was bombed to bits, my goods stolen. And I got into political trouble on top of that. No, I've had more than enough of an honest life. For me everything has its fixed price. Idealists can go and chase themselves so far as I'm concerned."

Thomas Lieven asked quietly: "I daresay you know a few other gentlemen in Madrid who are of your opinion?"

"Plenty!"

"And according to you everything has its fixed price?"

"Of course."

Thomas, with a smile, glanced up at the flickering newsreel. He murmured gently: "Listen, Luis. What would it cost—confidentially—to get a spontaneous little riot started?"

"What do you have in mind?"

Thomas Lieven told him what he had in mind.

[10]

"Aaaaaahhhhh!"

The black-haired, statuesque Consul Estrella Rodrigues woke up with a shriek, as Thomas Lieven entered her room at an advanced hour of the night. Quaking, she switched on the little red-shaded lamp behind the bed. One hand was pressed to her heart.

"Heavens, Jean, how you frightened me!"

"Sorry, darling, we were talking late—and then I saw the man with the passport to his plane . . ." He sat down wearily on the edge of the bed. She threw herself into his arms.

"Kiss me . . ." She hugged him tight. "Oh, thank God you are here at last! I've been waiting for you for hours—I thought it would kill me—I thought I should have to die . . ."

"Because you missed me so much?" he inquired, flattered.

"Yes, that too."

"I beg your pardon?"

"I was hoping all the evening that you would come and let me have a little more money, so that I could go to Estoril."

"H—m—m."

"I rang them up. Elevens and tens and twelves were coming up at all the tables! Can you imagine it? Those are my favorite numbers! I might have won a fortune today!"

"Estrella, tomorrow I am going to introduce you to an absolutely first-rate forger. You can give him your passorts to sell on commission. He is ready to go fifty-fifty with you on the proceeds."

"Oh, Jean, how wonderful!"

Thomas went into the bathroom. She called tenderly after him: "I had such a strange dream last night."

"Oh, what was that?" he inquired from the bathroom.

"I dreamed you were a German—you, my lover! A German! And I, who hate the Germans so! I thought it would kill me. I thought I was going to die . . . Jean, can you hear me?"

"Yes. Every word."

"Then why don't you answer?"

She heard him cough. "You gave me such a shock I swallowed half the water in my tooth glass."

That made her laugh. "Oh, you're so sweet! Come to me! Come quickly to your loving Estrella . . ."

A little later the German-hating lady with the glorious figure awoke to hear Thomas laughing quite heartly in his sleep. She shook his shoulder violently.

"Jean, Jean! What's the matter?"

"Eh? Oh, I had such a funny dream."

"What about?"

"About a spontaneous little riot," he said, laughing again.

[11]

On September 5, 1940, in Madrid, Inspector Filippo Aliados of the Secret Police composed the following confidential report to his chief:

> TOP PRIORITY. At 1403 hours today the duty officer of the Fourteenth Precinct informed me that about fifty persons had assembled outside the British Embassy, No. 16 Calle Fernando el Santo, and were making hostile demonstrations.

I at once proceeded to the spot with five men and found that the rioters were all from the lower strata of the population. They were shouting insults, in chorus, against England. Four (4) windows in the Embassy had been smashed and three (3) flower boxes had been pulled to the ground. The Commercial Attaché had come out into the street, at the request of the Ambassador, to interview the rioters.

On my arrival the Attaché, who appeared greatly excited, said: "These men admit that they were paid by German agents to start a riot here."

Most of the demonstrators fled on being energetically charged by a police detachment. But we were able to arrest three persons. Their names are Luis Tamiro, Juan Mereira and Manuel Passos.

The arrested men repeated in my presence the statement that they had been paid by German agents, whom they named as follows: Helmut Löffler, Thomas Weise and Jakob Hart, all three residents at the Palace Hotel.

The British Commercial Attaché insisted upon an immediate investigation of the matter, which he said would be the subject of a formal protest by his government.

In view of repeated official instructions to take every step to safeguard Spanish neutrality I immediately proceeded to the Palace Hotel and arrested the three above mentioned German tourists. They resisted arrest and had to be handcuffed before being taken into custody.

At the Station hearing they all indignantly denied having financed the demonstration. They were confronted by the three demonstrators arrested, but without recognition on either side. I then dismissed the rioters after warning them that they would be charged with a breach of public order.

The three Germans, however, are already known by us to be agents of German Military Intelligence and for that reason may well have inspired the demonstration.

They are still in my custody. I beg to request that I may be informed as soon as possible what is to be done with them, as the British Commercial Attaché telephones me hourly to inquire what steps I am taking.

(Signed)
Filippo Aliados
INSPECTOR.

[12]

A German fist came crashing down on a desk of German oak. The desk stood in one of the rooms in a house on the Tirpitz Embankment in Berlin. The fist belonged to Admiral Canaris. He was standing behind the desk. In front of the desk stood the liverish Major Fritz Loos from Cologne.

The face of the major was very pale. The face of the admiral was very red. The major kept very quiet. The admiral's voice was very loud.

"This is too much, Major! Three of our people expelled from Spain! Protest by the British Government! A gift to the enemy press. And that sly Herr Lieven of yours is laughing himself sick in Lisbon!"

"Herr Admiral, I really don't understand what that fellow, once again, has to do with it!"

Canaris retorted bitterly: "While our people were under arrest in Madrid for hours on end Major Débras left the country. Undoubtedly with a forged passport. He reached Lisbon without the slightest trouble. And do you know whom he embraced in public at the Estoril Casino and whose cheek he kissed? Your friend Lieven's! And do you know with whom he consumed a prodigious meal afterward? Your friend Lieven!"

"Oh no . . . Oh, God, no . . . surely not!"

"No doubt of it. Our people watched the whole touching scene of their reunion. What could they do about it? Nothing!"

Major Loos became aware of painful internal twinges and burning pains. There goes my liver again, he thought despairingly. That infernal scoundrel of a Thomas Lieven! Whatever possessed me to rescue him from the clutches of the Gestapo in Cologne?

"Herr Major, do you know what they are already calling you in the service? 'Let-'em-down Loos!' "

"Herr Admiral, with respect, that seems to me very unfair."

"Unfair? You pay the fellow ten thousand dollars for lists of the names of all the most important French secret agents and when we check on them here we find that they're all dead! I told you to bring the man back with you!"

"Portugal is a neutral country, Herr Admiral."

"To hell with that! I've had enough of all this, I tell you! I want that Herr Lieven here in my office! In this room! And alive! D'you hear?"

"Very good, Herr Admiral."

[13]

On September 6, 1940, at 1847 hours the secret service monitoring department reported to M.I.5 in London as follows:

> Since 1515 hours intense radio activity between Berlin Intelligence and the German Embassy in Lisbon. Messages in clear, not in code, but obviously camouflaged to mislead. The Berlin messages were directed to the German Commercial Attaché in Lison, ordering him to take steps for the repatriation of a merchant named Jonas as soon as possible. An important kidnapping operation obviously in view. "Jonas" must be a personage of the greatest possible interest to Berlin Intelligence . . .

[14]

On September 6, 1940, at 2230 hours a conference was going on in the Casa Senhora de Fatima, the luxurious residence of the chief of the Intelligence Department at the German Embassy in Lisbon. The chief had sent away his fascinating mistress, the long-legged, chestnut-haired dancer Dolores. He, the naval attaché and the air attaché of the German Embassy were sipping champagne. The last two had also given their mistresses the evening off.

The news service chief declared: "Gentlemen, time presses. Berlin wants Lieven. And fast. Suggestions, please."

The air attaché answered: "I suggest we drug the man and fly him to Madrid. Thence he could be transferred by courier aircraft to Berlin."

"I'm against that," said the naval attaché. "We've just been having trouble in Madrid. We know that the airfield there is positively swarming with British and American agents. We know that they photograph all passengers. We can't afford to risk any further diplomatic difficulties in Madrid."

"I'm entirely of your opinion," said the news chief.

The naval attaché went on: "I suggest accordingly that we abduct him by submarine, gentlemen. We could get in touch immediately by radio with Werner's anti-blockade office in Madrid. He works in close liaison with submarine staff headquarters and can easily identify the location of any of their units. He would be in a position at any time and with the greatest promptitude to direct a submarine to an agreed grid outside Portuguese territorial waters."

"And how do we get 'Jonas the merchant' there?"

"We could hire a boat."

"And how do we get him into the boat?"

"Well, I've got an idea about that." The naval attaché told them what his idea was.

[15]

An old man was shuffling through the airport restaurant, trying to sell dolls in regional costume. He had big ones and little ones, but no luck. It was nearly midnight on September 8, 1940, and only about two dozen weary passengers were waiting for the departure of their aircraft to be announced.

The old man approached a table by the window. Two gentlemen were sitting drinking whisky there.

"Lovely dolls, gypsy, Spanish, Portuguese . . ."

"No, thank you," said Thomas Lieven.

"Genuine, like in peacetime!"

"All the same, no, thank you," said Major Débras, who called himself, just then, Rafaelo Puntareras.

The old man shuffled away. Outside, on the arc-lit runway, the plane which was to take Débras from Lisbon to Dakar was being refueled.

The major gazed with a sentimental expression at Thomas Lieven. "I shall never forget what you have done for me!"

"Don't mention it," said Thomas. He was thinking: When you find that I've altered the lists of your secret service agents, you certainly won't forget what I've done for you!

"You saved those lists for me and you got me out of Madrid."

Correct, thought Thomas. And for that reason you may one day forgive me for having swindled you. He asked aloud: "What have you done with the lists?"

The major winked, "I followed your example and made friends with our stewardess. She has the lists in her luggage."

"Attention, please," announced a loudspeaker, "Pan American World Airways request all passengers traveling by Flight 324 to Dakar to proceed to the passport and customs barriers. Ladies and gentlemen, we wish you a pleasant journey."

Débras emptied his glass and stood up. "Duty calls, my friend. Thanks once again. Till our next meeting."

"Please give Mme. Josephine Baker my very best regards," said Thomas Lieven. "And good-bye to you, Major. For we shall never see each other again."

"Who knows?"

Thomas shook his head. "The day after tomorrow I leave by steamer for South America. I shall never return to Europe." He allowed the major to embrace him once more and kiss his cheek.

A little later he watched him cross the runway toward the aircraft. Thomas waved. Débras waved back. Then he disappeared into the passengers' cabin.

Thomas ordered another whisky. When the machine began to taxi down the runway he suddenly felt very lonely. After a while he paid for the drinks, stood up and left the table.

It was dark in the forecourt in front of the airport building. Only a few lights were burning. A big car gradually caught Thomas up and stopped beside him. The driver put his head through the window. "Taxi, Senhor?"

Not a soul was in sight.

"Yes, please," said Thomas absently. The driver got out, opened the door of the car and bowed.

At that moment Thomas Lieven noticed that there was something queer, something very queer, about that taxi. He swung around. But it was already too late. The driver kicked him violently behind the knees, sending him flying into the back seat, where he was instantly seized by four powerful hands and flung to the floor of the car. The door banged. The driver dropped into his seat behind the steering wheel and accelerated.

A large damp cloth impregnated with a disagreeably sweet-smelling liquid was pressed down on Thomas Lieven's face. Chloroform, he thought. Choking, he gasped for breath.

With uncanny distinctness he heard a voice with a Hamburg accent exclaim: "Fine, fine. Now down to the harbor and we're through."

Then the blood in Thomas Lieven's temples began humming. Bells sounded in his ears. He sank into a faint, deeper and deeper, as though falling through the velvety darkness of a well.

[16]

Our friend slowly recovered consciousness. His head still hummed. He felt sick and cold. Thomas cautiously opened his right eye. He was lying in the bows of an unpleasantly odoriferous fishing boat with a fussily clucking engine.

At the helm stood a wrinkled, undersized Portuguese wearing a leather jacket and a peaked cap. An extinct, short-stemmed pipe was clenched between his teeth. Behind the figure of the seaman the shore lights bobbed up and down. The wind was rising. The boat was making for the open sea. With a sigh Thomas Lieven opened his left eye.

There were a couple of burly fellows sitting on the bench next to him. Both wore black mackintoshes and grim expressions. Both held heavy pistols in their big, ugly hands.

Thomas Lieven struggled into half-erect position and said with an effort but without hesitation: "The best of good evenings to you, gentlemen. I didn't have a chance to speak to you at the airport. You're a bit to blame for that yourselves, you know. You ought not to have been so quick about knocking me down and chloroforming me."

The Hamburger said: "I warn you, Lieven. The slightest attempt to escape and these guns will go off."

The other tough spoke with a Saxon accent. "The game's up, Herr Lieven. You're on the way home now."

Thomas asked in an interested tone, "You come from Dresden?"

"Leipzig. Why?"

"Just curiosity. I've nothing against this boat, gentlemen. But it's a pretty fair way home by sea from here, isn't it? Won't it be too much for us?"

"What a chatterbox you are," said the Hamburger. "You don't have to worry, Herr Lieven. We're only going as far as the three-mile limit in this smack."

The man from Leipzig added: "We're bound for Grid 135 Z."

Thomas noticed the boat was not showing any navigation lights. The sea was getting more and more agitated. So was Thomas, but he tried not to show it. "And what is going to happen at Grid 135 Z, gentlemen?"

"In a quarter of an hour a submarine will surface there. It'll all go like clockwork, you'll see. Can't fail."

"German organization, eh?" Thomas observed politely.

The little helmsman said in Portuguese: "We're out of territorial waters now. Where's my money?"

The Leipziger got up, staggered over to the helmsman and gave him an envelope. The fisherman lashed the helm and started to count the notes in the envelope. After that everything happened very fast.

Thomas was the first to see a big shadow loom up, for he was the only man looking astern. The menacing black phantom shot out of the night, straight at the rolling smack. Thomas meant to give a warning shout. But at the last moment he forced it back, biting his tongue. No, he thought. No shouting. Keep quite quiet now . . .

Searchlights shone out. A siren sounded three times in rapid succession. Then the shadow suddenly changed to a racing yacht, coming nearer and nearer till it began to look really dangerous. The Portuguese skipper, with a wild yell, flung the helm over. It was too late. With a sickening crash the yacht rammed the little fishing vessel at an acute angle, to port. The Hamburg gentleman's pistol flew out of his hand. The gentleman from Leipzig fell down.

Then everything went topsy-turvy, the boat capsizing as the yacht's bows ground into her beam. A gigantic invisible fist sent Thomas high into the air and then down into the black, ice-cold water.

He heard a raging babble of voices, shouts, curses, bawled orders and through it all the incessant howling of the siren.

Thomas swallowed sea water, went under, came up gasping and saw a lifebelt, with a line attached, come flying toward him from the deck of the yacht. The circular white object splashed into the water beside him. Thomas seized it. Immediately the line stiffened and he was being pulled in toward the yacht.

His eyes blinking, he stared at the letters on the lifebelt, indicating the name of the vessel. Thomas read the words *Baby Ruth*.

Good Lord, he thought, when I tell them that in the club, they'll say I'm lying . . .

[17]

"Whisky or rum?"

"Whisky, please."

"With ice and soda?"

"Only ice, please. And if you don't mind, fill it up half. I catch cold so easily," said Thomas Lieven. An extremely eventful quarter of an hour had just passed.

Only fifteen minutes ago Thomas had still been a prisoner of German Intelligence. Now, after being shipwrecked in the

Atlantic, he sat wrapped in warm blankets on a bed so soft as to seem unreal, in a cabin so luxurious as to seem equally so. A gentleman he had never seen before was standing at a cocktail cabinet mixing him a drink. Thomas was feeling slightly lightheaded. He thought, what extraordinary things do happen in life . . .

The gentleman brought him the whisky. He had meanwhile himself taken a good swallow of the stuff. Now he raised his glass with a smile. "Cheerio!"

"Cheerio," said Thomas and took an enormous gulp. Now at last I'm getting that disgusting taste of chloroform out of my throat, he thought. From the deck he could hear a confused sound of bellowing.

"Who's that?"

"Our helmsman and yours. They're discussing who was responsible for the accident," replied the stranger, who wore an immaculate blue single-breaster and horn-rimmed spectacles which gave him an intellectual appearance. "Of course it was all the fault of your helmsman. One simply doesn't go to sea after dark without navigation lights. A bit more ice?"

"No, thank you. Where are those other two fellows who were aboard with me?"

"Down below decks. I assume you wouldn't want them anywhere else."

No good beating about the bush, thought Thomas. I'd better take the bull by the horns right away. He said: "I must thank you for having saved my life. And I don't mean from drowning."

"Good health, Jonas, you merchant!"

"I beg your pardon?"

"You're Jonas the merchant to us. We don't yet know your real name." Thank God for that, thought Thomas. "And I don't suppose you want to tell me, do you?"

"No, I don't." A bit of luck, he was thinking, that all my papers are safely locked up at the villa of the fair Consul, Estrella. I had the feeling all the time that something like this might happen to me.

"I quite understand. I realize that you can only speak frankly at the highest level. A man like yourself, a V.I.P.—"

"A what?"

"A Very Important Person."

"Is that what I am?"

"I should think so, Jonas, if German Intelligence tries to get you out of Portugal in a submarine. You can't have any idea what a fuss has been made about you during the last forty-eight hours. All that scheming! Terrific! Berlin Intelligence, Lisbon Intelligence, submarine at Grid 135 Z! It's months since the German wireless got into such a flap! Jonas the merchant . . . Jonas the merchant . . . Jonas the merchant must be brought to Berlin at all costs . . . and then you ask me whether you are really a V.I.P.! It's too delicious! Hallo, what's the matter, Jonas?"

"Could I—d'you think I could possibly have another whisky, please?"

He was given one—and a pretty stiff one too. The man in horn rims poured himself out another, reflecting aloud: "It won't hurt the *Baby Ruth* to kill a bottle of whisky with five thousand dollars coming in."

"What baby are you talking about? What five thousand dollars?"

The bespectacled man laughed. "Surely you must realize by this time, Jonas, that you're talking to a secret service man?"

"Oh, yes."

"You can call me Roger. That's not my real name, of course. But one false name is as good as another. Isn't that so?"

Good God Almighty, here we go again, thought Thomas Lieven. I shall have to look out now. I got away from the Germans. Now I shall have to get rid of the British. I'll have to gain time, think it all over carefully and watch my step.

He said: "You are perfectly right, Mr. Roger. But I repeat: What five thousand dollars? And who is 'Baby Ruth'?"

"Well, Jonas, as soon as we—I mean we boys of British Intelligence in Lisbon—found what a hysterical row the German wireless was making, we at once contacted M.I.5 in London . . ."

"What's M.I.5?"

"Chief of our counterespionage service."

"I see," said Thomas. He sipped his whisky, thinking: Europe's turned into a sort of murderous nursery school. Heavens, how glad I shall be to leave this absurd and dangerous continent behind me.

"So then M.I.5 signaled, Open fire!"

"I understand."

"We obeyed like lightning . . ."

"Naturally."

". . . we made up our minds that the Nazis weren't going to

get Jonas the merchant! What ho! Let's drink another whisky to *Baby Ruth*'s health!"

"I wish you'd tell me one of these days who Baby Ruth is."

"Mrs. Ruth Woodhouse, aged sixty-five and nearly stone deaf. She's survived two heart attacks and five husbands."

"Good for her."

"Didn't you ever hear of Woodhouse steel, Woodhouse tanks or Woodhouse machine guns? It's one of the oldest American armament firms. Never heard of it?"

"No, I'm afraid not."

"Then your education's been badly neglected, I must say."

"Well, now you've filled the gap. Thanks."

"Don't mention it. Well, she owns this yacht. For the moment she's staying in Lisbon. As soon as we found out they were going to use a submarine, we had a chat with her. She at once leased her yacht to us for five thousand dollars." The man who called himself Roger returned to the bar. "Everything went like clockwork, Jonas. Couldn't fail."

I've heard those phrases once before tonight, thought Thomas Lieven. He observed politely: "British organization."

Roger was raiding the American armament millionaire's cocktail cabinet like a wolf among a flock of sheep. He called back jovially to Thomas: "We followed you step by step, Jonas. You were shadowed day and night. I lay in ambush here, in Grid 135 Z. I was told by wireless that the Germans had kidnaped you at the airport. Then that the trawler was under way. What ho!"

"And what's going to happen now?"

"Can't fail! Clockwork! We shall naturally charge the Portuguese helmsman with gross negligence in seamanship. He was obviously responsible for the accident. We've already wirelessed to that effect. A police boat will be here soon to take him and your two German friends into custody."

"What will be done with them?"

"Nothing. They've already explained that they only wanted to go for a little cruise."

"And what will you do with me?"

"I have orders to bring you, if necessary at the risk of my life, safe and sound to the villa of the chief of British Intelligence in Portugal. Or would you rather go with your German friends?"

"By no means, Mr. Roger, by no means," said Thomas Lieven. He smiled wryly, thinking: Is that still sea water on my forehead, or is it, once more, the sweat of fear?

[18]

The Germans had used a very old limousine to carry Thomas Lieven off out of Lisbon. The British brought him back to Lisbon in a new Rolls-Royce. *Noblesse oblige!*

He sat on the back seat in a blue silk dressing gown embroidered with golden dragons and wore slippers to match. That was all the *Baby Ruth* could supply in the way of clothes. Thomas Lieven's wet suit and undergarments lay on the seat beside the driver.

Next to Thomas sat Roger, with a tommy-gun on his lap. He announced through his teeth: "Nothing to be afraid of, Jonas, you won't get hurt. This car's armored and the windows are of bulletproof glass. No one can shoot in here."

"May I ask then, how, if the need arises, you'll be able to shoot out of here?" Thomas demanded mildly. To this question, however, the British agent did not reply.

The car sped on past the sleeping resort of fashionable Estoril, due east into a glorious sunrise. Sky and sea were the color of mother-of-pearl. In the harbor many ships were anchored. Today is September 9, thought Thomas Lieven. Tomorrow the *General Carmona* leaves for South America. Good Lord, I wonder if I shall ever make it?

The comfortable villa of the British Intelligence chief stood in a garden of palms. The house was furnished in Moorish style and belonged to a moneylender named Alvarez who possessed two others of the same kind. He had leased one to the chief of Intelligence at the German Embassy and the other to his American opposite number . . .

Over the entrance to the villa rented by the British appeared the words CASA DO SUL in gold lettering. A butler wearing pin-striped trousers and a green velvet waistcoat held open the heavy wrought-iron door, raising his bushy white eyebrows. He bowed silently to Thomas. He then closed the door and preceded the two visitors through a wide hall, past a chimney piece, a staircase and portraits of Herr Alvarez's ancestors, to the library.

There an elderly gentleman, with his back to shelves of books in variously colored bindings, awaited them. He looked as miraculously English as any of the illustrations in a magazine of the British tailoring trade. His well-groomed elegance, perfectly fitting dark gray flannel suit, carefully tended military mustache and stiff, equally military demeanor were sincerely admired by Thomas Lieven.

"Mission completed, sir," Roger informed the elderly gentleman.

"Well done, Jack," said the latter, shaking hands with Thomas. "Good morning, Jonas. Welcome to the soil of Great Britain. I've been very anxious to see you. Whisky on the rocks?"

"I never drink before breakfast, sir."

"I understand. Man of principle, eh? Good. Very good indeed." The gentleman in dark gray turned to Roger. "Go up to Charley and tell him to tune in to M.I.5. Code Cicero. Report: 'Sun rising in the west.' "

"Very good, sir." Roger left the room. The gentleman in dark gray said to Thomas: "You can call me Shakespeare, Jonas."

"Delighted, Mr. Shakespeare." Why not? thought Thomas. In France I once had to call one of your colleagues Jupiter. If that sort of thing amuses you . . .

"I understand you are French, Jonas?"

"Er—yes."

"I thought so right away. Got an eye for it. Knowledge of human nature infallible! *Vive la France, monsieur!*"

"Thank you, Mr. Shakespeare."

"M. Jonas, what is your real name?"

If I tell him, I'll never get aboard my boat, thought Thomas. He answered: "I'm sorry, but my situation is too serious for me to reveal my true identity."

"Monsieur, I guarantee on my word of honor your safe transport to London at any time, provided that you agree to work for my country. Don't forget that we have rescued you from the clutches of the Nazis."

What a life, thought Thomas.

He said: "I am exhausted, Mr. Shakespeare. I—I'm just about all in. I must get some sleep before I can make up my mind about anything."

"I quite see that, *monsieur*. A spare room is at your disposal. Consider yourself my guest."

Half an hour later Thomas Lieven lay in a soft, comfortable bed in a quiet, pleasant room. The sun had risen. Many birds were singing in the park. Golden sunbeams fell through the barred window. The door was locked on the outside. British hospitality, thought Thomas Lieven, is famous throughout the world. You can't beat it . . .

[19]

Attention, time signal. On the stroke of the gong it will be eight o'clock. Good morning, ladies and gentlemen. You will now hear the second news transmission by Radio Lisbon. London: last night strong forces of German bombers again made concentrated attacks on the British capital . . .

Breathing heavily and twisting her fingers together the statuesque, black-haired Consul Estrella Rodrigues was pacing rapidly to and fro in her bedroom. She looked exhausted. Her seductively arched upper lip was trembling.

Estrella was close to a nervous breakdown. She had not slept for a single minute the night before. The last few hours had been terrible. Jean, her beloved Jean, had not come home. She knew that he had accompanied her mysterious friend, the French major, to the airport. She had telephoned the place. But no one there knew anything about a M. Jean Leblanc.

In her mind's eye Estrella could see her beloved being kidnaped, arrested, tortured, in the hands of the Germans, dead! Her breast rose and fell in the excitement of her emotions. She felt at death's door . . .

She suddenly realized that the wireless was still switched on. She stood still and listened to the announcer's voice.

. . . early today the American yacht *Baby Ruth*, while cruising outside the three-mile limit, rammed a Portuguese fishing boat which sank. The yacht's crew rescued several survivors. At the same time units of our coastal patrol located a submarine close to the scene of the collision. The submarine immediately dived and made off.

Captain Edward Marks, in command of the *Baby Ruth*, has charged the helmsman of the smack with recklessly endangering his vessel. The three passengers in the boat, two Germans and a French citizen . . .

Estrella uttered a scream.

. . . refused to give any account of themselves. It is suspected that the occurrence may have something to do with a thwarted attempt at kidnaping in which at least two foreign secret services are involved. Investigations are proceeding. The *Baby Ruth* will not be allowed to continue her voyage until further notice. She belongs to the American millionaire, Ruth Woodhouse, temporarily in residence at the Hotel Aviz. You have been listening to the news. The weather forecast for today and tomorrow . . .

The Consul relaxed her frozen immobility. She switched off the radio and dressed at full speed. Jean . . . her instinct had been right, something had happened to him, something dreadful, something awful . . . what was the name of that millionairess?

Woodhouse. Ruth Woodhouse. Hotel Aviz.

[20]

The bushy white eyebrows of the butler were again raised as he entered the library of the luxurious Casa do Sul. In sonorous tones he announced to the chief of British Intelligence in Portugal: "Senhora Rodrigues to see you, sir."

With elastic step the man who called himself Shakespeare rose to his feet. Elastically he strode to meet the fair Consul, who wore a close-fitting dress of white linen, hand-painted with brightly colored flowers and birds, plus rather too much make-up and the expression of a curvaceous deer in flight.

Shakespeare kissed her hand. The butler withdrew.

The chief of the British Intelligence Service, offered Estrella a chair, a very splendid one, into which she dropped breathlessly, with heaving bosom. Excitement had robbed her of speech, a rare phenomenon in her case.

The man whom it pleased to make use of the name of England's greatest poet observed sympathetically: "I was speaking to Mrs. Woodhouse on the telephone about half an hour ago. I am aware that you have paid her a visit, senhora . . ."

Estrella, still speechless, nodded.

". . . Mrs. Woodhouse is—ahem—a very good friend of ours. She told me that you were anxious about—ahem—a very good friend of your own."

Estrella had no idea of the trouble her next words were going to cause. "Yes—I'm anxious about Jean—oh dear—my poor, unlucky Jean . . ."

"Jean?"

"Jean Leblanc. A Frenchman. He disappeared yesterday . . . I'm already nearly out of my mind with worry. Can you help me, do you know anything about him? Tell me the truth, I beg you!"

Shakespeare wagged his head mysteriously.

"You're hiding something from me!" the Consul burst out. "I feel it! I know it! Have pity, senhor, speak! Has my poor Jean fallen into the hands of those wretched Huns? Is he dead?"

Shakespeare lifted a slender, aristocratic hand, white as milk. "No, no, no, most esteemed senhora. Nothing of that kind. I believe I have good news for you . . ."

"Oh holy madonna of Bilbao, can that be true?"

"Well—er—as it happens, a few hours ago a gentleman came here who might well be the person you are looking for . . .

"Oh God, Oh God, Oh God!"

"The butler has just gone to wake him. He may be here at any moment . . ." Someone knocked at the door. "Ah, there he is. Come in!"

The door opened. The supercilious manservant appeared. Thomas Lieven walked past him into the library. He was wearing slippers. His legs were bare. He was swathed in the oriental dressing gown supplied from the *Baby Ruth*'s stores.

"Jean!"

Estrella's shriek rent the air. She rushed at her beloved, stumbling over a rug and threw herself on his chest. She clung to his stiff figure, caressed and kissed him breathlessly. Then she stammered: "Jean, Jean, my one and only sweet . . . just to know you're alive and here makes me the happiest woman in the world!"

Shakespeare bowed, smiling indulgently. "I'll leave you now with the Senhora, M. Leblanc," he remarked primly. "See you later."

Thomas Lieven closed his eyes. Through the hailstorm of Estrella's kisses he thought desperately: All over, finished, I'm through now. Good-bye freedom, good-bye *General Carmona*, good-bye lovely South America . . .

[21]

Charley, the wireless operator, sat in a top-floor room of the Casa do Sul. The fronds of the palms outside the window stirred in the morning breeze. Charley was engaged in manicuring his nails when Shakespeare burst in.

"Get going! To M.I.5. Very urgent. Real name of Jonas the merchant is Jean Leblanc stop request instructions."

Charley put the message into code, switched on the transmitter and began to send Morse signals.

Meanwhile Shakespeare sat down in front of a big loud-speaker and pressed down one of seven keys. It bore the legend LIBRARY MICROPHONE.

The instrument clicked and crackled. Then Shakespeare listened in to the following dialogue between Thomas and the fair Estrella.

". . . But how do you make out I'm to blame for your danger, darling? How could I . . ."

"You ought never to have come here."

"But I was half out of my mind with fright and anxiety—I thought I was going to die . . ."

"You ought never to have mentioned my name."

Shakespeare smiled thinly.

"Why not? Why not?"

"Because no one must know my name."

"But you're a Frenchman, a friend of the British, an ally!"

"All the same . . . keep quiet now." Footsteps sounded.

". . . I'm pretty sure there's one of those things somewhere here . . . ah, yes. Here it is, under the table." The loud-speaker whistled shrilly. There was a startling crash. Then the line went dead.

Shakespeare remarked with admiration: "There's a sly devil for you! Finds the mike and tears it out!" A few minutes later he saw the operator's fingers flying as he took down a message. "Answer from M.I.5 already?"

Charley nodded. As he finished decoding the message from London his healthy young features lost color. He muttered: "Good God!"

"What's up?" Shakespeare snatched the slip from his hand. He read:

> MI 5 to shakespeare lisbon alleged jean leblanc really thomas lieven german intelligence agent has just played us up with false lists of french secret service members keep this man in custody at all costs special agent on way to you by courier aircraft comply with his instructions message ends

Shakespeare dashed the slip to the floor with a resounding oath and ran from the room. He raced down the stairs to the library, taking the steps two at a time.

In the hall a sad spectacle met his gaze. The heavy front door stood wide open. So did that of the library. Between them lay a motionless figure, face downward on a magnificent oriental rug. It was the highly respectable butler.

Shakespeare rushed into the library. The room was empty. A whiff of perfume still hung in the air. Shakespeare rushed out into the park. A red taxi was just getting on the move, with screeching gears. Shakespeare rushed back into the hall. The highly respectable butler had just regained consciousness. He sat on the rug groaning and feeling his neck tenderly.

"How on earth did this happen?"

"The man's a judo expert, sir. When I saw him coming out of the library with the lady I tried to stop him. But he acted like lightning. Threw me down and I lost my senses, sir . . ."

[22]

The telephone bell rang and rang and rang.

Thomas Lieven, still in dressing gown and slippers, came padding into Estrella's bedroom. During the last quarter of an hour the driver of the red taxi and several passersby had been as amazed at his extraordinary get-up as Estrella's maid. But Thomas, who had all his life dressed with such extreme elegance, cared nothing for their astonishment. He didn't care what anybody thought now. He knew his life was at stake.

He picked up the receiver. "Hallo?"

Then he smiled in relief, for he knew the voice of the speaker. It belonged to a friend, the only friend now left to him.

"Leblanc? Lindner here . . ."

"Thank God it's you, Lindner. I was just going to ring you. Where are you?"

"At the hotel. Listen, Leblanc. I've been trying to get you for hours."

"No wonder! I've had a disagreeable experience, several of them in fact . . . Lindner, you must help me. . . . I'll have to lie low until our boat goes . . ."

"Leblanc . . ."

". . . I've got to keep out of sight, I . . ."

"Leblanc, let me speak, for heaven's sake!"

"Well?"

"The boat won't be leaving."

Thomas dropped onto the Consul's bed. She had come up

behind him, her little fist jammed in terror against her seductive mouth. Thomas groaned. "*What* did you say?"

"The boat won't be leaving."

The sweat stood on Thomas Lieven's brow. "What's happened, then?"

The Viennese banker's voice sounded hysterical. "I had had an uneasy feeling for some days. The shipping company was behaving very strangely. I didn't tell you, as I didn't want to worry you. But this morning I found out . . ."

"Found out what?"

"That the boat has been seized by the Germans."

Thomas closed his eyes.

"What's the matter? What's the matter?" cried the unhappy Consul in a panic.

Thomas spoke hoarsely into the mouthpiece. "What about another boat?"

"Impossible! All accommodation's booked for months ahead. We'll just have to face it, Leblanc. We're stuck here in Lisbon—hallo—Leblanc—can you hear me?"

"I can hear every word," said Thomas Lieven. "I'll be in touch with you, Lindner. Good-bye for now. Keep your tail up if you can."

He rang off and clapped his hands to his forehead. Suddenly he could smell chloroform again. Suddenly he felt sick again. Giddy. Weary to death.

What was to be done now?

Now he was caught in the trap. Now he could no longer count on escaping the lot of them, the Germans, the British, the French. He had tricked them all and now they had him.

"Jean, Jean!" The voice of the fair Consul rang in his ears. He glanced up. She had fallen to her knees beside him, shuddering and sobbing. "Speak, speak! I beg you! Do tell poor Estrella what has happened!"

He gazed at her in silence. Then his face cleared. He said in a low tone: "Send the maid away, darling."

"The maid . . ."

"I want to be alone with you."

"But what about lunch?"

"I'll prepare lunch myself," said Thomas Lieven. He stood up like a boxer who has been heavily punished but by no means knocked out and is coming up for the next round. "I've got to think over everything very carefully now. And I always have my best ideas when I'm cooking."

He made a Hungarian *lecso*. Deep in thought he slit half a

pound of onions into rings. Quietly and gently he shelled a couple of pounds of green paprika pods.

The Consul watched him. She was so nervous that she kept fiddling with her bracelet, an extremely fine one of heavy gold, set with diamonds of the purest water.

Estrella, shaking her head, exclaimed: "You're so quiet and casual. How *can* you cook at such a time . . ."

He smiled with compressed lips. His eye fell on the broad bracelet. Its stones sparkled and glowed, as they caught the light, in white, blue, green, yellow and red tints. He slit the paprika pods into finger-length strips.

"Why don't you speak to me, Jean?"

"I'm thinking, my sweet."

"Jean, why won't you trust me? Why won't you tell me the truth? Why do you believe you're surrounded by dangers? Why are you even afraid of the British?"

He began to skin tomatoes. "The truth, my sweet, is so frightful that I simply can't tell it to you."

"Oh!" She was rotating her bracelet quite fast now. It flashed and gleamed like fire. "But whatever it is I want to help and protect you—trust me, Jean. I'll do anything for you."

"Anything? Really anything?"

"Really anything, my dearest!"

He lowered the tomato he was holding. His face showed cordial affection and quiet confidence. "In that case," said Thomas Lieven in a friendly tone, "after lunch we'll first rest for a little while and then you can report me."

It was not surprising that these words startled the fair Estrella, who at first made no reply. She stared at Thomas Lieven with wide eyes and open mouth.

"*What* did you say?" she gasped, as soon as she was able to speak. "Report you? Report you to whom?"

"To the police, my darling."

"But, for heaven's sake, why?"

"Because I have robbed you, my dear," replied Thomas Lieven. "Now what did I do with that garlic sausage?"

MENU

Mushrooms on Toast
Hungarian Lecso
Pears and Cheese

9 SEPTEMBER 1940

During the preparation of this Hungarian meal Thomas conceived the idea that saved his skin.

Mushrooms on Toast

Wash small, firm mushrooms, remove any blemishes and slice. Braise in butter till tender. Salt and pepper. Fry thin slices of white bread in butter on both sides. Cover the fried bread with the braised mushrooms. Sprinkle them with lemon juice and finely chopped parsley. Serve on warmed plates.

This dish can be made extra special if the mushrooms are braised with chopped shallots to which sweet or sour cream is then added. The mushrooms on the fried bread can also be sprinkled with cheese and placed in the oven for a short time to bake. But Thomas Lieven decided to use the first-mentioned method of preparation, as in this case the main dish was a substantial one and he only needed a light appetizer to precede it.

Hungarian Lecso

Slice half a pound of onions into rings. Dice a quarter of a pound each of streaky bacon and garlic sausage. Cut one pound of lamb into pieces slightly larger than those of the bacon and sausage. Remove seeds from two pounds of green peppers and slice them into half-inch strips. Peel one pound of tomatoes.

Fry the onions, bacon and sausage together. Then add the meat and fry it from all sides. Next add the peppers and a little later the tomatoes. Cover the saucepan and braise over a low flame till all is tender. Half an hour before serving add half a cupful of rice. This ingredient merely thickens the gravy a little. If more rice is used the dish will become too mushy. Season with salt and red pepper. Serve with slices of French bread.

Pears and Cheese

Ripe, firm but juicy pears are served with a mild cheese such as Gervais or Bel Paese. At table each person peels a pear, cuts it into portions convenient for the mouth and eats this portion with one of cheese, both being placed in the mouth together. This combination of fresh fruit and cheese makes a particularly tasty and satisfactory final course after a heavy, highly seasoned main dish.

BOOK II

CHAPTER 1

[1]

Extract from the daybook of Precinct 17 of the Lisbon police at the station in the Avenida E. Duarte Pacheco under date 9 September 1940.

1522 hours. Telephone call from No. 45 Rue Marques da Fronteira. Female voice urgently requested help in a case of robbery. Sergeants Alcantara and Branco despatched in station van. 1607 hours. Sergeants Alcantara and Branco return with (a) Estrella Rodrigues, Roman Catholic, widow, born 27.3.1905, Portuguese citizen, Costa Rica Consul, resident at 45 Rua Marques da Fronteira. (b) Jean Leblanc, Protestant, unmarried, born 2.1.1910, French citizen, banker, temporarily of no fixed address. (Refugee, Portuguese transit visa.)

Estrella Rodrigues stated: "I demand the arrest of Jean Leblanc, who has robbed me. I have known Leblanc for two weeks. He has often visited me at my villa. Five days ago I missed a heavy gold bracelet (Eighteen-carat, finely jointed, 150 grams, set with large and small diamonds) bought at the shop of Miguel da Foz in the Rua Alexandre Herculano. Price about 180,000 escudos. I accused Leblanc to his face of the theft and he admitted it. I gave him until noon today to return the bracelet. But he has not done so."

The foreigner Jean Leblanc, on being questioned, stated: "I did not steal the bracelet but only took it, at the request of Senhora Rodrigues, to try to sell it. I gave it back to her a long time ago because I could not find a purchaser."

QUESTION. Senhora Rodrigues says that she has not got it now. Can you get it or do you know where it has been deposited?

ANSWER. No, because Senhora Rodrigues has hidden it, in order to do me an injury. She wants to have me arrested.

QUESTION. Why?

ANSWER. Jealousy.

REMARKS. The foreigner Leblanc appeared sullen, defiant and arrogant while being questioned. At times he uttered certain threats. He accused the complainant of immorality and grossly insulted the examining inspector. Finally he pretended to have lost his wits, laughed, talked nonsense and sang French comic songs.

Sergeants Alcantara and Branco state: "The foreigner resisted arrest. He had to be handcuffed. While taking him to the station we noticed several suspicious looking persons loitering in the street in front of the villa and watching everything we did very closely."

FURTHER REMARKS. It may be assumed that the foreigner Leblanc is connected with the Lisbon underworld. He will be retained in custody overnight at this station. Early tomorrow morning he will be transferred in the prison van to police headquarters and there turned over to the Department of Petty Larceny for disposal.

[2]

It was nearly six o'clock in the evening when the beautiful if not particularly intelligent Consul and German-hater, Estrella Rodrigues, suffering equally from exhaustion and excitement, returned to the Rua Marques da Fronteira. She went by taxi.

With heaving bosom, feverishly glittering eyes and flushed cheeks she reflected, as she sat in the cab, that everything had gone just as Jean had desired and foreseen. But, good heavens, what terrible situations that incalculable, wonderful and mysterious man landed her in . . .

They had locked him up. He would be safe from his pursuers in prison. But why were they after him? He had never told her. He had just kissed her and begged her to trust him.

What else can I do, she thought desperately. I love him so. As such a brave Frenchman he may be engaged in goodness knows what secret mission here. Yes, I shall trust him and do everything he has asked me to. I shall put the bracelet in that hiding place in the cellar, go every day to the harbor and try to book an overseas passage for him and never mention him to anybody. If I manage to book him a passage to South America, I'll rush to the magistrate, show him the bracelet, say I only mislaid it and withdraw my accusation . . . oh, how terrible the days and nights will seem now without him, without my dear, sweet, beloved Jean . . .

The taxi stopped. The Consul alighted and paid the driver. As she crossed the pavement to her garden gate a pallid, careworn man wearing a shabby suit with a pepper and salt pattern stepped from behind a palm, raised his ancient hat to Estrella and addressed her in broken Portuguese. "Senhora Rodrigues, I urgently request you to grant me an interview."

"No, no," cried the voluptuous Consul, recoiling.

"I must insist," he retorted, following her and lowering his voice. "It concerns Jean Leblanc."

"Who are you?"

"My name is Walter Lewis," he replied. "I come from London." This last statement was true. He had landed an hour before. But his first statement was false. His name was Peter Lovejoy and he was the man who had been sent by his chief at M.I.5 to put a final stop to the activities of that infernal nuisance Thomas Lieven . . .

"What do you want with me, Mr. Lewis?"

"We want to know where M. Leblanc is."

"What has that got to do with you?"

The man who had called himself Lewis did his best to arouse Estrella's sympathy by gazing at her with lusterless eyes rendered dim and melancholy by low wages and undernourishment. "He has betrayed me. He has betrayed my country. He is a scoundrel."

"Silence!"

"He is a person devoid of honor, morality and decency . . ."

"Go away! Or I shall scream for help!"

"How can you bear to help a German? Do you want Hitler to win the war?"

"Hit . . ." The name stuck in the swan-white throat of the lady, that frenzied gambler who had not been exactly dogged by good fortune. "What was that you said?"

"I said, how can you bear to help a German?"

"A German? No! No!" The Consul clapped both swan-white hands to her forehead. "You are lying!"

"I am not! That wretched fascist's real name is Thomas Lieven!"

Estrella almost fainted. But she thought, Jean a German? Impossible! Inconceivable! After all we have been through together . . . his charm, his tenderness, his . . . No! He *must* be French!

She moaned: "Impossible!"

"He has cheated you, senhora, as he cheated me and all of us. Your Jean Leblanc is a German agent!"

"That's an awful thing to say!"

"He's a reptile! He must be made harmless, senhora."

The Consul threw back her beautiful head and stiffened her beauteous figure. "Follow me to the house, Mr. Lewis. Show me your proofs. I want facts, plain, hard facts. If you can supply me with them, then I'll . . ."

"Yes, senhora, yes?"

"I'll have my revenge! No German is ever going to laugh at Estrella Rodrigues, not if I know it!"

[3]

"*Manha*"—that was the word Thomas Lieven was to hear most often during the weeks of his imprisonment. Tomorrow! "Tomorrow," promised the warders. "Tomorrow," promised the magistrate. "Tomorrow" was the word with which the prisoners consoled themselves. They had been waiting for months for something, anything, to happen to them.

Nothing did happen. But perhaps something would happen tomorrow. Warders, magistrates and prisoners alike shrugged their shoulders fatalistically, smiled mysteriously and repeated a catchword which might well serve as the motto of all southern penal systems. "*Eh-eh, ate a manha!*" It might be translated: "Tomorrow is tomorrow, and tomorrow—well, good heavens, anything might happen before then, so don't let's anticipate."

After Thomas Lieven's arrest he was first taken to the Criminal Investigation Remand Prison on the Torel, one of the seven hills on which Lisbon is built. The Torel appeared to be quite seriously overcrowded.

Accordingly, after a few days Thomas Lieven was transferred to the Aljube, a medieval building of five stories in the oldest quarter of the city. The arms of the Archbishop Dom Miguel de Castro were carved above the main entrance. That prelate, as all cultivated people are aware, sojourned in this vale of tears from 1568 to 1625 and relegated to this dreadful old dungeon members of his cloth who had been found guilty of penal offences.

There must have been, thought Thomas Lieven on his arrival, a high percentage of such clerical sinners in sixteenth-century Portugal, for the Aljube was a prison of monstrous size.

It now received lay offenders only, among whom were many allegedly undesirable aliens. But at least an equal number had simply fallen foul of paragraphs in the Portuguese statute book which were entirely unconcerned with politics. Some were still under remand. Others had already been sentenced. They were to be found sharing a cell, in solitary confinement or else in cells reserved for "well-to-do" prisoners.

The latter occupied the higher floors and had the most comfortable accommodation. All the windows overlooked the courtyard. An adjacent leather goods factory, run by a certain Teodoro dos Repos, involved the production of certain unpleasant smells which greatly afflicted, especially in hot weather, the ill-to-do prisoners on the lower floors.

Life was more tolerable for the well-to-do on the upper stories. They paid a weekly rent, just as in an ordinary hotel. The size of the figure was calculated in accordance with the amount of bail required by the remand court. It was exhorbitant. But just as in an ordinary hotel the best service available was provided for the well-to-do. The staff made every effort to anticipate their wishes. Newspapers and cigarettes were supplied as a matter of course. And the prisoners could also, as a matter of course, have their meals brought in from neighboring restaurants recommended by the warders.

Thomas had deposited, in anticipation of some such amiable customs, a substantial sum of cash with the prison management. He organized victualing in the following manner. Every morning he summoned Francesco, the fat cook, and talked over with him, in detail, the day's menu. Francesco then sent his assistant to market. The cook was absolutely delighted with Senhor Jean. The gentleman in Cell 519 was always passing new recipes and culinary tips on to him.

Thomas Lieven thoroughly enjoyed himself. He regarded his imprisonment as a brief, well-earned period of sick leave before his departure for South America.

He was not in the least disturbed at not having yet heard from Estrella. He felt sure that the darling would be doing her very best to book him an overseas passage . . .

A week after Thomas Lieven's arrival at the prison he was given a cell-mate. Juliao, the friendly warder whom Thomas had lavishly tipped, brought the newcomer into the cell on the morning of September 21, 1940.

Thomas sat up on his cot with a start. He had never seen such a hideous human being in all his life.

The stranger looked like the late sexton of Notre Dame. He was small, he had a hump, he limped and he was entirely bald. His face had a corpselike pallor. Yet his cheeks swelled out like those of a hamster. Finally, he suffered from a nervous twitching of the lips.

"Bom dia," said the hunchback with a grin.

"Bom dia," murmured Thomas in a strangled tone.

"My name is Alcoba. Lazarus Alcoba." The newcomer held out a clawlike hand, covered with black hair.

Thomas shook it with the greatest horror and repugnance. He did not suspect that a true and loyal friend, with a heart of gold, had come into his life.

Lazarus Alcoba, as he made himself at home on the second cot, said in a hoarse, grating voice: "They've picked me up for smuggling, the sods—but this time they won't be able to prove anything. They'll have to let me out one of these days. But I'm not in any hurry . . . *Eh-eh, ate a manha.*" He grinned again.

"I'm also absolutely innocent," Thomas began. But Lazarus interrupted him with a cheerful wave of the hand. "Ay, ay, they tell me you pinched a diamond bracelet. Sheer slander, eh? Tcha, tcha, tcha—what wicked, wicked people."

"How did you know . . ."

"Oh, I know all about you, my lad! You can treat me as a friend, you know." The hunchback scratched himself exuberantly. "You're French and you're a banker and the sweetie who ran you in is the Consul Estrella Rodrigues. You're fond of cooking . . ."

"Who told you that?"

"Friend, I picked you out, I'm telling you!"

"Picked me out?"

Lazarus beamed, till his hideous countenance looked twice as wide, "Sure. You're the most interesting man in this clink. Got to have some sort of spiritual uplift in stir haven't we, hey?" He leaned forward familiarly and patted Thomas's knee. "I'll give you a little tip for the future, Jean. Next time they turn you in, ask to see the chief warder right away. I do that every time I'm nicked."

"Why?"

"I tell that idle sod of a chief warder that I'll keep his books for him. So I can go through everyone's papers. And after a few days I know the first and last thing about all the other lags. So I can pick out the best of 'em as a cell-mate."

Thomas began to find the hunchback amusing. He offered him a cigarette. "And what made you pick on me in particular?"

"I could see you had what it takes. Unfortunately you're only a beginner. But on the other hand you have good manners. A bloke could learn something from you. You're a banker. You could show me how to play the market. You like cooking. And that might be useful to learn too. It's never a waste of time to learn anything, you know . . ."

"Yes," said Thomas pensively. "That's true." He was thinking, What a lot of things I've learned since fate snatched me out of my peaceful career! Goodness knows what I'll still have to go through. My secure, respectable existence, my London club and my comfortable flat in Mayfair, how far away they seem now, all vanished into an impenetrable sea of fog . . .

"What about ganging up together?" said Lazarus. "You teach me all you know and I teach you all I know. How's that?"

"First-rate idea," said Thomas, delighted. "What do you fancy for lunch, Lazarus?"

"I've been thinking of something as a matter of fact, but I'm not sure whether you know the recipe . . . that stupid lout in the kitchen certainly doesn't."

"Well, give us a lead!"

"Well, I've worked in pretty well every country in Europe, you know. I'm greedy, I quite admit it. And I prefer French cooking. But I've nothing against German. One time in Münster, when I was cleaning up some gents' pockets, I ate some stuffed smoked ribs of pork just before I started." He rolled his eyes and smacked his lips.

"Well, if that's all you need," remarked Thomas Lieven calmly.

"You know the recipe?"

"I also worked in Germany at one time," Thomas said, banging on the door of the cell. "Stuffed smoked ribs of pork I can do for you. We can make this a German day for once. If so, I'd recommend that the first course should be Swabian dumpling soup and after the pork—h'm, let's see—yes, chestnuts and whipped cream . . ."

The friendly warder named Juliao stuck his head through the doorway.

"Send me up the head chef," said Thomas, pressing a hundred-escudo note into Juliao's hand. "I want to fix up today's menu with him."

MENU

Swabian Soup with Liver Dumplings
Westphalian Stuffed Ribs of Pork
Chestnuts and Whipped Cream (Baden Style)

21 SEPTEMBER 1940

Good plain cooking. Best foundation for a daring coup.

Swabian Soup with Liver Dumplings

Beat a quarter of a cup of butter till creamy. Mix with one cup of finely chopped ox liver, three whole eggs, one soaked roll, one cup of bread crumbs. Season with marjoram, salt and pepper. Form small dumplings and place in boiling water for ten to fifteen minutes, till they rise to the top. Remove and drain. Serve in a strong beef broth.

Westphalian Stuffed Ribs of Pork

Take a large fresh piece of boned pork ribs. Peel, core and slice large cooking apples, mix with parboiled stoned plums, add a little grated lemon peel, a little rum and bread crumbs. This mixture is placed on the boned, salted and peppered meat, which is then rolled and the edges sewn up. The joint is then browned on all sides and after that slowly roasted in the oven. When cooked it is served with mashed potatoes.

Chestnuts and Whipped Cream (Baden Style)

Sound chestnuts are incised crosswise on the round side, placed on a baking sheet and put in a hot oven for a short time. This makes it easy to remove the shell. The chestnuts are then placed in boiling water until the inner skin can be removed. They are next placed in sweetened vanilla-flavored milk and cooked until soft. Then they are put through the mincer direct onto the serving dish, covered with whipped cream and garnished with cherries soaked in cognac.

[4]

"Well, how do you like it? Good as that time in Münster?" inquired Thomas Lieven four hours later. He sat opposite the hunchback at a carefully laid table in his cell. Lazarus wiped his mouth and moaned in ecstasy. "Better, my boy, better! After ribs of pork like that I'd guarantee to pinch the brief case of our respected President Salazar himself!"

"The cook could have put a drop more rum in it."

"The bastards always drink it all themselves," said Lazarus. "I'd like to show my gratitude straight away for this meal, friend. So here beginneth the first lesson."

"That's nice of you, Lazarus. A little more purée?"

"Sure. Now look here. We're well-to-do. We've got the dough. So we don't have to rack our brains to get a decent meal. But what do you do if you're broke next time they nick you? The most important thing in the clink is to be well fed. And you will be if you're diabetic."

"But how do I get diabetes?"

"That's just what I'm now going to tell you," rejoined Lazarus, with his hamster cheeks full up. "First of all you keep on reporting sick to the prison doctor. You simply say you never feel well. Watch for the chance and pinch one of his syringes. Next, get chummy with the cook. That won't be difficult in your case. Ask him to let you have a drop of vinegar to season your grub and then some sugar for your coffee."

"I see." Thomas banged on the door. The warder appeared. "Clear away, please," said Thomas. "And bring the last course."

Lazarus waited until Juliao had left the cell with their plates. Then he went on: "You mix vinegar and water in the proportion of one to two and sugar the solution well. Then you inject two cubic centimeters of it into your thigh."

"Intramuscularly?"

"Yes. But slowly, very slowly, mind. Or you'll get the devil's own swell-up."

"I see."

"You inject the stuff one and a half hours before you're due to see the doc. And be sure you don't piddle before then. Get me?"

"Sure."

Juliao the warder brought in the last course, was given a portion for himself and departed gleefully.

While they ate their chestnuts and cream Lazarus finished his lesson. "You tell the doc you were frightfully thirsty all night. He'll at once suspect you may have an excess of sugar and he'll ask you for a sample of urine. You'll have it all ready for him. On examining it he'll find that you really have a lot of sugar. So you'll be correspondingly well fed. Roast meat, butter, milk and white bread. Well worth the bit of trouble you've taken."

Such was the information Thomas obtained on the first day of his meeting with the hunchback. During the following days and weeks he added to it. He underwent a regular course of instruction in crime and how to make the best of prison. His brain registered with mathematical exactitude every tip and recipe he received.

For example: In order to produce in a short time the symptoms of a high fever, so as to be taken to the sick bay, from which it is so much easier to escape, work up an ordinary soap lather and swallow three teaspoonfuls of it an hour before medical examination. The result will be a bad headache and within an hour temperature will rise to about 41 degrees centigrade. But it will only last about an hour. For longer periods regular "pills" of soap will have to be swallowed. Again, for jaundice symptoms mix one teaspoonful of soot with two of sugar, add vinegar and leave the solution to stand overnight. Drink it next morning on an empty stomach. The symptoms will develop within two days at most.

Lazarus said: "This is a warlike age, you know, Jean. The time may well come one day when you will wish to avoid a hero's death. Need I say more?"

"You need not," said Thomas Lieven.

Those were happy weeks. Lazarus learned how to cook to perfection. Thomas learned how to simulate sickness to perfection. He also learned international thieves' slang and dozens of such confidence tricks as the White Waistcoat, the Loan-Gift, the Car Sale, the Diamond Business, Damages, the Suit to Measure, the Information Leak and the Breakdown Service.

He felt—heavens, how low he had sunk already!—that he might well need to resort to all these tricks at some future time or other. This expectation was to be proved one hundred per cent correct.

Thomas and Lazarus, each of them learner and teacher,

lived together in peace and harmony until the morning of that terrible, that appalling day, November 5, 1940 . . .

On the morning of November 5, 1940, Thomas Lieven was again, after a considerable interval, brought before the examining magistrate. This gentleman's name was Eduardo Baixa. He always dressed entirely in black and wore pince-nez on a black silk ribbon. A cultivated man, he always addressed Thomas in French. He did so that morning. "Now, monsieur, why do you keep me waiting so long for your confession?"

"I've nothing to confess. I'm innocent."

Baixa polished his glasses. "Tcha, tcha! Then it looks as if you'll be a good long time yet in Aljube, monsieur. We've circulated your description to all the police stations in Portugal. Now we shall have to wait."

"Wait for what?"

"For replies from all those stations, naturally. We don't know yet what other crimes you have committed in this country."

"I haven't committed any crimes at all. I'm innocent."

"Oh, dear, no, of course not . . . but just the same, M. Leblanc, we shall have to wait. Moreover, you're a foreigner . . ." Baixa riffled through a file. "H'm, a most unusual sort of lady, I must say."

"To whom are you referring?"

"To the complainant, Senhora Rodrigues."

Thomas Lieven suddenly experienced a queer tingling along his backbone. His lips felt dry as he asked: "In what way unusual, your honor?"

"She hasn't turned up."

"I don't understand that statement."

"I asked her to come and see me. But she hasn't come."

"My God," Thomas exclaimed. "I hope nothing has happened to her!" That would be the last straw, he was thinking.

On returning to his cell he sent at once for Francesco, the fat cook.

The latter entered beaming. "What are your orders for today, Senhor Jean?"

Thomas shook his head. "It's not about cooking. I want you to do me a favor. Can you get away from the kitchen for an hour?"

"Certainly."

"Ask the management to give you some money from my deposit, buy twenty red roses and take a taxi to the address I have written here. A certain Senhora Estrella Rodrigues lives there. I'm very worried about her. She may be ill. Ask for news of her and whether you can be of any assistance."

"Very good, Senhor Jean." The stout cook went out.

He returned a good hour later, looking distressed. When he entered the cell carrying a splendid bouquet of blood-red roses, Thomas knew at once that something frightful had happened.

"Senhora Rodrigues is away," said the cook.

Thomas plumped down on his cot.

"What do you mean by 'away'?" Lazarus demanded.

"I mean what I say, you idiot," the cook retorted. "Away. Out. Gone abroad. Disappeared. No longer there."

"Since when?" Thomas asked.

"Five days ago, Senhor Jean." The cook gazed at Thomas sympathetically, "I gathered that she didn't intend to come back, at least not for some time."

"Why do you think so?"

"All her clothes, jewelry and cash were gone."

"But she hadn't got any money!"

"Well, her safe was open . . ."

"Her safe?" Thomas shuddered. "How did you come to see it?"

"The maid took me all over the house. Pretty little half-breed she was too, I give you my word! Tip-top! Wonderful eyes!" The cook accompanied his words with appropriate gestures.

"That's Carmen," Thomas murmured.

"Yes, Carmen's her name. We're going to the movies together this evening. She took me to the dressing room. All the cupboards were empty. And to the bedroom. The safe there was empty too . . ."

Thomas groaned. "Quite empty, was it?"

"Yes, quite empty. A pretty little pair of black silk panties hung over the open steel door and that was all. . . . My God, Senhor Jean, aren't you feeling well? Water . . . drink a little water . . ."

"Better lie down quietly on your back," Lazarus advised.

Thomas sank back on his cot obediently. He mumbled: "All the money I had in the world was in that safe . . ."

"Women. Always trouble with women," Lazarus growled fiercely. "And now we shan't get any lunch either!"

"But why?" Thomas whispered. "I can't make out why. I never did her any harm . . . what did Carmen say? Does she know where the Senhora is?"

"Carmen said she had gone to Costa Rica."

"Good God Almighty," groaned Thomas.

"She also said that the villa would be sold."

Thomas suddenly started raving like a madman. "Don't keep shoving those blasted roses under my nose, confound you!" He pulled himself together. "Sorry, Lazarus. Pure nerves. And—and wasn't there any message for me? No letter? Nothing?"

"Yes, Senhor." The cook took a couple of envelopes out of his pocket. The first was from Thomas's friend, the Viennese banker Walter Lindner.

Lisbon, 29 October 1940.

Dear Herr Leblanc,

I write these lines in very great haste and much anxiety. It is now eleven o'clock. In two hours my boat leaves and I must go aboard. And still there is no sign of life from you! I can't think where on earth you have got to and I wonder whether you're still alive.

I only know what your unhappy friend the Consul has told me, that on the 9th September, after speaking to me on the telephone, you went out and never came back.

Poor Estrella Rodrigues! You have someone there who loves you from the bottom of her heart. How she grieved for you! How anxious she was about you! I have seen her daily since I succeeded in obtaining an overseas passage for myself and my wife. Every day we hoped to hear something about you, but in vain.

I write these lines in the villa of your beautiful friend, who is in despair. She is standing beside me in tears. Even today—our last—there is no sign of life from you. But I still hope, as I write, that at least you are not dead and will one day return to this house and the woman who loves you so ardently. If that hope should be fulfilled, you will find my letter waiting for you.

I shall pray for you. Still hoping to see you again I remain

Yours most sincerely,
Walter Lindner

That was the first letter.

Thomas let it fall. He was gasping for breath. His head had suddenly begun to ache as if it would burst.

Why didn't Estrella tell my friend where I am? Why didn't

she come here and fetch me away as arranged? Why has she behaved like this? Why? Why?

The second letter told him the answer.

Lisbon, 1 November 1940.

Vile scoundrel!

Now that your friend Lindner has left Portugal there will be no one here to help you, and I mean to take my revenge.

You will never see me again. In a few hours I shall be traveling by air to Costa Rica.

Your friend has written you a letter. I shall put mine beside it. One day the examining magistrate will send someone to look for me. Then you will receive both letters.

In case, as is very probable, the magistrate reads both letters before passing them on to you, I declare for the second time that you have robbed me, you ruffian!

And I also declare, as no doubt his honor will be interested to hear, the reason why I am now leaving you for ever. It is because I have discovered that you are a German, a German secret agent, a mean, conscienceless, unscrupulous, money-grubbing, cynical German scoundrel. Oh, how I hate you, you beast!

E.

[5]

"Oh, how much I still love you, you beast!" groaned the passionate, statuesque Estrella Rodrigues.

While Thomas Lieven, in his cell in the Aljube, Lisbon, an icy chill at the pit of his stomach, was reading her farewell letter, the black-haired Consul of the provocative figure was sitting on the other side of the globe, in the drawing room of the most expensive suite in the most expensive hotel in San José, the capital of the Republic of Costa Rica.

Estrella's eyes were red. She was trying to keep cool by fanning herself. Her heart was beating fast. Her breath came fast.

Jean, Jean, she thought, I can't stop thinking about you, you vile beast called Thomas Lieven, you contemptible liar, you who have betrayed me . . . My God, and I love you so . . .

The Consul, confronted with this tragic state of affairs, boldly risked her life by pouring a double Costa Rican brandy down her beautiful throat. Then she closed her eyes with a shudder and remembered, with a shudder, her latest experiences.

Once more she saw the British agent telling her the truth, the truth about Thomas Lieven. Then she saw herself after the Englishman had left her. A crushed, shattered, broken woman . . .

It was in a state of collapse that in the evening of September 9, 1940, she had crept to the big safe in her bedroom. With tears in her eyes she had spun the combination and, trembling in every limb, opened the heavy door. That scoundrel's fortune in cash lay before her. Marks, escudos, dollars. Almost blinded by her tears, betrayed, deeply unhappy, she had counted the money.

That evening the visitors to the Estoril casino had experienced a real thrill.

Estrella Rodrigues, more beautiful than ever, paler than ever and wearing a gown cut lower than ever, arrived with a capital of some twenty thousand dollars. The employees and croupiers knew her as a persistent loser. They all, by this time, felt so sorry for her. But this evening she won and won and won.

She gambled with Thomas Lieven's money as if in a trance. She staked only the maximum, each time. When she staked on No. 11 it came up three times running. She staked on 29 *en plein* (to win 35 times the stake) and *à cheval* (on the separating line, to win 17 times the stake if either number comes up) and won both times. She staked on the middle dozen, red, *impair* (odd numbers), *passe* (Nos. 19 to 36) and No. 23 *en plein* and *à cheval*, putting on the maximum in each case. No. 23 came up!

Whenever she played she won, whatever she staked.

Tears came into her beautiful eyes. Gentlemen in dinner jackets and ladies in the most costly mink furs watched this strange gambler with curiosity. For she sobbed as fast as she won.

Players rose from their seats at other tables in the hall, with its sparkling candelabra, enormous mirrors framed in white and gold and splendid paintings. They came from every direction to stand in serried ranks staring at the beautiful woman in the red evening gown winning incessantly and growing, apparently, more and more desperate all the time.

"You are too beautiful. You have too much luck in love. It would be unfair if you also had luck at play." These words, which Thomas Lieven had uttered on the evening they met, burned like fire in her memory. Too much luck in love! That was why she had always lost. And now—now . . .

"Vingi-sept, rouge, impair et passe!"

A cry of astonishment rose from the crowd.

Estrella sobbed aloud. For she had won again, the maximum allowed at the Estoril casino with that stake.

"I—can't—go—on," moaned the fair winner. Two attendants in pumps were needed to escort her to the bar. Two other attendants with wooden boxes were needed to take the counters she had staked to the cashier to be changed. The conversion produced a sum of $82,734.26. It would hardly be appropriate, just then, to say that ill-gotten gain never thrives.

Estrella took a check for the amount. In her gold-embroidered evening bag she found a stray counter worth ten thousand escudos. From the bar, she threw it over the heads of the players onto the green cloth of an adjacent table. The counter fell on red. Estrella called out, sobbing: "For betrayed loves!"

Red came up.

Yes, red came up, Estrella Rodrigues remembered, with tear-filled eyes, on November 5, 1940, in the drawing room of the most expensive suite in the most expensive hotel of San José. In San José it was half-past nine in the morning by Costa Rican time. In Lisbon it was half-past twelve in the afternoon by Portuguese time. In Lisbon Thomas Lieven was just swallowing a first double brandy in the attempt to forget the awful dismay he felt. In San José the fair Consul was already drinking her second double of the day. She had imbibed the first directly after breakfast.

During the last few days she had been imbibing oftener and oftener, earlier and earlier in the day and with more and more relish. She suffered from such awful palpitations that she simply had to drink.

For if she didn't she really couldn't bear the memory of Jean, the sweet, unique, wonderful Jean—oh, the beast, the brute—any longer. Brandy, for the time being, helped her to some extent.

She was rich now and had nothing more to worry about. She would never see her beloved one again. The humiliation of having yielded to him in the past had ceased to afflict her.

With trembling fingers Estrella drew from her crocodile-leather handbag a golden flask, and unscrewed it. With trembling fingers she refilled her glass. And as her tears began to flow afresh she cried aloud, alone in the splendid room: "Never, never shall I forget that man!"

[6]

"Never," said Thomas Lieven, "never shall I forget that woman!"

Twilight was falling, in shades of mother-of-pearl, over Lisbon. Thomas Lieven paced his cell like an irritated tiger.

He had told Lazarus the whole truth. Lazarus knew now what Thomas's real name was, what tricks he had been playing and what fate awaited him if the German, British or French secret service could lay hands on him.

The hunchback, as he smoked a cigarette, was watching his friend attentively. "That sort of hysteria in women," he said, "disgusts me. And what's more, you never know what people like that are going to do next."

Thomas paused briefly in his restless pacing. "Yes, that's just the trouble. Tomorrow she'll be quite capable of writing to the prefect of police and accusing me of some murder that's never been cleared up."

"Or several murders."

"What?"

"I said, or several undetected murders."

"Yes, I daresay. But there's no way out. My position's quite hopeless. Naturally she's taken that damned bracelet with her and it'll never be found. So I can just sit here until I rot."

"That's right," said Lazarus. "And for that reason you'll have to get out in double-quick time."

"Out of here?"

"Before she can do you any more harm."

"Lazarus, this is a prison."

"So what?"

"What about the bars and walls and thick iron doors? What about the magistrates, the warders and the bloodhounds?"

"Just so. It won't be quite so easy for you to get out as it was for you to get in."

Thomas sat down on the edge of his cot. "But is it even possible?"

"Of course. We'll just have to exert ourselves a bit, that's all. Didn't you tell me you've learned something about forgery?"

"Yes, and a good lot too!"

"M'm. Well, there's a printing press in the cellar here. It's used for all the forms required in court. We'll get hold of the right rubber stamp somehow. You yourself are going to be the chief problem, my friend."

"I? How do you mean?"

"You'll have to change your style."

"In what way?"

Lazarus smiled grimly. "In my way. You'll have to grow smaller. You'll have to limp. You'll have to sport a hump. And hamster's cheeks. And twitching lips. And of course your noddle will have to be quite bald. Shocked you now, haven't I?"

"N—not at all," Thomas Lieven lied gallantly. "F—freedom's w—worth every effort, isn't it?"

"It's the best thing life has to offer," Lazarus declared. "Now listen very carefully to what I'm going to tell you."

He spoke at some length.

And Thomas Lieven listened very carefully.

"Of course it's always easier to get into jail than out," said the hunchback Lazarus Alcoba. "And yet it's not so terribly difficult to get out again."

"Well, that's good news, at any rate!"

"It's lucky we're in Portugal and not in your part of the world. In Germany the trick wouldn't work. Everything's too well organized there."

"Yes, so I've heard. German prisons are the best in the world, eh?"

"I've been in the Moabit jug twice myself," said Lazarus, striking himself on the knee. "And I can tell you the Portuguese simply can't compete with the set-up there. They're much too good-natured. They lack the Prussian sense of duty, the German love of discipline."

"You're right there."

The hunchback banged on the door of the cell. The friendly warder Juliao, so lavishly tipped by Thomas, who treated him as if he were the floor waiter in a good hotel, appeared at once.

"Ask the cook to step up here a minute, will you, pal?" said Lazarus to the warder. Juliao, with a bow, disappeared. Lazarus turned to Thomas. "Your escape's going to start in the kitchen, see?"

A little later the hunchback was saying to Francesco, the fat cook: "Look here, you know we have a printing press in the cellar, don't you?"

"Sure. For printing all the forms required in court."

"Including the public prosecutor's orders of release, eh?"
"Certainly."
"D'you know any of the lags working down there?"
"No. Why do you ask?"
"We want one of those orders of release."
"Well, I'll keep my ears open," said the cook.
"Yes, do that, will you?" Thomas Lieven broke in. "I can guarantee anyone who does us that little favor a week's good feeding."
Two days later the cook reported. "I've found a bloke who's willing. But he wants a whole month's good chow for the job."
"Impossible," said Lazarus coolly. "Two weeks' and no more."
"I'll see what he says," replied the cook.
When he had left the cell Thomas said to the hunchback: "You needn't have been so stingy. After all, it's my money that'll pay for it."
"Matter of principle," retorted the hunchback. "You mustn't let 'em stick it on. But apart from that, I hope you were telling the truth when you said you could forge a rubber stamp?"
"I can forge any rubber stamp you like. I've studied under the best forger in the country," Thomas retorted. He was thinking, It's perfectly awful how low you can get. I'm still actually proud of it!
Next day the cook reported that the printer had agreed to the terms offered.
"Where's the form?"
"The printer says he wants the fortnight's good grub first."
"Trust for trust," growled Lazarus. "He can either send up the form straight away or he can forget the whole thing."
An hour later the form was delivered.
Lazarus had been reporting daily, ever since his arrival, to the chief warder, for work on the prison books and business correspondence. He typed dozens of letters every day. The chief warder read his newspaper and left the hunchback to his own devices.
Lazarus was accordingly able, without interruption, to fill in an order for his own release. He typed his name, his personal description and the number of his file. He dated the order for November 15, 1940, though that day was only the eighth. Lazarus and Thomas needed a good week for what they had in mind. A day would also be required to pass the form through

the official channels in the prison. Thus if all went well Thomas could be released on November 16. That would be a Saturday and the friendly warder Juliao always had that day off, so . . . But we must not anticipate!

Lazarus finally completed his order of release with the signature of the public prosecutor, which he could easily copy from a letter filed in the chief warder's office.

On returning to the cell he asked Thomas: "I hope you've also been busy?"

"I've been practicing all the afternoon."

It had been arranged that Thomas would report instead of Lazarus as soon as the forged order of release reached the prison chancellery and Alcoba's name was called. For this purpose Thomas would be obliged to disguise himself as the hunchback so far as possible. It would be difficult, considering that Lazarus Alcoba had a hump and practically no hair on his head, that his cheeks were like a hamster's, that he was smaller than Thomas and suffered from a nervous twitching of the lips. The hunchback therefore insisted upon Thomas practicing the disguise every day.

Thomas now crammed the space between cheeks and gums with pellets of bread, thus actually giving his cheeks the look of a hamster's. Then he began to twitch his lips nervously. He tried, though the bread was a hindrance, to imitate the hunchback's voice.

"Don't grunt like that, lad! And what sort of a twitch is that? You're twitching far too much up!" Lazarus seized his own lip. "Look, I twitch down, not up! Lower, man, lower!"

"Won't go any lower," Thomas mumbled, twitching for all he was worth. "Those blasted bread crumbs are in the way!"

"No bread, no hamster cheeks. Just keep on trying and it'll go lower!"

Thomas wiped the sweat from his brow. "Well, I must say that mug of yours is a menace."

"We can't all be as handsome as you are. And don't forget we've only just started. Wait till I've singed all your hair off."

"Singed . . ."

"Of course. D'you think they'd allow us razors and scissors here?"

"I'll never be able to stand that," Thomas groaned.

"Cut the cackle and get on with your practicing. Shrink! Put on my overcoat, so that you can see how much to bend your knees. Take that pillow and make a decent hump for yourself. And don't bother me now, I've got to make a few enquiries around here."

"What about?"

"I want to find someone who has a letter from the public prosecutor. With a stamp over it. So that you can counterfeit it."

Thomas Lieven put on the hunchback's old overcoat and went limping about the cell with bent knees. Meanwhile Lazarus began knocking on one of the walls with a shoe. He used the simplest of all the alphabets invented for that form of communication. Three knocks for *a*, two for *b*, and one for *c*. Then six for *d*, five for *e* and four for *f*. Then nine for *g*, eight for *h* and seven for i and so on.

After knocking for all the letters in his question he waited for an answer, turning to watch Thomas as the latter twitched, grunted and practiced walking with bent knees.

An hour passed. Then the prisoner in the next cell began to knock. Lazarus listened, nodding.

Finally he said: "There's a prisoner named Maravilha on the third floor. He's kept, as a sort of souvenir, the public prosecutor's notification of refusal of his application for release. There's a stamp on the thing."

"Fine," grunted Thomas, twitching his lips hard. "Offer him a week's decent grub for it."

[7]

November 1940 was very warm. It was still possible to swim in the Atlantic or lie in the sun on the beach at Estoril, although dress, by Portuguese law, had to be extraordinarily chaste. Police regulations required males to wear one-piece costumes and the authorities were even stricter with the ladies.

On November 9, towards midday, a sour-looking, bowlegged gentleman hired a so called *gaivola* on the beach. This contraption was an old-fashioned water-bicycle, consisting of two wooden runners, a sort of deck chair with pedals slung between them and a paddle wheel. The gentleman proceeded to pedal out to sea, somewhat laboriously, in his *gaivola*.

He was about fifty years of age and wore a brown swimming suit and a straw hat. After about fifteen minutes he sighted a second *gaivola* far out to sea, rocking gently, all by itself, on the slight Atlantic swell. He steered toward this second machine. After another quarter of an hour he had come near enough to it to recognize the gentleman reclining in it, who looked like a close relative of his own, equally embittered and overworked of aspect.

The second gentleman, who wore a black swimming suit, called out to him: "Thank God, I was beginning to wonder whether you would come."

The gentleman in the brown swimming suit drew alongside the other. "Well, as you telephoned to say that my life was at stake, of course I came."

He of the black costume replied: "Don't worry, Major Loos. Out here no one can hear us. No mikes here. Quite a brilliant idea of mine, eh?"

He of the brown costume treated the other to a hostile stare. "Oh, very brilliant. What did you want to see me about, Mr. Lovejoy?"

The British secret service agent sighed. "I wanted to make a proposal for the benefit of us both, Major. On the subject of that fellow Thomas Lieven."

"I thought that might be it!" The German Intelligence officer nodded grimly.

Lovejoy said in a morose tone: "You people are after him. He's played you up. He's played me up, too. You and I may be enemies, admitted. We're obliged to hate each other. All the same, Major, I should like your permission for us to work together in this case."

"Work together?"

"Major, we belong to the same profession. I appeal to you as a colleague. Don't you think that things have gone far enough when a lousy civilian suddenly pokes his nose into our affairs, a bloody outsider who cheapens the market, makes us look like fools and goes on as if we were born idiots!"

The major from Cologne muttered gloomily: "I'm likely to get the sack on account of that fellow."

"And what about me?" growled Lovejoy. "Either I bring him to London or they shove me into Coastal Patrol! Do you know what that means? I've a wife and two children, Major. I expect you have too."

"My wife has obtained a divorce."

"Well, we don't earn much in our job. But I don't see why we should have our whole lives ruined by a fellow like that."

"I only wish I'd let the Gestapo keep him that day in Cologne. Now there's no telling where he is."

"Oh, yes, there is."

"What do you mean?"

"He's in jail."

"But . . ."

"I'll explain the whole thing to you. He won't be there forever. I've bribed one of the staff to let me know immediately he comes out." Lovejoy threw up his hands despairingly. "But then what's going to happen? Then the rivalry between ourselves, you and me, will start all over again, with yachts and submarines, chloroform and revolvers! My dear Major, I'll be quite honest with you. I simply can't stand any more of that sort of thing."

"Nor is it particularly good for my liver, I might tell you."

"That's why I propose that we should collaborate. When he comes out, something's going to hit him. I've a man on the spot, as you can guess, to do the dirty work. Then I can report to my chief that you Germans have bumped him off. And you can tell your admiral that it was we, the British. You won't have to go to the front and I won't have to go to Coastal Patrol. Don't you think that's a good scheme?"

"Sounds too good to be true. . . ." The major uttered an abysmally deep sigh. Suddenly he ejaculated in an almost inaudible tone: "Sharks."

"No!"

"Just ahead there." Loos was numb with fright. Through the blue water two stiffly erect tail-fins were darting toward them. Then there were three. Then five.

"Now we're done for," said Lovejoy.

"Keep cool. Pretend to be dead," commanded the major. The first creature had reached them. It glided under the two water-bicycles and tossed them playfully in the air. The *gaivolas* somersaulted, splashed down into the sea and rocked wildly. Then another creature darted up and flung them up again.

The major went spinning into the water. He went under, came up again and immediately lay stock-still on his back. A gigantic beast slid past him, but apparently without seeing him, its jaws wide open. The major, who was versed in zoology, made a soothing discovery.

Then he heard a frightful scream and saw his British colleague whirl through the air and come down beside him.

"Lovejoy, listen to me. Those aren't sharks. They're dolphins."

"D—d—do—"

"Yes, we've fallen in with a herd of them. But dolphins don't attack human beings. They only play with them."

Play they did. They repeatedly circled around and around

the two gentlemen and sometimes jumped right over them, sending up columns of spray.

The mutually hostile agents clung side by side to one of the runners of Lovejoy's capsized *gaivola.* They tried to push it toward the shore. Lovejoy gasped: "I'm out of breath . . . what was it . . . you were saying just now . . . Loos?"

At that moment an enormous dolphin rose high into the air behind the major, executed a graceful leap over his head and drenched him with a minor deluge. The major spat out quite a lot of sea water and then yelled into Lovejoy's ear: "I was saying that I only wish I could shoot that rascal down with my own hand when he comes out of jail!"

[8]

In Portugal people don't eat many potatoes. All the same Francesco, the prison cook, came up with a dozen particularly fine ones when the well-to-do prisoners Leblanc and Alcoba ordered baked potatoes in their jackets for lunch on November 15.

As he had been directed, Francesco cooked the potatoes lightly in their skins and took them up, still quite hot, to the fifth floor, where he served them to Leblanc and Alcoba with Portuguese sardines in vinegar and oil. At the request of the well-to-do prisoners Juliao, the warder, cut the potatoes—they were not quite soft—into halves with a sharp knife.

When the gentlemen were left alone they made no attempt to partake of the meal. Thomas had something to do. On a small table under the window he laid out, side by side, the order of release which Lazarus had filled in on the typewriter and the letter in which the public prosecutor had refused to grant the application for release of the prisoner Maravilha. The letter bore the stamp of the public prosecutor's office.

With the valuable instructions in mind which the painter and passport forger, Reynaldo Pereira, had given him, Thomas set to work. Lazarus the hunchback was an interested spectator.

Thomas took the still hot half of a potato and pressed the cut surface on the mark of the public prosecutor's stamp for fifteen minutes. Then he lifted the halved potato. The cut surface showed, in reverse, the impress of the stamp.

"Now comes the big moment," said Thomas. Force of habit made him grunt the phrase. The corners of his mouth also twitched a little. For the last two days he hadn't always been able to stop it when he wanted to. One can't twitch and grunt from morning till night for a whole week without paying the penalty. "Let's have the candle, Lazarus."

The hunchback took a candle and some matches from under his mattress. He had stolen these articles from the chief warder's office. He also intended to use them later on for the removal of Thomas Lieven's hair.

Lazarus lit the candle. Thomas carefully bit a piece off the underside of the halved potato. Then he held the bitten end over the flame of the candle in order to warm it up again.

"The experts call this making a bell," Thomas explained to the awed Lazarus. "The potato is now warming up. See the impress getting damp again? Coming to life, they call it. Just a few seconds more and . . ." With an elegant gesture Thomas clapped the "bell" with its damp, hot impress of the stamp, onto the order of release at the exact spot where it had to be. He kept the potato there, under gentle pressure, for a quarter of an hour, while it cooled. Then he lifted it. A perfect counterfeit of the original stamp appeared on the order of release.

"Fantastic!" cried Lazarus.

"And now we'd better have a quick meal," said Thomas. "The rest we can do later."

The rest of the procedure was as follows. That morning, in the chief warder's office, Lazarus had opened quite a number of letters which had just arrived from the public prosecutor. He opened envelopes every day from that source. But on this particular morning he had taken the trouble to open one badly stuck-down envelope with special care. He succeeded in his object. He took the envelope away with him, together with a tube of adhesive.

After lunch Thomas carefully folded the now completed order of release for Lazarus Alcoba, placed it in the green envelope, which bore the postmark of the previous day, and gummed it carefully down again. That afternoon Lazarus laid the envelope on the chief warder's desk among others that had come with the afternoon delivery.

"Now it's do or die," said the hunchback to Thomas Lieven that evening. "The chief warder has already sent my order of release from the administration across to the discharge section. Early tomorrow morning they'll duly issue a discharge certificate and then they'll send for me here, so far as my past experience goes, about eleven o'clock. That means that your hair must come off tonight."

The singeing process lasted exactly half an hour—just

about the worst half-hour in Thomas Lieven's life. He sat with his head down in front of Lazarus, who singed it as one would a plucked fowl. He held the candle in his right hand. The flame burned off Thomas Lieven's strands of hair quite near the roots. In his left hand Lazarus held a damp cloth, which he used to dab the cranium as fast as he could in order not to damage the skin. But now and again he wasn't quite quick enough.

Thomas bellowed with pain. "Look out, you idiot, damn you!"

Lazarus retorted by quoting an old Portuguese proverb. "Who freedom craves must feel her thorn. It can't be helped, it must be borne."

At last the torture came to an end.

"What do I look like?" Thomas asked in an exhausted tone.

"If you stuff your cheeks with bread and do the twitching properly, you'll be the living image of me," replied Lazarus proudly.

They both slept exceptionally badly that night.

Next morning an unknown warder brought their breakfast. For the sixteenth was a Saturday and on Saturdays, as already mentioned, their friend Juliao always had the day off. Lazarus had of course borne this fact in mind when he dated the order of release on the sixteenth.

The hunchback took the breakfast tray from the unknown warder at the door. Thomas Lieven was still snoring on his cot with the blanket drawn over his head.

After breakfast Lazarus swallowed three white pills and lay down on Thomas Lieven's cot. Thomas put on the hunchback's short overcoat and once more practiced a general rehearsal of his part, not open to the public, between eight and ten o'clock. It was only then that he stuffed his cheeks full of bread pellets and pushed his thick pillow down his back, under the shirt, where he tied it tight to keep it in place. Meanwhile he twitched away industriously . . .

About eleven the unknown warder returned. Lazarus was asleep, with the blanket drawn over his head. The unknown warder was holding a discharge certificate in his hand. "Lazarus Alcoba!" he bawled.

Thomas rose. With bent knees and twitching lips he blinked at the warder. "Here, sir," he grunted.

The warder took a good look at him. Thomas broke into a sweat.

"You are Lazarus Alcoba?"

"I am."

"What's up with your pal there, then? Isn't he going to get up?"

"Had a bad night," Thomas mumbled indistinctly. "What you want me for, Mr. Warder?"

"You're discharged."

Thomas clapped his hand to his chest, groaned and dropped onto his cot, pretending to be quite overcome. "I always knew that justice would prevail," he grunted.

"Cut the cackle and come along with me. Look sharp now!" The warder pulled him to his feet—almost too high. Thomas was careful to subside again. "My God, that hurt! Still, it doesn't last long." He followed the unknown warder along a number of wide corridors to the administrative section of the prison. Heavy iron gates were opened to let him pass and closed behind him. The twitching's not so difficult now, he thought, it's practically automatic. But the knee-bending's a nuisance ... if only I don't get cramp and come a cropper ...

Up stairs, down stairs—I'll never stick it out, never!

More corridors. The unknown warder gave him a searching glance. "Are you feeling hot, Alcoba? You seem to be sweating a lot. Take that overcoat off."

"No. No, thank you. It's—er—only the excitement ... Quite the contrary—I—I'm freezing ..."

They reached the discharge section. Here the room was divided in half by a counter behind which three officials were at work. In front of the counter two other prisoners due for discharge were standing. Two circumstances immediately struck Thomas. In the first place the officials were lazy devils and secondly there were no chairs in front of the counter. That may be a good sign, he thought weakly. A clock on the wall showed the time to be ten minutes past eleven.

By five minutes to twelve the officials had not yet finished with the other two prisoners. Fiery circles were already revolving before Thomas Lieven's eyes. He felt ready to faint at any moment. The frightful pain in his knees had spread to his calves, thighs, ankles and hips. He surreptitiously supported his weight on the counter, first with one elbow, then with two. Heavens, what relief, what sweet rapture!

"Hey, you there!" barked the smallest of the officials. "Take your arms off the counter, will you? Can't you even stand up decently for these few minutes? Lazy guttersnipe!"

Thomas twitched his lips submissively. "Pardon me, gentlemen." He took one arm off the counter and instantly collapsed. He just couldn't stand the cramped posture any longer. He thought desperately, Don't faint. For God's sake don't faint or they'll take the overcoat off and find out about my legs—and the hump . . .

He didn't faint. And as it seemed clear that the poor prisoner had been overcome by weakness as a result of sheer excitement he was even given a chair. He had hardly sat down when he thought, Well, I might have done that sooner! What a fool I am!

Two of the officials went off to lunch at half-past twelve. The third at last came to attend to Thomas. Inserting a form into a typewriter he murmured benevolently: "This is only a formality. I shall have to take down your personal description again in order to ensure that there are no discrepancies."

Yes, you'd better be damned careful about that, Thomas thought. Now that he had been allowed to sit down he was feeling quite cheerful again. He rattled off his friend's particulars, which he knew by heart, in a hoarse drawl. "Alcoba, Lazarus, single, Roman Catholic, born in Lisbon on April 12, 1905 . . ."

"Last residence?"

"Rua Pampulha 51."

The official checked his data with those of a second form and typed on. "Gray hair, sparse—soon lost it, didn't you?"

"Such was my sad fate."

"H'm. Eyes black. Height? Stand up!"

Thomas stood up, bending his knees. The official looked him up and down.

"Special peculiarities?"

"Hump and also facial . . ."

"Yes, yes, I've got that. H'm. You can sit down again."

The official typed and scribbled. Then he took Thomas into an adjoining room and handed him over to the official in charge of prisoners' property. Thomas had been allowed to keep, since he was only in remand custody, his own suit, underclothing and beloved gold repeater. He now received his friend Lazarus's passport, private papers, money, pocket knife and laundry bag.

"Acknowledge receipt," said the official. Thomas signed clumsily: "Alcoba, Lazarus."

So the last of my cash and my nice bogus French secret service pass in the name of Jean Leblanc have gone to the devil, he thought gloomily. My friend the painter will have to make me a new one in quick time.

If Thomas had hoped, by about a quarter past two, to have at last come to the end of the fearful strain he was under, he was wrong. A warder led him through many more long passages to the chaplain's office. That officer, an elderly gentleman, spoke very earnestly to Thomas and was deeply touched when the discharged prisoner, in obvious distress, begged permission to kneel during his reverence's admonitions.

Tottering and staggering rather than walking Thomas at last, ten minutes before three o'clock on November 16, 1940, crossed the prison yard, which still reeked with the odors of the adjacent tannery, to the main gate. There, for the last time, he had to show his order of release. His lips were twitching in a most frightening manner and his hump stood out crookedly under the short, threadbare overcoat.

"Best o' luck, dad," said the man who opened the heavy iron gate. Thomas Lieven reeled through it into a more than uncertain, if free, future. He managed to keep on his legs as far as the nearest street corner, where he again collapsed. He crawled on all fours into a doorway, sat down on a staircase and began to weep with rage and exhaustion. His passport, money and property were all gone, like the steamer on which he had booked a passage.

[9]

The escape of the prisoner Jean Leblanc was discovered the same day. In his cell only the prisoner Lazarus Alcoba could be found, fast asleep as though drugged.

A doctor was immediately summoned and confirmed that Alcoba was not shamming, but had taken a heavy dose of soporifics. The diagnosis was correct, though Lazarus himself had administered the dose, with three pills which he had abstracted from the prison doctor's surgery while on a visit there.

Injections and black coffee enabled the prisoner to regain his senses sufficiently to be examined. It was soon proved that he was Alcoba and not somebody else. When the little man was undressed his hump was found to be real enough.

His evidence was as follows: "That damned Leblanc must have put something in my breakfast coffee, which tasted very bitter. My head ached and I felt giddy. Then I passed out. I had told him that I was to be released today. I had found that out from the chief warder, in whose office I have been working."

The warder on duty at the cell that day, on being confronted with Alcoba, exclaimed: "But I spoke to you this very morning when I brought in your breakfast! And later on I came and took you out of the cell!"

To which Alcoba replied, with a logic which even the examining officials found irrefutable: "If you had taken me out of the cell this morning I wouldn't be sitting here now."

The investigators gradually realized that Jean Leblanc had escaped disguised as Lazarus Alcoba. The latter, as logically as ever, declared through a series of yawns and still only semiconscious: "As the order of release, however, concerns myself alone, you are bound, in any case, to discharge me forthwith."

"Well, yes, of course . . . but all the same, pending inquiries . . ."

"Now listen to me. Either I am discharged early tomorrow morning or else I inform the public prosecutor of the marvelous efficiency with which you run this prison!"

"Pereira! Hey, Pereira!" Thomas Lieven was calling at that very moment. He banged on the door of the apartment of his friend the forger. But no answer came.

Either he's drunk again or else he's not at home, thought Thomas, who had recovered to some extent from his fit of weakness. Then he remembered that the depraved painter never locked his rooms. Thomas turned the handle of the door. It opened. He walked through the dark lobby into the big studio. Through its enormous window the last light of the day fell on the same hideous pictures still standing or lying about the place, which looked as neglected as ever. Loaded ash trays, tubes of paint, brushes, pens and palettes bewildered the eye with a multiplicity of colors.

Thomas looked into the kitchen. His bearded friend was not there either. So he wasn't at home. Probably he was getting drunk elsewhere.

That was a nuisance, of course. How long did Pereira's binges last? One night? Two days? Three? Thomas's experiences with the man made him fear the worst. A really good soak needs time.

I shall have to wait for him, Thomas reflected. My escape may have already been discovered and I can't show myself in the street. He laid his hand on his stomach. Yes, he was hungry. The moment of his deepest depression seemed to be over. He laughed a little at himself. As he did so he noticed that he was still twitching his lips. His knees, too, were still hurting. Forget it, he told himself. Don't think about it.

Let's first just see what Pereira's got in the kitchen. There were loaves of white bread, tomatoes, cheese, eggs, bacon and tongue, pistachio nuts, capers, paprika, pepper and anchovies.

Their variegated hues inspired him. I'll make a mosaic sandwich loaf and stuffed tomatoes, enough for Pereira too. He'll need something substantial when he comes home.

Thomas began cooking. Suddenly, while he was cutting up pistachio nuts and capers, he slashed into the board with the knife as though he had gone crazy. He couldn't help thinking of Estrella. What a beast! What a witch! What a fiend! He chopped the nuts as though he were lopping Estrella's head off.

The red paprika increased his wrath. The whole world's in a plot against me! Everyone's my enemy! And I've done nothing to deserve it. I used to be a decent human being, a sober citizen. And now . . .

We'll add pepper. Decent, respectable pepper. I'll make it burn like my own fury.

Damned secret service swine. A nice mess you've made of me. Now I've been to prison and I've broken out of prison. I can forge documents. I'm an expert on poisons and revolvers, explosives and invisible ink. I can shoot, signal in Morse, put on judo holds, box, wrestle, run, jump, fix microphones and counterfeit jaundice, fever and diabetes. What sort of achievements are those for a private banker to be proud of?

Catch me being sorry about anything or anybody now! No more of that. Can't take in any more. Now you're all going to be in for it, the whole lot of you, the whole world!

I'm going in to the attack now like a hungry wolf, with all my criminal know-how. Now it's I who am going to forge, counterfeit, signal in Morse and fix microphones. Now it's I who am going to threaten and betray you, just as you have betrayed and threatened me. Now it's my turn to wage war, a one-man war against you all. And there won't be one single armistice, pact or alliance in it, not with anybody.

More pepper! More paprika! Salt with it! And we're going to knock all the ingredients together into a formless lump, the kind of pulp I'd like to make of you, you swine . . .

At that moment he heard the door of the apartment open.

That must be Pereira, thought Thomas, startled out of his extravagant schemes. He shouted: "Come along in. I'm in the kitchen."

An instant later a figure appeared at the kitchen door. But it was not the unshaven, drunken painter Reynaldo Pereira. It was not a man at all. It was a woman.

MENU

Mosaic Sandwich Loaf
Stuffed Tomatoes

16 NOVEMBER 1940

A cold collation for a hot head.

Mosaic Sandwich Loaf

Cut off both ends of a French loaf and scoop out the crumb without damaging the crust. For the filling take one stick of butter, half a cup of diced ham, half a cup of diced ox tongue, one hard-boiled yolk, half a cup of diced cheese, half a teaspoonful of capers, one quarter of a cup of chopped pistachio nuts, a little anchovy fillet, mustard, salt and pepper. Cream the butter, mash the yolk, add the pistachio nuts, capers and meat. Mix all with the condiments. The filling is put into the scooped loaf and chilled for a few hours. Then it is cut into thin slices which are laid on a flat dish. To obtain more color, the mosaic sandwiches are garnished with stuffed tomatoes.

Stuffed Tomatoes

Remove pulp from firm, hard tomatoes. Sprinkle the inside with grated cheese. Place in each tomato half a hard-boiled egg, cut horizontally with the cut side upward. Sprinkle it with salt and paprika, chopped parsley and chives.

[10]

She wore a red mackintosh, red shoes and a red cap perched on her blue-black hair. The young woman's mouth was big and red, her eyes big and black. Her complexion was chalk-white. With her hands in the pockets of the mackintosh she stared hard at Thomas Lieven, addressing him in metallic and slightly vulgar accents. "Evening, Pereira. You don't know me."

"I—" Thomas began. But she interrupted him with a haughty toss of her head, which sent her beautiful long hair flying. "All right, take it easy. I'm not from the cops. Quite the contrary."

He stammered: "Who—er—gave you my address?"

The woman in red closed one eye as she stared back at him. "What's the matter with you? Nerves? Coke? Booze?"

"What do you mean?"

"What's this game you're playing with your phiz? Can't you keep your mouth still? You never stop twitching it."

"That's only temporary. I—I get it sometimes in the evening. I asked you just now who gave you this address."

The woman in red came close up to him. She was richly perfumed and very handsome. She said quietly: "The address was given me by a certain M. Débras."

Thomas Lieven was stupefied. Major Maurice Débras of the French secret service, he thought. It only needed that. The third man I played up. Well, of course that was only to be expected. Now there are three of them after me. French, British and German. Can't be a matter of more than hours now before I lose my life . . .

The next words of the woman in red seemed to come from very far away. Even her figure suddenly seemed indistinct and shadowy. Her question confirmed Thomas's worst fears.

"Do you know a certain Jean Leblanc?"

Thomas made quite a noise with pans and cutlery before he mumbled: "Jean Leblanc? Never heard of him."

"Don't talk driveling bilge, Pereira. Naturally you know the man." Handsome and insolent, she perched on one of the kitchen stools and crossed her long, slim legs. "No need to get diarrhea over it!"

Damn her impudence, thought Thomas. What a filthy, degrading situation this is. Why should I have to put up with it? I was once the youngest private banker in London. I was a member of one of the most exclusive London clubs. I've had the best possible education. I have the right ideas of honesty and good manners. And here I stand in a dirty Portuguese kitchen and have to listen to a bitch pretty enough to eat telling me not to get diarrhea. Well, I'll give her something to think about!

The well-bred Thomas Lieven retorted: "Now you can just shut your trap double-quick and buzz off. Otherwise there'll be trouble!"

The situation changed the very next minute. Heavy footsteps were heard and an unshaven man in stained velveteen trousers and an ill-fitting black pullover appeared in the kitchen. The man was very drunk indeed. Nevertheless, his broad toper's face brightened in a joyful grin as soon as he caught sight of Thomas. He blurted out: "Welcome to my humble abode! But boy, oh boy, what on earth have you done with your hair?"

Reynaldo the painter had come home.

Suddenly the three people in the little kitchen all spoke at once. The woman in red jumped up, glaring at Thomas and exclaimed: "What! You're not Pereira?"

"Of course he's not Pereira," roared the intoxicated painter. "What sort of booze have *you* been drinking? *I'm* Pereira and that's—"

"Hold it—"

"—my old pal Leblanc."

"Oho!"

"And who the—hic—are you, pretty lady?"

"My name's Chantal Tessier," said the young woman, without taking her eyes off Thomas. A hungry expression came into her feline countenance. She said slowly: "M. Jean Leblanc in person? What a bit of luck!"

"What do you want with me?"

"You once gave your friend Débras a bogus passport. Débras told me that if I ever needed one myself I was to go to Reynaldo Pereira in the Rua do Poco des Negros and mention the name of Jean Leblanc . . ."

"Is that what your friend Débras said?"

"That's what my friend Débras said."

"Did he say anything else?"

"Only that you were a good sport who had saved his life."

So it's only half as bad as I thought, Thomas reflected. He asked amiably: "Won't you stay to eat with us? May I help you off with your coat, Mlle. Tessier?"

"Chantal to you!" The feline countenance, wreathed in smiles, revealed a formidable row of tigerish teeth. Chantal Tessier had plenty of self-confidence she was wily, she was undoubtedly cold as ice. But she did not seem to be used to men helping her off with her coat.

The tigress wore a close-fitting black skirt and a white silk blouse. Some figure, thought Thomas. I shouldn't think she gets her shoes wet when it rains.

The moment of danger had passed. Thomas could be himself again. Well bred and chivalrous to women, all kinds of women!

They sat down beside the drunken painter, who had already begun eating. He ate with his fingers and talked with his mouth full. "If I could paint as well as you can cook, old Goya couldn't hold a candle to me!" He belched lightly. "Did you put pi—pistachio nuts in?"

"Yes, and capers. Cover your mouth when you do that. You need a passport, I suppose, Chantal?"

"No." Her eyes were now watering a little and her left nostril was quivering. That was a habit of hers.

"I don't need one passport, I need seven."

"May I say something, please?" demanded the unshaven painter, with his mouth full.

Thomas told him irritably: "Swallow your food before you speak. And don't keep on interrupting. The best thing you can do is to try to sober up a bit." To the fair tigress he added: "For whom do you want the seven passports, Chantal?"

"Two Germans, two Frenchmen and three Hungarians."

"I see you have a cosmopolitan circle of acquaintances."

Chantal laughed. "That's natural. I am a professional ... foreigners' guide."

"Where do you guide them to?"

"From France through Spain to Portugal. It's quite a lucrative business."

"And are your journeys very frequent?"

"Once a month. My groups get bigger and bigger. All with forged passports. Or none at all. Depends on circumstances."

"Talking of passports," the painter began once more. But Thomas silenced him with a gesture.

Chantal went on: "I only concern myself with the rich. I charge high prices. But none of my people ever get caught. I know every centimeter of the frontiers. And I know all the frontier guards. Well! So it happens that with my last party I brought in seven men who need new passports." She nudged the painter. "You can earn a gold nose for yourself, old cock."

"I also need a passport," said Thomas.

"Holy Virgin!" cried the unshaven one. "And I haven't got any left!"

Thomas said angrily: "What have you done with those thirty-seven old passports I brought you?"

"Six weeks ago, man! You've no idea what a rush there was for them. In a fortnight they were all gone! I'm really sorry, but I haven't a single one left. I've been trying to tell you so for the last half-hour."

[11]

All around the Largo de Chiado, a sleepy square shaded by ancient trees, stood the pasteleria marques, little cafés catering mostly to ladies and famous for sweet cakes. In an alcove of one of the confectionery shops, called the Caravela, two gentlemen were sitting, that evening of November 16, 1940. One of them was drinking whisky and the other eating ice cream. The former was the British agent, Peter Lovejoy. The latter, a stout, good-humored giant with twinkling little pig's eyes, and a rosy, infantile countenance, answered to the name of Luis Guzmao.

Peter Lovejoy and Luis Guzmao had known each other for two years and had already collaborated successfully on a number of occasions.

"Well, now it's time to act," said Lovejoy. "I'm told that he broke jail this afternoon."

"We shall have to get a move on if we want to catch him before he leaves Lisbon," said Guzmao. He took a spoonful of ice cream and smacked his lips. He could never get enough of the stuff.

"You're right," said Lovejoy in a low tone. "How are you going to fix it?"

"I think I'll use a rod with a silencer. How about the cash? Did you bring it with you?"

"Yes. You get five thousand escudos now and five thousand when you've . . . that's to say, later on."

Lovejoy took a long pull at his whisky. He thought with exasperation, That finicky Major Loos gave me five thousand as his share in the operation. He didn't mind paying out. But he drew the line at meeting this fellow Guzmao. Too much the fine gentleman for that!

Lovejoy washed down his vexation with the overfastidious German by taking another gulp of whisky. Then he said: "Now listen carefully, Guzmao. Leblanc got away disguised as a certain Lazarus Alcoba, a little hunchback, practically bald." Lovejoy described Alcoba as precisely as the British agent's confidant in the prison had described him. He added:

"Leblanc knows that we and the Germans are after him. So he'll certainly go to ground."

"Where?"

"He has a friend, a drunken painter who lives in the Old Town, Rua do Poco des Negros, Number sixteen. I bet he'll go there. He'll either continue pretending to be the hunchback, in order to put off the scent, or else he'll be Jean Leblanc again, in order to put the police off."

"What does Jean Leblanc look like?"

Lovejoy gave an equally exact description of Thomas Lieven.

"What about the real hunchback?"

"He's still in jail. You don't have to worry about him. But if you pick up a hunchback in the Rua do Poco des Negros sixteen with hardly any hair on his head and answering to the name of Leblanc you won't have to ask him any more questions . . ."

A few minutes after eight o'clock on the morning of November 17, 1940, the eleven times previously convicted Lazarus Alcoba, bachelor, born in Lisbon on April 12, 1905, was summoned to the presence of the governor of the Aljube prison.

The governor, a tall man of haggard aspect, told him: "I hear that you uttered a lot of crazy threats last night, Alcoba."

The lips of the little man with the hump twitched even when he spoke. "I only argued in my own defense, sir, when I was informed that I could not be released because I was believed to have had something to do with the escape of that fellow Jean Leblanc."

"I'm convinced that you did have something to do with that, Alcoba. And I hear that you said you intended to appeal to the public prosecutor."

"I shall of course only do so, sir, if I am not forthwith released. It's not my fault, obviously, that Leblanc escaped under my name."

"Now listen, Alcoba. We are going to discharge you today . . ."

Alcoba grinned broadly. "That's more like it!"

". . . but that's not because we're afraid of you, let me tell you. It's because we've had orders to do so. You must report daily to your local police station and not leave Lisbon."

"Very well, sir."

"Don't grin in that silly way, Alcoba. You're incorrigible. I'm sure you'll soon be back here again with us. You ought to be here all the time. Men of your type are always better behind bars."

[12]

The narrow, crooked streets of the Old Town, with their decaying rococo palaces and the citizens' houses with many-colored tiles, lay quiet in the noonday hour of siesta.

Spotlessly white undergarments hung from innumerable clotheslines. Stunted trees grew from broken stairways. Again and again gaps in the walls afforded a view of the adjacent river.

Thomas Lieven was also looking down at the river. He stood at the big window of the studio of his thirsty friend. Chantal Tessier was beside him. She had returned to the Rua do Poco des Negros to say good-bye. She had to go back to Marseilles and she wanted Thomas to go with her.

Chantal seemed strangely restless. Her left nostril was quivering again. She laid a hand on Thomas Lieven's arm. "Come and join me as my partner. I might have some work for you to do, not necessarily escorting foreigners. You can't do any business here. But in Marseilles—good heavens, we could expand my shop into something quite big!"

Thomas shook his head, still looking out over the waters of the Tagus. They were flowing slowly and sluggishly out to the Atlantic. And further downstream, where they met the ocean, all kinds of vessels lay at anchor, ready to set out for distant harbors, ready to transport the persecuted, the discouraged and the terrified to free, distant lands. There they lay, those ships, at the disposal of people with passports, entry permits and money.

Thomas had no passport now. He had no entry permit. He had no money. He had nothing but the clothes he stood up in.

He suddenly felt tired to death. His life was spinning around in a devil's dance from which there was no escape. "I am honored by your offer, Chantal. You are a beautiful woman. You are certainly also a wonderful comrade." He glanced at her, smiling. The woman, who looked so much like a tigress, blushed like an infatuated schoolgirl. She stamped her foot angrily and muttered: "Oh, don't talk rot . . ."

Thomas added, nevertheless; "I'm sure you have a good heart. But I used to be a banker, you know. And I should like to be one again."

Reynaldo Pereira was sitting at a table littered with color-boxes, tubes of paint, brushes, loaded ash trays and bottles. He was now sober and working at a rather bewildering picture. "Jean," he said, "there's a lot in what Chantal suggests. She can take you safe and sound to Marseilles. And in Marseilles it'll be easier for you to get a forged passport than it will be here, where the police are after you. To say nothing of those other pals of yours."

"But, good Lord, I've just left Marseilles! Have I come all this way for nothing?"

Chantal said in a harsh, aggressive tone: "You're a sentimental fool if you can't see the point. It's true you've had bad luck. So what? We've all had bad luck once in our lives. All you need now, for a start, is a bit of boodle again and a decent ticket."

If I hadn't had the advantage of Alcoba's private tuition in our cell, thought Thomas, I shouldn't know what the lady means. He answered gloomily: "With Pereira's help I shall be able to get hold of a new passport even in Lisbon. And as for money, I have a friend in South America to whom I can write. No, no. You just leave me to it, I'll manage, I'll . . ."

He never finished the sentence. For at that moment the noonday peace was shattered by the muffled barking of shots in the courtyard overlooked by the kitchen.

Chantal uttered a stifled cry. Pereira jumped up, knocking over a pot of paint. They exchanged amazed glances. Three seconds passed.

Then a chorus of alarmed male voices rang out. Women shrieked. Children screamed.

Thomas rushed into the kitchen and flung up the window. He looked down into the ancient courtyard. Men, women and children were running to join a group surrounding a figure prone on the dirty cobbles. The body was painfully contorted, hunchbacked and diminutive.

[13]

"Lazarus, Lazarus, can you hear me?"

Thomas knelt beside the little man on the cobbles. Strangers were milling about behind him. Blood trickled incessantly from Alcoba's wounds. He had been hit by several bullets in the chest and stomach. He lay motionless now, his eyes closed. The nervous twitching of his lips had ceased.

"Lazarus . . ." groaned Thomas Lieven.

At that the little hunchback opened his eyes. Their pupils

were already dim. But Lazarus had recognized the man bending over him. He murmured: "Get going, Jean, get going. That was meant for you . . ." A torrent of blood poured from his mouth.

"Don't talk, Lazarus," Thomas begged his friend. But the hunchback whispered: "The bloke called out 'Leblanc!' before he . . . taking me for you . . ."

Tears of rage and grief stung Thomas's eyes. "Don't talk, Lazarus. A doctor will be here in a moment . . . they'll operate . . ."

"It's . . . it's too late . . ." The hunchback looked steadily at Thomas. Then he suddenly grinned craftily and mumbled with an effort: "Pity, eh? We might have been able to pull a few more fast ones, you and I . . ." Then the grin abruptly vanished. The eyes darkened.

As Thomas Lieven rose from the side of his dead friend the crowd parted to allow him to pass silently through their ranks. They noticed that he was weeping.

Through a mist of tears he caught sight of Chantal and Pereira, who were standing to one side of the excited onlookers. As he staggered toward the pair he stumbled and would have fallen if the painter had not reached him in time.

Two policemen and a doctor came running into the courtyard from the street. While the doctor examined the dead man the whole crowd began talking at once to the policemen. More and more inquisitive onlookers arrived. A shrill jabbering of voices filled the ancient courtyard.

Thomas brushed the tears from his eyes and glanced at Chantal. He realized that if he did not act there and then it would be too late. In a split second, between the raising and lowering of his eyelids, he made up his mind.

Two minutes later the police had heard the evidence of the excited eyewitnesses, to the effect that a stranger had bent over the dying man and had been the last to speak to him.

"Where is the man?"

"He went over there," said an old woman. She pointed with a bony finger to the entry to the back premises. Pereira, the painter, was standing there. But now he was alone.

"Hey, you there!" called one of the policemen. "Where's that fellow who was talking to the dead man?"

"No idea," said Pereira.

The doctor was just closing Lazarus Alcoba's eyes. The hunchback's ugly face, in death, looked extraordinarily dignified.

[14]

It was cold in the Pyrenees. A piercing east wind swept over the barren, reddish soil of the range of mountains separating Aragon in Spain from the South of France.

At dawn on November 23, 1940, two isolated pedestrians, a young man and a young woman, were moving north toward the pass of Roncesvalles. They were both wearing mountaineering shoes, felt hats and padded wind jackets. Both carried heavy rucksacks. The woman walked ahead. The man followed her, through dense woods and undergrowth, uphill.

Never before in his life had Thomas Lieven worn such heavy shoes or a padded wind jacket. Nor had he ever before gone climbing up difficult and dangerous mountain paths. Like everything else during the last five days, this hour of daybreak, with its mists and gray shadows, seemed a fantastic nightmare, as he tramped on behind Chantal Tessier toward the French frontier with sore heels and blistered soles.

Chantal Tessier had behaved splendidly, like a true comrade, during those last five days. She knew Portugal and Spain like the back of her hand. She knew the customs officials and the police patrols by sight. She knew peasants who would shelter and feed strangers overnight without asking questions.

His trousers, shoes, wind jacket and hat had all been bought for him by Chantal. She had even given him the money in his pockets. Or rather "advanced" it, as she said.

From Lisbon they crossed by train to Valencia. There had been two passport examinations, both of which she had helped him to evade. They had crossed the frontier into Spain by night, going by way of Vigo, Leon and Burgos. There had been many more examinations and many more police in Spain. Nevertheless, all had gone well, thanks to Chantal.

Now they were about to cross the last frontier. Then they would be in France. The straps of the rucksack were cutting into Thomas Lieven's shoulders. Every bone in his body ached. He felt tired enough to drop. Thoughts flitted confusingly through his mind as he walked on, Chantal ahead of him.

Poor Lazarus Alcoba . . . who had shot him? Who had ordered him to be shot? The British? The Germans? Would the murderer ever be found? Will another murderer find me? How long can I expect to live? Here I am slinking through this dark wood like a smuggler, like a criminal . . . crazy,

crazy it all is, an unreal and grotesque nightmare, a feverish dream . . . and yet it's the cruel truth . . .

The path grew less steep. The trees were being left behind. They reached a clearing where a weather-beaten barn stood. Thomas was just following the obviously tireless Chantal past this big open shed where hay was stored when three shots rang out in quick succession, quite close.

Chantal swung around in a flash. In a flash she was beside him, her breath in his face. "In here!"

She dragged him with her into the shed. Both sank into the hay and stared at each other, panting.

Another shot cracked, then another. The wind carried the sound of a male voice to them. But the words were unintelligible.

"Keep still," Chantal whispered. "Keep lying quite still. Might be frontier guards."

It might also be someone quite different, thought Thomas bitterly. Probably it was. The gentlemen in Lisbon would not have taken very long to find out what a regrettable mistake they had made. A mistake which would have to be corrected . . .

Thomas could feel Chantal close to him. She lay perfectly still. But he could sense her excitement and the effort she was making to remain quiet.

At that moment he made up his mind. He had no business to endanger another human life. The death of the unfortunate Lazarus, he knew, would haunt him until he drew his last breath.

Enough, thought Thomas Lieven. I'm not playing this game any more. Better end with an instant of terror than endure this terror without end. You needn't look for me any longer, you murderous idiots. You needn't pursue me any longer, you idiotic murderers. I shall surrender and you can leave innocent people out of your dirty game.

He tore off the straps of the rucksack with a swift gesture and stood up. Chantal started up beside him. Her eyes burned in her white face. She hissed: "Lie down, you fool . . ." She tried with all her strength to pull him down.

"Sorry, Chantal," murmured Thomas. He put a judo hold on her which he knew would knock her out for a few seconds. With a moan she dropped back into the hay.

Thomas walked out into the open.

Two men, with rifles at the ready, approached him across the clearing, over the dead grass, through the damp mist.

He went to meet them. He was thinking, with an absurd sense of triumph, that at least they wouldn't be able to shoot him in the back "while trying to escape."

As soon as they caught sight of him they leveled their rifles. Thomas took another step forward, then another.

The men dropped the barrels of their rifles and walked quickly toward him. Thomas had never seen them before. They both wore corduroy trousers, hats, wind jackets and mountaineering shoes like his own. Both were undersized and rather slightly built. One had a mustache. The other wore spectacles.

They came close up to him and stood still. The bespectacled one raised his hat and said courteously in Spanish: "Good morning."

"Did you see him by any chance?" asked the man with the mustache.

Thomas began to feel giddy. The men, the glade, the grass and the trees started going around and around. He asked almost inaudibly; "See whom?"

"The stag," answered the man with spectacles.

"I hit him," said the mustached one. "I'm positive I hit him. I saw him go down. Then he staggered away somewhere."

"He must be somewhere near here," said the other.

"I didn't see anything," said Thomas in broken Spanish.

"Ah, so you're a foreigner," said the bespectacled one. "On the run from over there, I suppose."

Thomas could only nod.

The Spaniards exchanged glances. "We'll forget we ever saw you," said the man with the mustache. "Good day and a good journey to you." Both raised their hats. Thomas raised his in return. The hunters walked on, disappearing into the woods.

Thomas drew a few deep breaths and then went back to the barn. Chantal was sitting in the hay groaning and rubbing her neck, which had turned red.

He sat down beside her and said: "Forgive me for what I did just now, but I didn't want . . . I wasn't going to let them . . ." He started stammering and at last blurted out shamefacedly: "They were only hunters."

Suddenly Chantal flung her arms around Thomas and hugged him tight. They both dropped back into the hay.

Chantal, bending over him, whispered: "You wanted to protect me, you didn't want me to run any risks, you were thinking of me . . ." She stroked his face tenderly. "No man ever did that for me before—ever . . ."

"Did what?"

"Thought of me," whispered Chantal.

In the sweetness of her violent kisses Thomas forgot all his misery and fears. He thought no longer of the dark past or the dark future.

[15]

In 1942 six thousand German troops surrounded the old docks quarter at Marseilles and compelled the inhabitants, some twenty thousand people, to evacuate their accommodation within two hours, taking no more than thirty kilos of luggage. Over three thousand criminals were arrested. The entire quarter was blown up. In this way the most colorful breeding ground of vice in Europe, where the most dangerous criminal plots were hatched, disappeared.

But in 1940–41 the place was flourishing as never before. In the dark old houses behind the Town Hall lived representatives of all nations. There were refugees, black market dealers, murderers on the run, forgers, political conspirators and legions of prostitutes.

The police were helpless. If it were at all possible they simply refrained from putting in an appearance at all in the Old Quarter. The rulers of this sinister realm were the chiefs of rival gangs which waged implacable warfare among themselves. The members included not only Frenchmen but also North Africans, Armenians, Spaniards and many Corsicans.

Their leaders were known all over the quarter. In the narrow, colorful streets they were always accompanied by their bodyguards, two or three men to right and left of them, marching with their right hands in their jacket pockets and their forefingers on the trigger.

The municipality appointed a body called the Contrôle Economique to fight the prosperous black market trade. But the majority of the members of the Contrôle could be bribed and many of the rest suffered from cold feet. They declined to venture into the streets after sunset. But that was just when cheeses began to roll from one house into another and joints were dispatched from secret slaughterhouses to the restaurants.

It was from such obscure sources that Thomas obtained such delicacies as leg of lamb and French beans, from which, on the evening of November 25, 1940, he prepared a first-rate meal in Chantal's kitchen.

MENU

Mussels in White Sauce

Roast Leg of Lamb with French Beans and Small

Potato Croquettes

Fruit in Caramel

25 NOVEMBER 1940

After sampling this menu a woman confessed her secret.

Mussels in White Sauce

Fresh mussels are washed and scrubbed, then placed in a large pan in which there is a boiling solution of half water and half white wine. This is covered and allowed to stew, being frequently shaken. When mussels have opened, pour into colander and remove flesh from open shells. Meanwhile a white sauce is prepared from butter and flour. The liquid in which the mussels were boiled is added. More white wine is added, together with salt, pepper, lemon juice and some egg yolk. Then the mussels, with some chopped parsley, are placed in the sauce and it is brought to a boil again.

Roast Leg of Lamb

A fresh young leg of lamb is incised slightly at the knuckle end and a little garlic is inserted in the cut. The joint is placed in a baking tin, basted with plenty of brown butter and browned on the stove on all sides. It is then well seasoned with salt and pepper. Next, the tin is placed in the oven and given frequent basting.

Young French beans are topped and cooked until tender in a little water. They are then drained, placed in a saucepan with plenty of melted butter and kept hot. Before serving sprinkle with salt.

Boiled potatoes are mashed and mixed with whole eggs till they form a dough. Flavor with a little nutmeg. Small spheres are formed and dropped into very hot fat until they swell and take on a rich brown color.

Fruit in Caramel

Loaf sugar is placed in a thick pan, melted over a flame and stirred constantly until golden-yellow. Water is added and the resulting caramel is boiled. Peeled and quartered peaches and pears, with fresh whole grapes, are placed in the boiling caramel and left until soft. The fruit is left to cool and is then placed in individual glass dishes decorated with blobs of whipped cream and sprinkled with chopped blanched almonds.

Chantal lived in the rue Chevalier Rose. The dirty water of the rectangular Old Harbor could be seen from the window, together with the many-colored lights of the countless cafés surrounding the docks.

Thomas had been surprised by both the size and the contents of Chantal's flat. Much of the effect was barbaric, as for instance when expensive ultramodern light fittings were associated with genuine antique furniture. Chantal had obviously grown up entirely neglected and uneducated, like a regular savage.

That evening she wore a fashionable, high-necked, close-fitting gown of embroidered Chinese silk, yet over it, most unsuitably, a heavy, wide leather belt. She was inordinately fond of undressed leather and its odor.

Thomas politely refrained from criticizing any of Chantal's tasteless errors. For the first time in his life he was wearing someone else's suit, though as a matter of fact it fitted him perfectly.

Immediately after their arrival Chantal had opened a big wardrobe filled with men's shirts, underclothing, ties and suits. She had said to Thomas: "Take whatever you need. Pierre was about your height."

Thomas reluctantly took what he needed, which was really everything, if he were to look decent, for he had absolutely nothing of his own.

When he asked who Pierre was, Chantal retorted morosely: "You want to know too much. He was a lover of mine. But we quarreled. That was a year ago. He'll never come back . . ."

In general, for the last few hours, Chantal had been behaving very coldly. It was as if their passionate affair at the frontier had never occurred. Even now, while they were at supper, she sat in silence, a prey, apparently, to gloomy thoughts. She kept glancing up at Thomas while she ate her mussels. By the time they had reached the leg of lamb her left nostril had begun to quiver again. A church clock struck ten as Thomas was serving her with the fruit in caramel.

Suddenly she covered her face with both hands and muttered something he could not catch.

"What's wrong, my dear?" Thomas inquired, stirring his fruit.

She looked up. Her left nostril was still quivering. But otherwise her attractive features had hardened into rigid lines. She pronounced very quietly and clearly the words: "Ten o'clock."

"Well—?"

"They're all ready on the ground floor now. As soon as I start playing the gramophone record *'J'ai deux amours'* they'll come upstairs."

Thomas laid down his little silver spoon. "Who?"

"Colonel Siméon and his mob."

"Colonel Siméon?" he repeated feebly.

Only her nostril quivered as she answered: "Yes. From the Deuxième Bureau. I've squealed on you, Jean. I'm the meanest bit of muck in this world."

There was silence in the room, after that, for a while.

At last Thomas asked: "Would you by any chance care for another peach?"

"Jean! Don't go on like that! I simply can't bear it! Why don't you yell? Why don't you give me a sock in the jaw?"

"Chantal," he said, feeling as though drowning in a great wave of fatigue, "Chantal, why did you do that?"

"The cops here have got me in the bag. It's a pretty foul business, connected with Pierre. Big fraud . . . then suddenly this colonel fellow, Siméon, crops up and says: 'You get us Leblanc and we'll fix it for you.' What would have you done in my place, Jean? I didn't know you then."

Thomas was thinking: Well, that seems to be the truth about life. It goes on and on and on. Hunter and hunted. Traitor and betrayed. Kill if you don't want to be killed yourself.

He asked quietly: "Why does Siméon want me?"

"He's acting under orders . . . apparently you've landed his people with bogus lists or something, is that right?"

"Yes, that's right," he said.

She rose, came over to him and laid a hand on his shoulder. "I want to cry. But the tears won't come. Hit me. Kill me. Do something, Jean. Don't look at me like that."

Thomas sat quite still, thinking hard. Then he asked in a low tone: "What was that song you had to play?"

" *'J'ai deux amours,'* " she answered.

Suddenly a strange smile illuminated his pallid features. He stood up. Chantal shrank back. But he did not touch her. He went into the next room, where she kept her gramophone. A record was already in place. He smiled again as he read its title. He switched on the mechanism. He set the needle in the first groove. Introductory notes resounded. Then Josephine Baker's voice sang *"J'ai deux amours"* . . .

Footsteps could be heard approaching up the stairs. They came nearer, nearer still. Chantal came close up to Thomas. Her breath hissed between her parted lips. The teeth, so like those of a tigress, glistened moistly. Her bosom rose and fell rapidly under the thin green silk of the tight-fitting Chinese gown.

"Get going . . . you've still got time . . . there's a flat roof under the bedroom window . . ."

Thomas shook his head, smiling.

Chantal lost her temper.

"You idiot! They'll pack you full of lead! In ten minutes you'll be floating like a drowned rat in the Old Harbor!"

"It would have been considerate of you to have thought of that a little earlier, my sweet," replied Thomas affably.

She swung up her arm wildly, as though to strike him, and gasped out: "How can you trot out that silly talk at a time like this?"

But a second later she burst out sobbing.

A knock sounded at the door.

"Open up," he said sternly. Chantal, one fist pressed to her lips, did not stir.

The knocking was repeated, but more violently. Josephine Baker's voice was still ringing out.

A male voice familiar to Thomas shouted: "Open the door or we shoot the lock out!"

"Good old Siméon," murmured Thomas. "Still as hotheaded as ever!" He turned his back on the trembling Chantal and went into the hall.

The main door of the flat was now quivering under hammering fists. The door was fastened by a security chain. Thomas turned the handle and the door was pushed open as far as the chain permitted. A shoe was thrust into the resulting aperture. So was a revolver.

Thomas stepped on the shoe as heavily as he could and pushed up the barrel of the pistol. "I should be glad if you could remove these two objects, Colonel," he announced.

"I daresay you would," Siméon shouted back from behind the door. "Open up at once or we shoot!"

"Then you'll have to shoot," Thomas told him coolly. "For as long as you've got your hand and foot stuck in the door I can't move the security chain."

After some hesitation the colonel complied with Thomas Lieven's request. The shoe and the weapon were withdrawn. Thomas opened the door. Next moment he felt the barrel of a revolver in his ribs and found himself standing right up against the heroic Jules Siméon, whose mustache bristled as he threw back his impressive head with its Roman nose.

Thomas noted that the poor chap had still not made any money, even during the last few months. He was still wearing the same shabby old trenchcoat.

"Well, this is a pleasure, Colonel," said Thomas. "How are you? And what is our lovely Mimi doing these days?"

The colonel retorted, scarcely moving his lips in the intensity of his scorn: "Your game's up, you dirty traitor!"

"I wonder if you'd mind pushing that pistol barrel against some other part of my body, the chest for instance? I've only just had supper, you know."

"In half an hour all your digestion troubles will be over, you blackguard," Siméon rejoined with flashing eyes.

A second man entered the vestibule. He was tall and elegant, with graying temples and shrewd eyes. The collar of his overcoat was turned up, his hands were in his pockets and a cigarette in the corner of his mouth. He was Maurice Débras.

"Good evening," said Thomas. "I guessed that you would be somewhere about when Chantal told me the name of that record. "How are you, Major?"

Siméon hissed: *"Colonel!"*

But Colonel Débras himself made no reply. He merely jerked his head, with a brief, imperious gesture, in the direction of the door.

Next moment a furious shout made them all turn round. Chantal, crouching like a tigress on the threshold of the living room, was brandishing a Malay kriss in her right hand. "Out with you!" she yelled savagely. "Or I'll stick the two of you! Leave Jean alone!"

Siméon, in alarm, retreated two steps.

Thomas thought: I'm glad to see you're not quite such an imbecile of a hero as you were when Paris fell. Then he turned to Chantal. "Stop that nonsense, Chantal," he told her sharply. "Didn't you promise the colonel you were going to give me up?"

But Chantal only crouched lower and hissed even more fiercely: "I don't give a damn for that . . . I've behaved like a bitch . . . but I can make amends for it all now . . ."

"You can make a load of damp garbage," Thomas retorted. "They'll only lock you up, you stupid slut."

"Let them . . . it's all one to me—I shall still not have turned anybody in. Get behind me, Jean, quick! Run into the bedroom . . ."

She had come right up to him. Thomas sighed and shook his head. Then he kicked out with his right foot, high. The point of the shoe caught Chantal's right wrist. She uttered a cry of pain. The dagger flew out of her hand and stuck quivering in the doorpost.

Thomas collected his hat and coat, pulled the dagger out and handed it to Débras. "You can't imagine how painful it is for me to have to attack a woman," he said. "But at Mlle. Tessier's place, it seems, one can't avoid brutality . . . Shall we go now?"

Débras nodded without speaking. Siméon pushed Thomas out onto the landing.

[16]

The door banged. Chantal was left alone. She began to tremble convulsively and sank helplessly to the floor, where she tossed from side to side, sobbing and crying out. At last she rose and staggered into the living room. The record was finished. But the needle was carrying on rhythmically. Chantal seized the gramophone and flung it against the wall, where it smashed with a clatter.

That night, the worst she had ever experienced, she could not sleep. She tossed to and fro in the bed, restless, conscience-stricken and in despair. She had betrayed her beloved and was responsible for his death, since she was sure that Siméon and Débras would kill him.

At dawn she fell into an uneasy slumber.

A resonant male voice, singing out of tune, awoke her. With an aching head and limbs that felt like lead she sat up.

She could hear the man's voice quite distinctly. It was singing *"J'ai deux amours."*

Mad, I've gone mad, she thought in alarm. I can hear his voice—the voice of a dead man—O God, I've lost my reason . . .

"Jean!" she screamed.

There was no answer.

She stumbled out of bed and rushed from the room in her nightdress. Away—away from here . . .

Then she halted abruptly. The door of the bathroom stood open. And Thomas Lieven was sitting in the bath.

Chantal closed her eyes. Then she opened them again. Thomas was still sitting in the bath. She moaned: "Jean . . ."

"Good morning, bitch," said he.

She fell rather than walked through the doorway and sank down on the edge of the bath. "How—what—what are you doing here?" she stammered.

"I'm trying to soap my back. I wonder if you'd be kind enough to do it for me."

"But . . . but . . . but . . ."

"I beg your pardon?"

"But they must have shot you . . . you must be dead . . ."

"If I were dead I wouldn't be here trying to soap my back," he told her reprovingly. "What nonsense you do talk. Really, Chantal, you must pull yourself together a little. You're not living in a lunatic asylum or in the jungle. Not now."

He held a piece of soap out to her. She seized it and flung it back into the water. At the same time she cried shrilly: "Tell me this moment what's happened!"

In a dangerously quiet tone Thomas replied: "Get that soap out of the water instantly. You're going to get a thrashing in any case. God is my witness, Chantal, that up to now I've never hit a woman. But in your case I shall abandon my most sacred principles. Wash my back now. Get on with it. How much longer are you going to be?"

Chantal fumbled in the water, found the soap and did as he asked. Meanwhile she gazed at him in awed admiration.

"It's taken me a long time to find out how to deal with you," he said grimly.

"What happened, Jean?" she demanded hoarsely. "Tell me . . ."

" '*Please* tell me,' is the proper was to ask."

"Please, Jean, please . . ."

"That's better," he grunted, writhing luxuriously. "Higher.

Further to the left. Harder. Well, after those two had carried me off from here, they took me down to the docks . . ."

[17]

Siméon and Débras drove down to the harbor with Thomas Lieven. An icy wind whistled through the narrow lanes of the Old Quarter. Dogs were baying the full moon. No one was about.

Débras sat at the wheel of the ramshackle Ford. Siméon, still holding his revolver, sat in the back of the car next to Thomas. No one spoke.

Lights were still burning in the black market dealers' cafés on the Quai du Port in the Old Quarter. At the *Intendance Sanitaire* building Débras turned right into the Quai de la Tourette and drove past the venerable cathedral northward to the Place de la Joliette. He bypassed the huge black Gare Maritime along the deserted Boulevard Dunkerque. Then they were again at the waterfront, this time that of the Bassin de la Gare Maritime. The Ford jolted over railway lines and sleepers, pulling up at last on the dark Mole A.

"Out you get," said Siméon.

Thomas Lieven alighted obediently. The autumn gale cut him to the bone. The air stank of fish. The few lights strung out along the mole danced wildly. A ship's siren sounded in the distance. Débras had suddenly drawn a heavy pistol. He jerked his chin up.

Thomas moved off resignedly, marching out along the deserted mole. He was still smiling. But the smile was growing gradually stiffer.

Water glittered in the ashen light of the moon. White crests of foam rose and fell on the little waves. The fishy stench grew stronger. Thomas, as he shuffled along, heard Siméon stumbling and cursing behind him. This is awful, thought Thomas, naturally he's got his finger on the trigger all this time. I hope he doesn't stumble again. Quite a serious accident might so easily occur. . . .

Colonel Débras had still not uttered a single word. Now there was not another living soul anywhere near them.

Anyone who falls into the water here won't be found for a very long time, thought Thomas. Especially if he has a few bullets in his guts. The mole had come to an end at last. Suddenly there was nothing more ahead but a strip of concrete and beyond it the waters of the port. They looked very black.

"Halt," said Siméon.

Thomas halted.

Then Débras spoke for the first time: "Turn around."

Thomas turned around. He gazed at Débras and Siméon and heard the church clocks of Marseilles strike the three quarters of the hour, far off, muted by the wind, ethereal. Next moment he heard Siméon say in a preoccupied, urgent tone: "Quarter to eleven, chief. We'll have to hurry if we're to get him to Madame's by eleven o'clock."

Thomas gasped. His stiff smile relaxed. He coughed discreetly as he heard one colonel say to the other: "You utter idiot!"

With a smile, Thomas addressed Débras. "Don't be too hard on him, for spoiling your little game. I've suffered from him too. He once landed me in a terribly difficult situation in front of a German first lieutenant. All the same, he's a decent sort." He clapped Siméon, who was looking frightfully embarrassed, on the back.

Débras pocketed his pistol and turned away to hide a grin which he didn't want either Thomas or Siméon to see.

Thomas continued: "Apart from that, gentlemen, I had an idea, right away, that you only wanted to give me a devil of a fright and then, probably, get me to work for you again."

"Wh—what made you think that?" Siméon stuttered.

"As soon as I heard Josephine Baker's record I suspected that M. Débras was somewhere about. Then I said to myself, If the major—oh, pardon, colonel, and let me congratulate you, by the way, on your promotion—if, then, you had made a special journey from Casablanca, it could hardly have been simply in order to be present at my inglorious demise. Am I right?"

Débras turned back to Thomas. He nodded. "Damn you three times over for an insolent *Boche*!"

"May I suggest, then, that we leave this inhospitable spot? The stink's beginning to get me down. And we really ought not to keep Madame waiting. Also, I'd like to go around by the station if possible."

"The station?" repeated Siméon with a bewildered look.

"There's a flower shop there which keeps open all night," Thomas instructed him amiably. "I want to buy a few orchids . . ."

Josephine Baker seemed more beautiful than ever to Thomas Lieven. She received him in the drawing-room of her suite at the Hôtel de Noailles in the Cannebière, the principal street of Marseilles.

Josephine's blue-black hair was piled high in a shining crown. She wore huge white earrings. Her dark skin had the sheen of velvet. The colorful sparkle of a great ring with a rosette of diamonds flashed in Thomas's eyes as he bent to kiss the hand of the woman he so revered.

She looked serious as she took the cellophane carton containing three rose-red orchids. "Thank you, Herr Lieven. Please sit down. Maurice, may I ask you to open the champagne?"

There were only three of them present. For Débras, in a sudden access of impatience, had sent Colonel Siméon back to his quarters.

Thomas Lieven, glancing about the room, saw a big mirror and a grand piano with a heap of sheet music lying on it. He also noticed a poster which read:

Marseilles Opera
JOSEPHINE BAKER
in
THE CREOLE
An Opera in Three Acts
by JACQUES OFFENBACH

Opening Night: 24th December 1940.

Colonel Débras filled their cut-glass goblets. He said: "Let us drink to the woman to whom you owe your life, Herr Lieven."

Thomas bowed low to Josephine. "I always hoped, madame, that you would understand the reasons for my behavior. As a woman you must hate violence, war, bloodshed and murder even more than I do."

"Of course," the brilliantly handsome woman answered. "But I also love my country. You did us a lot of harm by destroying those genuine lists."

"Madame," Thomas rejoined, "would I not have done your country even more harm if I had not destroyed those lists, if I had handed them over to the Germans?"

Débras intervened. "You are right. No need to say any more on that subject. Nor do I forget that you helped me to leave Madrid. You're a borderline case, Lieven. But I swear to you that if you play us up just once more there won't be more champagne, however well Josephine may understand the reasons for your behavior. Next time you won't be returning from the mole."

"Look here, Débras. I'm fond of you. I really, honestly am. I'm also fond of France. But I swear to you here and now that if you compel me to work for you again I shall play you up again. For I'm not going to act against any country, even my own."

Josephine asked quietly: "Including the Gestapo?"

"I beg your pardon?"

"Would you also have any scruples about injuring the Gestapo?"

"I would do that, madame, with the very greatest of pleasure."

Colonel Débras lifted his hand. "I suppose you know that just now, with British support, we are building up a new secret service and a resistance movement in both occupied and unoccupied France."

"Yes, I know that."

"Colonel Siméon had orders from his new chief in Paris to lure you to Marseilles and liquidate you. But before acting he discussed your case with Josephine. She informed me of the plan and asked me to intervene."

"Madame," said Thomas, with a bow, "may I refill your glass?"

"Lieven, I have to return to Casablanca. Josephine will follow me in a few weeks' time. We have received certain orders from London. Siméon will then be left alone here. What is your opinion of him?"

Thomas replied courteously: "I would have to lie to answer you."

Débras sighed. "Siméon has a good heart. He is an ardent patriot."

"And a heroic soldier," Thomas added approvingly.

"Brave and energetic," Josephine approved in her turn.

"Yes, yes, yes," said Débras. "But unfortunately there's something lacking in him. We all know what it is. I need not mention it."

Thomas nodded regretfully.

"It's not only a ready fist that proves courage," said Josephine. "A head is also required. You, Herr Lieven, and Colonel Siméon, can supply both between you. You two would make a good team."

"Siméon will never be equal to his job on his own," Débras said.

"What job?"

Débras compressed his lips. "The position is serious, Lieven. I've no wish to represent my countrymen as better than they are. Even some Frenchmen are swine."

"There are swine everywhere," said Thomas.

"Those in both occupied and unoccupied France are collaborating with the Nazis. They are betraying us. They are selling their country. There are French swine in the pay of the Gestapo. I said Gestapo, Herr Lieven."

"I heard you," Thomas said.

"You are a German. You can get on with Germans. And you can also at any time pass for a native Frenchman."

"Oh Lord, there it goes again!"

"Those people are not only betraying their country, they are also plundering it," said Débras. "For example, only a few days ago two men arrived here from Paris to buy up gold and currency."

"Frenchmen?"

"Frenchmen working for the Gestapo."

"What are their names?"

"Jacques Bergier and Paul de Lesseps."

Thomas Lieven gazed into space for a while, reflecting. Then he said: "Very well, Débras, I'll help to find those two traitors for you. But I should like you to promise me that you will let me go when I have done so."

"Where do you want to go to?"

"You know that perfectly well. To South America. I have a friend there called Lindner, a banker. I have no more money myself. But he has plenty."

"Herr Lieven . . ."

"He has a million dollars. If I could obtain a new passport from you he would guarantee me a visa . . ."

"Herr Lieven, just a minute . . ."

"And as soon as I have the visa I can get a ship . . ." He stopped speaking abruptly. "What's the matter?"

"I'm sorry, Herr Lieven. I'm really sorry. But I'm afraid you'll never see your friend Lindner again."

"What do you mean? Give me the details, please, and don't keep anything back. I'm already gradually beginning to see myself as a modern Job. What's happened to my friend Lindner?"

"He is dead," Débras said.

"Dead?" repeated Thomas. His face changed color, going gray. Walter Lindner dead. My last hope, my last friend, my last chance to leave this crazy continent . . .

"You were in jail at the time. So you heard nothing about it," Débras said. "On November 3, 1940, near the Bermudas, Lindner's boat hit a floating mine and sank twenty minutes later. Only a few survivors were picked up. Lindner and his wife were not among them . . ."

Thomas Lieven sat huddled in his chair, twiddling his champagne glass.

"If you had gone aboard that boat you would probably be dead at this moment," Débras remarked.

"Yes," said Thomas Lieven. "That is, to be sure, an uncommonly consoling thought."

[18]

In the early morning hours of November 26, 1940, Thomas Lieven, silent and brooding, left the Hôtel de Noailles for the Old Quarter of Marseilles. He went back to the flat on the second floor of the house in the rue Chevalier Rose. In the company of Josephine Baker and Colonel Débras he had drunk a good deal more champagne and discussed at length certain plans for the immediate future.

For some seconds he had been tempted to wake Chantal, asleep in her rumpled bed, with a sound thrashing. Then he decided to take a hot bath first. Eventually his seductive mistress, led by the sound of his singing, had discovered him there.

While Chantal scrubbed away at his back, he told her a few details of his miraculous escape, though not many, only the most essential. For he no longer had unlimited confidence in her.

Finally he said: "They let me go because they needed me. I'm to do a job for them. And I need you, once more, to help me with it. If you agree to do so I think we might be friends again on that basis."

Chantal's still submissive gaze brightened. "You can forgive me?"

"I shall have to, because I need you . . ."

"I don't care whether you have to as long as you do," she whispered, kissing him. "I would do anything for you. What do you want me to do?"

"Get me some gold bullion."

"B-bullion? How much?"

"Well, some five or ten million francs' worth."

"Genuine gold?"

"Oh, no. Lead fillings, naturally."

"Well, if that's all you want."

"You damned slut!" he cried. "You miserable wretch! It's all your fault that I'm back again in this mess! Don't scrub so hard!"

But she scrubbed all the harder, exclaiming: "Oh, how glad I am that they didn't kill you, my sweet!"

"Will you stop that scrubbing?"

She uttered a low laugh and began tickling him.

"Stop it, or I'll dust your pants for you!"

"That won't be easy, I haven't got any on!"

"Just you wait!" He seized her. She shrieked. Water shot up. Then she was down on top of him in the warm, soapy bath water, screaming, squealing and gurgling, till she lay still in his arms.

Suddenly he found himself thinking of the unfortuante Lazarus Alcoba, of the unfortunate Walter Lindner and his wife, of the passengers aboard the sinking steamer, of the sailors, of the unfortunate soldiers in the trenches and of all the other unfortunate people in the world. How short their lives were, how lamentably they died and how little happiness there was anywhere.

[19]

On Wednesday, December 4, 1940, three men sat down to a vegetarian lunch in a private room at the Hôtel Bristol in the Cannebière. One of them had drawn up the menu with the prudence of an experienced connoisseur and attentively supervised its production in the hotel kitchen.

The three gentlemen in question were named Jacques Bergier, Paul de Lesseps and Pierre Hunebelle.

Paul de Lesseps, a taciturn, haggard, sharp-featured individual, was about thirty-seven.

Jacques Bergier, older, rosier, stouter and somewhat overdressed, with affected gestures, a high-pitched voice and a mincing gait, wore a dark red velvet waistcoat with his dark blue suit and a rather oppressive perfume.

Pierre Hunebelle, finally, he who had taken so much trouble over the lunch, was the living image of our hero Thomas

Lieven. Thomas had a new bogus passport in his pocket, supplied by the French secret service.

It was the first meeting of Bergier and de Lesseps with M. Hunebelle. Bergier in particular observed that charming young gentleman with growing approval. He never took his sentimental, girlish gaze off the fellow. Thomas had invited both gentlemen to lunch after telephoning to Bergier, who was a lawyer, to ask for an appointment.

"Perhaps we might discuss the affair over a good meal," he had proposed.

"With pleasure, M. Hunebelle. But no meat, if you please, on any account," the sensitive Bergier had replied in his high voice.

"You are a vegetarian?"

"One hundred per cent. And I don't smoke and I don't drink." Nor, thought Thomas, do you care much for ladies' society, my friend. You only work for the Gestapo, you pure soul . . .

MENU

Genevan Celeriac
Fungi Cutlets
Belle Hélène Pears

4 DECEMBER 1940

A special dish of fungi extracted a sum of several million francs.

Genevan Celeria

Well wash and brush a few medium-sized celeriacs, parboil in salt water, peel and cut into thin slices. Place some fresh butter in a deep casserole, cover with slices of celeriac. On the slices sprinkle grated Gruyère cheese and dabs of butter. Repeat the process till the celeriac is all used. Sprinkle top layer with cheese and butter as before. Place lid on casserole and the casserole itself on a saucepan of boiling water. Leave to steam for at least an hour. Serve in the same casserole.

Fungi Cutlets

One pound of fresh chanterelles are cleaned and quartered. Two large onions are chopped and braised in butter with chopped parsley and the chanterelles until the latter are browned. Two soaked and squeezed bread rolls are then added. The mixture is well stirred and left to cook a little while longer, after which it is passed through the mincer with one or two boiled potatoes. Stir well and when cool enough add one egg and a few bread crumbs if the mixture seems too soft. Then spice with a little anchovy paste and a few drops of soya sauce or any other extract made from yeast (not meat) such as marmite. Salt and pepper are next added and cutlets are formed, dipped in flour, egg and bread crumbs and fried in butter to a golden brown. They are then garnished with lemon slices and capers.

Belle Hélène Pears

Place portions of vanilla ice cream in individual glass dishes and cover each with half a tinned pear. Cover this with a thick, very hot chocolate sauce and serve immediately. For the sauce take four squares (ounces) of bitter chocolate, melt in a steamer and add as much milk or cream as will form a thick sauce.

Conversation began over the first course of Genevan celeriac. The well-groomed Bergier remarked: "Wonderful, M. Hunebelle, simply wonderful. The slices just melt on the tongue."

"That's only what they should do," replied Thomas gravely. "The celeriacs should always be fine specimens, but not too large."

"Not too large, eh?" repeated Bergier, devouring Thomas with his eyes.

"They have to be well washed and brushed and then cooked in salt water until soft, but not too soft."

"But not too soft," the lawyer echoed. His perfume tingled in Thomas's nose. "You must write the recipe down for me, monsieur." He wore four rings with differently colored stones on his well-manicured fingers. He watched Thomas incessantly, with ever more melancholy eyes.

That one will be an easy fish to play, thought our friend. I shall have to be more careful, though, with de Lesseps.

At that very moment de Lesseps demanded abruptly: "Well, monsieur, what can we do for you?"

"Gentlemen, Marseilles is a small city. I have heard rumors that you have come from Paris to settle certain business matters."

Just then an old waiter brought in the main course and Thomas said no more for a while. The lawyer moaned, looking at the plates: "Oh, but I specially said, no meat!"

De Lesseps interrupted him rudely. "What sort of business matters, M. Hunebelle?"

"Well—er—currency and gold. You're said to be interested in that sort of business."

Lesseps and Bergier exchanged glances. Quite a long silence ensued in the private room. Finally de Lesseps—in 1947 he was accused of collaboration by the French Government and found guilty—observed coldly: "That's what they say, is it?"

"Yes, that's what they say. Won't you have some soya beans, M. Bergier?"

"My friend," replied the lawyer, looking deep into Thomas's eyes, "you have impressed me. What I thought was meat is actually nothing of the kind and yet tastes marvelous. What is this stuff, really?"

De Lesseps interposed irritably. "M. Hunebelle, you mentioned gold and currency just now. Suppose we really were interested in such items, what then?"

Thomas turned to Bergier. "They are fungi cutlets. Delicate flavor, don't you think?" He turned back to de Lesseps. "I might have some gold ingots to sell."

"You have gold?" de Lesseps asked tensely.

"I have."

"Where?"

"I don't see why that should interest you," Thomas retorted coolly. "I for my part am not interested in the parties for whom you are acting."

De Lesseps' eyes reminded him of a shark's. "How much gold can you supply?"

"That depends on how much you want."

"I hardly suppose you have as much as that," de Lesseps told him.

The silken-smooth lawyer suddenly giggled. "We are ready to buy up to the value of two hundred millions," he announced.

My word, thought Thomas Lieven. This is going to be something colossal!

The old waiter, who was listening outside the door of the private room, also thought, My word, this is going to be something colossal! Clicking his tongue, he entered the small bar of the hotel, which was almost empty at this hour. A thick-set fellow with hair brushed straight up from his forehead was sitting at the counter drinking Pernod.

The waiter addressed him with a "Hey, Bastian."

The man looked up. He had small eyes like those of an elephant and big hands like those of a furniture mover.

The waiter told him what the gentlemen in the private room were talking about. The man, whose name was Bastian Fabre, whistled through his teeth. "Two hundred millions! Good God Almighty!" He slipped some money into the waiter's hand. "Go on listening. Remember every word. I'll come back."

"Right you are, Bastian," said the old waiter.

Bastian, who wore a leather jacket, a beret and gray trousers, left the bar, mounted an old bicycle and pedaled alongside the Old Port up to the Quai des Belges. Here stood the most famous cafés in the city, the Cintra and the Brûleur de Loup. In both establishments illegal transactions of all kinds were arranged. The Cintra was more up to date and had the better clientèle, consisting of rich Greek merchants, Turks, Dutchmen and Egyptians.

Bastian entered the smaller, more old-fashioned Brûleur de Loup. The dark-paneled room, with its great mirrors mistily reflecting the gray light outside, was occupied almost exclusively by native Frenchmen. Most of them were drinking *pastis* at this midday hour, a sweet apéritif which still cost only two francs in 1939 and now cost ten, a source of perpetual resentment for all patriots.

Wine merchants, forgers, smugglers, emigrants on the run and racketeers sat in the Brûleur de Loup. Bastian knew many of them. He distributed salutes and was saluted in return. On the handle of a door at the end of the room hung a card marked CLUB.

The big man knocked four times slowly and twice rapidly at this door. It opened and he entered the room behind it.

Here electric light was burning, there being no windows. One could have cut the fog of tobacco smoke with a knife. Fifteen men and one woman sat around a long table. The men looked a reckless lot. Some were bearded. Others had

had their noses knocked in or bore scars. There were Africans, Armenians and Corsicans among them.

The woman sat at the head of the table. She wore a red cap perched on her blue-black hair, trousers and a jacket of undressed leather. It would have been clear, in any stranger's first encounter with this peculiar version of the Round Table, that Chantal Tessier ruled her band of rascals with a rod of iron, that she was a lone she-wolf, an ungracious queen.

"Where the hell have you been?" she snarled at Bastian the moment he entered. "We've been waiting for you for the last half-hour!"

"Those three took their time," he stammered, with a cringing expression. "The lawyer was very late."

Chantal snapped: "How many more times am I to tell you to change that beret of yours? You people make me sick! Is everyone to see at a glance that you come from the gutter?"

"I'm sorry, Chantal," Bastian murmured humbly, putting his dirty beret away with an embarrassed air. Then he reported what the waiter had overheard. When he mentioned the figure of two hundred millions a wave of excitement surged through the room. Some of the men whistled. One banged the table with his fist. They all started talking at once.

Chantal's icy tones rose above the tumult. "Would you gentlemen be so very kind as to shut your bloody traps?"

Complete silence fell.

"No one's to say anything unless they're asked to, do you hear?" Chantal leaned back in her chair. "Give me a cigarette." Two of the gang hastened to comply with her request.

She blew out a cloud of smoke. "I want you all to listen to me carefully now. I'm going to tell you what you have to do."

Chantal Tessier, female boss and lover of undressed leather, issued her orders. And the whole gang listened very carefully.

[21]

On Thursday December 5, 1940, it was already very cold in Marseilles. Two gentlemen were standing in an ironmonger's shop in the rue de Rome.

One of them said: "Four baking tins please."

The saleswoman asked the other gentleman: "And you, sir?"

The other replied: "I'd like three baking tins, my dear, if you can spare them."

The first gentleman, a muscular giant with reddish hair

standing straight up from his forehead, was known as Bastian Fabre, which was in fact his real name.

The two gentlemen bought seven baking tins at the excessive wartime price. But they did not seem to intend them for baking cakes. For they next purchased, not butter, sugar, saffron and flour, but nine kilograms of lead, a large sheet of fire clay and a steel cylinder of propane gas, all at a junk shop in the short rue Mazagran.

They then set out for the Old Quarter. They hardly spoke on the way, for they had only just met.

Thomas Lieven was thinking: So now I'm off with this orangutan to manufacture bogus gold ingots. What a monstrous idea! And the worst of it is that I'm really curious to see the technical process.

Another thing Thomas didn't yet understand was Chantal's attitude. For when he told her about the two buyers he had met she had at once replied: "Well, that's fine, sweetie, that's fine! My organization will be at your disposal. Fifteen first-rate specialists. We'll put those two Gestapo swine in the cart, plus your Colonel Siméon and—"

"No. Leave the colonel out of it. I've promised to help him."

"You're crazy! Is that your German idealism, or what? Enough to make one weep! If that's your game then you can play it alone. Go and get your own gold. Not one of my mob will help you."

That had been three days ago. But since then she had apparently changed her mind. He had never known her so tender and passionate before. During one of the few quiet spells of the previous night she had whispered in Thomas Lieven's arms: "You're quite right. You must keep your promise . . ." She kissed him. "Oh, how much more I love you now for being so decent . . ." She kissed him twice. "I'll let you have Bastian . . . you can have the whole mob . . ."

As Thomas strolled beside the gigantic Bastian Fabre, who was pushing a wheelbarrow containing the articles they had bought, he wondered, while they made their way through the dirty, winding lanes of the Old Quarter, whether he could trust the bitch Chantal. She had already once lied to and betrayed him. She had something in mind. But what could it be?

Bastian Fabre could have told him, in detail. Bastian was thinking, as he pushed that barrow beside the slim, elegant Thomas: I'm not at all keen on this youngster. He lives at Chantal's place and it's quite clear what's going on there.

There have been plenty of others who did the same. But it's more serious with this fellow Pierre Hunebelle, obviously. The boss is much more open about the whole thing than she ever was before. Damn and blast it!

Bastian remembered what Chantal had let slip about the lad at the business meeting of the gang at the Brûleur de Loup. "He's a genius. Not one of you blockheads is fit to pass him the water jug."

"Well, well," Bastian had dared to remark.

Chantal had hissed at him like a rocket. "Shut your trap, you! From now on you're going to do whatever he tells you!"

"But just a minute, Chantal . . ."

"Hold your tongue! That's an order, do you hear? You're to go with him to Boule and get those ingots made. And you others are to arrange to have him watched day and night. And report to me everything he gets up to."

"So far as the night's concerned you ought to know best what he—"

"One more word and I'll sock your jaw for you! He's my man, d'you hear that? The boy's too decent by half. When he starts on those two Gestapo swine it's we who'll have to think for him. He doesn't know what's good for him . . ."

That was what Chantal had said.

Bastian thought grimly, as he shuffled along beside Thomas through the Old Quarter, I've got a feeling that the lad knows quite well what's good for him!

That was what Bastian thought. But he didn't say what he was thinking. He merely said: "Here we are." He stopped in front of No. 14 in the rue d'Aubagne. To the right of the door an old, cracked enamel plate bore the legend:

DR. RENE BOULE
DENTIST
Surgery 9–12 and 3–6

They entered the house and rang the bell of an interior door. It opened immediately.

"So there you are at last," said Dr. René Boule. He was the smallest and neatest man Thomas Lieven had ever seen. He wore white overalls, gold-rimmed pince-nez and an exceptionally fine, glittering set of false teeth.

"Come in, boys." The doctor hung a card on the doorknob with the inscription: NO CONSULTATION TODAY.

Then he closed the door and led the way through a surgery

containing an adjustable patients' chair and some gleaming apparatus to a laboratory beyond, with a small kitchen adjoining it. There Bastian hurriedly introduced the gentlemen to each other. He explained to Thomas: "The doctor works regularly for us. He has a standing contract with the boss."

"Yes, but only for the production of imitation gold," the little man murmured, looking hard at Thomas. "When you boys have something wrong with your teeth, you go somewhere else. Funny I haven't seen you before. Only just joined the mob, have you?"

Thomas nodded.

"He's only just out of stir," Bastian explained cheerfully. "The boss thinks the world of him. This work's to go on her private account."

"Right. You've brought the tins? Fine, fine. I'll be able to make seven ingots at once without having to wait every time for the muck to cool off." Dr. Boule unpacked the tins and stood them in a row. "All right for length," he remarked. "Each to weigh a kilo, eh? Yes, that's what I thought." He turned to Thomas. "You can watch if you're interested, young man. One never knows when knowledge of this kind may come in handy."

"You're right there," said Thomas, raising his eyes to the ceiling in a gesture of self-pity.

Bastian growled: "I've seen it all hundreds of times already. I'll just go out and get us something to eat."

"Something pretty solid, please," said the dentist. "This foundry work's rather exhausting."

"Well, the boss is paying. What'll it be then?"

The little man smacked his lips. "Henri, on the ground floor, has got hold of some nice little ducklings from the country. He's pushing 'em on the black market before the bloke from Economic Control picks 'em up. They're sweet little specimens. Not much fat and small bones. Three pounds weight each at most."

"Well then, I'll just go down and get us a couple off the hook," said Bastian. He went out.

Dr. René Boule informed Thomas: "The trouble with the production of bogus gold ingots is that gold and lead have very different melting points and specific gravities. Lead melts at as low as 327 degrees Celsius and gold not till 1063. Those cake tins won't stand such a high temperature. So we shall have to line them with fire clay."

The little man took precise measurements of the tins. Then

he ruled the outlines of their bases and sides on the fire clay, engraved the lines with a file and broke off, without effort, the superfluous portions. As he worked he went on talking. "Now we'll make a set of bricks out of plaster of paris to fit into the tins in such a way as to leave a space of three millimeters all round. We stick four matches through the plaster while it's still soft, at the base of each brick, so as to hold it three millimeters off the bottom layer of fire clay . . . Wouldn't you like to take some notes?"

"I have a good memory."

"Have you? Well, all right . . . As soon as the plaster bricks are in place on the fire-clay base we can start melting down the gold in a crucible."

"How is the high temperature obtained?"

"With an oxyacetylene torch and bottled propane gas."

"And what quality of gold do you use?"

"Twenty-two carat of course."

"Where do you get it?"

"At any analyst's. I collect the dust and exchange it for the twenty-two carat equivalent. As soon as the gold is melted we pour it into the spaces between the fire clay and the plaster and let it cool naturally. We don't, for instance, chill it with water. You really ought to be taking notes, you know. Then I take out the plaster, leaving a thin gold container of the same dimensions as a bar of gold weighing one kilo. This container is then filled with lead."

"Just a minute," said Thomas. "Lead is lighter than gold surely, isn't it?"

"Young man, I shall see to it that my bars weigh a kilo each, whatever's in them. Only the volume is different. I shall allow myself certain little differences in the width of each ingot, as compared with the real article. No one's going to notice that."

[22]

Bastian returned. He brought with him two plump little ducklings and two pounds of chestnuts and disappeared into the kitchen.

Thomas went on watching the talented dentist for a while at his work on production of the plaster bricks. Then he went into the kitchen to see what was going on there. He stiffened with repugnance. He didn't know anything about the production of imitation gold ingots. But he knew quite a lot about ducklings. And the way in which one of those birds was being treated roused his connoisseur's ire. Shaking his head, he approached Bastian, who was working under the window with his shirt sleeves rolled up. He had opened up one of the ducklings and was rubbing salt into both inner and outer fleshy parts.

"What are you up to?" demanded Thomas Lieven sternly.

"What d'you mean, what am I up to?" retorted Bastian with irritation. "I'm getting a duckling ready. What's wrong with that, may I ask?"

"You savage."

"What did you say to me?" The giant gulped.

"I said you were a savage. That bird is to be roasted, I suppose?"

"Of course it is."

"And that's just what I call savage."

"See here, you!" Bastian stuck his fists on his hips. He had forgotten Chantal's warnings. Reddening with rage, he roared: "What the hell do you know about cooking, you miserable little runt?"

"A bit," Thomas answered politely. "At any rate enough to tell you that what you are doing is a crime."

"I've been a ship's cook. And I've been preparing ducks for roasting all my life."

"Then you've been committing crimes all your life. Without mentioning what others you may have committed."

At the very last moment Bastian remembered Chantal's warnings. By a frantic effort he managed to control himself. He put both his mighty fists behind him, to prevent their taking action of their own accord and doing something rash. He spoke in a strangled tone. "And how—ahem—would you, M. Hunebelle, prepare a duck?"

"Only in the Chinese style, naturally."

"Ah—"

"Because only preparation with pineapples and proper seasoning retains the subtle flavor of a duck unadulterated. Actually, it even does more. It brings out the characteristic taste and emphasizes it."

"Rot," returned the giant. "Roasting's the only way."

"Obviously you know nothing of gastronomy," said Thomas. "Gentlemen prefer Chinese."

"Listen, golden boy, if you're trying to insinuate . . ." Bastian began. But he was interrupted by the little dentist plucking at his sleeve.

"What's up, Bastian? What are you two quarreling about? We've got two ducks, haven't we? Why not try out both styles, roast and Chinese? I've got hours of work to do yet."

Bastian growled: "You mean we have a competition?"

"That's what I mean," said the little man, smacking his lips again. "I'll judge it."

Bastian suddenly started grinning. He asked Thomas: "That suit you?"

"Sure. But I'll need a few trimmings. Mushrooms, tomatoes, pineapple, rice."

The dentist tittered. "Go down to Henri. He's got everything." He clapped his hands delightedly. "Now we're going to have fun! I'll be teaching you something and you'll be teaching me something. *Aux armes, citoyens!*"

Thereupon both the kitchen and the laboratory of Dr. René Boule became scenes of businesslike activity.

MENU

Chinese Duck with Pineapple
Roast Duck with Steamed Chestnuts
Trifle with Whipped Cream

5 DECEMBER 1940

Thomas Lieven's duck started a friendship which became a legend.

Chinese Duck with Pineapple

Clean and bone a fairly lean duck, prepare a strong stock from the duck bones and giblets. The duck meat is cut into small pieces, fried in a casserole till golden brown, sprinkled with flour and left to cook till flour is yellow. The stock is poured over the meat, a skinned fresh tomato, a few chopped mushrooms and a quarter of a teaspoon of glutamate are added and the whole is then left to braise for half an hour. Pineapple cubes are added and the mixture is left to cook another quarter of an hour. Plain boiled rice is served with this dish.

Roast Duck with Steamed Chestnuts

A young, fairly lean duck is cleaned and rubbed inside and out with salt. The inside may also be rubbed with garlic if desired and various herbs laid inside the duck. The bird is then placed breast downward on a grid in the oven and a roasting pan with some water is placed underneath. The duck is roasted in medium heat and braised with the fat which dripped into the roasting pan. The bird should be roasted, according to size, for between one and one and a half hours. For the last twenty minutes it is roasted with the breast upward. The well-browned skin is brushed with cold water and given another five minutes in a very hot oven. The skin will then be very crisp and tender.

As many chestnuts as one would normally take potatoes are cleaned and steamed in salt water. Care must be taken not to break them. They are then drenched in melted butter and served.

Trifle with Whipped Cream

Very dark bread crumbs, preferably pumpernickel, are placed at the bottom of a large glass dish and damped with cognac or kirsch. A layer of drained preserved morelia cherries are placed on top of the bread crumbs and the whole is covered with a layer of whipped cream. These layers are repeated and topped off with whipped cream as before. Grated chocolate is sprinkled over the top layer and it is decorated with cherries. This dish is chilled and left to stand for some time before serving.

While Bastian was rubbing his duck with garlic, adding herbs and turning the bird breast downward on the grid of the oven, Thomas Lieven jointed his, chopped up the bones and prepared from them and the giblets a strong stock. While waiting for the stock to boil he went to watch the little specialist at work in the laboratory.

Dr. Boule had meanwhile produced seven vats of gold leaf in the seven cake tins. He proceeded to fill the first of them with liquid lead. The dentist said: "We must let the lead cool. At present only one side of the gold lining is still open. We lay a sheet of fire clay on it to prevent the lead liquefying again when it comes in contact with the liquid gold. This last sheet of fire clay is very important, as it guards against discoloration of the gold surface, which would make any expert suspicious."

Thomas returned to the kitchen to look after his stock. After cutting up the duck meat he returned to the laboratory to look after his ingots.

Dr. Boule had meanwhile liquified more gold in a crucible and was now pouring it over the fire-clay sheet in the cake tin. He said: "We must now wait for the bubbles to disappear. The gold will set of its own accord. The surface has to have a low, raised edge round it, like that of a cake of soap. Then, before the metal has cooled, we quickly do the most important job of all, the punching."

"The what?"

"The punching. With a stamp certifying the bar's quality and content." Dr. Boule turned to the kitchen, calling out: "What stamp shall I use, Bastian?"

"Lyons Refinery," the giant called back. He was just brushing his bird with hot fat.

"Well, that'll be all right," said Dr. Boule. "I have a whole collection of punches in use by all sorts of refineries and banks." He showed them to Thomas. "I cut the negatives in linoleum and stuck the lino shapes on wooden blocks. Now watch carefully."

He picked up a counterfeit Lyons stamp and smeared the lino with olive oil. He then pressed the stamp into a corner of the still soft gold leaf of the first ingot. The film of oil burned up with a hissing sound. Dr. Boule snatched the stamp away before the hot metal could scorch the linoleum. The instant of pressure had sufficed. The impression of the stamp remained perfectly clear.

Quoth the dentist: "The irregularities, ashes and lumps left on the bar can stay there. Genuine ingots aren't polished either."

"What chances are there of the swindle being discovered?"

"Practically none." Dr. Boule shook his head. "The lead filling is now surrounded on all sides by a layer of gold three millimeters thick. The purchaser tests the bar with oilstone and acids. When he scratches a corner of the ingot with his oilstone a strip of gold will come off on it. He dabs the strip with various acid concentrations, one after another, appropriate to various carat contents. If the strip stays, the gold must be twenty-two carat. And that's just what it is, of course." The dentist suddenly began sniffing. "Holy Mother, that smells good! I wonder if it's your duck or his?"

An hour later the gentlemen sat down in silence to their meal. First they tasted the roast duck and then the Chinese. Next door the first three bars were cooling out. And it was ominously quiet in Dr. René Boule's little dining room. At last Bastian wiped his mouth and surveyed the dentist with half-closed eyes. "Well, come on, René, which was the best?"

Dr. Boule glanced in embarrassment from one cook to the other, from Thomas to Bastian and from Bastian to Thomas. Bastian's huge fists were stiffly opening and closing.

The little doctor stammered: "Impossible to say in three words, my dear Bastian . . . on the one hand your duck is . . . but on the other hand of course . . ."

"Yes, yes, yes," said Bastian. "You're sick in your stomach in case I beat you up, eh? All right, I'll do the judging for you. The Chinese was the best!" He grinned and gave Thomas such a thump on the back that the latter nearly choked. "I believe I'm the oldest of us two. So I'll give you leave, in return for your duck, to call me Bastian."

"Call me Pierre, Bastian."

"I've been a fool all my life about my roast duck. Wish I'd met you earlier, boy! Know any other recipes like that?"

"A few," answered Thomas modestly.

Bastian beamed. He gazed upon Thomas, all of a sudden, with the greatest sympathy and respect. The satisfaction of his greed had done away with his jealousy. "Pierre, d'you know what I think? I think we're going to be first-rate pals!"

Bastian was right. In 1957, at a villa in the Cecilien Allee, Düsseldorf, their friendship would be as vigorous and robust as on this first day. During the intervening seventeen years many of the mighty ones of the earth would learn to tremble before this pair of allies.

"But your duck wasn't bad either, Bastian," said Thomas. "Not at all bad, really. Incidentally, I also made some trifle with whipped cream. Help yourselves. I can't eat more. If I take another mouthful I shall drop dead!"

On the subject of death . . .

Cologne, 4 December
1940

FROM: Cologne Intelligence.
TO: Head of Berlin Intelligence.
SECRET 135892/VC/LU.

On my return from Lisbon I venture with respect to report for the attention of the Admiral the death of the double agent and traitor Thomas Lieven, alias Jean Leblanc.

The said individual was shot on the 17th November 1940 at 0935 hours (local time) in the courtyard of No. 16 Rua do Poco des Negros.

Lieven was disguised, at the time of his assassination, as a certain Lazarus Alcoba, with whom he had shared a cell.

Although the Portuguese authorities naturally did their best to suppress news of the event and draw a veil over its details, I have been able to ascertain beyond doubt that Lieven was shot by a paid professional killer acting under instructions by the British Secret Service. As the Admiral is aware, Lieven also sold the British bogus lists of the names and addresses of French agents.

I regret that it proved impossible for me to capture Lieven alive as directed. On the other hand his well deserved end means one source of trouble less for our own Service.

Heil Hitler!
Fritz Loos,
Major and Special Detachment Leader.

CHAPTER 2

[1]

In the afternoon of December 6, 1940, Messrs. Hunebelle and Fabre visited the Hôtel Bristol to call upon the stout, rosy-faced lawyer Jacques Bergier. He received them in the drawing room of his suite. The French buyer for the Gestapo wore a blue silk dressing gown with a dainty silk handkerchief in the breast pocket and was redolent of refreshing perfume.

At first he objected to Bastian's presence. "I don't understand this, M. Hunebelle. This gentleman is unknown to me. It is my intention to deal with you alone."

"This gentleman is a friend. I am bringing rather valuable merchandise with me, M. Bergier. I feel more secure in his presence."

The lawyer withdrew his objection. His spinsterish eyes gazed, with the expression of an invalid, upon the elegant Thomas. The vegetarian, non-smoker, and woman-hater Bergier then announced: "I must regret that my friend de Lesseps is unable to be here."

I don't regret it though, Thomas thought. He asked: "Where is he then?"

"He's gone to Bandol." Bergier pursed his rosy little lips as if he were going to whistle. "He will be buying another very large consignment of gold near there, you know. And currency also."

"I see." Thomas gestured to Bastian, who put a small case on the table and clicked open the lock. Inside lay seven gold bars.

Bergier examined them closely. He read the stamped impression. "H'm. Lyons Refinery. Excellent."

Thomas surreptitiously gave Bastian a second sign. The latter asked: "Might I wash my hands, please?"

"There's the bathroom."

Bastian went into the bathroom, which contained a multitude of pots and bottles. M. Bergier evidently paid much attention to his toilet. Bastian turned on one of the taps. Then he slipped noiselessly into the passage, removed the key of the apartment from the lock, took an old tin of beeswax out of his pocket, pressed both sides of the key into the wax, put the key back into the lock and the tin back into his pocket.

Meanwhile, in the drawing room, Bergier was testing the ingots. His methods were exactly the same as had been described by the little dentist. He used an oilstone and various concentrations of acids.

"Satisfactory," he announced after testing all seven bars. Then he gazed speculatively at Thomas. "I wonder what I ought to do in your case."

"I beg your pardon?" To Thomas's relief Bastian re-entered the drawing room at that moment.

"Well, I have to render a formal account to my principals of every purchase I make, naturally. We—er—keep lists of our customers."

Lists! Thomas Lieven's heart beat quicker. Those were just the lists he wanted! Lists of the names and addresses of collaborators in unoccupied France, people who sold their country, and often enough their countrymen and women also, to the Gestapo.

Bergier continued in the mildest of tones: "Of course, we don't compel anyone to give us information. . . . How could we?" He laughed. "But if you should ever feel inclined to do business with us later on, it might perhaps be useful if I took a few notes . . . naturally in the strictest confidence . . ."

In the strictest confidence with the Gestapo, thought Thomas. He answered: "Just as you like. I am hoping, in fact, to be able to make a few more deliveries to you. Of currency also."

"Please excuse me a moment," Bergier requested. With his mincing, feminine gait he crossed the *salon* and disappeared into his bedroom.

"Did you get the impression?" Thomas asked.

"Sure." Bastian nodded. "Tell me, is that lad a bit . . . ?"

"You don't miss a thing, do you?" Thomas commented.

Bergier returned. He was carrying a brief case with four locks, which he ceremoniously unfastened. He extracted several lists from the case, each of many names and addresses. He took out a gold fountain pen. Thomas Lieven gave his false name and a false address. Bergier wrote them down.

"And now the money, please," said Thomas.

Bergier laughed. "Don't worry. It's just coming. Please accompany me into my bedroom."

In the adjacent bedroom were three enormous wardrobe trunks. The lawyer pulled out a small drawer in one of them. It was chock-full of bundles of one-thousand and five-thousand-franc notes. Thomas had realized that Bergier and de Lesseps would have to carry great quantities of cash about with them. Undoubtedly the other drawers in the trunk also contained money. He therefore noted with the greatest excitement where Bergier proceeded to stow away the brief case containing the lists.

Bergier paid 360,000 francs for each ingot. The total for the seven bars therefore amounted to 2,520,000 francs.

As he handed over the bundles of notes to Thomas he smiled seductively at the latter and tried to catch his eye. But Thomas simply went on counting the francs.

At last Bergier inquired: "When shall we meet again, my dear fellow?"

Thomas looked astonished. "Why, won't you be returning to Paris, then?"

"Oh no. Only de Lesseps is going. He'll be passing through here on the Paris express at half-past three tomorrow afternoon."

"Not stopping?"

"No, he'll be going straight on from Bandol with the merchandise. I shall be taking your gold to him in his compartment. But after that you and I might have a meal together, don't you think, dear boy?"

[2]

"Fifteen-thirty hours at the St. Charles station," said Thomas an hour later in the library of a big old house on the Boulevard de la Corderie. The house belonged to a man named Jacques Cousteau, destined many years afterward to become famous as a deep-sea diver and for his book and film, *The Silent World*. In the year 1940 this former major of marine artillery was an important figure in the recently reorganized French secret service. Young and full of energy, black-haired and black-eyed, he was trained to a hair and a keen sportsman.

Cousteau sat in a deep armchair with rows of books bound in glowing colors behind him and smoked an ancient pipe, perforce only half full of tobacco.

Colonel Siméon sat beside him, the elbows and knees of his black suit pitifully shiny. When he crossed his legs a hole in the sole of his left shoe became visible.

That absurd, poverty-stricken, pitiful French secret service, thought Thomas. I, a foreigner forced to turn agent, am for the time being richer than the whole Deuxième Bureau!

Thomas Lieven, elegant and well groomed, was standing beside the bag in which he had brought the gold ingots to M. Bergier. The bag now contained 2,520,000 francs.

"You must be very wide-awake," said Thomas Lieven, "when the express comes in. I've found out that it only stops for eight minutes."

"We'll be awake all right," said Cousteau. "Don't you worry, M. Hunebelle."

Siméon twisted his Adolphe Menjou mustache and asked anxiously: "And you think de Lesseps has a lot of the stuff with him?"

"According to Bergier he has a huge quantity of gold, currency and other valuables. He's been buying up the stuff in the South for days. He's bound to have a lot with him or he wouldn't be going to Paris. Bergier will be handing him my seven ingots. I think the best thing to do would be to arrest the pair of them just at that moment."

"Everything's fixed," said Cousteau. "We've given our friends in the police the tip."

Siméon turned to Thomas. "But how are you going to get hold of those lists?"

Thomas answered with a smile: "You don't have to rack your brains over that, Siméon. But all the same, if you could supply three lads in Hôtel Bristol staff uniforms, I'd be obliged."

Siméon opened his mouth and eyes wide. It was obvious that he was thinking hard. But before any ideas occurred to him Cousteau said: "We can do that. The Bristol employs the Salomon laundry to wash the staff's uniforms. The deputy manager of the laundry is one of our boys."

"That's fine," said Thomas.

He glanced at the haggard Siméon, with his worn-out shoes and shabby suit. He glanced at Cousteau, drawing economically at the chewed up mouthpiece of his pipe, with so little tobacco left in his pouch. He glanced at the bag of francs. And then our friend performed a touching act. It proved that his heart was in the right place. But it proved also that he had still not learned to live according to the heartless rules of the heartless world into which a cruel fate had thrust him.

[3]

When Thomas Lieven left the house on the Boulevard de la Corderie half an hour later he saw a shadow detach itself from a recess in a wall and follow him through the hazy twilight. Thomas turned a street corner and halted abruptly. His pursuer ran straight into him.

"Oh, pardon," he exclaimed politely, lifting an ancient, dingy hat. Thomas recognized him. He was one of Chantal's mob. The man mumbled something unintelligible and shuffled away.

Thomas's black-haired, tigerish mistress received him at their apartment in the rue Chevalier Rose with enthusiastic kisses and embraces. She had made herself look particularly attractive for his benefit. Candles were burning. Champagne was on the ice. "At last, darling! I've been so longing for you!"

"I was . . ."

"Yes, I know. At your colonel's. Bastian told me."

"Where is Bastian, by the way?"

"His mother was suddenly taken ill. He had to go to her. He'll be back tomorrow."

"Tomorrow," Thomas repeated with a guileless air. "I see." He opened his little bag. It was still quite full but not so full as it had been when Bergier had filled it. Chantal whistled joyfully through her teeth.

"Don't whistle too soon, my dear," said he. "It's half a million short."

"What?"

"Yes, I gave that much away to Cousteau and Siméon. They're broke, poor devils. I felt quite sorry for them, you know. We can say it's my share of the swag they've got. The rest, quite a decent sum of two million twenty thousand francs, is for you and your colleagues."

Chantal kissed the tip of his nose. She withstood his attack of kindheartedness with ominous alacrity. "My gentleman! You're so sweet . . . Now you won't get anything out of it, will you?"

"I get you," he said affably. But he added without a change of tone: "Chantal, why are you having me followed?"

"Followed? I? You?" She raised her cat's eyes to the ceiling. "Darling, what do you mean by such nonsense?"

"One of your mob fell right over me."

"Oh, that could only have been a coincidence . . . oh Lord, why on earth are you so suspicious? Whatever can I do to make you quite sure that I love you?"

"You could tell the truth for a change, you slut. But I know there's absolutely no sense in making such a request," he retorted.

As the Paris express, punctually at half-past three on December 7, 1940, came in at platform III of the St. Charles station, a man of about thirty-seven stood at the open window of a first-class compartment. Paul de Lesseps had a lean, sharp-featured countenance, with cold shark's eyes and sparse ash-blond hair.

His gaze traveled anxiously along the platform. Then he saw the plump, conspicuously dressed lawyer Bergier standing near a small bag.

Paul de Lesseps lifted a hand.

Jacques Bergier lifted a hand.

The train stopped. Bergier hurried to his friend's compartment. After that everything happened very fast. Before a single passenger could alight, thirty plainclothes detectives stepped forward out of the crowds on both sides of the train. The detectives picked up two long ropes which had been lying on the permanent way and formed a cordon to prevent any passenger alighting.

An inspector spoke to Bergier, who had turned as white as a sheet, and arrested him on strong suspicion of gold and currency smuggling. Bergier still held the bag containing the seven gold ingots.

Meanwhile two other detectives rushed into the coach, one at each end, and arrested Paul de Lesseps in his compartment.

At the same time three men in the green uniforms of the Hôtel Bristol staff were striding along a corridor on the fourth floor of that establishment. Two of them looked like members of Chantal Tessier's gang. The third looked like Thomas Lieven. None of them looked particularly well in their uniforms.

The man who looked like Thomas Lieven opened, without difficulty, the door of a certain suite. With an energy seldom to be observed in hotel attendants they dragged three enormous trunks out of the bedroom of the suite to the staff elevator, went down with them to the courtyard, heaved them into the back of a delivery van belonging to the Salomon laundry and drove away without interference. But they did not drive to the laundry in question. They drove to a house in the rue Chevalier Rose.

An hour later a beaming Thomas Lieven, once more normally clothed, returned to the house of Jacques Cousteau on the Boulevard de la Corderie. Cousteau and Siméon were awaiting him.

Thomas extracted from the brief case of the charming M. Bergier the lists upon which the precise names and addresses of spies, collaborators and soul-sellers had been noted. He waved the sheets on high, in triumph. Cousteau and Siméon, to his astonishment, received this manifestation without emotion.

Thomas demanded, in some anxiety: "What's wrong? Did you get them both?"

Cousteau nodded. "In the lockup."

"And those seven ingots?"

"We've got them too."

"Well . . . ?"

"But that's all we have got, M. Hunebelle," said Cousteau slowly. He was staring very hard at Thomas. Colonel Siméon was also watching Thomas with a very strange expression.

"What do you mean by that? De Lesseps must have had a fortune on him in gold, currency and other valuables!"

"Yes, that was what we were led to suppose, wasn't it?" Cousteau was chewing his underlip.

"Didn't he have anything then?"

"Not a gram of gold, M. Hunebelle. Not a dollar. Nothing of any value at all. Funny, wasn't it?"

"Well—but—surely he must have hidden the stuff in his compartment or somewhere else aboard the train. He must have been working in with the railway staff. You'd better search the train and all the passengers."

"We've done that. We've even shoveled all the coal out of the tender. But we've found nothing."

"Where's the train now?"

"It's gone on. We couldn't hold it up any longer."

Siméon and Cousteau noted that Thomas was suddenly beginning to smile grimly, shake his head and move his lips soundlessly. If they had understood lip reading, they would also have understood what Thomas was muttering, viz, "That damned slut!"

Siméon didn't understand it. He stood up, arched his chest

and demanded in a sternly ironical and menacing tone: "Well, Lieven, have you by any chance any idea where that gold can be?"

"Yes," said Thomas Lieven slowly. "I think I have some idea."

[4]

His blood boiling with rage, Thomas Lieven struggled, with clenched teeth and hunched shoulders, against an ice-cold northeasterly gale, as he turned into the rue de Paradis, Marseilles, just as evening was coming on, that December 7, 1940.

That slut Chantal!

That ruffian Bastian!

It blew harder and harder. The wind shrieked and whistled, moaned and roared, through the streets. It was just the right weather for Thomas Lieven's vengeful mood.

Near the Old Stock Exchange a tall, shabby house stood in the rue de Paradis, with a restaurant known as Chez Papa on the first floor.

It belonged to a man whose real name no one knew but whom the whole town called "Olive." He was fat and rosy like the pigs he slaughtered for the black market.

Thick clouds of smoke hung in the rooms of the restaurant, which had fluorescent lighting. At this early evening hour Olive's clients were talking business over apéritifs and getting into the right mood for an evening meal provided by the black market.

With a cigarette in the corner of his mouth Olive was leaning over the wet counter when Thomas Lieven entered. The man's little eyes twinkled good-humoredly. "Good evening, monsieur. What's it to be? Drop of pastis?"

Thomas Lieven had heard a rumor that Olive made his own schnapps, starting with a somewhat sinister product, to wit, the alcohol used at the Anatomical Institute. Thomas had nothing against alcohol. But Olive was alleged to use spirit which, before being stolen, had already served, at the Anatomical Institute, for the preservation of certain portions of corpses. It was said that some of Olive's clients had been seized by acute attacks of mania after partaking of his pastis.

Thomas therefore replied: "Give me a double brandy. But the real thing, mind!"

He got it.

"Listen, Olive. I have to see Bastian."

"Bastian? I don't know him."

"Of course you know him. He lives just behind your place here. I know that one can only reach his rooms by going through this dive of yours. I also know that you have to announce all his visitors."

Olive blew out his fat cheeks. His eyes suddenly grew truculent. "You don't fool me, you little runt of a bogie. Buzz off, boy. I've a dozen men here to give you a going-over if I whistle 'em, see?"

"I'm not a bogie," Thomas said. He took a sip of the brandy. Then he drew out his beloved repeater. He had retained it throughout all his dangerous adventures, even saving it from the Costa Rican consul, and brought it with him from Portugal right across Spain to Marseilles. He made it strike the hour.

The owner of the restaurant looked on in astonishment. Then he demanded: "How d'you know he lives here?"

"He told me himself. You go and tell him that his dear friend Pierre wants to speak to him. And if he doesn't let his dear friend Pierre in on the dot, then something's going to happen here in five minutes by my ticker . . ."

[5]

With outstretched arms and a beaming smile Bastian Fabre approached Thomas Lieven. They stood in the narrow passage connecting the kitchen of the restaurant with Bastian's rooms. The latter smote Thomas on the shoulder with his huge palm. "What a pleasure to see you, old lad! I was just going out to look for you!"

"Take your flippers off me this minute, you swindler," said Thomas fiercely. He pushed Bastian aside and entered the latter's apartment.

The front room looked pretty rough. Tires, petrol cans and cigarette cartons lay all over the place. In the back room there was a big table with a complete model railway on it, run by electricity, with winding tracks, level crossings, mountains, valleys, tunnels and bridges.

Thomas remarked contemptuously: "Started a kindergarten, have you?"

"It's my hobby," said Bastian in an offended tone. "Please don't lean on that box or you'll put the transformer out of action . . . and would you mind telling me what on earth you're in such a rage about?"

"You've got the nerve to ask me that? Yesterday you vanished. Today Chantal vanished. Two hours ago the police arrested those two buyers for the Gestapo, Bergier and de Lesseps. De Lesseps had been in Bandol with gold, jewelry, coin and paper currency. But he arrived in Marseilles with neither paper nor coin currency, with neither jewelry nor gold. The police turned the whole train upside down without finding anything."

"You don't say!" Bastian, with a grin, pressed a button of his apparatus. One of the toy trains started running toward a tunnel.

Thomas snatched a plug out of the wainscot. The train stopped. Two of the coaches had just emerged from the tunnel.

Bastian rose to his full height, looking like an enraged ape. "You'll get one in the kisser if you're not careful, my lad. What d'you want here anyhow?"

"I want to know where Chantal is. And I want to know where that gold is."

"Next door, of course. In my bedroom."

"What?" Thomas gave a great gasp.

"You didn't think they'd be anywhere else, did you? Did you suppose she'd run off with the loot? All she wanted was to doll everything up with candles and so on, just to give you a nice surprise." Bastian called out in a louder tone: "Ready, Chantal?"

A door opened. Chantal Tessier, looking more attractive than ever, stood on the threshold, wearing tight green trousers of undressed leather, a white blouse and a black belt. Her tigerish teeth glittered in a beaming smile.

"Hallo, sweetie!" she cried, seizing Thomas's hand. "Now baby boy's going to get such a nice present!"

Thomas followed her, without resistance, into the next room. Five candle ends were burning in five saucers. Their soft light illuminated the old-fashioned bedroom, with its great double bed.

On a closer view of this place of repose Thomas caught his breath convulsively. For there lay, glistening and sparkling in the candlelight, a good two dozen gold ingots, countless gold coins and rings, together with chains and bracelets, ancient and modern, an antique crucifix encrusted with jewels, a small icon inlaid in gold and bundles of dollar and pound notes.

Thomas Lieven felt as though his legs had turned into jelly.

Seized with a sudden fit of faintness he collapsed into an old rocking chair, which at once got into motion at high speed.

Bastian, standing beside Chantal, was rubbing his hands, elbowing the lady and chuckling with pleasure. "That one caught him all right! Just look at him there! Flat out, that's what he is!"

"It's certainly a great day for all of us," said Chantal.

Thomas, in his stupefaction, could only see their faces as white spheres bobbing about in rushing water. They kept jumping up and down. He braced his feet against the floor to stop the chair rocking. Then he could see their two faces clearly. They looked like those of children, perfectly innocent of any dissimulation or deceit.

He groaned: "So I was right. You two knocked the stuff off."

Bastian struck himself on the belly with a gross chuckle. "We did it for all three of us!"

Chantal ran to Thomas and rained kisses on him, brief but ardent. "Oh," she cried, "if you only knew how sweet you're looking now. I could gobble you up! Darling, I'm crazy about you!" She sat on his knee and the chair started rocking again. Once more Thomas began to feel faint.

Chantal's voice reached his ears as through a sea of cotton wool. "So I told the boys, we'll have to go it alone this time, my sweetie's too goodhearted for it, he's got too much of a conscience. We mustn't bother him with it at all. When we flop the boodle down under his nose, he'll be as pleased as any of us!"

Thomas, shaking his head and still feeling very faint, inquired: "And how did you get at the stuff?"

Bastian reported. "Well, yesterday, when I went with you to see that queer chap, Bergier, I heard him say his pal de Lesseps was away in Bandol, pretty well loaded up. So what else could I do but take three of the boys with me down to Bandol? I had some of my mates there, you know. I found out that de Lesseps was in with some of the railwaymen. He was scared sick of being caught with the stuff he had. He wanted to stick it under the coal for the engine that would be taking him to Paris, see? In the tender, I mean."

After mastering, with some difficulty, a hoarse fit of laughter, Bastian continued: "Well, we let him do it, for a start. Then we arranged for a smart little bird to keep him busy for the evening. Luckily the randy bastard's easier to provide for than his pal Bergier! So that kid did just what we told her and fairly turned him inside out! A pretty thorough job. He was still drunk and weak at the knees when he showed up at the station next morning."

"Good for her," murmured Chantal, her long red fingernails busy in Thomas Lieven's hair.

Bastian beheld this scene sadly but appreciatively. "I envy you, boy," he observed, then continued in a brisker tone: "Well, while our pal de Lesseps was busy elsewhere the boys and I started playing trains. It's my hobby, as I've already told you. There are plenty of tenders, you know, in any station. And one looks just like another."

"But didn't de Lesseps have his tender guarded?"

"Sure he did. He put two railwaymen on it." Bastian raised his hands and let them fall again. "He gave each of them a gold ingot. But we gave each of them another two we happened to have about us and that was that."

"The power of gold," said Chantal, biting Thomas in the left ear lobe.

"Chantal!"

"Yes, sweetie?"

"Get up, please," Thomas requested. She rose, looking disconcerted, and went to join Bastian. He laid an arm about her shoulders. The pair stood there motionless, like mischievous children suddenly frightened.

Beside them the gold bars sparkled, the coins glittered and the chains, rings and jewels glistened.

Thomas, too, stood up. In a tone of deep depression he informed them: "I'm most sincerely sorry to have to spoil your pleasure and wreck the surprise you arranged for me. But it just can't be helped."

"What can't be helped?" demanded Bastian, in a dry, level voice.

"Passing on this stuff to Cousteau and Siméon. It's impossible for us to keep it."

"C-c-crazy—" Bastian's lower jaw dropped. He looked at Chantal in utter bewilderment. "He's gone crazy!"

[6]

Chantal stood perfectly still. Only her left nostril quivered. Thomas said quietly: "I've just left Siméon and Cousteau. We came to a clear agreement. They are to have the lists of spies and collaborators, together with all the stuff Bergier and de Lesseps have seized or extorted by blackmail down here. We are to retain all the money contained in the three wardrobe trunks we took from Bergier's bedroom. After all, that amounts to pretty nearly sixty-eight millions, you know."

"Sixty-eight million francs!" exclaimed Bastian, wringing his hands. "Francs! Francs! When their value's falling day after day!"

"And for that you're going to give up all this?" Chantal spoke in a very low tone, almost a whisper, motioning toward the bed. "There's at least one hundred fifty million's worth of francs there, you fool!"

Thomas retorted angrily: "It's French property, stolen from France! The money in the trunks is Gestapo money. We can keep it with a clear conscience. But that stuff there, the jewels, the crucifix, the gold from the Bank of France—my God, am I, a German, to remind you of your duty as French patriots?"

Bastian rejoined hoarsely: "That's our swag. We pinched it. The Gestapo's lost it. In my opinion we've done enough for our country."

Bastian and Thomas argued the point, growing more and more heated over it. Chantal, on the other hand, became quieter and quieter, dangerously quiet, in fact.

With her hands on her hips and her thumbs in her leather belt, she tilted her right shoe backward and forward, her left nostril quivering. At last she interrupted Bastian in a very low tone. "Don't get excited. This is your flat. Before anything happens this little idiot must get out of here and Cousteau and Siméon must come in."

Thomas shrugged his shoulders and walked to the door. In a moment Bastian had barred his way, holding a heavy revolver. "Where are you off to?"

"Chez Papa. I'm going to telephone."

"One more step and you've had it." Bastian was breathing noisily. The safety catch of his weapon clicked back.

Thomas took two more steps forward. The barrel of the revolver touched his chest. He took two more steps forward.

Bastian groaned. He retreated two steps. "Be reasonable, lad . . . I—I really mean to do you in . . ."

"Let me go, Bastian." Thomas made another step forward. Bastian now had his back against the door. Thomas reached for the handle.

Bastian moaned: "Wait, man! What are the bastards going to do with all that glorious swag? They'll waste it and squander it, sell it on the black market—so-called police—government—secret service—so-called patriots—so what? They're all nothing but a lot of blackguards!"

Thomas turned the handle. The door opened behind Bastian, who had grown very white in the face. He glared at Chantal, moaning: "Chantal, do something—help me, for God's sake—I—I just can't kill him—"

Thomas heard a peculiar noise and turned round. Chantal had dropped down on the edge of the bed. She was hammering with her little fists at the gold bars, the crucifix and the coins.

Her voice sounded shrill and broken. "Let him go, let the fool go . . ." Tears were raining down the tiger's cheeks. She was sobbing wildly. She looked up at Thomas. "Go on, call Siméon . . . he can have everything . . . oh, you beast, I wish I had never met you . . . and yet I did love it all so . . ."

"Chantal!"

". . . I wanted to go away with you—far away, to Switzerland. I couldn't think of anything but you . . . and now . . ."

"Chantal, my dearest—"

"Don't call me that, you wretched creature!" she screamed, falling forward in a faint. Her forehead struck the heap of coins, making an unpleasant rattle. She lay there weeping incessantly, as though she would never stop.

[7]

Just then the handsome young constable Louis Dupont was saying: "Strip, please." He was standing in the reception room of the police prison in the Marseilles Prefecture. Two prisoners had just been brought in to him. One was the rosy-faced, well-groomed and well-scented Jacques Bergier. The other, the younger, was the haggard Paul de Lesseps.

"What's that you say?" de Lesseps demanded truculently. His cold shark's eyes narrowed to slits, his lips to two bloodless lines.

"You must undress," said Dupont. "I want to see anything you may have concealed in your clothing or on your persons."

Bergier giggled. "What on earth do you think we may have on our persons then, my young friend?" He stepped forward and opened his waistcoat. "Come along, search me for weapons." He took off his tie and undid his shirt buttons. Dupont helped him off with his jacket.

Bergier shrieked. "Oh, don't, please, dear boy! I'm so frightfully ticklish!"

"Let's end it now," said Paul de Lesseps.

"Eh?" Dupont turned around.

"I've had enough of this. Call up the prison governor and ask him to come here at once. This instant."

"Don't take that tone to me, you . . ."

The voice of Paul de Lesseps sank to something very like a whisper. "Hold your tongue. Can you read? Look at this." He showed the young constable a pass. It was printed in both German and French and stated that M. Paul de Lesseps was employed on behalf of the German Public Security Head Office.

"Oh, that reminds me," said Bergier, extracting from his hip pocket, with fastidious gestures, a mauve wallet which smelled of Russian leather. He drew from it a pass like that of his friend. Both documents had been issued by a certain Walter Eicher, *Sturmbannführer*, Security Service, Paris.

De Lesseps added disdainfully: "The Sturmbannführer is to be informed of our arrest immediately. If you don't instantly take that step you'll have to put up with the consequences."

"I—I'll speak to my superior officer," Louis Dupont stammered. After he had seen this couple's credentials he disliked them more than ever. Marseilles was in unoccupied France. But all the same . . . Security Service . . . Gestapo . . . Dupont didn't want any trouble. He picked up the telephone at his elbow.

[8]

. . . 7 dec 1940—1739 hours—trunks—marseilles prefecture to CID paris—today 1530 hours st. charles station arrested (1) paul de lesseps (2) jacques bergier—charged gold and currency smuggling—(1) has german sd pass no. 456832 series red (2) german sd pass no. 11165 series blue—both issued by sd sturmbannfuhrer walter eicher—request immediate confirmation whether prisoners actually employed by sd—message ends—

[9]

"De Lesseps? Bergier?" Sturmbannführer Walter Eicher leaned back in his office chair, going red in the face. He bellowed wrathfully into the mouthpiece of the instrument he was holding to his ear. "Sure, I know them all right. Sure, they're working for us. Tell Marseilles to keep them both in custody. We're coming to fetch them."

The French official at the other end of the wire thanked his correspondent politely for the information.

"Don't mention it! *Heil Hitler!*" Eicher banger the receiver down into its rest and yelled: "Winter!"

His adjutant dashed in from the next room. The macabre activities of these gentlemen were proceeding on the fourth floor of a sumptuous villa in the Avenue Foch, Paris. The man called Winter rasped: "Sturmbannführer?"

"De Lesseps and old Aunty Bergier have been picked up in Marseilles," snapped the man called Eicher.

"Good God! How did that happen?"

"I don't know yet. It's enough to drive one crazy. Apparently we can only get idiots to work for us. Imagine what Canaris would say if he came to hear of it! Just the sort of thing he'd enjoy! Security Service buying up unoccupied France—"

The Security Service office and Canaris's Intelligence Department hated each other like cat and dog, one as bad-tempered as the other. The fears of Sturmbannführer Eicher were well founded. He growled: "Have the black Mercedes ready, Winter. We're driving down to Marseilles."

"Today?"

"Within the hour, man. So that we can be there first thing in the morning. We'll have to get those two idiots out before they start jabbering!"

"Very good, Sturmbannführer!" bawled Winter. He slammed the door as he went out. Nothing but trouble. Bloody awful job this was. He'd have to put off dear little Zuzu once again. Twelve hours on the road with that ogre. Not a wink of sleep. For crying out loud!

Twenty-four hours later Chantal Tessier was presiding at a business meeting of her gang in the back room of the Brûleur de Loup café in Marseilles. The meeting, to put it mildly, was a bit noisy.

The French black marketeers, the Spanish passport forgers, the Corsican prostitutes and the killers from Morocco, all busy with their various trades in the front room, often glanced with disapproval at the door at its far end, with the card inscribed CLUB dangling from the handle.

Pretty riotous sort of club that was! At last the door in question opened and the occupants of the café, whose sentences, if the police could ever catch the lot of them, would amount at a modest estimate to about five hundred years' penal servitude, saw Bastian Fabre, who was well known to them all, go to a telephone booth near the counter. He looked agitated.

Bastian dialed the number of Chez Papa. Olive, the owner, answered. Bastian wiped the sweat from his brow, pulled nervously at his black cigar and said hurriedly: "Bastian here. Is the man who came to see me yesterday afternoon still there?" He had asked Thomas to wait in the restaurant until the result of the meeting was known.

Olive's voice sounded muffled. "He's here, yes. Playing poker at my regular customers' table and wining all the time."

"Ask him to speak to me, will you, please?" Bastian took a long pull at his cigar and opened the door of the booth to let out the smoke. That damned Pierre, he was thinking. The man simply didn't deserve to have so much trouble taken over him.

Twenty-four hours ago the fellow had called up those two secret service characters and they had come and fetched all that splendid swag away. Or rather, not quite all, thank God. While Thomas was on the telephone Bastian and Chantal had quickly hidden a few jewels and quite a tidy sum in gold coins. But that wasn't much compared with the millions they had lost. Didn't bear thinking about . . .

"Hallo, Bastian! Well, old lad, how's tricks?"

Bastian noted the carefree accent of that slippery rogue with grim vexation. He said: "Pierre, I am your friend, in spite of everything. So I'm going to give you some good advice, which is: Hop it. This instant. There isn't a minute to lose."

"Well, well! And why is that?"

"The meeting's gone all haywire. Chantal's resigned!"

"Good Lord—"

"She burst out crying—"

"Bastian, if you only knew how painful all this is for me—"

"Don't interrupt me, you bastard. She said that she loves and understands you . . . then quite a lot of the mob got all sentimental—"

"Ah, *l'amour! Vive la France!*"

". . . but not all. Lame François and his pals stuck out. You know him. We call him Hoofy—"

Thomas didn't know him. But he had heard of him. Hoofy was the oldest member of the gang. His nickname was derived in about equal parts from his lameness, his tendency to violence and his methods of amorous conquest.

". . . he's in favor of killing you . . ."

"Charming of him . . ."

". . . he's nothing against you personally, he says, but he considers your influence over Chantal disastrous. You're softening her, he says . . ."

"Well, well!"

". . . you're the ruin of the mob, he says, and in order to protect Chantal you'll have to be done in . . . Pierre, I'm telling you, shove off, make yourself scarce!"

"On the contrary."

"What?"

"Now listen to me carefully, Bastian," said Thomas Lieven. His friend listened. He began by shaking his head. For some time he remained doubtful. Finally he agreed. He growled: "All right, if you think you can bring it off. In an hour, then. But you take full responsibility, mind."

He hung up and went back into the smoke-filled back room. The lame François, nicknamed Hoofy, was in the middle of a passionate speech advocating the dispatch to a better world of Jean Leblanc, Pierre Hunebelle or whatever he liked to call himself.

". . . in the interests of us all," he was just saying, stabbing the table, as he spoke, with the point of an uncommonly thin and sharp jackknife. Then he let fly at Bastian. "Where have you been?"

"I've been on the phone to Pierre," retorted Bastian calmly. "He's invited us all to a meal. In two hours' time, at my place. He says we can then talk everything over at our leisure."

Chantal uttered a faint shriek. Everyone began talking at once. "Shut up!" yelled the lame François. Silence fell.

"Bloke's got guts, I must say," François commented with a certain respect. Then he grinned spitefully. "Okay, boys. Let's take him at his word."

[10]

"Welcome, gentlemen," said Thomas Lieven. He kissed the hand of their white-faced boss, whose nerves were strained to breaking point.

The fifteen ruffians crowded into Bastian's apartment. Some were grinning. Others looked grim and menacing. They stared at the festively appointed board, Bastian's big table for his miniature railway. Thomas had got it ready with Olive's help. He had removed the mountains, valleys, bridges, rivers and stations. But a single pair of rails ran along the white tablecloth, from one end to the other, among the glasses, plates and cutlery.

"Come along then," exclaimed Thomas, rubbing his hands. "May I ask you all to sit down? Chantal at the head of the table. I shall have to be at the other end, for certain reasons. Please, gentlemen, make yourselves at home, and put off your plans for my assassination for the time being."

The men sat down, whispering and muttering to one another and still very suspicious of their surroundings. In front of Chantal's place stood a bowl of red hothouse roses. Thomas had thought of everything.

MENU

Cheese Soup
Rabbit Stew with Noodles
Surprise Pie with Mushroom Sauce

8 DECEMBER 1940

A strange meal which saved Thomas's life.

Cheese Soup

A large quantity of grated Parmesan cheese is soaked in milk and whisked. The mixture is then carefully poured into boiling beef stock. The soup is removed from the flame and yolks of egg are stirred in.

Rabbit Stew with Noodles

A large young skinned rabbit is cut into medium-sized portions. In a casserole three quarters of a cup of diced fat bacon is fried. Portions of rabbit are added and browned on all sides. Last of all add the liver, with a few small shallots, chopped onions and a crushed clove of garlic. When all is brown some flour is sprinkled over the rabbit and two cups of boiling water or stock are added. This is then flavored with salt, pepper, mixed spices and some lemon peel. Also half a bottle of red wine. The stew is then simmered until the rabbit is soft. The other half of the red wine is added and the stew is left to simmer a little longer. It is served with plain boiled noodles to which, after draining, a little butter has been added.

Surprise Pie with Mushroom Sauce

Three fillets of veal, pork and beef respectively, their size depending on the number of persons present, and their length not exceeding that of half the diameter of a large cake tin, are skinned and fried lightly on all sides, then salted and peppered. The bottom and sides of the cake tin are lined with flaky pastry and the cooled fillets are arranged in such a way that the narrow ends point to the center. The fillets should be so distributed that each third of the bottom of the tin is covered by a different fillet. A mark should be made in the top of the pastry where one fillet starts and the other finishes and transferred to the top edges of the tin. A lid of pastry is then placed on the top of the tin and the three marks transferred to the lid. From the marks pastry-leaf decoration is carried to the center, thus trisecting the pastry lid. Pastry models of a pig, an ox and a calf are placed on the relevant sections. The pastry is the then brushed with egg yolk and baked at medium heat until golden.

A mushroom sauce is served with the pie.

A few finely chopped shallots are braised lightly in butter and plenty of thinly sliced mushrooms are added. A little flour is sprinkled over, well stirred in and stock is added. Care has to be taken no to darken the sauce. It is flavored with salt, pepper, lemon juice and an egg yolk. A little white wine may be added if desired.

Olive and two of his waiters served the first course of cheese soup. Thomas had prepared it in the Chez Papa kitchen. The restaurant had also supplied the crockery and cutlery.

"Good appetite!" cried Thomas heartily. He sat at the end of the table, with certain mysterious objects beside him. No one could guess what they were as they were covered with napkins. The ends of the railway tracks were also hidden under these little heaps of cloth.

The men sampled the soup in silence. Nevertheless, as Frenchmen, they knew how to appreciate good food.

Chantal never took her eyes off Thomas. An entire gamut of feeling was reflected in them. Hoofy ate with bent head, mute and sullen.

Then came the rabbit stew. Next, Olive and his waiters trundled in, with considerable effort, a dish which looked like a colossal pie. It was placed on a side table next to Thomas Lieven.

Thomas seized a prodigious knife. While he sharpened it, be observed: "Gentlemen! I now venture to set before you a novelty, my own invention, so to speak. I know there are considerable differences of temperament among you. Many of you are good-natured and ready to forgive me. But others have hot tempers and would like to make an end of me." He raised his hand. "That's understandable. There's no accounting for tastes. But for that very reason I should now like to serve a dish which will appeal to all tastes." He pointed to the pie. "And there it is—the Surprise Pie!"

He turned to Chantal. "My dear, would you prefer beef, pork or veal?"

"Ve . . . ve . . . veal," Chantal croaked. Then she cleared her throat violently and almost shouted: "Veal!"

"Just coming!" Thomas gave the pie a keen look, turned it round a little and cut out of a certain third of it a fine slice of veal with its accompanying pastry and laid it on a plate.

Then he removed the napkins and revealed the objects hidden beneath them. Bastian's model locomotive, its tender and a big goods truck, flanked by an electrical switchboard, came into view.

Thomas placed the plate of veal on the truck and switched on the current. With a whirring sound the engine proceeded to pull its tender and the truck carrying the plate along the whole length of the table, past the fifteen astonished gangsters. The train stopped in front of Chantal. She took the plate from the truck. Some of the men uttered surprised laughs. One clapped.

Thomas reversed the engine, with its empty truck. Then he inquired calmly: "What would the gentleman on Chantal's left like to have?"

A savage-looking fellow with a patch over one eye shouted back, with a ferocious grin: "Pig!"

"Pig, by all means," replied Thomas. He again glanced keenly at the enormous pie, turned it, cut a slice of pork out of a second third and dispatched it in the same way as before.

The men began to be amused. They exchanged comments on Thomas's idea. Then one called out: "Beef for me!"

"With pleasure," rejoined Thomas, serving him. Several of the men now clapped.

Thomas glanced at Chantal, closing one eye. She couldn't help smiling in return. The noise round the table increased, growing more and more exuberant. Orders poured in pell-mell. The little train ran backward and forward along the table.

At last only François, alias Hoofy, was left with an empty plate. Thomas turned to him. "And you, monsieur?" he demanded, resharpening his great knife.

François gave him a long, brooding stare. Then he stood up slowly, fumbling in his jacket pocket. Chantal screamed. Bastian surreptitiously drew his revolver. He had perceived that Hoofy now had that dreaded knife of his in his hand. The blade flashed out. Hoofy took a single, noiseless, limping step toward Thomas. Then another and another, till he stood quite close to him. The room grew deathly still. For ten seconds François looked Thomas steadily in the eye, while the latter stood quietly before him. Then the cripple suddenly chuckled. "Take my knife," he said. "It's sharper than yours. And give me some pork, you damned rascal!"

[11]

On December 8, 1940, Sturmbannführer Eicher and his adjutant Winter—in civilian clothes—arrived at Marseilles, where they demanded the surrender of de Lesseps and Bergier, whom they immediately took back with them to Paris. Once there, the two buyers were subjected to a grueling investigation.

On December 10, 1940, the Paris Security Service office sent out a search warrant to all its branches.

On December 13, accordingly, in a room of the discreetly camouflaged Hôtel Lutetia, Paris, serving as Intelligence headquarters, Captain Brenner of Section III read the order issued by his German competitor. He read it once casually, then gave a start and read it again more carefully.

The wanted man was a certain Pierre Hunebelle, accused in the order, rather vaguely, of "betraying Security Service personnel to French authorities."

Captain Brenner read the description a third time. "Pierre Hunebelle, narrow face, dark eyes, close-cropped black hair, height five and a half feet, slim build, in possession of gold repeater watch with which he often plays. Special peculiarity: fond of cooking."

H'm.

Fond of cooking.

Captain Brenner rubbed his forehead. Wasn't there a ... yes, there certainly was ... a general who had been double-crossed by someone who was fond of cooking. That was about the time of the fall of Paris. There was a file on the subject.

File ... file ...

An hour later Captain Brenner had found what he was looking for. There wasn't much in the file. But the captain's memory had not played him false. There was the man's name. Thomas Lieven, alias Jean Leblanc. About five and one half feet tall, narrow face, dark eyes, dark hair. In possession of an old-fashioned gold repeater. Special peculiarity: passion for cooking.

The fever of the chase arose in Captain Brenner. He had private correspondents in the Security Service. He cultivated them for three days. Then he knew why Sturmbannführer Eicher was searching so grimly for Herr Hunebelle, alias Leblanc, alias Lieven. Brenner, with a grin, drew up a report to the most eminent of his superiors.

Admiral Wilhelm Canaris read Captain Brenner's report in his Berlin office on the Tirpitz Embankment with ever growing satisfaction. The joy which his subordinate in Paris had felt communicated itself to the admiral. What a game, eh? Security Service head office plundering unoccupied France! I'll rub Herr Himmler's nose in *that!*

And the Security people were played up by a certain Hunebelle, alias Leblanc, alias ...

The admiral grew serious. He read the last paragraph again. He read it a third time. Then he sent for his secretary. "Fräulein Sistig, my dear, would you please bring me the Thomas Lieven file?"

Fifteen minutes later he had it. A big black cross had been drawn on the cover.

On the top sheet he read:

Cologne, 4 December
1940

FROM: Cologne Intelligence.
TO: Head of Berlin Intelligence.
SECRET 135892/Vc/40/LV

On my return from Lisbon I beg respectfully to inform the Herr Admiral of the death of the double agent and traitor Thomas Lieven, alias Jean Leblanc ...

Canaris sat motionless for a long time. Then he lifted the telephone receiver. His voice sounded quiet but ominous. "Fräulein Sistig, be so good as to get me Cologne Intelligence, Major Fritz Loos . . ."

[12]

On the stormy evening of December 28, 1940, Thomas Lieven was listening to the 10:30 P.M. French broadcast from London. He listened to the London radio every evening. It was necessary for a man in his position to be well informed.

He was sitting in Chantal's bedroom. His beautiful mistress had already gone to bed. Her hair was piled high on her head and she wore no make-up. Thomas preferred her that way.

She was stroking his hand as he sat beside her. They were both listening to the broadcaster's announcements.

". . . resistance to the Nazis is on the increase in France. Yesterday afternoon a German troop train was blown up on the line between Nantes and Angers, near Varades. The engine and three coaches were entirely destroyed. At least twenty-five German soldiers were killed. Well over a hundred were wounded, some seriously."

Chantal's fingers continued to stroke Thomas Lieven's hand.

". . . by way of reprisal the Germans immediately shot thirty French hostages . . ."

Chantal's fingers ceased to move.

". . . yet the struggle still goes on, in fact it has only just begun. Merciless underground activity continues against the Germans day and night. We hear from reliable sources that substantial stores of gold, currency and other valuables recently fell into the hands of the Marseilles resistance group. These articles were the proceeds of robbery and plunder by the Nazis and will enable the struggle to be extended and broadened in scope. The action at Varades will be followed by others of a similar kind . . ."

Thomas had turned pale. He couldn't bear to listen any longer and switched off. Chantal lay on her back, motionless, looking at him. And suddenly he found that he could no longer bear that either.

With a groan he dropped his head in his hands. The words "twenty-five Germans, thirty Frenchmen, more than a hundred wounded, only a beginning, the struggle goes on, financed with substantial quantities of Nazi gold and Nazi currency, seized in Marseilles," re-echoed in his brain. Misery, blood and tears. Financed by whom? With whose help?

Thomas Lieven lifted his head. Chantal was still looking at him without moving. He said quietly: "You were right, you and Bastian. We ought to have kept that stuff. You two saw the truth instinctively. A betrayal of Siméon and the French secret service would have been by far the lesser evil."

"Not one of the jobs we did in my gang ever cost an innocent life," Chantal said in a low tone.

Thomas nodded. "I can see," he said, "that I shall have to change my way of life. My ideas are outmoded. My notions of honor and loyalty are false and dangerous. Chantal, do you remember what you once suggested to me in Lisbon?"

She sat up quickly. "Yes, that you should be my partner."

"I will be, Chantal, from today on. No more mercy or pity. I'm fed to the teeth. It's the swag I'm after now."

"Sweetie, I couldn't agree with you more!"

She flung her arms round his neck and kissed him passionately.

That kiss sealed a very remarkable partnership and collaboration which is still talked of in Marseilles, and with good reason. For between January 1941 and August 1942 southern France was afflicted with a positive earthquake, a regular flood, of criminal activities. It sounds almost fabulous, but they had one feature in common. No one felt any pity for the victims.

The first was the Marseilles jeweler Marius Pissoladière. If it hadn't been raining on January 14, 1941, in Marseilles, that gentleman might perhaps have been spared the tragic loss of over eight million francs. But unfortunately it poured from morning till night and fate took its inevitable course.

Marius Pissoladière's smart shop was situated in the Canneblère, the main street of Marseilles. M. Pissoladière was an enormously rich man, fifty years old, rather stout and always dressed in the height of fashion.

In former years Pissoladière had built up his fortune by dealings with the Riviera international set. But recently a new but equally international circle of customers had opened its ranks to him. He now dealt with refugees from all the countries invaded by Hitler. Pissoladière bought up these people's jewelry. They needed money for further emigration and to bribe officials, for entry permits and forged passports.

In order to pay the lowest possible prices to the refugees, the jeweler had recourse to an extremely simple system. He haggled with the sellers for days and weeks on end. At last the poor devils came to the point when they must have money or perish. Pissoladière would have been only too glad to see the war last another ten years.

But even as it was, he really couldn't complain. His business was doing splendidly. And no doubt it would have gone on doing so if it hadn't rained on January 14, 1941, in Marseilles.

On January 14, 1941, just before eleven o'clock in the morning, a gentleman aged about forty-five entered Marius Pissoladière's shop. The customer wore a Homburg hat, an expensive fur-lined overcoat, spats and thoroughly respectable trousers, striped black and gray. Naturally enough, too, he carried an umbrella.

Pissoladière considered the narrow, pale, aristocratic features of the visitor. Strikingly refined, they suggested exhaustion, wealth and ancient lineage, precisely those characteristics the jeweler preferred in his clients.

Pissoladière was alone in the shop. Rubbing his hands and bowing respectfully, he wished the visitor a good morning.

The elegant gentleman acknowledged Pissoladière's greeting with a weary inclination of the head and hung his umbrella, which had an amber handle, on the edge of the counter.

When he spoke, his accent sounded slightly provincial. Aristocrats, Pissoladière reflected, probably talk like that in order to prove their liberal views. That they are people just like you and me. Splendid! The gentleman announced: "I should like—h'm—to buy a little jewelry here. I was told at the Bristol that you had a good selection."

"The finest in Marseilles, monsieur. May I ask what you had in mind?"

"Well—er—a sort of—er—diamond bracelet or—h'm—something of that sort."

"We have such articles at all prices, monsieur. About what price would monsieur wish to pay?"

"Well—er—something between—h'm—two and—er—three million," replied the gentleman, yawning.

My word, thought Pissoladière. This is the day! He went to a big safe and spun the combination, remarking: "We have of course some very fine pieces at about that price."

The thick steel door swung back. Pissoladière chose nine diamond bracelets and laid them on a black velvet tray, which he placed on the counter for the customer's inspection.

The nine bracelets glittered and glowed in all the colors of the rainbow. The gentleman examined them for a long time in silence. Then he lifted one of them in his small, well-manicured hand. It was a particularly fine specimen, with costly flat bands and six two-carat stones.

"How much is—er—this one?"

"Three million francs, monsieur."

The bracelet had belonged to the wife of a Jewish banker from Paris. Pissoladière had acquired it, or rather extorted it by blackmail, for four hundred thousand francs.

"Too much," said the gentleman.

Pissoladière at once perceived that his client was an experienced purchaser of jewelry. Only amateurs agree without argument to any price first named by the seller. Some stubborn bargaining began, neither party yielding much ground.

Suddenly the door of the shop opened. Pissoladière looked up. A second gentleman had entered. He was not quite so well dressed as the first, but pretty nearly. Seemed a retiring sort. Clothes and demeanor quite decent. Herringbone tweed overcoat, gloves, spats, hat and umbrella.

Pissoladière was just going to ask this second visitor if he could wait a little, when the latter said: "I only want a new watch strap, please." So saying, he hung his umbrella as close as it would go to the umbrella of the gentleman in the fur-lined overcoat, who was apparently unknown to him.

At that moment Marius Pissoladière was already, so to speak, lost and done for.

[13]

The two gentlemen who met on the morning of January 14, 1941, in Pissoladière's jewelry shop as perfect strangers were in reality old friends. But during the last two weeks they had each undergone a metamorphosis both outwardly and inwardly.

Only a fortnight ago they had been in the habit of swearing like cabmen, spitting on the floor, wearing bright yellow shoes and putting far too much padding in the shoulders of their jackets. Their fingernails had always been black and their hair always too long. They would have been clearly recognizable as active members of that mysterious, antisocial caste usually called by respectable citizens, with a shudder, the "underworld."

Who could possibly be entitled to the credit of having turned two hardened rascals, in such a short time and by so evidently strenuous a course of intensive training, into two new-born gentlemen?

The intelligent reader will have already guessed. The credit was due to none other than Pierre Hunebelle, alias Jean Leblanc, alias Thomas Lieven.

In order to prepare the two rogues mentally, as a start, for the proposed fishing expedition to Pissoladière's, Thomas Lieven had invited them, two weeks ago, to a meal.

It took place in a back room of the famous or infamous black market restaurant known as Chez Papa, in the rue de Paradis, near the Stock Exchange. Thomas Lieven and his mistress were the only others present. The two ruffians selected appeared in their original persons and under their right names, Fred Meyer and Paul de la Rue.

They had belonged to Chantal's mob for years but worked at a distance, in Toulouse. The organization had several branches. It had been built up on a sound basis.

Paul de la Rue, descended from a Huguenot family, was tall and slim, by profession an expert picture faker. He spoke with a southern accent. In spite of his disreputable appearance there was something aristocratic about his narrow cranium.

Fred Meyer had learned the safe-cracker's trade. But he also dabbled in the kindred spheres of burglary, hotel thieving and smuggling. He, too, spoke in the accents of southern France.

These two arrived for the meal rubbing their hands and grinning. The Huguenot black sheep blurted out: "What about another little snifter afore we stoke up, hey?"

"Before we eat," rejoined Thomas Lieven icily, "you gentlemen will not be taking another little snifter but going downstairs to the barber, where you will be shaved, have your hair cut and wash your necks and hands. You can't sit down to table in your present state."

"To hell with that," growled Fred, who, like his companion, was not yet well acquainted with Pierre Hunebelle. "We don't take orders from you. Chantal's the boss here."

Chantal said primly: "Do what he says. Go to the barber. You look like a couple of pigs." The two men departed, muttering oaths.

Alone with Thomas, Chantal proved that, although she had changed her characteristic style of dressing in some respects for his sake, she hadn't changed her true character. She hissed at him like a wildcat: "I didn't want to make you look like a fool. I'd lost all my authority over the boys if they saw me quarreling with you. But you'd better realize that it's still my mob and not yours!"

"I'm sorry, but if that's your attitude we'd better drop the idea altogether."

"What do you mean by that?"

"I'm not your employee. We're either equal partners or we're not partners at all."

She stared at him with half-closed eyes. She murmured something unintelligible. Then she punched his shoulder, mumbling half in vexation and half with delight: "All right then, blast you!" She added immediately: "But don't you go imagining things, see? Thinking I've fallen for you or something like that. That would only make me laugh. All I need is another man I can trust and that's the lot. Get me?"

"Sure," said Thomas. He blinked facetiously at her. They drank an old brandy each in token of reconciliation.

After three quarters of an hour Paul and Fred returned. They now looked much more civilized. Over the first course Chantal explained: "Get this, boys. Anyone who says anything against Pierre will have me to deal with, d'you hear?"

"Hell, Chantal, this is the first time you ever—"

"Cut that out! Pierre's my partner."

"Poor kid, you've got it badly, haven't you?" commented the safe-cracker. Next movement he felt a stunning box on the ear. Chantal hissed at him: " Mind your own damn business!"

"Can't we even talk to you now?" Fred protested.

"Not if you can't keep a civil tongue in your head." Chantal, obstinate as she was, had already learned something from Thomas. "You'd do better to try and eat decently, you oaf. Manners, man! Look at the bastard cutting up spaghetti with a knife!"

"Well, this grub keeps slipping off the fork!"

"Allow me to give you a tip," Thomas said amiably. "If you find you can't twist spaghetti round a fork, then just stick your fork into a little of it, take a spoon in your left hand and press the prongs of the fork into the hollow of the spoon. Like this." He demonstrated. "Now turn the fork. See how easy it is?"

Fred imitated the trick. It worked.

"Gentlemen," said Thomas. "It will really be necessary for us to go exhaustively into this question of good manners. They are the alpha and omega of any decent swindle. Did you ever see a banker who had bad manners?" My God, thought

Thomas, I'd better not mention bankers. My bank, my club, my beautiful home, gone, all gone with the wind . . .

MENU

Spaghetti Bolognese
Cutlets Robert with Fried Potatoes
Sacher Torte

3 JANUARY 1941

A lesson in gastronomy by Thomas Lieven in preparation for a jewel robbery.

Spaghetti Bolognese

Take one pound of spaghetti and one half pound of meat, preferably a mixture of beef, pork and veal. Cut the meat into cubes. Take the same quantity of onions, cut into fine rings, and braise in a little oil or butter. Add the meat, a crushed clove of garlic and some herbs. Fry the mixture well. Add seeded tomatoes or tomato purée. Let the whole simmer on a very low flame until a sauce is formed. The spaghetti should be boiled, but not too soft, in salt water, then rinsed in cold water and, when dry, mixed with the well-seasoned sauce. Grated Parmesan cheese is served with this dish.

Cutlets Robert

Take medium thick pork chops, cut in the rind and beat lightly. Place, without adding any fat, in a thick, previously well-heated frying pan. Brown the chops for three minutes on each side, salt and pepper them, add a large piece of butter to the pan and leave them to fry for a further minute on each side. Remove cutlets and place them on a warm dish. Meanwhile mix equal quantities of red wine and sour cream with a tablespoonful of mustard. Pour this into the pan and cook fast till boiling. Then pour this sauce over the cutlets and serve immediately with fried potatoes.

Fried Potatoes

Peeled potatoes are cut into finger-thick chips, washed and

well dried in a cloth. Then fry small quantities in a large pan with hot lard or oil. As soon as they begin to color remove them and place them on a sieve, where they are left to drain and cool. Shortly before serving, the fat must be reheated and the chips once more fried until they are golden-yellow. They are then placed on blotting paper to dry off and sprinkled with salt. They are then ready for serving.

Sacher Torte

Take half a cup of butter, stir until foamy. Add three quarters of a cup of sugar, one and a half cups of sieved flour, five yolks, a little vanilla and three quarters of a cup (6 ounces) of melted chocolate.

Mix all well, add the beaten whites of the five eggs, place mixture in a cake tin and bake in medium heat for half an hour. For icing use half a cup of melted chocolate, one and a quarter cups of confectioners' sugar and two tablespoonfuls of hot water. Mix well over heat. Spread apricot jam on the cake and cover it with the icing, replacing it in the oven for one or two minutes to harden. The cake must be well cooled before serving.

"Yes, good manners are the thing now," said Chantal imperiously. "The wind's blowing from quite another quarter these days, d'you hear? My partner and I have talked it all over. We're going to nobble the boodle . . . I mean, our operations will not now be directed, against just anybody . . ."

"Against whom, then?"

"Against any swine who deserve it. Nazis, collaborators, secret agents, anyone like that. And for a start we're going after that skunk Pissoladière . . ." She stopped speaking as Olive, the stout proprietor of Chez Papa, personally brought in the main course.

Olive, who admired Thomas for his culinary art, gave him a broad smile. "I dipped the fried potatoes in the oil twice, of course, M. Pierre!"

"I never thought you would do otherwise," said Thomas cordially. He was thinking, Good heavens, how fond I'm getting of this underworld. How's it all going to end, if it begins like this?

He distributed the cutlets, but immediately raised his eyebrows. "M. de la Rue, please don't use your pastry fork."

"How the hell am I to find my way about all this hardware?"

"As to hardware, gentlemen," said Thomas, "you must always work from outside to in. The cutlery you need for the last course is put nearest your plate."

"I'd like to see the coal cellar in which you were brought up," said Chantal scornfully. She turned, in a most ladylike manner, to Thomas. "Please go on, dear."

"Gentlemen, in pursuance of our altered regulations we have, as has just been announced, got our peepers on, I mean we have in view, the jeweler already mentioned, who's quite a nasty bit of work—M. Meyer, it just isn't done to pick up your cutlet in your hands and gnaw the bones—now where was I?"

"Pissoladière," Chantal prompted him. She was now watching Thomas most affectionately. Sometimes she loved, sometimes she hated him. Her feelings changed so abruptly that she hardly knew herself any more. But she did know for certain that she wouldn't want to live without that wretch, that beast . . .

"Pissoladière, yes, that's right." Thomas described the jeweler's base character. Then he continued: "I hate violence. I detest bloodshed. Breaking in through the ceiling, attacks with leveled revolvers and so on are therefore not to be considered for a moment. Believe me, gentlemen, modern times require modern methods. Only the imaginative will survive. There's simply too much competition in the old fields. M. de la Rue, one doesn't handle fried potatoes. One uses a fork."

Fred Meyer demanded: "How are we going to get the loot out of Pissoladière then?"

"With two umbrellas."

Olive brought in the last course.

"I should like you gentlemen to get into the habit at once," said Thomas, "of eating pastry with your small forks, not with your spoons."

Chantal said: "You two will have to put in some real hard studying in the next few days. No boozing and loafing and womanizing, do you hear?"

"But, damn, it, Chantal, now we've managed to get to Marseilles at last—"

"Business before pleasure, my friends," said Thomas. "You'll have to learn how gentlemen dress, walk, stand and speak. And if possible drop your accents. You'll have to learn too how to make articles disappear unobtrusively."

"It won't be as easy as lapping up honey, I can tell you that," Chantal declared. "You'll be at the disposal of my partner from morning till night."

"But not during the night itself," said Thomas. He kissed her hand. She instantly turned crimson, lost her temper and aimed a blow at him. "Don't go on like that in front of other people, man! I can't bear that damned hand-kissing!" The bitch in Chantal had flared up again.

[14]

Things really happened very fast after that.

The jeweler produced a number of watch straps for Fred Meyer at the lower end of the counter. At the top end Paul de la Rue was bending over the nine sparkling diamond bracelets. Beside him hung the two umbrellas.

His next movement had been practiced for hours under the supervision of Thomas Lieven. He picked up, without a sound the bracelet priced at three million francs, leaned forward and dropped it, just as noiselessly, into the slightly open umbrella of his friend Meyer. Its ribs had of course been previously enveloped in cotton wool. Then he took two more diamond bracelets and disposed of them in the same way.

He then walked a considerable distance away from the umbrellas, right to the end of the shop, where some gold bangles were on view. Paul de la Rue examined them with admiration, while he stroked his recently groomed hair with his right hand.

On this already agreed signal Fred Meyer decided quite suddenly to purchase a watch strap priced at 240 francs. He paid for it with a five-thousand-franc note.

Pissoladière stepped to the cash register. He booked the transaction, obtained Meyer's change and called across to Paul de la Rue: "I'm free to attend to you now, monsieur."

The jeweler handed the watch-strap purchaser his change. The latter picked up his umbrella and left the shop. If Pissoladière had gone to the door with him he would have noticed that this customer, though it was raining hard, did not open his umbrella. Not just then at any rate . . .

The jeweler hurried back to wait on his aristocratic client. "And now, monsieur," he began. But he did not finish the sentence. He had seen at a glance that three of the most valuable bracelets were missing.

Pissoladière at first believed that his customer had abstracted them as a joke. He knew that degenerate aristocrats occasionally went in for weird hoaxes of this sort. He smiled wryly at Paul de la Rue and said with a chuckle: "You gave me quite a shock then, monsieur!"

Thomas Lieven's excellent training enabled Paul to raise his eyebrows quite inimitably as he answered: "Eh, what's that? You don't feel well?"

"I didn't say so, monsieur. And I think this joke has gone far enough. Please put those three bracelets back on the tray."

"Eh? Not drunk, are you? Are you implying that I've got those three . . . ah, yes, I see. What on earth's happened to those most remarkable . . ."

Pissoladière turned purple. He exclaimed shrilly: "Now then, sir! If you don't instantly put those bracelets back here on the counter, I shall have to call the police!"

Thereupon Paul de la Rue bungled his part slightly. He began to laugh.

His laughter deprived the jeweler of the last traces of his self-control. He pressed the button under the counter which set off the burglar alarm. Heavy iron shutters came rattling down in front of the showcases, the street door and the back exit.

A big pistol suddenly appeared in Marius Pissoladière's hand. He screeched: "Hands up! Don't move . . . keep still!"

Paul de la Rue, obediently raising his hands, drawled negligently: "You poor silly fool! You're going to regret this."

The flying squad arrived shortly afterward.

Paul de la Rue, with the utmost coolness, handed them a French passport made out in the name of René, Vicomte de Toussant, of the Bois de Boulogne, Paris. It was a flawlessly forged document, the work of the best experts in the Old Quarter. All the same, the detectives stripped Paul de la Rue to the skin, went through all his pockets and undid the lining of his overcoat.

All in vain. Nothing came to light. Not a single diamond, not a single fragment of the three missing bracelets.

The police asked the Vicomte to prove that he had been in a position to pay out three million francs.

The accused man smilingly requested them to ring up the manager of the Hôtel Bristol. The manager declared that the Vicomte had deposited a sum of six million francs in the hotel safe. This was a master stroke. Paul de la Rue had of course really put up at the Bristol and deposited six millions of the gang's capital.

The detectives became noticeably more polite.

But they put through a trunk call to the Paris police, who confirmed that a certain René, Vicomte de Toussant, in fact resided in the Bois de Boulogne, that he was very wealthy, hand in glove with the Nazis and the Vichy Government, and for the time being absent from Paris, probably in southern France. Thereupon the flying squad released the accused man with many apologies.

Marius Pissoladière, in a state of utter collapse and white to the lips, also stammered out his profound regrets.

The unobtrusive watch-strap purchaser, of whom Pissoladière could only give a very vague description, could not be traced.

The whole transaction had been foreseen by Thomas Lieven when he picked out Paul de la Rue on account of his appearance and had a passport forged in the name of the Vicomte. The Perpignan *Messenger* of January 2, 1941, had also been useful. For under the heading. "Rural Notes" Thomas had seen a photograph of the Nazi-loving aristocrat with the caption: "René Vicomte de Toussant, the Paris industrialist, has arrived to take the waters at the picturesque village of Font Romeu at the foot of the Pyrenees."

The umbrella trick could not of course be repeated in Marseilles. That sort of thing gets talked about sooner or later. But it could be played in Bordeaux, Toulouse, Montpellier, Avignon and Béziers. During the next few weeks jewelers and dealers in antiques in those towns had melancholy and financially disastrous experiences with gentlemen carrying umbrellas. But oddly enough the victims were invariably persons of the same kind of reprehensible and stingy mentality as Marius Pissoladière.

As already noted, this was the feature that all these proceedings had in common. No one could feel sorry for those who suffered from them. On the contrary rumors soon began to go round southern France that a sort of super Robin Hood was operating in secret in that part of the world.

Through a certain chain of events with which Thomas Lieven was not altogether unconcerned the police were set off on a false scent. They had come to the conclusion that those responsible for the impudent jewel robberies were to be found in the ranks of "Baldy's" gang.

One of the oldest of the Marseilles criminal establishments

was controlled by a certain Dantes Villeforte, a Corsican who for obvious reasons was known as Baldy.

When the transport of refugees to Portugal was organized Villeforte and his mob were in on the racket. But Chantal's activities in this direction suddenly started on a colossal scale. Her operations, moreover, defied all the recognized regulations. She acted in accordance with a motto which had quite wrongly fallen into disuse: low prices, big turnover, good profit. Sometimes her slogan was even: escape now, pay later.

It was intelligible that Baldy's temper did not improve when he found that Chantal was completely ruining his racket. For the vast majority of potential clients were now applying to her, while he could book hardly anyone.

One day someone told him that all these innovations were due to the farsightedness and intelligence of Chantal's lover, in whom she had the fullest confidence. He was alleged to be the brain of her gang and a first-rate brain too, apparently.

Baldy resolved to take a certain amount of interest in this fellow.

[15]

In July 1942 he called a plenary session of his gang at No. 4 in the rue Mazenod, where he lived.

"I've had enough now, boys," he said. "That gang of Chantal's sticks in my throat. She was always a bit of a pest when she was alone. She played us up and did us down over and over again. But now, with that blasted Pierre or whatever his name is behind her, it's past a joke."

Murmurs of approval greeted this exordium.

"What I say is, we could come to terms easily enough with Chantal. She's not too bad to deal with. Now, I hear that she's fallen for this character Pierre. How could we best give her a hell of a big jolt?"

"We could rub her sweetie out," said one of the men.

"You crazy?" Villeforte shouted at him. "Rubbing out's all some of you prize idiots can think of. What's the good of our being in with the Gestapo if we don't take advantage of it? I've found out that the beggar calls himself Hunebelle among other things. And the Gestapo is looking for someone called Hunebelle. We can all line our pockets if we . . . don't have to say any more, do I?"

He didn't have to say any more.

In the evening of September 17, 1942, a thunderstorm burst

over Marseilles. Chantal and Thomas had meant to go to the movies. But in view of the weather they decided to stay at home.

They drank calvados and played gramophone records. Chantal was in a most unusually soft, sentimental and submissive mood.

"It's amazing how you've changed me," she whispered. "I can hardly recognize myself sometimes."

"Chantal," said Thomas. "We'll have to get out of here. I've had bad news. Marseilles is no longer safe from the Germans."

"Let's go to Switzerland, then," she suggested. "We've got enough money over there to live on. We'll have a wonderful time."

"Yes, my sweet," said he, giving her a kiss.

She murmured with tears in her eyes: "Oh, darling, I've never been so happy as now. It can't last forever, nothing does. But just for a while, just for a little while . . ."

Later on she suddenly felt she would like some grapes.

"Well, the shops are closed now," Thomas said. "But I may be able to get some at the station."

He stood up and put on his overcoat. "Oh, but it's crazy to go out in this weather," she protested.

"Not at all. You've got to have your grapes. Just because you love grapes and just because I love you."

Tears came into her eyes again. She struck herself on the knee with her little fist and swore. "Damn this bloody nonsense, it's too silly! Here I am crying because I love you so . . ."

"I'll be back in a few minutes," said Thomas, hurrying out of the room. He was wrong there.

For twenty minutes after he had left the house in the rue Chevalier Rose to buy grapes Thomas Lieven, alias Jean Leblanc, alias Pierre Hunebelle, found himself in the hands of the Gestapo.

[16]

It's funny, thought Thomas, how used I have got to living with Chantal, I can't imagine living without her now. Her crazy moods, her tigerish behavior, like that of a prowling man-eater, positively enthrall me. So do her pluck and her intuitions. And she doesn't tell lies. Or at least hardly ever . . .

Thomas Lieven crossed the deserted Place Jules Guesde,

with its asphalt pavement shining under the rain, and turned into the narrow rue Bernard du Bois. The small, old-fashioned Serviette Cinema, which he often visited with Chantal, was situated in that street.

A black Peugeot was parked in front of the cinema. But Thomas did not notice it. He walked on, followed by two shadowy figures. As they passed the black Peugeot one of them tapped briefly on its nearside window. Immediately the car's headlights flashed on, though only for an instant. Then they were extinguished again. At the further end of the narrow, badly lit street two other shadowy figures got into motion.

Thomas did not notice them. He saw neither the men who were coming toward him nor those who were following him. He was thinking, I must have a quiet talk with Chantal soon. I've heard from reliable sources that American troops will be landing in North Africa this year. The French underground movement is giving the Nazis more and more trouble. It's based in southern France. The Germans will undoubtedly soon occupy the rest of the country. So Chantal and I ought to be off to Switzerland as soon as possible. In Switzerland there are no Nazis, no war. We can live in peace there . . .

The two shadows ahead of him drew nearer. So did the two behind him. The engine of the black Peugeot started. The car moved forward at a walking pace, without lights. And still Thomas Lieven did not notice anything.

Poor Thomas! He was intelligent, fair-minded, good-natured, charming and obliging. But he was no Leatherstocking, Napoleon or male Mata Hari, no sort of a superman. He was not the kind of hero one reads of, who is never frightened and always victorious, a heroic hero of heroes. He was only a man perpetually on the run from pillar to post, never left alone and always forced to try to make the best of a bad job, as we all must.

Consequently, he did not perceive the danger that was threatening him. He was not in the least perturbed when two men suddenly confronted him. They wore raincoats and were obviously French.

One of them said: "Good evening, monsieur. Would you be good enough to tell us the time?"

"With pleasure," answered Thomas. With one hand he was holding up his umbrella. With the other he extracted his beloved repeater from his waistcoat pocket. He touched the spring of the lid. As he did so the two shadowy figures which had been following him reached the group.

"It is now precisely eight . . ." Thomas began. Then a stunning blow descended on the nape of his neck.

His umbrella went flying. His repeater—luckily it was attached to a chain—dropped from his hand. He fell to his knees with a groan. He was just opening his mouth to call for help when a hand holding a huge wad of cotton wool struck his face. Nausea surged in his throat at the sickly sweet stench in his nostrils. It was only too familiar. He had had a similar experience in Lisbon. Then things had turned out all right in the end. But now, he thought, in his last flash of consciousness, now it wasn't going to turn out that way.

After he had fainted his abductors encountered only technical difficulties in stowing him away in the Peugeot. It was a mere furniture mover's problem.

CHAPTER 3

[1]

The Fresnes Central Prison, about a dozen miles outside Paris, was a collection of shabby buildings of medieval aspect, surrounded by high walls. There were three principal sections, each with a number of subsidiary wings. Massive and isolated, the prison stood in a desolate plain dotted with stunted trees, a waste of abandoned pasture and neglected plowland.

Section 1 was occupied by German prisoners, either political offenders or deserters. No. 2 housed French and German members of resistance groups. French prisoners only were detained in the No. 3 section.

The governor was a German reserve captain. The staff were a mixed lot, consisting of both French and German warders, the latter without exception elderly non-commissioned officers from Bavaria, Saxony or Thuringia.

In Wing C of Section 1 there were only German warders. The wing was under the exclusive control of the German Security Service in charge of Paris. In the cells for prisoners in solitary confinement the electric light burned day and night. Their occupants were never allowed exercise in the courtyard. The Gestapo had discovered a simple way of keeping their charges beyond the reach of even the most eminent authorities. The occupants of Wing C were never registered. They were dead souls. For practical purposes they had ceased to exist.

In the morning hours of November 12, a young man with a narrow face and shrewd black eyes sat motionless on his cot in Cell 67 of Wing C. Thomas Lieven was a pitiable sight. His complexion had turned gray. His cheeks had fallen in. He wore an old convict's uniform, much too big for him. He felt frightfully cold. The cells were never heated.

He had been sitting in that hideous, stinking cell for more than seven weeks. During the night of September 17–18, his abductors had handed him over to two Gestapo agents at Chalon-sur-Saône. They had taken him to Fresnes. Since then he had been waiting for someone to come and question him. But in vain. He was beginning to lose his reason under the strain of the delay.

Attempts to make contact with the German warders had proved useless. So had the exercise of charm and bribery in the interests of obtaining better food. There was nothing to eat but thin cabbage soup, day after day. He had tried also to smuggle a note through to Chantal, but in vain.

Why didn't they come, after all this time, and put him up against a wall? Every morning about four o'clock they came and took men from the cells. He heard the tramp of heavy boots, ringing words of command and the feeble cries and whimpering of those marched off. And the shots when they were executed by shooting. But nothing when they were hanged. Generally one heard nothing.

Suddenly he sprang to his feet. Footsteps were approaching. The door flew open. A German sergeant-major stood on the threshold. Beside him were two huge fellows in Security Service uniform.

"Hunebelle?"

"Yes."

"You're wanted for examination."

At last, Thomas thought, at last!

He was handcuffed and taken down to the courtyard. A big, windowless bus was waiting there. One of the Security men pushed Thomas into a dark, narrow passage which ran down the middle of the bus and had many doors on each side. Behind the doors were tiny cells in which one could only sit huddled up.

Thomas was showed into one of them. The door was banged and locked. He could hear that all the other cells were also occupied. The whole vehicle stank of sweat and terror.

It clattered off along a street full of potholes. The journey lasted half an hour. When the bus stopped Thomas could hear voices, footsteps and curses. Then his cell door was flung open. "Outside, you!"

Thomas, giddy with weakness, stumbled into the open air behind a Security man. He immediately recognized the magnificent Avenue Foch in Paris. Several of its buildings, he knew, had been confiscated by the Security Service.

His escort led Thomas through the hall of No. 84 into a library which had been refurnished as an office.

Two men were sitting there, both in uniform. One was short, jovial and red-faced, the other looked unhealthily pale. The first was Sturmbannführer Walter Eicher and the second his adjutant Fritz Winter.

Thomas halted before them in silence.

His escort announced him and left the room.

The Sturmbannführer roared in execrable French: "Well, Hunebelle, what do you say to a cognac?"

Thomas felt very sick. But he answered: "No, thank you. I'm afraid I haven't got the right digestive foundation for it."

Sturmbannführer Eicher was not quite sure what Thomas had said, since he had spoken French. His adjutant, therefore, translated it. Eicher laughed loudly. Winter continued in a prim tone: "I believe we can speak German to this gentleman, can we not?"

Thomas had seen a file marked HUNEBELLE lying on a side table as he came in. There was no point in lying. "Yes, I can also speak German."

"Ah, wonderful, wonderful! Perhaps you're even a countryman of ours, eh?" The Sturmbannführer shook a playfully threatening finger at him. "Come on, you little rascal! You may as well confess!"

He blew a cloud of cigar smoke into Thomas's face. Thomas remained silent.

The Sturmbannführer grew serious. "Look here, Hunebelle, or whatever you like to call yourself, I daresay you think we enjoy locking you up and examining you. No doubt you've heard a lot of atrocity stories about us, haven't you? But we don't like the difficult job we have to do, I can assure you. It goes against the German grain, Hunebelle." He nodded sadly. "But the country demands it. We have taken an oath to the Führer. After final victory our people will have to take over the leadership of all the nations of the earth. That sort of thing has to be prepared for. Everyone will be needed then."

"Even you," added Winter, the adjutant.

"I beg your pardon?"

"We know how you've swindled us, Hunebelle. At Marseilles. That business with the gold and jewelry and currency." The Sturmbannführer chuckled. "Don't contradict me. We know all about it. I must say it was a clever trick. You've got brains, my boy."

"And because you're such a brainy boy you're now going to tell us what your real name is and where all that stuff de Lesseps and Bergier had has got to," Winter added quietly.

"And who was in it with you," said Eicher. "We have to know that too, of course. We've already occupied Marseilles. We can put your colleagues in our pockets right away."

Thomas said nothing.

"Well?" asked Eicher.

Thomas shook his head. He had been expecting this.

"You won't talk?"

"No."

"Everyone talks here sooner or later." Eicher's jovial good-humor and the grin on his face vanished abruptly. His voice grew hoarse. "You filthy rogue! You little skunk! I've wasted enough time with you!" He stood up, bending and straightening his knees, threw his cigar into the fireplace and said to Winter: "Carry on. Put him through it."

Winter took Thomas down into an overheated cellar, where he gave orders to two men in plainclothes. They tied him to the boiler of the central heating system. Then they "put him through it."

This process continued for three days in succession. First came the bus journey from Fresnes to Paris. Then came the examination, followed by putting the prisoner "through it" in the cellar. Then he would be taken back to his unheated cell.

The first time they made the mistake of thrashing him too fast and hard, whereupon he fainted.

The second time they were more careful. So they were the third time. After the third session Thomas had lost two teeth and had many open wounds on his body. He was then transferred to the prison hospital at Fresnes for a fortnight.

After that the whole thing started all over again.

When the windowless bus brought him once more to Paris on December 12, Thomas Lieven had reached the end of his resistance. He couldn't stand the torture any more. He thought, I'll jump out of the window on that third floor where Eicher always examines me now. Yes, I'll jump out of that window. With any luck I'll kill myself. Oh, Chantal, Bastian, I would so much like to have seen you again . . .

Just before ten o'clock in the morning of December 12, 1942, he was escorted to Herr Eicher's office. A man Thomas had never seen before stood next to the Sturmbannführer. He was tall, lean and white-haired. He wore the uniform of a colonel of the German Army, with many rows of ribbons. Under his arm he a carried a thick file on which Thomas Lieven could decipher the letters GEKADOS.

Eicher looked angry.

"There's your man, Colonel," he said sulkily, coughing.

"I'll take him with me right away," said the much decorated colonel.

"Well, if it's a GEKADOS case I can't stop you, Colonel. Sign the receipt, if you please."

Thomas felt as if everything was whirling around him, the room, the men and everything else in it. He stood there in his pitiable convict's dress, hardly able to keep on his feet, choking and gasping for breath. He thought of a sentence he had once read in a book by Bertrand Russell. "In our century it is only the unexpected that happens."

[2]

Thomas Lieven, handcuffed, sat beside the white-haired colonel in an army limousine. They drove through the Cité quarter of Paris, which did not seem to have altered much since the German occupation. France, apparently, was ignoring that event. The streets were very animated. Thomas saw smart women and hurrying men. The German soldiers mingling with them looked curiously embarrassed and bewildered.

The colonel remained silent until they had reached the residential suburb of St. Cloud. Then he said: "I hear you like cooking, Herr Lieven."

Thomas stiffened at the mention of his real name. Rendered nervous and ultra-suspicious by the torture he had undergone during the last few weeks, he wondered what was behind this remark, what new trap might be in store for him. He stole a side glance at the officer. The colonel's features pleased him by their shrewd and skeptical cast. The eyebrows were bushy, the nose aquiline, the mouth sensitive. So what? In Germany, Thomas reflected, many murderers play Bach in their spare time.

He said: "I don't know what you are talking about."

"Oh, yes, you do," said the colonel. "My name is Werthe and I belong to the Paris branch of Military Intelligence. I can save your life. But whether I do so or not depends on you."

The car stopped beside a high wall surrounding a large estate. The driver sounded his horn three times. A massive gate opened, apparently of its own accord. The car drove through the gateway and up a graveled avenue leading to a villa of yellow brick, with french windows and green shutters.

"Raise your hands," said the colonel who had called himself Werthe.

"Why?"

"So that I can unlock your handcuffs. You can't very well cook with those on. I should like a Cordon Bleu if that's all right with you. With Crêpes Suzette. I'm going to take you to the kitchen, where Nanette, the maid, will help you."

"Cordon Bleu," Thomas repeated in a faint voice. His head again began to whirl as Colonel Werthe unlocked the steel handcuffs.

"If you please."

Now I'm alive, thought Thomas. I'm breathing again. I wonder what's going to come of it this time. Feeling his normal interests stirring, so to speak, in their sleep, he replied: "Good. Then perhaps we might have stuffed aubergines as a first course."

Half an hour later Thomas was explaining to Nanette, the maid, how to prepare aubergines. She was an uncommonly attractive brunette, wearing a white apron over her uncommonly close-fitting black woolen dress. Thomas sat beside her at the kitchen table. Colonel Werthe had gone away. There were bars, however, on the kitchen window.

Nanette repeatedly came quite close to Thomas. Once her bare arm touched his cheek. Once her rounded hip brushed his arm.

As a patriotic Frenchwoman she guessed where he had come from. And Thomas, despite all the torture and deprivation he had endured, still looked a useful sort of fellow.

"Oh, Nanette," he sighed at last.

"Yes, monsieur?"

"I really ought to apologize to you. You are so young and pretty that under normal circumstances I wouldn't be sitting here so quietly. But I'm done for. I'm a wreck . . ."

"Poor monsieur," whispered Nanette. Then she gave him a very quick, very light kiss, blushing as she did so.

The meal took place in a large, darkly paneled room with windows opening on a park. The colonel had changed his uniform for a very well-cut flannel suit.

MENU

Stuffed Aubergines
Cordon Bleu with Small Garden Peas
Crêpes Suzette

PARIS, 12 DECEMBER 1942

A preliminary to Thomas's pact with the "Devil's Admiral."

Stuffed Aubergines

Large firm aubergines are peeled thinly and halved lengthways. The pulp is carefully removed and put through the mincer with beef, pork, one onion and a soaked crustless roll. An egg, salt, pepper, paprika and a little anchovy paste are added, well mixed to a forcemeat and the aubergines stuffed with the mixture. A little stock is poured into the bottom of a well-buttered casserole. The stuffed aubergines are placed in it, well sprinkled with grated cheese and butter flakes and baked at medium heat for half an hour.

Cordon Bleu with Small Garden Peas

Tender fillets of veal are well beaten and half of each is covered with a slice of ham, on top of which is placed a thin slice of Gruyère cheese so as to leave half an inch uncovered round the edge. The edges are then brushed with white of egg and the uncovered half of each fillet is folded over the covered half, the edges being well pressed together. Then each turnover is first rolled in flour, next in lightly salted and peppered egg yolk and lastly in bread crumbs. It is fried in deep hot butter until golden-brown. The fillets are served with small garden peas previously sprinkled with salt and chopped parsley.

Crepes Suzette

Plenty of wafer-thin pancakes, prepared with water instead of milk, are fried. At table, on a chafing dish over a spirit flame, a fair-sized portion of butter is heated, but must not get brown. The juice of an orange or tangerine together with its finely chopped peel are added to the butter. A small quantity of kirsch and maraschino, with either curaçao or cointreau and a little sugar are added and heated. One pancake at a time is laid in the liquid and heated quickly. It is then removed to a heated plate, rolled up and served immediately.

Nanette was in attendance. Her pitying glances fell again and again on the man in the crumpled, dirty prison garb, who nevertheless behaved like an English aristocrat. He was obliged to eat with his left hand, two fingers of his right hand being bandaged.

Colonel Werthe waited until Nanette had served the aubergines. Then he said: "Delicate, really delicate, Herr Lieven. What top dressing did you use, may I ask?"

"Grated cheese, Colonel. Why have you brought me here?" Thomas ate little. He felt that he ought not to overload his stomach after the weeks of starvation he had undergone.

Colonel Werthe ate with relish. "You are a man of principle, I hear. You would prefer to be thrashed to death rather than reveal any information to the Security Service, let alone work for those—ahem—for that organization."

"Yes."

"What about the Canaris organization?" The colonel helped himself to another aubergine.

Thomas asked quietly: "How were you able to get me away from Eicher?"

"Oh, that was quite easy. We've a good man in Intelligence here, a Captain Brenner. He's been watching your career for some time. You've been putting on quite a show, Herr Lieven." Thomas bent his head. "Oh, you needn't be so modest. When Brenner discovered that the Security people had arrested you and taken you to Fresnes, we put on a little show of our own."

"A little show?"

Werthe pointed to the file marked GEKADOS, which lay on a side table under the window. "We get people out of the hands of the Security Service by means of files like that. We take a number of old espionage cases and cook up a new one, purely imaginary, out of them, adding a few fresh pieces of entirely fabricated evidence. We cover the whole file with all sorts of signatures and stamps to make it look impressive. In this particular instance we've included statements by various witnesses to the effect that one Pierre Hunebelle was involved in the perpetration of a series of attacks with explosives in the neighborhood of Nantes."

Nanette brought in the Cordon Bleu.

She glanced affectionately at Thomas and silently cut his portion into small pieces before leaving the room. Colonel Werthe smiled. "You've made a conquest there. Where was I? Ah, yes. That little show of ours. Well, after we had got our bogus file ready I went to Eicher and asked him whether his department had arrested a certain Pierre Hunebelle. I played the perfect innocent. Yes, he said at once, we've got him in Fresnes. Then I showed him my file with the initials GEKADOS, meaning 'Secret Army Headquarters Case.' I dropped a lot of dark hints about the interest of Canaris, Himmler and so on, swore him to secrecy and finally let him read the file. After that it was quite simple for me to take over the custody of a spy so important to German interests as Hunebelle."

"But why, Colonel? What do you want of me?"

"The best Cordon Bleu I ever tasted! Well, seriously, Herr Lieven, we need you. We are faced with a problem which only a man like yourself can solve."

"I hate secret service work," said Thomas Lieven. He thought of Chantal, Bastian and all his other friends. His heart ached for them. "I hate and despise all the secret services in the world."

Colonel Werthe said: "It's just half-past one. At four o'clock I have an appointment with Admiral Canaris in the Lutetia. He wants to talk to you. If you consent to work for us, our GEKADOS file will get you out of the clutches of the Security Service. If you refuse, I can do nothing more for you. I shall have to hand you back to Eicher."

Thomas stared at him. Five seconds passed.

"Well?" demanded the colonel.

[3]

"Forward, roll!" yelled Sergeant-major Adolf Bieselang in the vast hall of the gymnasium. With a groan, Thomas Lieven somersaulted forward.

"Backward, roll!" yelled Sergeant-major Adolf Bieselang. With a groan, Thomas Lieven somersaulted backward. Eleven other men groaned with him. There were six Germans, a Norwegian, an Italian, a Ukrainian and two Indians.

The Indians kept their turbans on while they somersaulted. The custom did not admit of infringements.

Sergeant-major Bieselang wore the uniform of the German Air Force. He was forty-five years old, lean, sallow and always, apparently, on the point of bursting with fury. The mere sight of his enormous open mouth with its many lead-filled teeth struck instant terror into the soul. Sergeant-major Bieselang kept his mouth open almost permanently, what with yelling by day and snoring by night.

A widower of two years' standing with an extraordinarily pretty marriageable daughter, Bieselang operated some sixty miles northwest of Berlin, near the village of Wittstock on the River Dosse.

His job was to train parachute troops, although, to his rage, not in uniform but in plainclothes, a set of extremely peculiar blokes with extremely peculiar assignments, both Germans and foreigners, a repulsive lot of typical bloody civilians.

"And forward ro-o-oll!"

Thomas Lieven, alias Jean Leblanc, alias Pierre Hunebelle, somersaulted head first.

The date was February 3, 1943.

It was cold. The sky over the Marches of Brandenburg looked like a gray cloth. The roar of low-flying practice aircraft never ceased.

Thomas Lieven, pacifist and gourmet, who loved women and hated war, the man who detested secret services, had made up his mind to work for a secret service once again. He had driven with Colonel Werthe to the Hôtel Lutetia in Paris, where he had met Admiral Canaris, the mysterious chief of German Intelligence.

Thomas Lieven knew that if he were handed back to the Gestapo he would be dead in a month. Traces of blood had already appeared in his urine.

Thomas Lieven considered the most horrible of lives to be preferable to the most honorable of deaths. All the same, he had not denied his principles even in the presence of the white-haired Admiral. "Herr Canaris, I will work for you because I have no choice. But I warn you that I will neither kill, threaten, terrorize, torment nor kidnap anybody. If that is the sort of work you have in mind for me I would rather go back to the Avenue Foch."

The admiral shook his head gravely. "Herr Lieven, the mission I would like you to take up is intended to prevent bloodshed and save human lives, so far as it remains within our power to achieve that aim." He raised his voice. "Both German and French lives. Is that what you would like to do?"

"I would always like to save human lives, irrespective of nationality or religion."

"We have to try to subdue dangerous groups of French partisans. One of our people has reported that a newly organized and strong resistance unit is attempting to get in touch with London. As is well known, the British War Office supports the French resistance movement and directs many of its groups. The unit I have mentioned needs another radio set and a decoding book. I wish you to deliver both articles, Herr Lieven."

"I see," said Thomas.

"You speak fluent English and French. You have lived for years in England. You would be dropped with the transmitter over partisan territory, posing as a British officer. It would be a special type of transmitter."

"I see," said Thomas for the second time.

"A British aircraft will bring you to the locality. We have a few captured RAF planes which we use in these cases. Of course we shall have to give you some parachute training first."

"I see," said Thomas for the third time.

[4]

Thomas knew that the Germans had occupied Marseilles. He wondered what had happened to Chantal. Was she still alive? Had she been deported, arrested or perhaps tortured like himself?

He lay sleepless when he woke from terrifying dreams about her. In the hideous dormitory of the barracks six men snored and groaned. Chantal, he thought . . . we were just going to Switzerland to live in peace . . . in peace.

Weeks ago he had tried to get letters through to her. In Paris, at the Hôtel Lutetia, Colonel Werthe had promised to see to it. Thomas had given another letter to an interpreter he had met at the language school, who was going to Marseilles. But Thomas's own address had been perpetually changing for the last few weeks. There wasn't much chance of a letter from Chantal reaching him. Meanwhile the ferocious sergeant-major, Bieselang, drove his twelve pupils pitilessly on. After practice indoors they went out to the frozen fields, where the ground was as hard as iron. After buckling on their loose parachutes they had to stand in the airstream created by an aero-engine mounted on a pedestal. The parachute flew open in the blast and carried the helpless trainee off across country. He had to learn how to swing the parachute around and throw himself on top of it to expel the air.

Cuts and scratches, bruised knees and sprained wrists abounded. But Bieselang kept his twelve novices hard at it from six in the morning till six in the evening. The next stage involved jumping from a considerable height through a structure resembling the trap door of a Ju 52 onto a blanket held by four other pupils.

"Straight knees, you scum! Straight knees!" bawled the sergeant-major.

If the knees weren't kept straight you fell on your face or strained every muscle in your body. Bieselang taught his pupils everything they had to know. The trouble was that his methods were too brutal.

The night before their first real jump he ordered them all to make their wills and leave these documents behind in sealed envelopes. All their property also had to be packed up before they went to bed. "So that we can send the stuff away to your families if you get it tomorrow morning!"

Bieselang considered that he was laying a psychological trap for them by this explanation. He wanted to see which of his squad would get the wind up. They all did, except one. Bieselang bellowed at him: "Where's your will, Number Seven?"

Thomas answered, meek as a lamb: "I don't need one. A man who has had the benefit of your training, sergeant-major, can easily survive any jump!"

Next day however Bieselang at last exceeded his instructions. About nine o'clock in the morning they all climbed into an obsolete old rattletrap of a Ju 52 and went up to a height of about five hundred feet. The twelve trainees, their ripcords loose, stood one behind the other in the rear of the aircraft. The pilot's buzzer sounded.

"Get ready to jump!" roared Bieselang, who was standing to leeward of the open trap door. All the apprentices were now wearing steel helmets, in the case of the two Indians underneath their turbans. All were grasping heavy tommy-guns.

Number One, the Italian, stepped forward. Bieselang struck him on the shoulder. The man spread his arms wide and sprang into the void, parallel with the left-hand wing of the aircraft. His ripcoard, which was fastened to a steel hook, went taut and tore open his parachute. He immediately dropped away downward behind the aircraft.

Number Two and Number Three followed. Thomas noticed a dryness of his lips and wondered whether he would faint during the drop or kill himself. Oddly enough he suddenly longed inordinately for a mouthful of goose liver. How I wish I could have stayed with Chantal, he thought. We were so happy together . . .

Number Six, the Ukrainian, unexpectedly shrank away from Bieselang, bumping into Thomas and screaming in sudden panic: "No—no—no—"

Typical nervous breakdown, thought Thomas mechanically. Induced by fear. Perfectly intelligible. It was laid down in the training regulations that no one must be compelled to jump. If anyone refused to jump on two successive flights, he was to be dismissed.

Sergeant-major Adolf Bieselang, however, couldn't have cared less about printed instructions. He roared: "You skunk! You cowardly son of a bitch, get on with it, will you?" He seized the shaking recruit, pulled him to the trap and delivered a mighty kick against his backside. With a shriek the wretched man went spinning into the void.

Before Thomas could recover from his indignation at this scene he found himself being jerked forward. The sergeant-major's boot crashed against his own hindquarters and he too dropped down, down, down through the empty air.

[5]

Thomas survived the first parachute jump of his life without serious injury.

As he was returning to the barracks on the evening of February 27, he passed a high barbed-wire fence which separated the secret agents' enclosure from that of the air force trainees. A paratrooper on the other side of the barrier whistled to him. "Hey, hey!"

"What's the matter?"

"You look like a fellow a man called Bastian was describing to me."

In a second Thomas, who had been dog-tired, was wide awake. "Bastian?"

"Is your name Pierre Hunebelle?"

"Yes, that's me . . . do you know—did you hear anything about a certain Chantal Tessier?"

"Tessier? No. I only know this man called Bastian Fabre. Gave me three of those gold coins of theirs to take you this letter . . . here, I must be off now . . . sergeant-major's coming . . ."

Thomas Lieven found an envelope in his hand. He sat

down on a milestone. The light was fading and the air felt cold. But he didn't notice it. He tore open the envelope, pulled out the enclosure and began to read, with his heart thumping like a sledge hammer.

Marseilles.
5.2.43.

Dear old Pierre,

I don't know how to begin this letter. You may be kicking up the daisies as I write.

These last weeks I've been looking about and bumped into a guy who's got a pip on each shoulder. Works for both the resistance and the Germans. He'd heard from Paris what happened to you. If I ever meet one of those cursed Security swine I'll strangle him with my own hands. Then you went to another mob, so this bloke said. How the hell did you manage it? Now, apparently, you're being trained as a paratrooper somewhere near Berlin. Well, if that isn't enough to make a man sick! My old pal Pierre a German paratrooper! I could laugh if I didn't want to cry over it.

I got to know a German soldier in Montpellier, a decent sort. But I made sure by lining his pocket for him. He's off to Berlin today so I gave him this letter.

Chantal got two letters from you. But we had no one we could trust to take an answer.

I'm fond of you, boy. You know that. So it's specially hard for me to write what's been happening here. On the 24th January German Headquarters ordered the Old Port to be cleared.

That day they arrested about 6000 people in our quarter. You know many of them. They also closed over 1000 bars and knocking-shops. Regular set-tos there were with some of the girls. You never saw anything like it.

We were only given four hours to clear out before the demolition squads moved in. Chantal, Hoofy and I hung on to the last minute. She was raving mad to get her hands on Baldy, the piss-begotten sod who turned you in to the Gestapo.

Well, so that evening we waited for him in the entry to a house in the rue Mazenod, opposite his hideout. We knew he was lying low in the cellar there. Chantal said he was bound to leave when they started dynamiting. So we waited there for hours. Boy, was that an evening! Smoke and dust everywhere. One house after another going up. Men yelling, women shrieking, children howling . . .

[6]

Smoke, dust explosions, yells, shrieks and howls . . .

When it grew dark the sinister red glare of the burning buildings lit up the scene. Chantal stood motionless in a dim doorway. She wore tight-fitting trousers and a leather jacket, a red scarf over her dark hair. Under the jacket she gripped a tommy-gun. Her white, feline features were rigidly set.

Another house went up. Bricks and mortar rained down. Screams, oaths in German, shouts and the trampling of field boots resounded.

"For Christ's sake, Chantal, let's get going," Bastian urged. "The Germans will be here at any moment. If they see we're armed—"

Chantal shook her head sullenly. "You shove off. I'm staying here." Her voice sounded hoarse. She coughed. "I know Baldy's over there in the cellar. He's bound to come out, the swine. And I'm going to rub him out if it's the last thing I do."

A shrill outburst of feminine shrieks rang out. Some way up the street soldiers were driving a mob of women toward them, some dressed only in kimonos or peignoirs. They were hitting out right and left, biting, kicking and scratching at their escorts.

"Yvonne's gang," said Hoofy, as the tumultuous group, yelling obscene curses in both male and female voices, drew level with the doorway.

Bastian suddenly roared: "There he is!"

Dantes Villeforte and three other men were emerging from the house opposite. Baldy was wearing a short fur jacket, his bodyguard thick pullovers. The butts of revolvers protruded from the pockets of their trousers.

Bastian leveled his own pistol. But Chantal struck the barrel down, shouting: "No! You'll hit that girl!" The women were still tussling with the German soldiers in front of the entry.

After that things happened fast.

Dantes Villeforte, bending low, made a dash for one of the soldiers, a non-commissioned officer. The Corsican took care, as he went, to keep either a soldier or one of the women between himself and Chantal.

He showed the Security man a pass signed by a certain Sturmbannführer Eicher of the Paris Gestapo. Talking fast, Villeforte pointed to the doorway where Chantal, Bastian and Hoofy were standing.

Chantal instantly leveled her tommy-gun, but hesitated for a moment, as two or three women were still standing between her and the Corsican.

That hesitation cost Chantal her life. With a fiendish grin Villeforte, ducking behind one of the girls, aimed his own gun and fired a long burst.

Without uttering a sound Chantal staggered and dropped to the littered pavement. A stream of blood dyed the leather jacket red. She lay motionless. The life drained out of her splendid eyes.

"Come on!" yelled Hoofy. "Through the courtyard! Over the wall!"

Bastian knew that every second counted now. He swung around, firing at Villeforte. He saw the Corsican reel, clutching at his left arm and squealing like a stuck pig.

Then Bastian and Hoofy ran for their lives. They knew every inch of the Old Quarter, every short cut. Behind the yard wall there was a grating giving access to a sewage pipe. By climbing down into the drainage system they could get clear away from the quarter.

[7]

Bastian's letter continued: "We managed to escape through the old sewer."

Thomas Lieven let the letter fall. He stared away into the violet shadows of the gathering dusk and wiped the tears out of his eyes.

Then he read on.

> I went to ground in Montpellier. If you're ever that way, ask for me at Mlle. Duval's, No. 12 Boulevard Napoleon, that's where I hang out now.
>
> Pierre, old pal, our dear Chantal is dead. I know of course, how thick you two were. She told me once that you might have married her. You know that, as your friend, I'm as hard hit by this as you. Life is a filthy business. I wonder if we shall ever see each other again

and if so when and where. All the best, old pal. The thing makes me sick. Can't write more.

Bastian.

It was quite dark now. Thomas Lieven sat on the milestone. It was cold. But Thomas did not feel the cold. The tears were running down his cheeks.

Dead. Chantal was dead. Suddenly he buried his head in his hands and groaned aloud. God, how he longed for her! It was terrible to think of her wild moods, her laughter and her love.

He did not hear the voices calling him from the barracks, where he had been missed. He sat in the cold, thinking of his lost love and weeping.

[8]

On April 4, 1943, shortly after midnight, a British aircraft of the Blenheim type flew in at a height of 750 feet over a lonely, wooded stretch of country between Limoges and Clermont-Ferrand. After describing a wide arc the aircraft flew in a second itme. Two fires blazed up on the ground below, followed by three red lights and finally the white flash of an electric torch, the agreed signal.

Two Luftwaffe pilots and a Luftwaffe wireless operator sat in the machine, which bore the blue, white and red circles of the Royal Air Force. Behind the uniformed men stood another in brown overalls of English manufacture, with a parachute, also made in England, buckled to his belt.

He possessed expertly forged British papers in the name of Robert Almond Everett, together with a captain's military pass. In addition to his walrus mustache and long, thick side whiskers he had British cigarettes, British rations and British medical supplies with him.

The senior pilot glanced around and nodded at him. Thomas Lieven took out his old-fashioned gold repeater from the pocket of his overalls and pressed the spring: 0028 hours.

The wireless operator helped him to drop a bulky package, also equipped with a parachute, through the trap. Thomas shook hands with him and followed the parcel.

Crouching as he had been taught, Thomas swore an oath. If I ever get out of all this, he told himself, and meet Dantes Villeforte anywhere again on this earth, I'll avenge you, Chantal, I'll avenge you. He added aloud, foolishly enough: "I love you so much, Chantal."

Then he spread his arms wide and jumped toward the left-hand wing of the aircraft, out into the dark night.

Below he could see two fires glowing in a small glade and the red dots of three pocket torches.

During the next ten seconds of the drop he thought, I'll have to land in the triangle formed by those red dots. The clearing is free of trees there. If I don't land in that triangle it's highly probable I shall get an oak branch in the . . . My God, and this month I shall be thirty-four! Steer a bit with the arms now. That's fine, I'm over the triangle again. Those decent French partisans down there with their red torches think I've been sent to them by Colonel Buckmaster in London. If they had the slightest idea that I've been sent to them by Admiral Canaris in Berlin—

During the last ten seconds of the drop he thought, A walrus mustache like this is just about the most repulsive thing on earth, really. The hairs are always getting into one's mouth. And then these long sideburns those Intelligence characters made me grow. Typical secret service idiocy! They think a walrus mustache and sideburns make me look English. As if a genuine English captain intending to drop into German-occupied France on a secret mission wouldn't immediately shave off his sideburns and walrus mustache in order to look less English! Imbeciles, the whole lot of them. They can all . . .

Thomas Lieven, alias Captain Everett, came to earth with a painful thump, face downward, with a fair amount of mustache hairs in his mouth. But he remembered at the very last moment to swear in English, not German.

Then he rose slowly to his feet. Four people stood before him in the light of the two flickering fires. There were three men and one woman. They all wore wind jackets.

The woman was young and pretty. She had fair hair drawn strictly back from her forehead. The cheekbones were high, the eyes slanting and the mouth attractive.

One of the three men was short and fat, one tall and thin and one as shaggy as a Stone Age specimen.

The short, fat man addressed Thomas in English. "How many rabbits has my mother-in-law got in her garden?"

Thomas replied with a marvelous Oxford accent: "Two white, eleven black and one piebald. They must soon go to Fernandel. The hairdresser's already waiting for them."

"Do you like Tchaikovsky?" the severe-looking blonde asked in French. Her eyes glittered and her teeth gleamed in the reflected light of the fire beside her. She was holding a heavy pistol at the ready.

He replied dutifully, in French but with an English accent, uttering the sentence Colonel Werthe had taught him in Paris at the last moment. "I prefer Chopin." This statement seemed to satisfy the blonde, who put away her murderous tool. The stout little man demanded: "Can we see your papers?"

Thomas handed them his forged papers. The tall thin partisan announced with an air of authority: "That will do. Welcome, Captain Everett."

They all shook hands with him vigorously.

So it's as easy as that, thought Thomas. If I ever allowed myself to play such silly games on the London Stock Exchange for a single day I'd be flat broke the same evening, that's certain.

[9]

It really had not been so very difficult to carry out the plan. German Intelligence had discovered that a new and strong resistance group of French partisans had been organized in the highly picturesque woodland region on the other side of the Creuze Valley. The group was called the Crozant, after the small village of that name south of Gargilesse.

The Crozant group was most anxious to get in touch with London and go into action against the Germans under British orders. Its members were peculiarly dangerous because they operated in territory almost impossible to control and full of important railways, roads and power stations. Ravines and rocky hills impeded any serious counteraction by the Germans, even with tanks.

The new group had affiliations with that of Limoges, which possessed a transmitter and communicated regularly with London. But the wireless operator was a double agent who also worked for the Germans. It was through him that German Intelligence in Paris learned of the desire of the Crozant group to possess its own transmitter.

The treacherous wireless operator who had told the Germans instead of London what the Crozant group wanted next received messages which purported to come from London but really emanated from German Intelligence in Paris. These messages requested the Limoges group to inform that of Crozant about the projected arrival of a Captain Robert Almond

Everett by parachute over a glade in the Crozant woods shortly after midnight on April 4, 1943.

"Where is the parachute we dropped with the radio equipment?" asked Thomas Lieven in his new character as Captain Everett. He was anxious about the apparatus in question. German technicians had been working on it for a long time.

"It's already hidden," said the severe-looking beauty, who never took her eyes off Thomas. "Allow me to introduce my friends to you." She had a rapid, resolute way of speaking and obviously dominated the men just as Chantal had dominated her own gangsters. But instead of passion and temperament the blonde employed a chilly intellectuality in exercising her control.

The little fat man turned out to be Robert Cassier, the mayor of Crozant. The tall, shrewd-faced, taciturn fellow was introduced as a former lieutenant named Bellecourt. The third partisan, a potter from Gargilesse, was presented by the mysterious blonde as Emile Rouff.

Thomas wondered why that peremptory little fair-haired bluestocking of a partisan kept eyeing him with such apparent distaste. Or could it be that she was sensually attracted by him? She seemed a weird sort of creature in any case.

The potter, heavily bearded and shockheaded, announced: "I swore nine months ago that I wouldn't cut my hair until that Hitler scum has been liquidated."

"We mustn't be too optimistic, M. Rouff. I think it will be a year or two yet before you'll be seeing a barber." Thomas turned to the girl. "And may I ask your own name, mademoiselle?"

"Yvonne Dechamps. Assistant to Professor Débouché."

"Débouché?" Thomas started slightly. "The famous physicist?"

"I expect you've heard of him in England," said the blond Yvonne proudly.

And in Germany too, thought Thomas. But I'd better not say so. He inquired politely: "I was under the impression that the professor taught at the university of Strasbourg?"

Bellecourt's lean figure confronted him. The ex-lieutenant informed him in an expressionless tone: "Strasbourg University has been transferred to Clermont-Ferrand. Didn't you know that in London, Captain?"

Damn, thought Thomas. That comes of talking too much. He answered coolly: "It's certain to be known, of course. Not by me, unfortunately. Gap in my education. Sorry."

A rather uncomfortable pause ensued. Thomas thought, Sheer cheek's the only hope now. He stared haughtily at the ex-officer and rapped out: "Don't let's waste time. What's the next move?"

Bellecourt stared calmly back at him. "Professor Débouché," he retorted deliberately, "is waiting for us in the mill at Gargilesse."

"There are too many Vichy militia about in the villages," said Yvonne. She glanced briefly at the ex-lieutenant with an expression which Thomas didn't like at all. I shan't have any trouble with the mayor and the potter, he thought. But those other two are dangerous. Very dangerous.

"Who's the wireless operator of your group?" he demanded.

"I am," answered the blonde, tight-lipped.

You would be, he thought. Worse and worse.

[10]

Professor Débouché resembled Albert Einstein. Small and slight, with the massive cranium of a scholar, he possessed a white, leonine mane, kind, melancholy eyes and an occiput of unusual size. He surveyed Thomas Lieven for some time in silence. Thomas forced himself to return the professor's calm, penetrating gaze. The effort made him feel hot and cold alternately, as he stood in the center of that mute group of five.

At last Débouché laid both hands on Thomas Lieven's shoulders and said: "Welcome!" The scene of this meeting was the living room of the mill at Gargilesse.

The professor addressed the others: "The captain is all right, my friends. I know a good man when I see him."

The attitude of the four partisans changed from one second to the next. After being so formal and taciturn they suddenly all began talking at once, slapped Thomas on the shoulder, laughed and became his friends.

Yvonne came up to him with her eyes shining. They were sea-green and very beautiful. She threw her arms round Thomas and kissed him. He flushed, for Yvonne had kissed him with the passion of a patriot thanking a national hero. Then she said, beaming: "Professor Débouché has never yet been mistaken in his judgment of anyone. We trust him. For us he is God Almighty."

The old man raised his hands deprecatingly.

Yvonne was still standing quite close to Thomas. She said in a provocatively hoarse tone: "You have put your life at our service. Yet we were suspicious of you and that must have pained you. Please forgive us."

Thomas looked at the kindly, white-haired scholar, the primitive Rouff, the laconic lieutenant, the stout, comical mayor, who all loved their country. It is for you to forgive me, he thought, all of you. I am thoroughly ashamed of myself. But what should or could I have done? I wanted then and I want now to save your lives—and mine too.

He had brought with him genuine British army rations, genuine English cigarettes and pipe tobacco and bottles of scotch whisky stamped "For Members of His Majesty's Royal Air Force Only." All these agreeable items came from stores captured by the German Army.

The partisans opened one of the bottles and toasted him as if he were a hero, while he kept thinking how disgracefully he was behaving. The whisky tasted like oil. He felt wretched, now that they were all treating him like a friend and comrade, with the greatest respect and admiration. The worse of it all was that even Yvonne, the cool, intellectual Yvonne, looked at him in that way, with a moist gleam in her eyes and parted lips.

"What we most urgently need," said the long-haired potter, "is dynamite and ammunition."

"You have weapons then?" Thomas inquired casually.

Bellecourt told him that the members of the Crozant group, about sixty-five in all, had raided two French depots and one German. "We possess at this moment," he declared with some pride, "three hundred and fifty French Lebel rifles, caliber 7.5, sixty-eight British Sten guns, thirty German fifty-millimeter trench mortars, fifty German FN machine guns and twenty-four French army machine guns."

Well, I hope you'll enjoy having them, thought Thomas.

"And I nearly forgot our nineteen Hotchkiss models," the lieutenant added.

"But there's no ammunition for any of them," said the mayor.

Thank God for that anyway, thought Thomas.

The old professor observed: "We'll report the whole position to London. Could you now please explain the code and transmission data to us, Captain?"

Thomas complied. Yvonne immediately understood the code system. It was based on much letter-transposition and the substitution of letter groups for individual letters. Thomas grew more and more melancholy as he reflected that he was responsible for all this, had hoped that it would work and now it was working . . .

Switching the apparatus on, he said: "It's now five minutes to two. At two o'clock precisely London will be expecting our first message. Frequency 1773 kHz." The transmitter had been adjusted to that frequency by German technicians. Thomas went on: "You will always report as 'Nightingale Seventeen.' You will ask for Room two-thirty-one at the London War Office. Colonel Buckmaster of the Special Operations Branch will answer." He stood up. "Please take over, Mlle. Yvonne."

They had already encoded their first message. Now they were all looking at their watches. The second hand was approaching the last minute before two A.M. Fifteen seconds more, ten, five, one . . .

Now!

Yvonne began to transmit in Morse. The men stood around her in a close circle. The stout, comical mayor, the lean lieutenant, the old professor and the long-haired potter watched the girl intently.

Thomas stood a little apart from them.

Well, now we're off, he was thinking. Can't stop now. God help them all. And God help me too.

[11]

"Whoops, here they come!" announced the Viennese corporal, Schlumberger. Seated with earphones adjusted before his receiving apparatus he began to take down the message. At an adjoining table Corporal Raddatz was studying with critical attention a French nudist magazine.

He now rose and came to sit by his colleague, adjusting earphones in his turn. Both men scribbled down the text that was reaching them from hundreds of miles away, through fog and darkness, transmitted in dots and dashes by a girl sitting in an old mill on the River Creuze.

The text corresponded exactly with the script which Schlumberger had before him. It had been handed to them by their strange new chief, Thomas Lieven, eight hours before, when he left Paris.

"gr 18 34512 etkgo nspon crags" began the text on Schlumberger's desk. The Morse signals being received on Frequency 1773 also read "gr 18 34512 etkgo nspon crags."

"Fits like a glove, eh?" grunted the Viennese.

"What about those guys in London?" demanded the other corporal, who came from New Cologne. "Think they're listening in?"

"I doubt it, on this frequency," Schlumberger retorted.

They were sitting in a room on the top floor of the Hôtel Lutetia, headquarters of German Military Intelligence in Paris.

Schlumberger's earphones ceased buzzing. He leaned back, then tapped out, as he had been instructed: "We'll be back."

Raddatz growled: "Why don't the bastards give up? That's what I'd like to know."

"They can't, George. Hitler 'ud stick 'em all up against the wall."

"Hitler," groaned the other. "What's the good of talking about Hitler? We're all Hitlers. We elected him didn't we? Christ, I think we've all gone crazy with our 'Heil Hitlers.' Oughta think more, that's what we oughta do. And yell less."

The two men went on talking in this not particularly patriotic fashion for quite a time. Then Schlumberger began to tap out in Morse, duly coded, the message his special task commander, Lieven, had left with him.

> from room 231 war office london to nightingale 17—message understood—welcome you as new member of our special operations branch—from now on report daily at time specified—instructions will be transmitted—we shall be collecting captain everett to-day the 4th april 1943—

[12]

"—in a lysander aircraft at dusk about 6 P.M. from the clearing where he landed—vive la france—vive la liberte buckmaster—message ends." Such was the message in Morse decoded by five men and one girl in a mill on the River Creuze. After deciphering it they jumped up and embraced one another in a frenzy of delight.

Just before three A.M. they all retired to bed.

Yvonne had asked Thomas to bring the instruction leaflet for the transmitter to her room. He knocked at her door a few minutes later with the leaflet, which was printed in English, in his hand. He felt tired and depressed. He couldn't get Chantal out of his mind.

"One moment," Yvonne called from the other side of the

door. He thought she had probably already undressed and would be putting something on before opening the door. He waited a moment. Then he heard her voice. "You can come in now, Captain."

He opened the door.

His assumption had been wrong. If Yvonne had been putting something on when he knocked, she had taken it off again afterward. For she stood there before him, in the small, overheated room, with its rustic furniture, naked as the day she was born.

Oh, no, thought Thomas. No! This is really too much. First she suspected me. Now she trusts me and wants to prove it . . . no, no, I simply can't . . . oh, Chantal, my beloved, dead Chantal . . .

He put the leaflet on a crudely fashioned chest of drawers, turned as red as a schoolboy and mumbled hurriedly: "A thousand pardons, mademoiselle."

Then he left the room.

Yvonne stood motionless, her lips quivering. But no tears came. She clenched her fists. From one moment to the next her feelings changed completely. That miserable wretch, she thought. That cold-blooded Englishman. I'll make him pay for this.

Between the opening and shutting of a door a woman ready for love had replaced it by deadly hatred.

Next morning she had disappeared. None of the men knew where. They found a note in her room to the effect that she had gone on ahead to Clermont-Ferrand.

The fat mayor lost his temper. "That's a nice thing! Who's going to cook for us now? Just when we were going to give you a farewell meal, Captain!"

"Gentlemen, if you will permit me to do the cooking—"

"Good heavens, can you cook, then?"

"A little," said Thomas modestly. Accordingly, he prepared the only kind of meal suitable in the circumstances, viz., a thoroughly English one, though he knew he was taking a certain risk in doing so among Frenchmen.

MENU

Roast Beef, Vegetables and Yorkshire Pudding
Apple Pudding

AT THE GARGILESSE MILL, 4 APRIL 1943

How Thomas softened up the partisans.

Roast Beef

A well-hung, boned sirloin is placed in a roasting pan, basted with plenty of hot butter, mixed with suet and fried quickly on all sides, then salted and peppered. The pan is then placed in a preheated oven at a high temperature and left to roast for forty-five minutes, with frequent basting. The heat is then reduced. No water should be added. The joint can be turned a few times. But during the last part of the roasting the layer of fat should face upward. When removing from oven do not carve immediately, as the juices will then run out and the joint will look gray. Leave it to stand for a few minutes. If the sirloin is baked on the rack, the drippings can be used to cook the Yorkshire Pudding.

Yorkshire Pudding

Mix five or six eggs thoroughly with one cup of flour, two cups of milk and a little salt. Pour the mixture into the hot fat from which the sirloin has been removed. Leave it to bake for ten minutes in a hot oven until the bottom of the pudding is brown and the top lightly set. Cut it into portions and place them round the slices of roast beef. It is also possible to prepare the pudding with cubed bacon and serve it separately from the roast beef.

Apple Pudding

Take four cups of flour, one and a half cups of soaked and finely chopped suet, a heaped teaspoonful of powdered ginger and a little salt. Mix well with cold water to a dough until it no longer sticks to the hands. Roll a round of it. Put a cloth in a pudding basin, dust it with flour and put the round of dough on it. Fill it up with quarters of peeled, tart apples. Pull the dough over the apples, press well and tie cloth. Boil for two hours in water containing two tablespoonfuls of salt. Serve sprinkled with fine sugar and without sauce. The pudding can be much improved if the apples are mixed with butter, half a cup of each of sultanas and currants, a quarter of a cup each of finely chopped orange and lemon peel, a little sugar and rum. This mixture should be steamed a little before being placed in the basin.

Nevertheless, everyone considered his roast beef tasted excellent. Only the vegetables which were served with it were criticized by the mayor. "Tell me, is all that stuff invariably cooked in salt water?"

"Yes, we English prefer it that way," answered Thomas, pulling a few mustache hairs out of his mouth. He was conducting two conversations at once, for at the same time Professor Débouché was telling him that the production of forged documents in Clermont-Ferrand had run into trouble. "Lately the authorities have invariably demanded passports as well as ration cards. Is there anything we can do about that?"

The greedy mayor simultaneously wanted to know the ingredients of Yorkshire pudding.

"One thing at a time," Thomas Lieven retorted. "The dough is made of eggs, milk and flour, thoroughly mixed. It is sometimes called 'dripping cake' when served with roast beef."

He turned to Professor Débouché. During the next few seconds he founded a first-rate factory for the forging of documents. "The papers must be forged flawlessly, Professor. No doubt you have friends in every government office in the country. Every item must agree with all the others. Passports, army passes, pay books, census certificates, ration cards and tax cards must all bear the same false name, which must also be registered at all the offices concerned."

This suggestion by Thomas Lieven was taken up and fully exploited to such an extent that it gave the Germans a terrible headache. France was flooded with such "genuine" forged documents. They saved many human lives.

[13]

At dusk on April 4, 1943, a Lysander aircraft landed on the small clearing over which Thomas Lieven had been dropped by parachute eighteen hours before. A pilot in British uniform sat in the machine. He came from Leipzig, and had been chosen by German Intelligence because he spoke English, though unfortunately with a Saxon accent.

For this reason he spoke little, confining himself for the most part to saluting, but making Thomas Lieven's blood run cold by doing it all wrong.

He laid his palm smartly against his cheek in the German fashion instead of turning the palm outward, as the British custom is.

None of Thomas Lieven's new French friends seemed to notice this mistake. Embraces, kisses, vigorous handshakes and good wishes were exchanged.

"Good luck!" shouted the partisans as Thomas climbed into the aircraft. At the same moment he hissed into the pilot's ear: "You idiot! You prize ass!"

Then he turned, to see Yvonne standing motionless at the edge of the forest. Her hands were plunged into the pockets of her jacket. He waved to her. But she did not reciprocate. He waved again. But she didn't move.

He realized as he sat down that this girl had by no means finished with him yet. Not by a long way!

The Nightingale 17 scheme worked just as smoothly as Thomas had hoped.

Every evening at nine o'clock the Crozant group reported to Corporals Schlumberger and Raddatz at the Hôtel Lutetia, waited until the message had been decoded and then received replies from "Colonel Buckmaster, Room 231, War Office, London."

Two other men were present at the Lutetia on these occasions. They were Colonel Werthe, who had rescued Thomas from the clutches of the Gestapo, and Captain Brenner, who had for a long time been following our friend's career with so much interest.

Thomas found Captain Brenner to be a typical professional soldier, dry, obstinate, pedantic, not unmannerly, not a Nazi, but just the same a parade-ground type, blindly obedient to orders, a military machine that worked without feelings, without capacity for criticism and almost without a heart.

Brenner, a little man with meticulously parted hair, gold-rimmed spectacles and a brisk way of moving, consequently understood nothing, right from the start, about "all that Nightingale Seventeen melodrama," as he called it.

At first Thomas sent the Crozant group instructions to mark time. But Nightingale 17 demanded action. The resistance men wanted to hit out. They clamored for ammunition.

Thereupon the German crew of a captured British aircraft dropped four cases of ammunition, on a warm May evening, into the woods between Limoges and Clermont-Ferrand. There was only one thing wrong with the ammunition in question. It was unsuitable in type and caliber for use with the weapons of the Crozant group.

Prolonged discussions by radio followed. Several more days went by. "London" regretted the mistake. It would be corrected, they signaled, as soon as the right ammunition for the Crozant weapons, many of which were of German and French origin, became available.

"London" next instructed the Crozant group to lay in provisions. It was known that the population of those inaccessible districts was starving. And hungry men might well become dangerously aggressive.

Once more captured machines with German pilots took off. This time they dropped packages of captured British rations, medical supplies, whisky, cigarettes and coffee.

Captain Brenner couldn't understand this policy at all. "We liquor up with substitute Pernod and those much respected partisans scoff real whisky! I smoke Gauloises and I daresay they have Henry Clays! We're coddling up those rascals to make them tough and fat! It's sheer lunacy, gentlemen, sheer lunacy!"

"It's nothing of the kind," Colonel Werthe retorted. "Lieven is right. It's the only way to stop those people from constituting a danger to us. If they once start blowing up railways and power stations, they'll be off all over the place and we'll never lay hands on one of them."

In June 1943, Nightingale 17 grew so restless that Thomas changed his tactics. Captured British aircraft with German crews began to drop munitions over the territory of the partisans which really suited their weapons.

But shortly afterward the Crozant group were told: "marseilles maquis about to sabotage and attack on grand scale—absolutely necessary for your weapons and ammunition to be temporarily at the disposal of your comrades."

The group protested energetically.

But "London" remained inexorable. Precise directions were given as to the time and place of the transfer.

One stormy night in the woods by the road leading from Belac to Montemart the equipment changed hands. Its new owners, who had behaved like real Frenchmen, drove away in several heavy trucks. But as soon as they were on their own again they relapsed into their customary lingo, that of the German Army.

At the beginning of July, Colonel Werthe learned from the treacherous wireless operator of the Limoges group that the Crozant partisans were "fed up with London." A certain Yvonne Dechamps, he said, was the ringleader in this attitude, suggesting that they might not have been in touch with the real London at all and that she herself had always thought "Captain Everett" a phony. She had also suspected the "RAF pilot" who had collected "Everett" and saluted "like a *Boche*."

"Damn it," said Thomas Lieven when he heard the news. "I thought that would happen sooner or later. There's only one more chance now, Colonel."

"And that is?"

"We must order Nightingale Seventeen to carry out a perfectly genuine act of sabotage and give them the means and opportunity for it. We shall have to sacrifice a single bridge, railway or power station in order to preserve, possibly, a great many from destruction."

Captain Brenner, who was present at this conversation, shut his eyes and groaned. "Cracked, Special Operations Commander Lieven, absolutely cracked!"

Colonel Werthe, too, looked worried. "There are limits, you know, Lieven. Really! What do you want me to do?"

"Give me a bridge, Colonel," cried Thomas in a sudden access of excitement. "Hang it all, there must be a bridge somewhere in France we could dispense with!"

BOOK III

CHAPTER 1

[1]

The elevator gates on the top floor of the Paris Hôtel Lutetia, commandeered by German Intelligence, clashed back. A man of thirty-four stepped out. He was of medium height, slim and had a walrus mustache.

George Raddatz, the lean Berliner, stuffed the latest issue of the French nudist magazine *Régal* into his pocket, sprang to his feet and clicked his heels. "Heil Hitler, Herr Sonderführer!"

"Corporals Raddatz and Schlumberger on wireless duty, Herr Sonderführer!" bawled the Viennese, assuming an exaggeratedly rigid posture.

The undoubtedly strangest special operations commander ever produced by the Third Reich, answered with a grin: "Heil Hitler, you shining lights! London on the air yet?"

"Yessir!" reported the Viennese, still standing stiffly to attention. "Just gone off!"

For weeks these three had been meeting every evening. And every evening, before anyone else arrived, they used the rceivers of an excellently equipped German wireless station for a forbidden purpose. They listened in to London every evening.

The stout Schlumberger announced: "Churchill made a speech. He said that if the Italians go on backing us now that Mussolini's folded they'll really get it."

On July 25, five days before, King Victor Emmanuel of Italy had ordered the arrest of Mussolini. On the same date daylight attacks had been made on Kassel, Remschied, Kiel and Bremen.

"Pretty fast work now, boys," sighed Raddatz. "In Russia we get a bellyful at Lake Ladoga and retreat from the Orel junction. In Sicily the Italians are getting it in the neck."

Thomas sat down. "And yet the gentlemen in Berlin are still shooting off their big mouths. They go on and on and on."

The two veteran, disillusioned corporals nodded sadly. They had heard a few things about Thomas Lieven. They knew that he had been tortured by the Gestapo before Colonel Werthe had rescued him from certain death in the cellars of the Security Service under the Avenue Foch.

He had since more or less recovered from his imprisonment and savage treatment under interrogation. His body still bore certain ugly scars. But they were not visible when he was dressed in the immaculate clothing to which he had now reverted.

"Colonel Werthe and Captain Brenner will be here shortly," he said. "Meanwhile, may I ask you to code this message, please?" He laid a sheet of paper on Raddatz's desk.

The Berliner, after reading it, uttered an exclamation of astonishment. " 'Struth! Wonders never cease! That's a nice way to win the war! Just look at this, Karli!"

The Viennese read the message and scratched his head, commenting briefly: "I give up."

"Don't do that," said Thomas. "It would be so much better to code the message." It read:

> to nightingale 17—raf bomber will parachute special container plastic explosive 1 august 23 to 2315 hours over grid 167—on 4 august midnight precisely blow pont noir between gargilesse and eguzon—be exactly on time—best luck—buckmaster.

"Come along, boys," said Thomas Lieven. "What are you making those big eyes for?"

"It's the same old leg-pull again, George," said the man from Vienna. "Only a piffling little bridge what don't matter, see?"

"That bridge, gentlemen," Thomas told them with a weary smile, "leads across the Creuze to Route Nationale Twenty and is one of the most important in central France. It's near Eguzon and the dam that supplies most of central France with current."

"And that's the very bridge you want blown up?"

"If God wills," said Thomas. "It took me long enough to get it scheduled."

[2]

On July 11, Thomas had visited the headquarters of the Todt building organization, where he had been directed to call upon one Heinze, a member of the Board of Works. Just before eleven A.M. Thomas pushed open a door with that name printed on it. The office contained two large drawing boards and two large men hotly arguing in front of them. The dispute had grown so fierce that neither of the men noticed Thomas Lieven's entrance. They were both dressed in long white coats and were shouting at the tops of their voices.

"I decline all responsibility! Any tank that crosses the thing may bring it down!"

"But the next bridge over the Creuze is at Argenton!"

"I don't give a damn about that. Let them go the long way around. I tell you, that Pont Noir at Gargilesse is a menace. There are yard-long cracks underneath the fairway. My statics engineer nearly fell through it himself!"

"You can reinforce it with concrete."

"For God's sake—a fat lot of good that would be—"

They're talking about the Gargilesse bridge thought Thomas. Fantastic! Absolutely fantastic! It's as though reality were chasing my wishes and dreams. Now it's caught them up . . .

"Think of the power station, the dam! If we blow that bridge, the supplies of current will be cut—"

"Not if we blow it ourselves. We could disconnect and switch over before blowing. But if the thing collapses tomorrow of its own accord you can start worrying about cuts all right! I tell you—what the devil are *you* doing here?"

Thomas Lieven's presence had at last been discovered. He bowed, saying quietly: "I came to see Herr Heinze."

One of the men exclaimed: "I'm Heinze. What's the matter?"

"My dear sir," replied Thomas. "I think we are going to be of the greatest mutual assistance to each other . . ."

And that was really what happened. As early as July 15 the plans of the Todt and Canaris organizations respectively regarding the future of the Pont Noir, south of Gargilesse, had been fully co-ordinated. Thomas then gave the following instructions, as "Colonel Buckmaster, War Office, London," to the Crozant group: "list all important bridges your area plus full details local troop movements."

The partisans lay in wait day after day and night after night. They squatted under bridges, crouched in the tops of trees and in the attics of old windmills and laborers' cottages. They had binoculars, paper and pencils with them. They counted German tanks, trucks and motorcycles. And every evening at nine they reported their observations to London. They reported bridges at Feurs, Macon, Dompierre, Nevers and the big Pont Noir south of Gargilesse, close to the Eguzon dam.

On July 30, at nine P.M. Yvonne Dechamps and Professor Débouché, Cassier the mayor, Lieutenant Bellecourt and Emile Rouff the porter were sitting in the living room of the old mill at Gargilesse. You could have cut the cigarette smoke with a knife.

Yvonne had her headphones adjusted. She was taking down the coded message which the somewhat overweight Corporal Schlumberger was tapping out in Paris.

"sv. 21 54621 lhyhi rhwea riehr ctbgs twoee . . ."

The men standing around Yvonne Dechamps were drawing short, regular breaths. Professor Débouché was polishing his eyeglasses. Lieutenant Bellecourt repeatedly licked his lips.

". . . sante siane krodi lygap" Schlumberger sent out in Morse on the top floor of the Hôtel Lutetia in Paris. The men standing around him, Thomas Lieven, the diminutive Captain Brenner with his neat hair style, and the taciturn Colonel Werthe were drawing short, regular breaths. Captain Brenner took off his gold-rimmed spectacles and gave them a thorough polishing.

At twenty minutes past nine "London" stopped sending. In the picturesque old watermill on the bank of the Creuze the Crozant leaders began decoding the message: "to nightingale 17—raf bomber will parachute special container plastic explosive . . ."

As soon as they had the message in clear they all, except Yvonne Dechamps, began talking at once. The girl sat motionless in front of the receiving apparatus, her hands folded in her lap. She was thinking of the enigmatic Captain Everett, whom she had so deeply suspected.

She paid little attention to what Débouché was saying. What she was thinking and feeling appeared senseless and perverse to herself. Yet she knew, with painful certainty, that she would see Captain Everett again some time, somewhere.

The voices about her grew louder. Yvonne gave a start. She realized that a dispute had arisen between the mayor, the potter and the professor. The self-important Cassier struck the table with his fist. "This is my area! I know it inside out! I insist on being in charge of the operation!"

Professor Débouché said quietly: "There's no need for table thumping, my friend. Lieutenant Bellecourt will be in charge of the operation. He specializes in work with explosives. You will have to obey him."

"I'm sick of everything being handed over to the lieutenant," cried the mayor furiously. "Who founded this group? It was I and Rouff and some of the local farmers."

"Yes, that's right," the potter agreed. "At first we were all local people. You others only came in later."

Yvonne forced herself to stop thinking about Captain Everett. She said coldly: "Stop quarreling. What the professor says goes. It's true we only turned up later. But it was we who first put the group on a proper footing. If it hadn't been for us you would never have got this receiver. And it was I who showed you how to use it."

Neither the mayor nor the potter replied. But they exchanged glances over Yvonne's head, the sly looks typical of elderly peasants.

[3]

On August 3, 1943, about ten minutes past eleven P.M., a British bomber captured by the Germans parachuted over Grid 167 a big, specially constructed package containing captured British plastic explosive.

On August 2, 1943, a certain Heinze, member of the board of works of the Todt organization in Paris, appeared at the Eguzon power station. He discussed with the chief German engineers, in the greatest detail, the consequences of the steps which would have to be taken if the bridge adjoining the dam were blown up.

On August 3, Heinze visited the commander of the German battalion occupying the Gargilesse area, swore him to secrecy and impressed upon him that all German sentry posts should be withdrawn on August 4 between 11:15 P.M. and 12:30 A.M.

On August 4, at eight minutes past midnight, the Pont Noir duly blew up with earsplitting din. No one was hurt.

On August 5, at nine P.M., Corporals Schlumberger and Raddatz crouched, sweating, over their equipment in the Hôtel Lutetia, Paris. Behind them stood Thomas Lieven, Colonel Werthe and Captain Brenner.

Nightingale 17 reported punctually. Schlumberger murmured, as he scribbled: "The girl's not signaling today. It's one of the boys this time . . ."

Nightingale 17 sent a longer message than ever before. While Schlumberger was still taking down the signals, Raddatz was already decoding them. The first part of the message was just what Thomas had expected.

> . . . mission pont noir duly carried out—whole bridge completely destroyed—twenty men actually on job—lieutenant bellecourt broke leg prior to operation—being cared for by friends at eguzon—emile rouff transmitting—professor debouche and yvonne deschamps in clermont ferrand . . .

Werthe, Brenner and Thomas looked over Raddatz's shoulder as he decoded.

That confounded fool down there, thought Thomas, losing color. What's he giving names for?

Before Thomas could do anything more, Raddatz kicked him. Glancing down at the corporal's face, he saw that it expressed disgust and amazement. Just at that moment Schlumberger passed him another sheet to decode. Raddatz cleared his throat with a kind of groan of despair.

"What's happened?" Brenner demanded, thrusting his weasel-sharp features forward.

"I—I—nothing—" the Berliner stammered.

Brenner snatched the paper from him. "Give me that!" he shouted. He waved the sheet in the air, his spectacles flashing. "Just listen to this, Colonel!"

Thomas felt as though an icy hand was gripping his heart, as he listened to Brenner reading out what Raddatz had just decoded.

> We request that general de gaulle may be informed of the operation and made aware of the identity of our most important and daring members—appreciation and bestowal of medals would greatly assist morale . . .

Good God, thought Thomas, I simply can't believe it!

... chief services in the operation were rendered after retirement of lieutenant bellecourt by mayor cassier resident in crozant—seconded by emile rouff of gargilesse—and ...

Corporal Schlumberger looked up agitatedly from his memorandum block.

"Go on taking the message, man!" Brenner shouted at him. Then the captain swung around to Thomas. "Didn't you once say, Herr Sonderführer, that those fellows could never be caught because their real names and addresses weren't known? Hey?" He laughed harshly, "Well, now we shall soon know who *you* are!"

The room seemed to start going around Thomas. Those wretched creatures down there, he thought. Conceited idiots! I always thought only Germans could behave like that. But Frenchmen are no better. All I've done has been in vain.

Colonel Werthe suddenly looked very grim. He said very quietly: "Leave the room, Herr Lieven."

"Colonel, I beg of you to—" Thomas began. But the look in Werthe's gray eyes showed that nothing he could say could ever now have any effect on the man.

In vain! Everything had been in vain on account of a few silly imbeciles who wanted to strut about after the war with a few pieces of lead on their chests.

Five minutes later Corporals Schlumberger and Raddatz, dismissed in their turn, came down to the lounge, where Thomas was waiting for them.

Schlumberger looked very woebegone.

"That stupid ass goes on and on and on. He's given away twenty-seven names up to now."

"And from those twenty-seven it'll be easy enough to find all the rest," Raddatz added.

"What about a meal together, boys?" Thomas suggested. They went to Henri's, as they often had during the last few months. It was a small restaurant which Thomas had discovered in the rue Clement Marot. The manager came to their table in person and greeted them warmly. Whenever he saw Thomas his eyes grew moist.

Henri's sister-in-law was a German Jewess who had taken refuge in a rural district with forged papers supplied by Thomas. There were many good opportunities of getting hold of forged documents in the Hôtel Lutetia. Thomas took advantage of such occasions from time to time. Colonel Werthe knew all about it. But he held his tongue.

"Something light, Henri," Thomas said. It was already late in the evening and he felt he needed calming down. They concocted the menu together.

"I say, Herr Lieven," Schlumberger requested. "Translate for us. Tell him we'd like a few pancakes."

MENU

Lamb Kidneys on Croutons
Sole à la Grenoble
Apricot Pancakes

PARIS, 5 AUGUST 1943

Thomas had an inspiration, with the fish, that saved sixty-five lives.

Lamb Kidneys on Croutons

Remove fat and skin from small lamb kidneys and cut into halves lengthways. Cut thin slices from a French loaf, butter them lightly on both sides and place on each half a kidney with the cut side down. Mix strong mustard, sour cream, a little butter, one yolk, salt and cayenne pepper to a thick cream and spread it over the kidneys. Place on a baking sheet and put into a medium oven for ten minutes. Test with a sharp fork. When no more red juices appear, the kidneys are cooked. Serve hot.

Sole à la Grenoble

Ask the fishmonger to skin and fillet the soles. Cover for at least half an hour with lemon juice, pepper and salt, to keep the fillets firm and white. Dry well and fry quickly on both sides in hot brown butter. Place on a warm serving dish. Next heat small lemon cubes and a few capers quickly in the butter left in the pan. This sauce is then poured over the fillets. They are served with boiled potatoes sprinkled with parsley.

Apricot Pancakes

Cook fine, thin, medium-sized pancakes. Spread apricot jam on one side, roll up and fry quickly in the hot butter. Serve immediately and sprinkle to taste with grated almonds. Pancakes are best when the prepared butter is made at least an hour before cooking and left till wanted.

Thomas translated. Henri disappeared. A leaden silence settled upon the three friends. Not until the lamb kidneys appeared did the Viennese mutter: "Brenner's called up Berlin. Early tomorrow morning at latest a 'special detachment' will get to work. Not much doubt about what will happen to those people then."

Thomas was thinking of Professor Débouché, the beautiful Yvonne, Lieutenant Bellecourt and so many, many others. They were still living and breathing. But soon they would be arrested. Soon they would be dead.

"Boy," said Raddatz, "I've had four years of active service now and haven't yet killed a single soul. It makes me puke to think that all of a sudden we're going to be responsible for . . ."

"We're not responsible," Thomas said. He was thinking, No, you two aren't. But what about me? Inextricably involved already in lies and treachery, deception and plotting . . . how can I deny reponsibility?

"Herr Lieven," said Schlumberger, "we can't possibly go to the help of partisans who kill our comrades."

"No," said Thomas, "that you can't do." What can one do, he thought. What ought one to do? How can one remain a decent human being?

"Karli's right," the Berliner said. "I'm no Nazi either, you know. But honestly now, if the partisans happen to pick me up in the woods, would they believe me if I swore I wasn't a Nazi?"

"Not they," said the other corporal. "They'd shoot. For them a German's a German and that's that."

Thomas toyed meditatively with his sole. Suddenly he jumped up. "There's still one chance," he exclaimed. "Just one!"

"What's that?"

"It's a chance to do something and still stay decent," Thomas said. He went to the telephone booth in the restaurant, called up the Hôtel Lutetia and asked for Colonel

Werthe. The latter's voice, when he answered, sounded preoccupied.

Thomas could also hear many other voices. Apparently the colonel was in conference. Thomas sweated as he thought, Must stay decent, to decent men in my own country and decent men in this. Don't be a traitor or a crank or a sentimentalist. Just save lives . . . save lives . . .

He said hoarsely: "Colonel, this is Lieven. I have a proposal of the greatest importance to make to you. It won't be possible for you to act on it alone. I beg you to listen to me and then immediately inform Admiral Canaris."

"What's all this nonsense about?"

"Colonel, when do they start in down there?"

"First thing tomorrow morning. Why?"

"I want you to let me take charge of the operation."

"Lieven! I'm in no sort of mood whatever for joking. I've had enough of all this—"

"For heaven's sake listen to me, Colonel. Do please hear what I have to propose . . ."

[4]

At a quarter to five in the morning of August 6, 1943, a genuine British Lysander was heading for Clermont-Ferrand. The glowing orb of the sun was just rising through seething clouds of mist.

The pilot, separated from his passenger by a partition, spoke on the intercommunication line. "Landing in twenty minutes, Herr Sonderführer."

"Thanks," said Thomas Lieven. He clicked down the receiver at his elbow. Then he sat motionless in his tiny cabin, staring out at the absolute purity of the sky and the whitish-gray veils of mist that still hid the squalid earth, its wars and intrigues, its baseness and stupidity.

Thomas Lieven looked ill. He was hollow-cheeked, with dark circles under his eyes. He had just passed the worst night of his life. The worst day of his life lay ahead of him.

Ten minutes later the aircraft began to lose height, dropping down through the early morning haze. Clermont-Ferrand, a cathedral and university town, became visible, lying asleep, without a sign of life in the streets.

By a quarter-past five Thomas was drinking hot coffee in the office of the Tyrolese Captain Oellinger. The sturdy little commander of the Alpine troops garrisoning the city studied Thomas's secret service pass with close attention.

"I've had a long message from Colonel Werthe by teleprinter," he said. "And only an hour ago he telephoned to me. My people are at your disposal, Herr Sonderführer."

"For the moment I only want a car to take me into town."

"You can have an escort of ten men."

"No, thank you. What I have to do I must do alone."

"Oh? But—"

"Here's a sealed envelope. If you haven't heard anything of me by eight o'clock, open it. You will find full instructions there from Colonel Werthe as to how you are then to proceed. Good-bye for the present."

"Till our next meeting, then—"

"I hope there will be one," said Thomas, touching wood.

A Citroën, confiscated by the Germans, but still carrying its French number plates, bumped over the deserted Place Blaise Pascal. Thomas sat next to the sleepy, silent driver. He had slipped a trenchcoat over his gray flannel suit and wore a white hat.

Thomas was bound, at this early morning hour, for the residence of Professor Débouché, spiritual leader of the resistance in central France. The professor had accommodation assigned to him in one of the buildings of the widespread University City. Thomas alighted at its main entrance in the Avenue Carnot. "Drive around the corner and wait for me," he told his companion.

He went up to the closed gate. God help me now, he was thinking. God help us all now.

He was obliged to ring again and again before at last the elderly janitor, wearing slippers, with an overcoat covering his nightshirt, opened the door, swearing volubly. "God Almighty, have you gone crazy? What on earth do you want at this hour?"

"I want to speak to Professor Débouché."

"Now look here, young man—" The janitor ceased speaking. A five-thousand-franc note had changed hands. "All right then, I suppose it's urgent. Whom shall I announce?"

"Have you a telephone in your quarters?"

"Yes, monsieur."

"Then I'll talk to him myself."

Thomas sweated freely in the janitor's cramped basement flat as he listened to the telephone bell ringing in Professor Débouché's quarters.

The janitor's wife had got out of bed and was standing close to her husband, whispering to him, while both stared with frightened expressions at Thomas. At last the latter heard a voice he knew. "Débouché speaking. What's the matter?"

Thomas croaked out: "Everett."

He heard the professor gasp. "Everett? Where—where are you?"

"At the university. In the janitor's quarters."

"Tell him to bring you to me at once. I—I shall be expecting you . . ."

Thomas hung up. The janitor said: "This way, monsieur." As he went out Thomas saw him nod to his wife. What he did not see was that the wrinkled, gray-haired old woman went over to the telephone as soon as they had gone and picked up the receiver.

[5]

"What in heaven's name induced you to be so crazy as to come here, Captain Everett?" The famous physicist who looked so much like Albert Einstein confronted Thomas against the background of a towering bookshelf in the professor's library.

"Professor, the Crozant group has blown up the bridge at Gargilesse."

"Yes, in accordance with their instructions."

"Have you seen any of them since?"

"No. I have been here with my assistant for a week now. I had lectures to give."

"But I suppose you know that after Bellecourt's accident Cassler and Rouff took charge of the operation?"

"Good, gallant fellows, both of them."

"They were wretched, stupid idiots," Thomas retorted bitterly. "Vain, irresponsible fools!"

"Captain, if you please—"

"Do you know what those god-damned imbeciles did last night? They sat down at the transmitter and reeled off the names and addresses of the members of their group! They named themselves, they named you, they named Yvonne Deschamps and Bellecourt and over thirty others . . ."

"But, for God's sake, why?" The old man's face was white.

"To make themselves important. So as to make certain that General de Gaulle himself should know who had been the most gallant heroes and who had earned the highest decorations . . . A thickheaded lot you have up there in the hills, Professor!"

The old scholar stared at Thomas for a long time. At last he said: "It was wrong, of course, to give those names away. But was it a crime? Did it endanger London in any way? I don't see how it could . . . So that can't be the reason why you have come here at the risk of your life . . ." Professor Débouché came very close up to Thomas. The scientist's eyes widened in a searching gaze as he whispered hoarsely: "Why did you risk your life, Captain Everett?"

Thomas drew a deep breath. Suppose he kills me, he thought. Suppose I don't survive this day. Then at least I should have died in the attempt to remain a decent human being in this squalid age. He suddenly felt perfectly calm, as when he had resolved to evade further Gestapo interrogation by suicide.

He said quietly: "Because I am not Captain Everett. My name is Thomas Lieven."

The old man closed his eyes.

"Because I don't work for London, but for German Intelligence."

The old man opened his eyes. He gazed at Thomas with an expression of infinite melancholy.

"And because for months the Crozant group has not been in communication with London but with the Germans."

A long silence ensued. The two men stared at each other.

At last Débouché whispered: "That would be too terrible. I can't believe it. I refuse to believe it."

At that moment the door flew open. Débouché's assistant, Yvonne Dechamps, stood on the threshold. She was out of breath. She wore no make-up and had scarcely anything on under her blue raincoat. Her abundant fair hair fell loosely about her shoulders. Her sea-green eyes were wide with shock. Her beautiful mouth quivered. "So it was true . . . Captain Everett . . . it was really you . . ."

She reached Thomas in three strides. Débouché started violently. She glared at Thomas, stuttering: "The janitor's wife called me up . . . she knew I lived here . . . Captain Everett, what has happened? What has happened?"

Thomas, compressing his lips, remained silent. Suddenly she seized his hand and held it tight in both of hers. It was not until then that she realized Débouché's presence. He was seated in a broken, senile attitude, despair in his face.

"What has happened, Professor?" cried the girl shrilly, in a sudden access of panic.

"My child, that man whose hand you are holding is a German agent."

Yvonne Dechamps moved very slowly away from Thomas. She reeled as though drunk, then dropped into a chair. Débouché told her in a low tone what he had just heard from Thomas.

She listened without taking her eyes off Thomas. Their green depths grew darker and darker, till they were filled with hate and scorn. Her lips scarcely moved when at last she spoke. "I consider you the basest and vilest of mankind, Herr Lieven. I consider you the most odious of scoundrels, a truly hateful creature."

"I don't care in the least what you consider me," said Thomas. "It is not my fault that not only we Germans but also you French produce such vain, selfish idiots as Rouff and Cassier. For months everything was all right . . ."

"You call that all right, you brute?"

"Yes," said Thomas. He felt himself growing steadily calmer. "I do call it all right. For months no one was shot in that area. No Germans and no French. It could have continued that way. I could have protected you all right up to the end of this accursed war . . ."

Yvonne suddenly uttered a scream as piercing and hysterical as a child's. She leaped clumsily to her feet and spat into Thomas's face. The professor dragged her forcibly back.

Thomas wiped his cheek with a pocket handkerchief, surveying Yvonne in silence. She's right, he was thinking. From her standpoint she's right enough. We are all right from our respective points of view, even I. For I only want to behave decently to everybody. . . .

Yvonne started to rush to the door. Thomas pulled her back. She crashed heavily against the wall and snarled at him, showing her teeth.

"You stay here." Thomas barred the way to the door. "When the names came through last night German Intelligence at once informed Berlin. It was decided to send in the Alpine troops in charge of the city. I then again spoke to the head of Paris Intelligence."

"Why?" asked Professor Débouché.

Thomas shook his head. "That's my affair."

The professor gave him a strange look. "I didn't mean to offend you."

That man, thought Thomas, that admirable man, is beginning to understand. He is beginning to understand me . . . if I have any luck, if we all have any luck . . .

"I represented to Colonel Werthe that the proposed operation by the Alpine troops would undoubtedly involve loss of life on both sides. While our own side would attack with determination, yours would offer a desperate resistance. Blood would flow and human beings would die. Both Germans and French. The Gestapo would torture the prisoners and they would betray their comrades."

"Never!" cried Yvonne.

Thomas swung around. "You keep your mouth shut!"

The old man said: "Some tortures are terrible." The glance he shot at Thomas suddenly seemed as wise and sad as that of some Old Testament prophet. "I think you know that, Herr Lieven. I think I understand a lot now. I feel that there is nothing to retract. Do you remember? I once said that I considered you a decent sort. . . ."

Thomas said nothing. Yvonne was breathing noisily.

"What else did you say to your colonel, Herr Lieven?"

"I made a suggestion to him which was later approved by Admiral Canaris."

"What was the suggestion?"

"You are the spiritual leader of the resistance here. The members obey you. If you summon a meeting of the group in the Gargilesse mill and explain that capture is inevitable, the troops will be able to take them prisoner without firing a shot."

"And what then?"

"In that case Admiral Canaris will give his word of honor that none of you will be handed over to the Security Police but that you will be taken to an ordinary prisoners-of-war camp."

"That's bad enough."

"In the circumstances it's your best chance. The war won't go on forever."

Professor Débouché did not answer. He stood with bent head, facing the rows of books.

Thomas was thinking: May God grant that this war may now at last be coming to an end. It is so terribly difficult to remain decent among Nazis. May they perish now once for all. And may I at last be left to live in peace.

But it was going to be very long indeed before such hopes could be fulfilled.

The professor asked: "How am I going to reach Gargilesse?"

"With me, by car. We haven't much time, Professor. If you decline my suggestion, the troops will begin operations at eight o'clock without us."

"What about Yvonne? She is the only woman in the group . . . a woman, Herr Lieven. . . ."

Thomas smiled sadly. "I shall take Mlle. Yvonne as my personal prisoner—please allow me to finish—to a cell in the town jail. She will stay there until the operation is over. She will be prevented in this way from causing any disturbance with her patriotic enthusiasm. I shall then come to get her and take her to Paris. And on the way there she will escape."

"What?" Yvonne stared at him.

"You will succeed in getting away," Thomas said quietly. "That will be the second favor I shall have received from Colonel Werthe. It will be an escape guaranteed, so to speak, by German Intelligence."

Yvonne walked straight up to Thomas. She was panting with excitement. "If there is a God, He will punish you . . . you will perish slowly and miserably . . . I am not going to escape! And Professor Débouché will never agree to your suggestion, never! We shall fight and die,all of us."

"Oh, of course," said Thomas wearily. "And now suppose you go and sit down again and try to hold your tongue for once, you tintype heroine."

[6]

secret—1435 hours—9 august—intelligence paris to head intelligence berlin—alpine troops battalion clermont ferrand zone under sonderfuhrer lieven captured crozant group about 22 hours 7 august near gargilesse mill—members of group under professor debouche made no resistance—sixty-seven (67) men arrested—prisoners taken in accordance with instructions to army prisoners of war camp 343—messages ends.

[7]

On September 17, 1945, Professor Débouché declared before an Allied Investigations Committee in Paris:

"All the members of the Crozant Resistance Group were considerately treated in Army Camp 343. They all survived the war and returned to their homes. I must emphasize that we all probably owe our lives simply to the courage and humane feeling of a German whom we first met in the guise of a British captain and who came to visit me in Clermont-Ferrand on August 6. He said at that time that he was known as Sonderführer Thomas Lieven. . . ."

Officials of the committee immediately began a search for Sonderführer Lieven. But they couldn't find him. For in the autumn of 1945 organizations of a character very different from that of an Allied Investigations Committee were after Thomas Lieven. For this reason he had just . . . But we are anticipating. Let us return to August 1943.

[8]

"Gentlemen," said Colonel Werthe. "I have just received the necessary instructions from Berlin. Captain Brenner, for your services in respect of the liquidation of the Crozant resistance group, you are promoted to major with retrospective effect to August 1. Furthermore, in the name of the Führer and Commander in Chief I bestow upon you the War Service Cross, First Class, with Swords."

That was little Captain Brenner's finest hour. Behind the flashing spectacles his eyes sparkled like those of a happy child on Christmas Eve. He stood stiffly to attention, chest out, stomach in.

"Bravo!" exclaimed Lieven, the civilian. That day he was wearing a surperbly cut blue summer suit, a white shirt and a tie with subdued gray and pink stripes. "Congratulations, Major!"

The newly fledged major murmured confusedly: "Of course I owe it all to you!"

"Nonsense!"

"No, it's not nonsense, you alone were responsible. I confess that I often opposed you in the question of this operation, in fact that I thought the whole thing crazy and didn't trust you in the least . . ."

"If you trust me from now on all will be well," Thomas assured him indulgently. And in fact Major Brenner subsequently proved a devoted admirer of Thomas and never quailed at the wildest and most daring schemes of his strange special operations chief.

Colonel Werthe had been awarded a bar to the Iron Cross, First Class, which he had won in the First World War.

"Think of that," Thomas commented to the new major. "The two world wars we started came so close together that a strong, healthy man had every chance of experiencing both in all their heroic grandeur."

"Oh, dry up," said the colonel. "I don't know what we're going to do with such a queer fish of a special operations chief as you are. You're a typical civilian, aren't you?"

"And I hope I always shall be."

"But there's a query here from Berlin. What sort of decoration would you like?"

"I don't take any interest in decorations, Colonel," replied our friend. "But could I just make one request?"

"Go ahead!"

"I'd like a different sphere of activity. I don't want to be employed again in action against partisans, gentlemen. I'm gay and cheerful by nature. But I've lost my gaiety during these last few weeks. If I really have to go on working for you I should prefer a pleasanter, more entertaining sort of job."

"I believe I have exactly the right assignment for you, Sonderführer Lieven."

"And that is?"

"Supervision of the French black market," Werthe said. And in fact from that moment, at any rate for some time, all the dark clouds disappeared from Thomas Lieven's horizon and our friend went tumbling head over heels into a carnival of grotesque new adventures . . .

"Never in the whole history of mankind," said Colonel Werthe, "has so vast, crazy and dangerous a black market existed as we have here and now in Paris." Thomas learned with amazement what went on behind the superficial frivolity of the City of Light on the Seine. "All the establishments here support it, the Todt organization, the Fleet, the Air Force, the Army and its motorized forces, even the Security Police, are in the racket now."

According to Werthe, Goering himself was in favor of taking measures against the *marché noir*. For competition between rival German buyers had been forcing prices up to astronomical heights. An ordinary lathe, for instance, normally worth forty thousand francs, now cost, owing to the intervention of five or six agents, a whole million.

The Security Police had therefore set up a Counter-Black-Market office in the rue des Saussaies, with accommodation in the Sûreté building, and an SS Untersturmbannführer in charge. Representatives of the Security Police from all parts of France were called in to Paris for training.

But the new office did not prove very efficient. The counter-black-market experts, once they were trained, soon found they could come to profitable terms with the *marché noir*. They worked in with the French. The most scandalous rackets were organized.

For example, fifty thousand sweaters were sold in a single day not once but four times over. The first three buyers were simply assassinated. The fourth was himself in with the group of swindlers. Consequently the sweaters could again be offered for sale later on. Meanwhile the amount realized from the first three sales was already in the bag, viz., three times the price of fifty thousand pullovers.

People disappeared. Locomotives disappeared. Hundreds of thousands of kilos of the best cigarette paper disappeared. Wilder and wilder grew the activities due to the corruption of the Security Police in the Counter-Black-Market office. Agents continually arrested or assassinated one another. Gestapo officials masqueraded as French gangsters and the latter as Gestapo officials.

All this was explained in detail by Colonel Werthe to Thomas Lieven, who could hardly believe his ears. Finally the colonel inquired:

"How would that sort of job suit you, Lieven?"

"Very well indeed, I should think, Colonel."

"Not too dangerous?"

"Well, you know, I had quite a strenuous training in that particular field when I was in Marseilles," Thomas Lieven replied. "And I'm already in possession of all the necessary resources. I still have my villa in the Bois de Boulogne. I'm still a partner, as I was before the war, in a small bank here. I should be considered exceptionally trustworthy."

He was thinking, And then at last, too, I should have a private life again. And at last I could loosen my ties with you, dear friends, and not see quite so much of you. Who knows? I might even contrive to get away, after all, to Switzerland . . .

[9]

Thomas Lieven found his bank again, feeling like the man in the fairy tale who returned to his village after a long, enchanted sleep and discovered that seven years had passed. In the case of Thomas Lieven only three years had passed. The chief clerk and most of the older employees were still working at the bank, though many of the younger men had gone.

Thomas accounted for his long absence by declaring that he had been imprisoned by the Germans on political grounds and only recently released.

He next asked for news of his treacherous English partner, Robert E. Marlock. But no one had the least idea of what had become of the rascal.

Thomas drove out to the Bois de Boulogne. The sight of the little villa in which he had spent so many delightful hours with sweet little Mimi Chambert really depressed him.

The thought of Mimi reminded him of Colonel Siméon. Were they in Paris? He felt inclined to look for them, and also for Josephine Baker and Colonel Débras. From far, far away in the great sandy desert of time they seemed to smile at him. Then there were Bastian and Hoofy of Marseilles, Pereira, the forger of genius, Lazarus Alcoba, the dead, loyal hunchback, Estrella Rodrigues of Lisbon, the hysterical female consul. And furthest away of all, inaccessible, the melancholy smile of the woman for whom Thomas still hopelessly longed . . .

Rousing himself abruptly from these memories he wiped the moisture from his eyes and went into the little garden of the villa, whence he had escaped three years before in a Chrysler with an American flag on its roof.

A pretty young housemaid opened the door to him. He asked to see the master of the house. The girl showed him into the drawing room. "The staff paymaster will be here in a moment."

Thomas glanced about. He could recognize his own furniture, carpets and pictures. They were, alas, neglected, the worse for wear. But still his.

The staff paymaster entered. He had a confident, well fed and self-important air. "Höpfner is my name. Heil Hitler! What can I do for you?"

"Thomas Lieven. You can leave these premises immediately."

The staff paymaster turned crimson. "Is this some silly hoax?"

"No. It happens to be my villa."

"Rubbish! This villa's mine. I've been living here for a year."

"Yes, that's obvious. I never saw such a filthy mess."

"Look here, Herr Lieven, or whatever you call yourself, be off this instant or I call the police."

Thomas rose. "I'm on my way. Incidentally, I see that you're not quite properly dressed."

He went to see Colonel Werthe. Two hours later Staff Paymaster Höpfner received from his immediate superior orders to evacuate the villa in the Bois de Boulogne without delay. He spent the night in a hotel. The whole thing seemed incomprehensible to him.

[10]

While Staff Paymaster Höpfner lost a villa, Colonel Werthe lost, about the same time, a first-rate domestic employee, the pretty, black-haired Nanette. The little French girl had met and admired Thomas Lieven when he had arrived at the house, escorted by Colonel Werthe, on December 12, 1942, after being rescued in such a pitiable condition from the Gestapo. Now Nanette suddenly gave the Intelligence colonel notice. A few days later he met her at Thomas's villa.

"Please don't be angry, sir," she piped. "I've always wanted to work in the Bois de Boulogne."

Thomas had soon re-equipped his former residence to his taste. The cellar was filled with black market liquor, the kitchen with black market provisions. Black market countermeasures could begin at any time.

The first, somewhat mysterious, key figure recommended for his attention by Colonel Werthe was a certain Jean-Paul Ferroud. This white-haired giant owned, like Thomas himself, a private bank in Paris. It seemed that the biggest, most impudent frauds were being perpetrated through his agency.

Thomas asked his fellow banker to dinner.

In 1943 there were two steps which Frenchmen only took under most exceptionable circumstances. They very rarely visited Germans or invited visits from them. Representatives of the two nations met in restaurants, bars and theaters, but not at one another's houses unless there were very good reasons indeed for doing so.

The Ferroud affair began, accordingly, with a surprise for Thomas. The banker accepted his invitation.

Thomas Lieven and Nanette took five days to get the meal ready. Ferroud arrived at half-past seven. Both gentlemen wore dinner jackets.

MENU

Ham in Red Wine with Celery Salad
and Boiled Potatoes
Savarin with Fruit

PARIS, 10 SEPTEMBER 1943

Thomas Lieven's black market merry-go-round began with ham.

Ham in Red Wine with Celery Salad

From a whole fresh ham remove skin and some of the fat. Mix to a cream some grated onions, ground pepper, ginger, bay leaf and juniper berries. Rub the cream by hand well into the ham until latter goes brown. It is then placed in a pot, to which is added a bottle of red wine and half a bottle of vinegar. This is left to soak for from five to eight days during which it is occasionally turned. Before roasting it is well rubbed with salt and baked in half the liquid. When this first half of liquid has boiled away add the rest gradually. Bake the ham to a good brown color. Prepare the gravy and serve with a celery salad (no mayonnaise) and boiled potatoes. The ham requires, according to size, three to five hours' cooking time.

Savarin with Fruit

Take two cups of flour, exactly half a cup of milk, one envelope of dry yeast, one stick or half a cup of butter, one third of a cup of sugar, three eggs and a little salt. Make a yeast dough with a quarter of the flour and leave it to rise. Mix into it the melted butter and other ingredients and beat till bubbles form. Grease a flan tin with butter, fill three quarters of the tin with the dough and leave to rise until tin is full. Bake for thirty minutes. Meanwhile heat some tinned or bottled apricots in halves and a quarter of a cup of apricot jam. Prepare a liquid from half a cup of the fruit juice, two tablespoonfuls of white wine, one tablespoonful each of kirsch, sherry, maraschino and lemon juice, with half a teaspoonful of rum and a little powdered vanilla. Place the baked yeast cake on a warm dish, pour the hot liquid over it, spread it with the hot apricot jam and sprinkle it with two tablespoonfuls of chopped pistachio nuts. Pile the hot fruit high in the middle. The cake can be baked the day before and reheated before application of the liquid and other additions.

They drank very dry martinis in the drawing room, then sat down to dinner by candlelight.

Nanette served the ham.

Ferroud ate like a connoisseur. He licked his lips delicately. "Really wonderful, monsieur. Cooked in red wine, I take it?"

"For five days. But the most important part of the preparation was the rubbing with juniper berries, ginger, bay leaf, ground pepper and onions. The ham has to be rubbed until it is nearly black."

"And you only use red wine?" Ferroud looked very handsome, like an aristocratic father in a French play.

"I added half a bottle of vinegar. Very glad you accepted my invitation."

"The pleasure is mine," said the other, with a generous load of celery salad on his fork. "After all, it's not every day that one is invited to dinner by an agent of German Intelligence."

Thomas went on calmly eating.

"I have made certain inquiries about you, M. Lieven. It's really not possible to be quite sure about your true identity, since I heard so much about you that amounted actually to so little. But one thing seems certain. Your attention has been drawn to me because I am supposed to be a big wire-puller in the black market. Isn't that so?"

"Yes," said Thomas. "Do help yourself to another slice of ham. There's one thing I don't understand."

"What, may I ask?"

"Well, I wonder why, if you distrust me and know what my object is, you nevertheless came to see me. There must be a reason for that."

"Of course there is one. I wanted to meet the man who might perhaps be my enemy. And I should like to hear you quote a figure. We may be able to come to some arrangement, monsieur."

Thomas raised his eyebrows. He retorted with a certain arrogance: "You don't seem to be so well informed about me after all. That's a pity, M. Ferroud. I'd been looking forward to meeting an adversary of my own caliber. . ."

The banker flushed, laying down his knife and fork. "Then I take it no mutual agreement is possible. So it's my turn to say, what a pity. I fear you underestimate the danger in which you will be living from now on, monsieur. You will understand that I cannot allow anyone to see my cards. Not even men who cannot be bribed . . ."

[11]

Thomas Lieven had only just gone to bed at his villa in the Bois de Boulogne, Paris, when the telephone rang. It was fourteen minutes to two A.M. on September 13, 1943, a historic moment. For in retrospect that telephone call could be seen to have released an avalanche of events. For it meant that he would:

(a) resume an acquaintance with a lady from which, after an extremely short period of bliss, he would barely escape with his life;

(b) make a friend of a man who would save the said life a few months later;

(c) be enabled to reveal not only a highly intelligible though at the same time reprehensible murder, but also, in connection therewith, the biggest black market swindle of the year, and:

(d) earn the eternal gratitude of a desperate housewife and an aged female cook by rescuing them from a situation peculiarly dreadful for domestically minded women.

A thoroughly mixed program, evidently enough, with a number of plus and minus signs. Nevertheless, if Thomas had suspected what was in store for him, he would have let that telephone bell ring until the Day of Judgment. But he never expected anything of the sort. So he lifted the receiver. "Yes?"

"M. Lieven?"

He knew that voice. It was that of Jean-Paul Ferroud.

Thomas inquired politely after the banker's health.

Ferroud said he was all right.

"And your respected consort?"

"She is also quite well, thank you. Herr Lieven, I feel I owe you an apology for behaving so—ahem—coldly and aggressively toward you . . ."

"Don't mention it, I beg of you!"

"But I must, I must! Especially after having enjoyed such an exquisite loin of pork . . . I'm most anxious to make amends." The devil you are, thought Thomas. "Would you give my wife and myself the pleasure of dining at our house this evening?"

Good God, thought Thomas.

The banker continued with suave irony: "I assume that, as an Intelligence agent, you know exactly where I live. Or am I wrong?"

Little jokes of that sort had long ceased to irritate Thomas. The retorted promptly: "But of course I know, monsieur. You live in the Avenue Malakoff, No. 24, quite near here. You have a very beautiful wife, Christian name Marie-Louise, maiden name Kléber. She owns the most valuable jewelry possessed by any lady in Paris. You have a Chinese butler named Shen-Tai, a cook named Thérèse, a maid named Suzette and two bulldogs named Cicero and Caesar."

He heard Ferroud laugh. "Shall we say about eight then?"

"At eight, monsieur." Thomas hung up.

Before he could begin to conjecture the meaning of this strange invitation, someone knocked at the bedroom door. His extremely pretty maid Nanette burst in, quite out of breath. She spoke in German, as she always did when she was particularly excited. "Monsieur . . . monsieur . . . I've just heard on the radio that Mussolini has been rescued . . . and he's already on the way to Berlin—to Hitler—to go on fighting the war as his ally . . ."

"Benito must be very pleased about that," said Thomas.

Nanette laughed. She came right up to the bed. "Oh, monsieur . . . you are so nice . . . I am so happy you let me be here . . ."

"Nanette, don't forget your Pierre!"

She pouted. "Oh, Pierre—he's so boring . . ."

"He is a very nice young man," said Thomas pedantically. He got out of bed. She was coming a bit too near him. "Off you go now, Nanette! Kitchen!" He slapped her playfully. She laughed as though he had tickled her. Then she reluctantly left the room. What does that banker want, Thomas was wondering.

[12]

The villa in the Avenue Malakoff proved to be a regular museum of works of art, both European and from the Far East. Ferroud must be a millionaire.

The little Chinese butler received the visitor with the eternal smile characteristic of his race, yet with a certain arrogance and coldness in his bearing and speech. The maid behaved in the same way when Thomas handed her a cellophane carton of three pink orchids for her mistress.

Finally, the master of the house himself gave a similar impression of arrogance and coldness. He let Thomas wait quite a while—seven minutes, as the guest checked, with wrinkled brow, from his gold repeater—in the drawing room. Then he appeared, elegant as ever, shook hands with Thomas and began to mix martinis. "My wife will be here in a minute."

Thomas thought it all a bit queer. He examined the statue of Buddha, the small inlaid cabinet, the heavy, many-branched candlesticks and the rugs. Jean-Paul Ferroud, he thought, is not dependent on anyone. He's in a position to ignore me. But if so, why does he invite me to dinner? And if he invites me to dinner, why does he behave in such a way that I am slowly getting more and more angry?

Suddenly the white-haired banker dropped two small ice cubes. He was standing at a bar decorated with fantastically painted mirrors and filling a silver cocktail shaker. He cleared his throat with an embarrassed laugh. "Hand's trembling. Getting old! It's the booze."

A light suddenly broke it on Thomas. The man was not just putting on airs. He was nervous, frightfully nervous. So were the Chinese butler and the maid . . . The idea he had formed of them at first was all wrong. They all had the jitters, they were afraid of something. But of what?

The mistress of the house entered the room. Marie-Louise was tall, slender and flawless in her beauty. Her eyes were blue, with long lashes. Her fair hair was marvelously waved. She wore an off-the-shoulder black gown and magnificent jewelry around neck and arms. There could of course be no comparison, Thomas thought involuntarily, between that stuff and the swag we took off Pissoladière in Marseilles. I say, what a degenerate I am already, he told himself.

"'Madame . . ." He bowed deeply, kissed her hand and noted that the slim, white, delicately perfumed fingers were trembling.

He straightened, looked into her cold blue eyes, and detected panic in them also, controlled only with an effort.

Madame thanked him for the orchids, declared that she was pleased to meet him and accepted a martini from her husband. Suddenly she put the glass down on a hexagonal bronze table, pressed her fist against her lips and burst into sobs.

The white-haired Ferroud made a dash for his beautiful

spouse. "Good God—Marie-Louise—what the—control yourself, what will Herr Lieven think of you?"

"Oh, dear," sobbed Mme. Ferroud. "Forgive me, Jean, forgive me . . ."

"It's just nerves, darling . . ."

"No, it's not nerves . . . it's not even that other thing . . . something else has happened!"

Ferroud's expression hardened. "Something else—what do you mean?"

"Our dinner—it's ruined!" With a great sob the mistress of the house seized her handkerchief, blew her nose in it and exclaimed: "Thérèse has dropped the fish!"

Ferroud, the banker deeply suspected by German Intelligence of being one of the most dangerous key figures of the fantastic French *marché noir,* lost his temper. "Marie-Louise, I won't have this! You know perfectly well what's at stake this evening. And yet you go and burst into tears about some idiotic fish! You're behaving like a . . ."

"M. Ferroud!" Thomas interrupted him in a quiet but resolute tone.

"What do *you* want—er—I mean—I beg your pardon?"

"Would you allow me to ask Madame a question or two?"

"I . . . er . . . well . . . certainly, of course."

"Thank you. Madame, you say Thérèse has dropped the fish?"

"Yes—she's so old, you know. Her sight's so bad. The fish fell on the stove as she was taking it out of the water. It simply broke up—oh dear, I feel so awful—into a lot of little pieces!"

"Madame, there's only one sin that matters in this world and that's to lose heart. Courage, madame! You had the pluck to invite a German agent to dinner. Don't let a French fish get you down!"

Suddenly Ferroud seized his handsome head in both hands and groaned: "Oh, this is too much . . ."

"I don't see why," said Thomas. He turned to the lady. "Forgive my indiscreet question. But what were we going to have before the fish?"

"Ham and Cumberland sauce."

"H'm." He assumed the expression of a great surgeon called in consultation. "And—er—afterward?"

"Chocolate coffee cream."

"Aha," said Thomas, helping himself to an olive. "That'll do nicely."

"What will do nicely?" The lady, who must have had quite seventy carats' worth of precious minerals on her, asked in a barely audible whisper. Thomas bowed. "Madame, you seem to me to be suffering from two quite distinct anxieties. I can easily relieve you of one of them if you will permit me to visit your kitchen."

"You . . . you think you can still do something with what's left of the fish?" Marie-Louise stared at him in utter stupefaction.

"But of course I can, madame," said our friend. "May we take the glasses and the cocktail shaker with us? One can cook so much better over a sip or two. Really excellent, this martini. Genuine Gordon's gin, eh? I can't imagine how you can still get the stuff in this fourth year of war, M. Ferroud . . ."

MENU

Boiled Ham and Cumberland Sauce
Baked Fish Soufflé
Chocolate Coffee Cream

PARIS, 13 SEPTEMBER 1943

Thomas rescues first a fish and then a blonde.

Cumberland Sauce

Mix one cup of red currant jelly with half a cup of red wine, the juice of two oranges, one teaspoonful of English mustard and the peel of one orange cut into thin strips after removing the pith. This mixture should be kept cold. It can be used as a sauce for any kind of cold meat, especially game.

Baked Fish Soufflé

Boil a while fish, remove skin and bones and cut the flesh into pieces. Prepare a *roux* with butter and flour, add sour cream, white wine, grated Parmesan cheese and a little fish stock. Cook to a thick white sauce. Season with salt and pepper. Add some cooked mushrooms and a few capers. Place the pieces of fish in a well-buttered soufflé dish, pour the sauce over it, sprinkle it thickly with grated Parmesan cheese and small flakes of butter. Then bake in oven till golden-brown. Before serving garnish with *fleurons*, i.e., crescents of baked puff pastry. This dish can be prepared from all firmly fleshed fish, such as cod and any shellfish.

Chocolate Coffee Cream

Boil six ounces of squares of cooking chocolate, and a little sugar in four cups of milk. Three yolks and a flat tablespoonful of corn flour are well beaten in a pan. The boiling liquid is added to the mixture and it is stirred continuously. Cook on very small flame until thick, without bringing to the boil. Add a soupspoonful of coarsely ground coffee (not pulverized) and the egg whites, beaten stiff, to the cream after removing it from the flame. Chill and serve.

[13]

What, then, was really the trouble at Ferronds'?

Thomas could not guess even in the gigantic, tiled kitchen. With an apron tied over his dinner jacket he neatly eliminated all traces of the catastrophe with the fish. The group of admiring spectators consisted of the humiliated, short-sighted old cook, the pallid mistress of the house and its equally pallid master. The strange pair had forgotten, for the time being at any rate, their intense nervousness. Thomas thought, well, I can wait. Till the small hours, if they like to keep it up so long. Some time or other they're bound to start talking.

He boned, skinned and sliced that disastrous fish. Then he took a sip of his martini and observed: "I have learned by bitter experience during these difficult years, ladies, that life usually allows just one more chance. A fish in bits is always better than none at all. We'll start making a really good sauce now. Have you any Parmesan cheese, Thérèse?"

"As much as you would like, monsieur," the old cook piped up. "Oh, I feel so terrible about what has happened, it was all my fault!"

"Pull yourself together, my friend. Take a sip of that stuff. It will do you good." The master of the house handed the cook a full glass. Thomas added: "White wine, sour cream and butter, please."

He got what he wanted. Everyone watched him preparing the sauce. Then a sudden tumult broke out in another part of the house. Two high-pitched voices, male and female, could be heard. The mistress of the house grew paler still. Ferroud rushed to the kitchen door. On the threshold he encountered the Chinese butler. The latter had a simple way of keeping what he had to say secret. He jabbered it in Chinese.

He also pointed back over his shoulder. Mme. Ferroud, who obviously understood Chinese, uttered a scream. Her husband admonished her sternly in the same language. She dropped onto one of the kitchen stools. Ferroud followed Shen-Tai without excusing himself, banging the door behind him.

Well, well, thought Thomas. I suppose this sort of thing must happen even in well-bred French families. Don't see what I can do about it. He decided to keep calm whatever happened. "Have you any capers, Thérèse?"

"O Mary Mother of God, my poor mistress!"

"Thérèse!"

"Capers—yes, we have some."

"And mushrooms?"

"Ye-yes . . . madame, can I do anything for you?"

Mme. Ferroud spoke with an effort at self-control. "Herr Lieven, please excuse all this excitement. Shen-Tai has been with us for ten years. We have no secrets from him. We engaged him in Shanghai, where we lived for a long time . . ."

Raised voices from another room could be heard, followed by the crash of overturned furniture. Thomas thought, As my friend Corporal Karli Schlumberger would say, "Wait for it!"

"And put this lot in the stove, Thérèse."

"My cousin is rather a trying girl, Herr Lieven."

"I'm sorry to hear that, madame. Bake with a small flame now."

"We wished her to dine with us, you know. But just now she wanted to run out of the house. Shen-Tai only just managed to stop her."

"Certainly rather disturbing for you. But why did your respected cousin want to run away?"

"Because of you."

"Because of—*me?*"

"Yes. She didn't want to meet you." Mme. Ferroud rose. "My husband will be in the drawing room with her now. Please come with me. I'm sure Thérèse will be able to manage now."

"Sprinkle thickly with Parmesan, capers and mushrooms, Thérèse," said Thomas. He picked up his martini and the cocktail shaker. "*Madame,* I look forward to meeting your relative. When a lady tries to avoid me before she has ever met me, I feel terribly flattered!"

He followed the mistress of the house. As he entered the drawing room, he did a thing he had never done before. He dropped his martini. The liquor seeped into the thick carpet.

Thomas, rooted to the spot as though paralyzed, stared at the slender young woman seated in a chair of antique design. Ferroud stood at her elbow like a bodyguard. But our friend could only see the girl's pale face, compressed lips, slanting green eyes, severely combed fair hair and high cheekbones. He heard her say hoarsely: "Good evening, Herr Sonderführer."

"Good evening, Mlle. Dechamps," said he with an effort. Then he bowed to the former assistant of Professor Débouché and former Crozant partisan, who hated Germans so much, who had spat in his face at Clermont-Ferrand and wished him a prolonged and agonizing death . . .

Jean-Paul Ferroud picked up the glass Thomas had dropped and said: "We did not tell Yvonne who was coming to visit us this evening. But she . . . she heard your voice while we were going into the kitchen and recognized it. Then she wanted to leave the house . . . you can imagine why."

"I certainly can."

"Well, we're at your mercy now, Herr Lieven. Yvonne's life is in danger. The Gestapo are after her. Without help, she will be done for."

The eyes of Yvonne Dechamps narrowed to slits, as she stared at Thomas. He could read shame and anger, bewilderment and hate, fear and indignation in her beautiful face. He was thinking: I have deceived her twice over, once as a German and once as a man. She will never forgive me that last deception. That's why she hates me. If I had only stayed in her room that night at the Gargilesse mill . . .

He heard Ferroud say: "You are a banker like myself. I am not concerned with the emotional, but only with the practical aspect of this matter. You require information about the black market. I require the safety of my wife's cousin. Is that clear?"

"Quite clear," said Thomas. His lips had suddenly become as dry as parchment. He addressed Yvonne: "How is it that the Gestapo are after you?"

She threw her head back and glanced aside.

Mme. Ferroud called our sharply: "Yvonne!"

Thomas shrugged his shoulders. "Your cousin and I are old

enemies, madame. She can't forgive me for letting her escape at Clermont-Ferrand. I gave her at that time the address of a friend of mine named Bastian Fabre. He would have hidden her. But unfortunately it appears that she made no attempt to find him."

"She went to the leader of the Limoges resistance group," said Ferroud, "so that she could go on fighting for France."

"Our dear little patriotic heroine," Thomas commented with a sigh.

Yvonne suddenly darted a calm, frank look at him. For the first time there was no hatred in it. She said quietly: "France is my country, Herr Lieven. I wanted to go on fighting for it. What would you have done?"

"I don't know. Perhaps the same. Then what happened?"

She lowered her head.

Ferroud said: "There was a traitor in the group. It was the wireless operator. The Gestapo caught fifty-five of the others. Six escaped. One of them is sitting here."

"Yvonne has relatives in Lisbon," said Mme. Ferroud. "If she can get there she will be all right."

The two men looked at each other without speaking. Thomas realized that a successful collaboration was about to begin. But heaven only knows, he reflected, how I can induce my colonel to agree to it!

The Chinese butler appeared, bowing. "Dinner is served," said Mme. Ferroud.

She preceded the others to the dining room. As they followed her Thomas Lieven's hand touched Yvonne's arm. She started as if she had received an electric shock. He looked at her. Her eyes had suddenly grown dark. Her cheeks reddened.

"You'll have to stop all that at once," he said.

"What—what do you mean?"

"Starting and blushing like that. As a German Intelligence agent you'll have to exercise more self-control."

"As—as *what*?" she whispered.

"A German Intelligence agent," retorted Thomas Lieven. "What are you worrying about? Did you suppose I could take you to Lisbon as a French partisan?"

[14]

The regular night express to Marseilles, leaving Paris at 9:50 P.M., included three sleeping cars. Adjoining central compartments of one were reserved on the evening of September 17, 1943, for members of German Intelligence.

Ten minutes before the departure of the train a smartly dressed civilian appeared in the corridor of the car in question, accompanied by an elegant young lady, and beckoned to the French guard. The lady wore a camel-hair overcoat with an upturned collar and a hat like a man's, with a broad rim, at that time the latest fashion. It was rather difficult to see her face.

The gentleman showed his reserved ticket to the guard and tipped him lavishly.

"Thank you, monsieur. I'll bring the glasses at once . . ." The guard opened the doors of the two compartments reserved for German Intelligence. In one of them a silver ice bucket contained a bottle of Veuve Clicquot. On the adjustable table by the window stood a vase of twenty red carnations. The communicating door between the compartments was open.

Thomas Lieven closed both the doors into the corridor. Yvonne Dechamps took her big hat off. She was again blushing deeply.

"I've told you not to blush like that," said Thomas. He pulled up the window blind and looked out onto the platform. Two non-commissioned officers of the German Army Railways Control Service were just passing. "H'm." Thomas pulled down the gleaming black curtain again.

"What's the matter?" he asked. "What are you looking at me like that for? Have I been betraying France again?"

"That champagne—and the flowers . . . why do you do that?"

"Oh, just to calm your nerves a bit. You're nothing but a bundle of them at present. You jump at every sound. You look back at everyone we pass. And yet you're perfectly safe, you know. Your name is Madeleine Noël and you're a German Intelligence agent. You have a German Intelligence pass."

In order to get that pass Thomas had been obliged to talk himself black in the face at the Hôtel Lutetia for a whole day. At last Colonel Werthe, with a sigh, had shaken his head. "Lieven, you'll be the death of Paris Intelligence. You're just about all we needed to put us out of business!"

"Ah, here come the glasses," cried Thomas gaily. "Just put them down, Emile. I'll open the bottle myself."

He did so. They were just drinking their first glass when,

two minutes before the train left, the two non-commissioned officers of the Railway Control Service appeared in the compartment.

Yvonne proved that she did not always behave hysterically. She remained perfectly calm. The soldiers were very polite. They asked to see the passengers' passes, saluted, wished them a pleasant journey and departed.

"Well, there you are," said Thomas Lieven. "Everything's going according to plan!"

[15]

After the first bottle of Veuve Clicquot, Yvonne stopped worrying. Her hysterical stiffness came near to relaxing. The conversation grew almost cheerful. At one moment they were both laughing when Yvonne suddenly fell silent, moved away, stood up and looked in another direction.

Thomas understood what she was feeling. He had once rejected her advances. No woman ever forgets such a thing. No woman wants such a thing to happen again.

Accordingly, they bade each other good night at about half-past eleven. It's best that way, thought Thomas . . . or is it? As it happened, he didn't feel too sober and Yvonne seemed to him extremely attractive. When he kissed her hand at parting she drew back, smiled stiffly and again seemed to turn to stone.

Thomas undressed in his own compartment, washed and had just pulled on his pajama trousers when the engine braked violently and slewed around an abrupt curve. Thomas lost his balance, reeled across his compartment and crashed heavily against the communicating door, which flew open. He fell rather than staggered into Yvonne's compartment. She was already in bed and sat up in alarm. "For heaven's sake!"

He regained his footing. "I beg your pardon. I didn't do it on purpose—really I didn't . . . I . . . good night . . ." He turned back to the open door. Then he heard her call out in an agitated tone: "Wait!"

He looked around. Yvonne's eyes were half closed and very dark. Her lips were parted. She gasped: "Those scars!" She was staring at the bare upper half of his body. Right across the left side of his chest ran three ugly, swollen weals of a peculiar shape, inflicted by blows with a rubber-covered steel spring.

"Oh—that—" Thomas turned his head away, involuntarily raising an arm to cover the scars. "I had an accident . . ."

"That's not true . . ."

"I beg your pardon?"

"I had a brother who was twice arrested by the Gestapo. The second time they hanged him. The first time they tortured him. When"—her voice broke—"when he came home, that first time, from hospital, he had . . . scars like yours . . . and you . . . I cursed you . . . I suspected you . . . you of all people . . ."

"Yvonne . . ."

He went to her. The lips of a beautiful woman kissed the scars of wounds which a brutal man had inflicted. Then for Thomas and Yvonne the hostility of the past was swept away in a flood of tenderness. The engine's whistle sounded. The wheels of the train clattered incessantly. The vase of red carnations rattled almost inaudibly.

[16]

The twin-engined courier aircraft with the German markings rushed faster and faster down the runway of the Marseilles airfield. The morning was overcast. A light rain was falling.

At one of the windows of the airport building a man with many false names was standing. His real name was Thomas Lieven. Both his hands were plunged in the pockets of his fleecy overcoat, the thumbs and forefingers pressed together.

Yvonne Dechamps sat in the courier aircraft. She was bound for Madrid and then on to Lisbon.

They had only spent a single night of love together. And yet now, as the aircraft disappeared into the clouds, Thomas felt lonely, forsaken and very old.

He shivered. Good-bye, Yvonne, he was thinking. In your arms, for the first time in months, I forgot Chantal. But we could not remain together. This is not an age for lovers. It tears them apart or kills them. All the best, Yvonne. I don't suppose we shall ever hear from each other again.

But he was wrong there.

On September 22, 1943, Thomas Lieven returned to Paris. His pretty black-haired maid, Nanette, who so much respected him, announced: "M. Ferroud telephoned four times while you were away. He said he must speak to you on urgent business."

"Come to my house about four o'clock this afternoon," Ferroud requested, when Thomas called him up at his bank.

As soon as our friend arrived the white-haired, elegant man of millions embraced him with tears in his eyes.

Thomas coughed. "M. Ferroud, Yvonne is safe. But you are not. You are in more danger than ever."

"What do you mean?"

"Before we get down to our own affairs—I have fulfilled my side of the bargain and now you must fulfill yours—I'd better tell you quickly what my investigation of your transactions has so far revealed."

Thomas had discovered Jean-Paul Ferroud to be a lawbreaker of a peculiar kind. Like other black market dealers he had cornered enormous quantities of materials required for war purposes, not, however, in order to sell them to Germans but in order to keep them out of German hands. He was thus the very opposite of the ordinary racketeers who were selling up French property. His object was, on the contrary, to preserve it. That was why he had falsified balance sheets, showing the wrong production figures for undertakings managed by his bank, and negotiated fictitious sales, on a vast scale, to German buyers.

All these operations by Ferroud were now described to him by Thomas to his face. Ferroud blanched. He began by protesting, but finally ceasing speaking and turned his back on the other.

Thomas concluded: "It was absolutely idiotic, monsieur, to behave in such a way. The almost immediate consequence will be the expropriation of your factories. And then what will happen? From the French point of view your behavior is intelligible enough. And for that reason I'll give you a private tip before they catch up with you. Appoint German trustees at once. Then they'll leave your factories alone . . . and I don't suppose you'll have any difficulty in getting the trustees to play ball with you—or will you?"

Ferroud swung around. He nodded. He swallowed hard, twice. Then he said: "Thanks."

"Not at all. Well, now to our own business. But I warn you, Ferroud. If your information turns out to be useless to us, I'll blow you sky-high."

Ferroud took a step toward him. "And what I am going to tell you may help you to crush one of the biggest black market rings of all time. It is an organization which has already done very great damage to both our countries. During the last few months German Treasury bills have been pouring into France in unprecedented quantities. You know what bills I am talking about?"

Thomas did know. They were a kind of occupation currency, used in every country invaded by the Germans. The object of such bills was to prevent excessive disbursement of genuine German bank notes abroad.

Ferroud continued: "Those bills are numbered in series. Two of the figures used—they are always to be found in the same place—indicate in which country they are to be employed. Well, my friend, during the last six months French goods to the value of about two milliards have been bought up in the black market with German Treasury bills. But over a milliard's worth of the bills were not earmarked, in their serial numbers, for France, but for Rumania."

"Rumania?" Thomas gave a start. "How could bills for Rumania reach France in such enormous quantities?"

"That I don't know," Ferroud went to his desk and took from it two thick bundles of German Treasury bills to the value of ten thousand marks each. "All I know is that here they are. Look, these are the figures that mean 'for Rumania.' But in my opinion, monsieur, no *Frenchmen* would be in a position to let loose a flood of this stuff, meant for Rumania, into their own country . . ."

[17]

"Ferroud doesn't know how those Rumanian bills got into France," Thomas reported to Colonel Werthe in his office at the Hôtel Lutetia two hours later. Thomas was talking fast. The fever of the chase was in his blood. He didn't notice that Colonel Werthe and the ambitious little Major Brenner, who was also listening, were exchanging significant glances. Quite carried away, he rattled on: "But Ferroud is quite certain that the bills could only have been brought into France by Germans and consequently that Germans must be running the whole racket!"

"So that's what your M. Ferroud believes, is it?" drawled Colonel Werthe, with a glance at Brenner.

"Hey, what's going on here?" Thomas had now perceived that something was wrong. "What do these ominous glances mean?"

Colonel Werthe sighed: "Tell him, Brenner."

Major Brenner bit his lips. "Your friend Ferroud is in serious trouble. Security Police have been in his villa for the last half-hour. He's been under house arrest ever since they arrived. If you had stayed talking to him a bit longer you'd have been able to say good afternoon to your old friends Sturmbannführer Eicher and his adjutant Winter."

Thomas's blood ran cold.

"What has happened then?"

"Two days ago a certain Untersturmführer Erich Petersen was murdered in Toulouse. Shot in his hotel. The Hôtel Victoria. The murderer got away. The Security people are convinced that the motive was political. The Führer has already ordered a state funeral."

"Himmler has called for a thorough investigation," said Colonel Werthe.

"The Toulouse Security Office has contacted the French police," Brenner said. "And they've given the Gestapo a list of fifty Communists and one hundred Jews. Some of them will be shot in retaliation for what is believed to have been the assassination, on political grounds, of Petersen."

"Most obliging of the French police, was it not, Herr Lieven?" Colonel Werthe commented sarcastically. "Always keep well in with the Gestapo, even at the cost of the lives of your fellow countrymen"

"Just a moment, please," said Thomas. "I don't quite follow all this yet. Why such a fuss about Herr Petersen?"

"Because he had the Order of the Blood," Brenner replied. "That's why the Security head office is raising hell. That's why Bormann dashed off in person to Himmler and demanded bloody vengeance."

"Ah," said Thomas. "Now I see. But I have a second query. What has my banker Ferroud got to do with a murder in Toulouse?"

"The Toulouse Gestapo have been interrogating a whole lot of witnesses. One of their pets, a moneylender in a small way named Victor Robinson, swore that your pal Jean-Paul Ferroud had instigated the murder of Untersturmführer Petersen."

Our friend's brain started working at top speed. Petersen, a member of the Order of the Blood, murdered. Ferroud suspected. I know a lot about him. But he also knows a lot about me now. Has he turned me in? Did he tell the truth? What will happen to him? And to me? And to the fifty Communists? And to the one hundred Jews?

He had to cough before he could speak. "Colonel, Ferroud

is convinced that Germans are at the head of a gigantic swindle with German Treasury bills." He spoke hesitantly, seeking for the right words. "Isn't it rather strange that the Security people dropped on that banker Ferroud just at the very moment when we were beginning to be interested in him?"

"I don't understand a word of all that," said the worthy Major Brenner.

"I didn't suppose you would," said Thomas, not at all disagreeably. He added, to Werthe: "I can't prove I'm right, but I have the feeling that we ought not to abandon Ferroud just yet. Intelligence ought to be on the ball with the rest of the team in this affair."

"How do you suggest we act, then?"

"Colonel, as you know, I used to live in Marseilles. At that time I got to know two men who came from Toulouse, Paul de la Rue and Fred Meyer . . ."

These were the two formerly hardened gangsters who had been trained by Thomas, in a grueling crash course, to become gentlemen, before they relieved the jeweler Marius Pissoladière of bracelets to the value of about eight million francs.

Thomas Lieven described in discreet language the true nature of his dealings with these two underworld characters and added: "I should like, therefore, to go to Toulouse."

"Why?"

"Because those two couldn't possibly know nothing of a crime committed in their own home town. And they'll tell me, if no one else, what they know."

"And how are we to handle the Gestapo?"

"I suggest you go to Eicher yourself, Colonel, and explain that for the moment Ferroud is extraordinarily important to us. After that you could offer Eicher the collaboration of Intelligence in the investigation of the murder of Untersturmführer Petersen."

Little Major Brenner took off his spectacles and polished them thoroughly. Biting his lips, he thought, I burned my fingers in that crazy partisan affair. Then I tried crossfire and chanced a big bluff. The consequence was—Major Brenner glanced down at the braid of his left epaulette. "On mature consideration I am of Herr Lieven's opinion. We really ought not to allow ourselves to be played off the field. We really ought to keep on the ball. That Treasury bills case is too important . . ."

Thomas turned his head away to hide a covert grin.

Colonel Werthe demanded in an exasperated tone: "So you want me to go crawling to those swine again and sit up and beg?"

"No need to sit up and beg, Colonel," exclaimed Brenner. "Try the old trick again. Go across in full uniform and show them a top secret army file!"

"You're crazy, both of you," said Colonel Werthe. "That fellow Eicher goes purple in the face the moment he lays eyes on me."

"Colonel, we rescued Herr Lieven with a forged 'Gekados.' What's to stop us taking a hand in the Petersen affair with a real one?"

[18]

"That thrice-accursed god-damned swine of a Lieven," said the jovial, undersized and red-faced Sturmbannführer Walter Eicher. He was sitting in his office in the former library of No. 84, Avenue Foch. Confronting him were his adjutant Fritz Winter and Obersturmführer Ernst Redecker, a blonde esthete who loved Rilke and Stefan George.

It was a few minutes to seven P.M. on September 23, 1943. Sturmbannführer Eicher had finished work. He often liked to linger an hour or so after the day's labor, over a drop of the best, with his adjutant. Nor did he object at all to the presence of Obersturmbannführer Redecker on these occasions. For that ambitious officer had a special point in his favor. He was actually the brother-in-law of the Reichsführer SS and Chief of the German Police, Heinrich Himmler. From time to time Redecker received personal letters from "Reichsheini," which he preserved with loving care and passed around with very natural pride. Eicher was of the opinion that such people must be kept sweet and he acted on this principle.

Yet this time he was not in the right mood for chatting around the fire. "There's fresh trouble every day," he growled. "Colonel Werthe, of Intelligence has just been to see me." Again the Sturmbannführer cursed. "That god-damned swine of a Lieven!"

"The one we had in hand?" asked the adjutant, with glittering eyes.

"Unfortunately we didn't have him in hand long enough. My apologies, Obersturmführer. I don't usually go on like this. But that sod gives us nothing but trouble."

"What's it about this time?" Winter demanded.

"Oh, the Petersen murder."

The actual brother-in-law of "Reichsheini" put down his glass of brandy with a bang. His features twitched. He lost color. It was generally known that a warm friendship had existed between Obersturmbannführer Redecker and Erich Petersen, who had been shot in Toulouse. The former's agitation was therefore understandable.

Eicher explained that Colonel Werthe had called to tell him that German Intelligence took a very deep interest in the banker Ferroud, suspected of complicity in the assassination, and a key figure of the highest importance in a formidable currency-smuggling ring to which it was evident that even Germans belonged.

Redecker took another sip of brandy. He had suddenly grown so nervous that he spilled some of the liquor. He demanded hoarsely: "So what? What had Petersen to do with currency smuggling?"

"Nothing, of course. But Werthe wanted me to agree to the collaboration of Intelligence with ourselves in the investigation of that vile assassination of our comrade."

Redecker asked in considerable excitement: "Naturally you refused, did you not, Sturmbannführer?"

"Naturally I refused—at first. But Werthe immediately began talking about 'Gekados' and so on. He insisted upon telephoning to Canaris from my office. Canaris obviously consulted your brother-in-law. For half an hour later I had a teleprinter from Security headquarters. The investigation is to be conducted in common with Intelligence."

For some obscure reason drops of sweat suddenly came out on Redecker's forehead. No one noticed it. He stood up, turned his back on the other two and wiped the perspiration away. At the same moment Eicher's angry voice rang out. "Werthe's already gone down to Toulouse. And who went with him? Herr Lieven! A blasted double agent! A swine who's put it across us, the Security Police! He ought to have been in a mass grave years ago!" Eicher took a pull at his brandy in great excitement. "If I ever get my hands on that fellow again . . . Yes, what is it?"

One of his subordinates had just entered.

CHAPTER 2

[1]

In Toulouse Thomas had already learned that Jeanne Perrier, the sandy-haired proprietress of that discreet hotel where he had once lived, was no longer in Toulouse. He would have been only too delighted to pay her and her girls a visit, of course only to exchange old memories.

He stopped in front of a shabby house, entered its shabby vestibule and climbed to the third floor. One of the doors bore the legend: PAUL DE LA RUE—FRED MEYER. REAL ESTATE.

Thomas grinned as he rang the bell. Real estate! When I first met them, he thought, they were still picture fakers, hotel thieves and safebreakers. Now they've entered a profession!

Footsteps approached the door from the inside. It was opened. Paul de la Rue, the descendant of Huguenots, stood on the threshold. His clothes were in good taste and his hair had been well trimmed.

His tall figure and narrow head lent him a remarkably aristocratic air. He began with a polite phrase. "Good morning, sir. What can I do for you?" Then he uttered a yell. "*Nom de Dieu!* Pierre!"

He gave Thomas, whom he had known by the name of Pierre Hunebelle, a boisterous thump on the shoulder. For a few seconds he forgot his good manners. "Well, I'll be buggered! You got away then? They told me the Gestapo had rubbed you out!"

"Nice little place you have here," Thomas remarked, extricating himself from the other's embrace and entering the apartment. "I see my training has been quite effective. But you'll have to get rid of all that bric-à-brac, of course, that little fawn, the goblin and the girl dancer . . ."

Paul stared at him. "Where the hell have you been? How is it you've landed up here?"

Thomas explained. Paul listened in silence. From time to

time he nodded. At last Thomas said: "So I came down with my colonel in hope that you two might be able to help me. I see you're a posh outfit these days, the pair of you . . ."

"Posh outfit be damned! That real estate notice on the door is just a blind. We're in the market, naturally, like everyone else here. But we use a bit more savvy, thanks to you. You did us a good turn in those days."

"Yes," said Thomas calmly. "And now you can do me a good turn. I've got to know who plugged that Untersturmführer Petersen. I've got to know whether it was one of the maquis boys."

"Couldn't have been the resistance. Nothing political in it."

"You'll have to prove that. Who shot Petersen, how and why?"

"But look here, Pierre. You can't expect me to squeal on a Frenchman who plugs a Nazi. That's not reasonable."

"Listen to me, Paul. The Nazis have arrested a hundred and fifty Frenchmen, some of whom will be shot in revenge for Petersen. We shall only be able to stop them doing it if we can prove that politics had nothing to do with his murder, that the fellow had blotted his copybook some other way, see? Can you get that into your thick skull, hey?"

"For Christ's sake don't yell at me like that! I'm quite willing to have a bit of a snoop around . . ."

[2]

Three days later, on September 27, 1943, three gentlemen sat down to lunch at Paul de la Rue's place. They were Paul himself, Thomas Lieven and Fred Meyer.

Paul had rung up Thomas at his hotel. "I think we've some information for you. Come and see me. Fred will be there. Perhaps you could cook us something a bit extra? The Marseilles boys told us you once put up a real stunner for them."

"Okay," Thomas had answered. He had worked for three whole hours that morning in Paul de la Rue's kitchen. The two gangsters wore dark suits in honor of the reunion, with white shirts and light gray ties. They had been so well trained that they tried to eat the first course—stuffed celery—with their knives and forks and found it extremely difficult.

MENU

Stuffed Celery
Spanish Frico
Flambé Peaches

TOULOUSE, 27 SEPTEMBER 1943

A tasty meal that led to the breakup of a racket worth millions.

Stuffed Celery

Wash well fresh, firm stalks of celery. Mix well equal quantities of butter and Gorgonzola or Roquefort cheese to make a creamy paste. Cut the natural lengthwise groovings of the celery stalks a little way down, fill the stalks with the cheese mixture and chill. Serve upright in a glass vase with the small green leaves on top. Fill the spaces in the vase with chips of ice.

Spanish Frico

Cut small steaks from a fillet of beef and beat until tender. Spread them with mustard, salt and pepper. Cut peeled potatoes into thin, round slices. Fry sliced onions in butter till golden-brown. Sprinkle bread crumbs in a well-greased, fireproof casserole. Place a layer of potato slices, with dabs of butter and salt and pepper, at the bottom of the casserole. On this base place a layer of the steaks. Cover them with onions and a layer of the potato slices. Continue this process till the casserole is full. The top layer should be potatoes dabbed with butter. Mix half a cup of red wine, cream and stock in equal proportions and pour it over the potatoes. Cover well and steam for one and a half hours. Turn out onto a large dish.

Flambé Peaches

Prepare a light caramel with a little butter, granulated sugar and blanched almond chips. Pour into it the freshly pressed juice of oranges and lemons, in the proportion of one to two. Add one dash each of cointreau, maraschino and cognac. Place fine drained halves of tinned or bottled peaches in the liquid. Baste them continuously until they are heated through. Then pour on more cognac and light it. Place the hot peaches on a plate over a portion of vanilla ice cream, pour the liquid over them and decorate with whipped cream.

To prepare this dish a strong, thick frying pan of stainless steel should be used on the dining table itself, over a spirit burner.

"With this sort of food," said Thomas, "it is absolutely correct, by way of exception, to take the stalks in one's fingers."

"Thank God for that," said Fred. "What kind of cheese is this?"

"Roquefort," said Thomas. "Now, who killed Petersen?"

"A certain Louis Monico, a Corsican, called the Dreamer."

"In the maquis?"

"Good Lord, no. He's a thoroughgoing crook. Quite young. But a serious tubercular case. He's already done four years for manslaughter. According to what we have been told—and our informants are absolutely reliable—that fellow Petersen was a most fearful swine. Order of the Blood and Gestapo agent my foot! Don't make me laugh! Petersen came down here as an ordinary citizen, see? And do you know what he was up to? He was buying gold!"

"Well, well, well!"

"In any quantity. He paid good prices, too. Must have been in pretty big time. The Dreamer had already sold him a few bits and pieces, never very much at a time, now and then."

Thomas thought, So Herr Petersen of the Security Police was an illicit gold buyer. And the Führer has ordered him a state funeral. And hostages are to be shot. And Germany has lost a hero. Glory be!

"Well, after a time the Dreamer began to trust Petersen. And one day he turned up at Petersen's hotel with a really big consignment of gold . . ."

[3]

The pallid, slightly built Louis Monico placed two heavy boxes of gold coins and ingots on the rococo table in the drawing room of Suite 203 at the Hôtel Victoria. The effort made him pant. The breath came whistling from his chest. His eyes shone feverishly.

A short man in a gray flannel suit was standing opposite the Dreamer. He had watery eyes, an almost lipless mouth and a mathematically exact parting through his cropped fair hair. All that Louise knew of him was that he called himself Petersen and bought gold. Good enough, thought Louis. That was all one needed to know.

"What's the quantity this time?" Petersen asked.

"Three hundred louis d'or and thirty-five gold ingots." The Dreamer opened the two boxes. Gold glittered in the electric light from the chandelier.

"Where's the money?"

Petersen put his hand in his inside breast pocket. When he drew it out it held a pass. He spoke in icy tones. "I am Untersturmführer Petersen of the Security Police. You are under arrest."

Louis Monico had kept his right hand in his jacket pocket while Petersen was speaking. He did not remove it. He fired from the pocket. Three bullets struck Erich Petersen, Member of the Order of the Blood, in the chest. He died instantly. He lay staring at the ceiling with the light fading from his eyes.

The Dreamer said to the dead man: "You picked the wrong sucker tonight, you bastard." Then he stepped over the corpse, crossed to the double doors of the suite and opened them. The corridor was empty. The Dreamer picked up his two boxes of gold and went down to the lounge, where no one took any notice of him.

[4]

"No one noticed him in the lounge," Fred Meyer concluded his report.

"And who told you all that?" Thomas asked.

"The Dreamer's brother."

"He didn't attempt to suppress anything?"

"No, because meanwhile the truth had ceased to matter to him. I told you the Dreamer's lungs were affected, didn't I? Well, three days ago he burst a blood vessel. He's in the hospital now and won't live to the end of the week."

"You can go along there with your colonel," said Paul. "The lad's ready to make a statement."

At 1615 hours on September 27, 1943, the telephone on little Major Brenner's desk tinkled. He lifted the receiver and recognized the voice of his chief. "Werthe here. I'm speaking from Toulouse. Listen carefully. What I'm going to tell you is of the most vital importance."

"I'm listening, sir."

"We've found Petersen's murderer." Werthe described the consumptive Louis Monico and the confession he had made. "Lieven, two Security Police officers and I were at the bedside."

"Good God Almighty, sir!" exclaimed Brenner. His heart was beating wildly. That Lieven! That devil of a Lieven! Thank God I backed up his idea right away this time.

Something else occurred to Brenner. "That moneylender, Victor Robinson—he falsely accused Ferroud."

"We've accounted for that too, now. Robinson was in on Petersen's racket. He had formerly been employed by Ferroud, who had dismissed him. Robinson wanted to pay him out. But that still isn't all, Brenner. Here's the main point. So far as Lieven could ascertain Petersen used the gold to get in on a gigantic swindle in connection with German Treasury bills . . . Brenner, are you listening?"

Brenner licked his dry lips. Good heavens, those Treasury bills! It's getting more and more complicated. And, good Lord, here I am in the middle of it! He called back tensely: "Yes, sir. I'm listening."

"We don't yet know the details. But there's not a second to lose now, Brenner. If we can prove that Petersen was in on the Treasury bills racket, there'll be a simply terrific scandal. The Security people will of course do their utmost to hush everything up. For the moment we're ahead of them, though only for a few hours at most. Major Brenner, you are to take five reliable men—"

"Yes, sir!"

"Petersen has an apartment at No. 3 Avenue Wagram. It's his official residence. You will first search the premises."

"Yes, sir!"

"Lieven has discovered that Petersen also has a secret hideout in the Avenue Mozart, No. 28, of which the Gestapo apparently know nothing. You are also to visit those premises."

"Yes, sir!"

"Turn both places inside out. Do what you like. Lieven is already on the way back to Paris to contact you. Put all suspected material under seal before the Security people can make it disappear. D'you hear me?"

"Yes, sir!" cried Brenner.

As the result of this conversation the little major plunged into an adventure which was to make his honest chubby cheeks turn red with shame. It was a shocking, a truly Parisian adventure. It is to be hoped that Major Brenner's adventure can now be related in the necessary discreet language.

[5]

With screaming tires the army Mercedes came to a halt outside No. 3, Avenue Wagram. Out sprang little Major Brenner. He squared his shoulders and straightened his gold-rimmed spectacles with a resolute gesture.

A gray army truck pulled up behind the Mercedes. Five men in uniform climbed down into the street, which was reflecting the last sunshine of a fine, warm autumn day. It was 1646 hours on September 27, 1943.

"Follow me!" ordered the little major, pulling the pistol in his belt around to the front. Then he raced, with his five picked men, into the house. But the official residence of the dead Petersen was empty. The doors stood open. The carpets and furniture had disappeared.

The fat concierge explained, shrugging her shoulders: "Everything was taken away early this morning."

"Taken away? By whom?"

"By furniture movers, of course—and a German officer, a friend of Herr Petersen's, who often came here. Name of Redecker."

"Redecker?" Little Major Brenner had his connections with the Security Police. He knew Obersturmführer Redecker, own brother-in-law to the Reichsführer SS and Chief of the German Police, Heinrich Himmler.

Brenner became distinctly uneasy. Were Redecker and Petersen so intimate? If so, then there really wasn't a second to lose. He had been too late at the official residence. But the hideout in the Avenue Mozart was allegedly unknown to the Security people. So that must be the next port of call.

The five reliable men tore down the stairs behind their major and out into the street. Accelerators roared. The vehicles shot forward. Major Brenner's heart was beating wildly. He felt just like the Demon King. Hey, presto! Here I come!

In the fashionable Avenue Mozart, a few minutes later, Brenner tried to explain to the concierge of No. 28 in his schoolboy's French that he had orders to search the apartment of Herr Petersen on the second floor.

"But, monsieur," the porter's wife objected, "the ladies are there just now."

"Ladies? What ladies?"

"Mme. Lily Page and her maid."

"Who is Mme. Page?"

"M. Petersen's mistress, of course. He's been away for the last few days.

Brenner made a lightning deduction. Hereabouts, obviously, nothing was yet known of the murder of the member of the Order of the Blood and illicit gold buyer. He dashed off again with his five men, but this time up to the second floor.

An uncommonly pretty maid opened the door to his ring. Brenner explained his mission, without however—must keep one's head!—letting slip a word about the sad fate of the member of the Order of the Blood. The pretty maid appeared confused and called her mistress.

Mme. Page arrived in a sketchy costume which even in the dim light of the hall could not be otherwise described than as bewilderingly transparent. She seemed to be about thirty-three years old, most attractive and of a rather full figure. In all she made a stimulating impression with her almond eyes and snow-white skin.

The major perceived that the eyes of his five realiable men were popping out of their heads. Fritz Brenner had never in his life so far dealt with ladies of this kind. He cleared his throat in some embarrassment and explained in polite but definite language the purpose of his visit.

Then he marched, the very incarnation of conscientiousness, straight into the drawing room, which was furnished with extraordinary elegance and lavishness. On the walls certain extremely indecorous pictures were to be observed. Brenner, naturally, did not observe them.

Meanwhile Lily Page strolled gracefully to the window and drew down the sun blind, though at this time of day it was really no longer necessary.

I'm not a born idiot, thought Brenner. That must be a prearranged signal to someone in the street. Accordingly he crossed the room to the side of the opulent Lily, drew the sun blind up again and pronounced with cast-iron gallantry the words: "I beg to be allowed to contemplate madame's beauty in the full light of day."

"Charmant!" smiled the lightly clad Lily. She dropped into a deep, soft armchair and crossed her legs. "Please begin your search, Major."

Brenner's five men had obviously already started it. He could hear them banging about next door and chaffing the maid. Confound the fellows! No seriousness, no sense of duty! What a conception of the Service . . .

In this mood of irritation and also embarrassed by the proximity of the lady, Brenner opened a tall mahogany cabinet. Its contents made him blush to the roots of his hair. He gasped for breath. The dark-haired Lily smiled sardonically. The major shut the cabinet with a bang. For the second time he felt distinctly uneasy.

Major Brenner had of course heard it alleged that certain books, drawings, photographs and other objects existed which had to shun the glare of publicity. But he had never been able to imagine what they might be like. Now that his unsuspecting glance, when he opened that cabinet, had fallen upon such filth, he felt sickened to the very soul. Atrocious! Monstrous! Decadent! Corrupt! No wonder such a people had lost the war . . .

Carefully suppressed caterwauling and guffaws from the next room made the major wince. The almond-eyed lady murmured languidly: "Your men seemed to have found the library."

Brenner rushed into the adjoining room. Four of his picked men were crowding around a bookshelf. The major shuddered when he saw what was causing their hilarity. He turned to look for the fifth picked man and found him in the maid's room.

Brenner forbade the group of four to go near the bookshelf and forbade Number Five to go near the maid. The situation began to get a bit beyond him. For this apartment was turning out to be a positive museum of the unspeakable.

The major's face assumed permanently the color of an overripe tomato. Drops of sweat stood out on his brow. In desperation he dashed to the telephone and put through an urgent call to Toulouse through the army exchange Leander 14.

Thank God! Werthe was still there. Brenner groaned with relief when he heard his colonel's voice. Breathlessly the major explained what a cesspool he had fallen into.

Colonel Werthe, in Toulouse, also groaned—over his ultra-respectable major. But Brenner did not notice the groan. He only heard Werthe demand: "What about material? Treasury bills and so on? Didn't you find anything?"

"No, sir."

"Look here, Brenner. Lieven will be in Paris very shortly. You must stay where you are and not say anything to anyone about Toulouse."

"I understand, sir. I stay here and keep absolutely mum."

"Call up the Lutetia and Lieven's villa. The moment he gets to Paris he's to join you."

Brenner replaced the receiver. Lieven! Thomas Lieven! A ray of hope at last, the Sonderführer! If only he'd come quickly . . .

Major Brenner heard the maid squeal, as though she were being tickled. In a rage, he rushed off to apprehend the malefactor. Heavens, what a disagreeable situation!

[6]

The secret hideout of the member of the Order of the Blood had so far revealed to the major and his men—apart from the obscene collections—some valuable items of jewelry, large quantities of gold coins, and a number of rare prints and wood carvings from the Far East, but no proofs whatever of any participation by Petersen in the German Treasury bills swindle.

Mme. Page made repeated efforts to get at one of the sun blinds. She only ceased when any such movement was strictly forbidden by the major.

One and a half hours had now elapsed since the search of the apartment had begun. Suddenly the front doorbell rang. Lily turned as white as a sheet.

Brenner drew his revolver. "Silence!" he hissed. He backed away through the hall, then suddenly swung around and snatched the door open, seizing the man who stood outside.

He was young, handsome and olive-complexioned. He had smooth black hair, a small mustache, long eyelashes and two scars on his right cheek which might have been inflicted by a knife. At the moment he looked as pale as a corpse.

"You fool!" the voluptuous Lily shrieked at him. "What did you come up here for?"

"Why shouldn't I?" he shouted back. "The sun blind was up!"

"Aha!" cried Brenner in triumph. He searched the man for weapons, but found none. His identity card gave his name as Prosper Longtemps, his profession as that of impresario and his age as twenty-eight.

Brenner interrogated him formally. But the young man sullenly refused to give any further account of himself.

Lily suddenly burst into a wild fit of sobbing. "Monsieur le Commandant," she cried. "I will tell you everything. Prosper is—the only man I love. I have been deceiving Petersen with him for a long time now . . . don't you believe me?"

"No, I don't," retorted Brenner icily. He was thinking, that's the way Lieven would have answered—icily. Then he locked Prosper Longtemps in the bathroom.

It was now half-past seven and already dark outside. The major put a second call through to the Lutetia and then to Lieven's villa. But Thomas Lieven had not yet arrived at either address.

Brenner dared not send even one of his five picked men to the railway station to meet Lieven. It was quite possible that the Security Police might have traced the apartment by this time. If they tried to get in he would have to hold it like a fortress.

What on earth was he to do next? Everything had begun in such a brisk and promising way and yet now here he sat in this stuffy apartment, filled with unspeakable things but empty of the proofs he was looking for. He had certainly taken one prisoner. But he couldn't make head or tail of the fellow. Would he, Brenner, ever learn the truth?

And on top of it all there was that disturbing Mme. Page with her extremely pretty maid and five men who could only be kept away with the greatest difficulty from those unspeakable collections and the maid herself. He fervently wished he were back at his desk in the Hôtel Lutetia. Theoretical work on the General Staff, that was his strong suit, not the direct, practical application of tactics and strategy.

He gave a sudden start. Mme. Page had suggested that her maid might really start cutting some sandwiches for the hungry men.

He hesitated. Ought he to allow such a thing? Were not madame and her maid his enemies? On the other hand the men must certainly be hungry and he did not wish to appear tyrannical. He therefore permitted the maid to go to the kitchen, posted one of his men to keep an eye on her and sternly warned him to behave with the most absolute propriety.

The men were soon munching away with bulging cheeks and drinking champagne which they had found in the refrigerator. Brenner had at first austerely declined either to eat or to drink. But later on he took a modest bite and sip or two.

Nine o'clock struck, then ten. There was still no news of Thomas Lieven. The ladies requested permission to go to bed.

Brenner granted their request. He organized sentry duty.

One man was posted at the door of the maid's room, one before her mistress's door and one at the bathroom door. Two men kept watch at the front door. The major himself stayed in the drawing room, beside the telephone.

He intended to keep awake, comparing himself with a rock in the surf, impregnable, impervious, imper—

But he did drop off after all.

When he awoke it was dark in the drawing room. He became aware of soft hands gently caressing him . . .

"Don't move," Lily Page whispered. "Everyone's asleep . . . I'll do anything you like, but please let Prosper go . . ."

"Madame," said Brenner sternly, seizing her arms in a vise-like grip, "take your hands off my revolver this instant!"

"Oh," sighed Lily in the darkness. "I don't want your pistol, you silly boy . . ."

At that moment the front doorbell rang.

[7]

Thomas Lieven had reached Paris at ten minutes past ten that night. At the Hôtel Lutetia he was excitedly informed that Major Brenner had been impatiently awaiting him for hours at No. 28, Avenue Mozart. It was added that the major had set out with a raiding party.

"H'm," said Thomas. He was wondering what on earth Brenner had been doing for hours in that racketeer Petersen's secret hideout.

In the lounge of the hotel he caught sight of his two old friends Raddatz and Schlumberger, the war-weary and somewhat cynical wireless operator corporals, whom he had got to know and like during his adventure with the Crozant resistance group. The Berliner and the Viennese greeted him with delight. They had just come off duty.

The lean man from Berlin, who was so fond of French magazines, exclaimed rapturously: "Why, look, Karli, there goes our Herr Sonderführer!"

"Come and join us, Herr Sonderführer!" cried the slightly overweight Viennese. "We're just off to the rue Pigalle to find us a couple of nice little dicky-birds!"

"Listen, boys," said Thomas Lieven. "Put off your praiseworthy intentions for a little while and come along with me. I may need your help."

Accordingly, a few minutes before eleven o'clock the three friends found themselves standing at the front door of No. 28

in the Avenue Mozart. Thomas rang the bell. He heard several voices inside the apartment, then a certain amount of banging about. At last footsteps approached. The door was flung open. Major Brenner stood on the threshold. His face was a deep crimson, he was out of breath, his hair was standing on end and there were traces of lipstick on his neck. Behind him Thomas and his friends caught sight of a lady who was wearing a dream of a nightgown over nothing at all.

Major Brenner stammered: "Herr Lieven . . . thank God you're here at last . . ."

Thomas Lieven gallantly kissed the hand of the lady in the nightgown.

Major Brenner then explained the position. He described what he had unfortunately found in the apartment and also what he had unfortunately not found. Finally he referred to the prisoner.

"Prosper is my lover," Lily Page interrupted. She had meanwhile added a morning wrapper to her somewhat inadequate clothing. Looking Thomas deep in the eyes, she continued: "He knows nothing whatever about Petersen's business affairs."

"He hasn't any," Thomas told her bluntly. "Erich Petersen has been shot dead in Toulouse by one of his business partners . . ."

Lily's seductive lips pouted in a seductive smile. She looked angelically happy as she murmured: "At last they've caught up with him, the vile blackguard."

"Try not to grieve over it too much, madame," Thomas implored her.

The little major looked bewildered. "But," said he, "but I thought . . ."

"Hey!" The sonorous tones of Corporal Raddatz interrupted him. "Here's something worth looking at, I must say!"

"How dare you interrupt me!" shouted Brenner. Then he turned around. The lean corporal was standing at the big mahogany cabinet which the major had opened that afternoon and then closed again in utter disgust.

Corporal Raddatz had also opened the cabinet. But he had not closed it again in utter disgust. He began taking out the contents of the drawers, examining them with amazement and delight. Finally he took out all the drawers and emptied them out on the floor, still chuckling. But suddenly he stopped laughing. He exclaimed in bewilderment: "Well, I'll be damned! Just look at this! What the hell are Treasury bills doing in among this caboodle?"

A sudden deathly silence fell in the room. At last Thomas said quietly: "Well, well." He bowed to Mme. Page. "May I ask your permission to recommence the search?"

The beauty gave him a weary smile. "With pleasure. And I'll also be glad to tell you where you'd better look. It's wherever the major ordered his men to stop looking."

Treasury bills of the Rumanian issue to the value of five million marks were brought to light. They were found in rosewood cabinets containing strange objects from the ingenious Orient, behind pornographic books in the library, among the "unspeakable" collections and behind the indecent pictures on the drawing-room walls.

Thomas then dismissed Mme. Page to her bedroom and proceeded to interrogate the pallid, terrified Prosper Longtemps. Ten minutes later he went into madame's room.

She was lying in bed with feverishly burning eyes. Thomas sat down on the edge of the bed. She whispered: "I'm going to tell you the truth . . . Prosper is the only man I love. It was only for his sake that I stood it here with Erich—the dirty swine . . . but I'm sure you don't believe me . . ."

"I believe you," said Thomas Lieven. "Now, madame, I am ready to protect Prosper under one condition—"

"I understand," she interrupted, with a wry smile and a languid gesture.

"I don't think you do," Thomas replied amiably. "Petersen was involved in illicit dealings with Treasury bills. I have to know how they got into France. If you help us to find out I'll look after your friend Prosper."

Lily slowly sat up in bed. A most beautiful woman, thought Thomas.

Lily Page said: "Do you see that picture over there, of 'Leda and the Swan'? Take it down."

Thomas did as she said. A small wall safe with a combination lock was revealed.

"Dial the number 47132," said the woman in the bed. He did so. The door of the safe opened. The steel interior contained a book bound in black leather, but nothing else.

"Erich Petersen was a disagreeable, pedantic sort of creature," said the woman in the bed. "He kept records of everything. Of men, of women and of money. That's his diary. Read it. Then you'll know everything about his affairs."

That night Thomas Lieven slept little. He was reading the

diary of Untersturmführer Erich Petersen. By daybreak he knew all about one of the greatest swindles of the war.

That same morning, with bleared eyes, he reported to Colonel Werthe, now back at the Lutetia. "The whole set-up was involved. Top men at Security headquarters in Berlin, top Gestapo officials in Rumania, probably even Manfred von Killinger, the German ambassador in Bucharest and here in Paris, Obersturmführer Redecker, Heinrich Himmler's brother-in-law. They were all in it."

"God Almighty," murmured Colonel Werthe in a faint voice. Major Brenner squirmed restlessly in his chair, tense with expectation.

"It was really Redecker who started the whole show," Thomas went on. "In 1942 he was working at Security headquarters in Bucharest . . ." At that time the Rumanians were obliged to accept German Treasury bills as legal tender. But they were happy if they could find anyone who would pay them in dollars, sterling or gold for the bills. Even at rock-bottom prices. They didn't care how little they received for that rubbishy paper so long as they got rid of it.

Then Redecker was transferred to Paris. There he met Untersturmführer Petersen. The pair of them discovered that they had a very great deal in common. Redecker described his Rumanian experiences. They built up quite a big business together.

"The facts are exactly as surmised by that banker Ferroud," Thomas Lieven concluded. "Only Germans could have arranged so gigantic a fraud. With the bills they had acquired so cheaply in this way Redecker and Petersen bought up anything they liked in France with perfect impunity. But Petersen never quite trusted Redecker. So Lily Page told me. That was why Petersen kept a secret hideout and a diary in which he recorded all the operations in which Redecker had been concerned. He wanted to have a hold over Redecker." Thomas lifted up the black leather book. "But Redecker's name is not the only one in these pages. Many others are mentioned. With this book in our hands, gentlemen, we can blow the whole racket sky-high."

"But just a minute, Lieven," growled the colonel irritably. "Don't you realize whom we're up against in this affair? There's Himmler's brother-in-law, there's an ambassador and there are all those top-ranking Security bosses! You told us so yourself!"

"That's why our next steps will have to be very carefully

considered, sir. And where can one consider important steps more carefully than over a good meal? I've already made all the necessary arrangements at my own place. I shall expect you, therefore, at my villa in an hour's time."

But alas, a good deal can happen in an hour.

[8]

Colonel Werthe and Major Brenner looked pale and upset when they arrived, sixty minutes later, at Thomas Lieven's charming little villa in the Bois de Boulogne. The major seemed about to burst into tears. The colonel stared glumly into space while the pretty Nanette served the first course.

MENU

Melon Slices
Parmesan Cutlets
Chocolate Pancakes

PARIS, 28 SEPTEMBER 1943

Over dessert Thomas Lieven evolved a plan to bring even a Reichsführer to reason.

Melon Slices

Iced slices are served from a firm, ripe melon. Each guest peppers and salts his own to taste.

Parmesan Cutlets

Medium-sized pork cutlets, preferably from near the neck end, are beaten, peppered and salted. They are then placed in a well-buttered, fireproof dish, and sprinkled liberally with grated Parmesan cheese. Pour thick sour cream on the cutlets, but not so as to cover them. They are then baked in the oven for twenty to thirty minutes, till light brown. The cutlets are served in the same fireproof dish with boiled potatoes and a green salad.

Chocolate Pancakes

Extra-fine, thin pancakes are baked. The batter should have been prepared at least an hour before cooking. Cream three yolks with three tablespoonfuls of fine sugar till frothy. Melt three squares of chocolate in one cup of milk over a flame, adding a little vanilla sugar and a pinch of salt. Mix all together. Cook over a very low flame to a thick cream and spread over pancakes. These are then rolled, sprinkled with coarse sugar and ground almonds or pistachio nuts and served immediately, very hot.

Thomas waited until she had left the room. Then he inquired: "Why so melancholy, gentlemen? Can it be that you feel a natural human sympathy, all of a sudden, with the impending fate of Reichsheni's brother-in-law?"

"If it were only that fellow who was going to catch it," Werthe grunted gloomily.

"Well, who else is in for it, then?" asked Thomas, popping a piece of melon into his mouth.

"You," said Werthe.

One doesn't talk with one's mouth full. So Thomas swallowed down his morsel before demanding: "A joke, sir?"

"Unfortunately not, Lieven. The Security Service is determined to run you in. I expect you know that Brenner has certain connections with that department. So after we parted today he paid another visit to the Avenue Foch. After all, we had just solved the mystery of Petersen's murder at Toulouse. So he had a chat with Winter. To begin with he made the reassuring discovery that Paris Security knew nothing of the Treasury bills swindle. But then Winter began to talk about you, Lieven."

"Did he, though? And what did he say?"

"He said . . . well, ahem . . . he said that now at last you were in the bag."

The door opened.

"Aha, here comes our dear Nannette once more," cried Thomas, rubbing his hands. "And so do the Parmesan cutlets!"

The girl blushed to the roots of her hair. "M. Lieven, please don't call me 'dear Nanette' when I'm serving. Otherwise I'm sure to drop the plates and ruin everything!" As she offered the dish to Werthe she murmured: "M. Lieven is the most charming man in the world!"

The colonel nodded dumbly and helped himself to salad. When the maid had left the room again Thomas said: "I hope the cutlets haven't been overpeppered? You think not? Good. So I'm in the bag, am I? And how do they make that out?"

It appeared that during Thomas's search for a bridge to be blown up by the Crozant resistance group he had accidentally run into a certain lady, a chief staff clerk at the Paris Ministry of Labor, who had treated him with such insufferable Nazi arrogance that he had been obliged to inform her that he represented Admiral Canaris and could not therefore take orders from her. This lady, it seemed, had not forgotten him. She had caught sight of him in the Paris express with Yvonne, sent a couple of military police to investigate their passes and reported the circumstances, which she considered suspicious, to Sturmbannführer Eicher.

The latter, who detested Thomas, had soon found out that Lieven's companion, after traveling to Marseilles as Madeleine Noël of Paris Intelligence, was now living in Lisbon as Yvonne Dechamps.

That name seemed to ring a bell in Eicher's memory. He searched his records. Then a triumphant grin broke over his face. Yvonne Dechamps, Professor Débouché's assistant, had been wanted by the Gestapo for weeks as a dangerous member of the resistance. And Thomas Lieven had enabled her to reach safety with a German Intelligence pass!

"Winter told me that Eicher had already communicated the facts to Berlin," said Brenner, cutting a boiled potato, most improperly, with his knife. "To Himmler in person."

"To the brother-in-law of Herr Redecker," said the colonel. "Himmler spoke to Canaris. And Canaris called me up half an hour ago. He was furious. You know how strained our relations are with the Security Service. And now a thing like this! I'm sorry, Lieven. You're a decent fellow. But I can't see any way out of this. The Security Service has lodged a criminal charge against you. You'll be court-martialed and that'll be the finish . . ."

"Oh, no, it won't," said Thomas.

"I beg your pardon?"

"I think there are a lot of things we can still do, Major. Don't eat too much of that pork, I warn you. There's another specialty coming. Chocolate Pancakes."

"For God's sake, Lieven, don't keep chattering away like that about food or you'll drive me crazy," shouted Werthe. "What on earth can we still do?"

"The Security Service wants to put me on the spot. Very well then, we'll put Herr Redecker on the spot too. What's to-day, Tuesday? Right. Then I'll call on Sturmbannführer Eicher tomorrow afternoon and put an end once for all to the trouble over that forged pass."

"What? You'll actually go to Eicher?"

"Yes, of course. I'm really most awfully sorry to have caused Admiral Canaris such inconvenience."

"But why—why should you go to Eicher now of all people?"

"Because tomorrow is Wednesday, gentlemen," said Thomas amiably. "And according to my little black book Wednesday is the day in every week on which German Treasury bills are flown from Bucharest to Berlin. All we have to do now, after lunch, is to draw up an exact time schedule. But really nothing whatever can go wrong now . . ."

[9]

With the tenderest of smiles the extremely pretty black-haired maid, Nanette, helped her beloved master into his camel-hair overcoat. Thomas glanced at his repeater. It was half-past four on September 29, 1943.

Thomas looked out of the window. "Do you think there'll be any fog later on today, my dear?"

"No, monsieur. I don't think so . . ."

"Well, let's hope it keeps fine," said Thomas. "For in that case quite a few gentlemen will find themselves in the soup this evening."

"Pardon, monsieur?"

"Never mind, Nanette. I've fixed up a little race for this afternoon. And I should certainly like to win it."

Thomas Lieven had really arranged for a race and now he was going to take part in it. He'd set an avalanche in motion and he'd have to be damned careful that it didn't overwhelm him. He was just off, in fact, to Paris Security Service headquarters in the Avenue Foch, to visit Sturmbannführer Eicher.

The operation which Thomas was now hoping to bring to a victorious end in person had begun twenty-four hours previously. In the praiseworthy effort to save his crazy Sonderführer's life, Colonel Werthe had sent a long report by teleprinter to Admiral Canaris. An hour later the white-haired head of German Military Intelligence had begun an hour's interview with Heinrich Himmler. The admiral brought bad news to the Reichsführer SS and Chief of the German Police.

"I shall take the most ruthless measures," Heinrich Himmler declared wrathfully.

At 6:30 P.M. on September 28, a special committee of high-ranking SS officers set to work. Three of its members flew that night, via Vienna, to Bucharest.

On September 29 at a quarter-past seven in the morning these three SS officers arrested Unterscharführer Anton Linser, a Security Service courier, on the airfield at Bucharest, as he was about to take off for Berlin. His extensive luggage contained several parcels of "Secret Headquarters Material," which were opened. German Treasury bills earmarked for Rumania were found, to the value of two and a half million marks.

At 8:30 A.M. the three SS officers called at the offices of the Bucharest Security Service, situated in an unobtrusive wing of the German Embassy in the main street of the city, the Calea Victorei. Here great quantities of louis d'or gold coins and enormous piles of German Treasury bills could be safely hidden. Two persons were arrested.

At ten minutes to two on September 29, 1943, the courier aircraft from Bucharest arrived at the Staaken airfield in Berlin. Members of the special committee arrested an Untersturmführer named Walter Hansmann, who had been asking the crew, with every sign of the utmost anxiety, for news of the Bucharest courier, Linser. After a brief interrogation Hansmann broke down and confessed that he was involved in the German Treasury bills affair. He gave the names of four high-ranking members of the Security Service who were in on the racket in Berlin. By two o'clock these four men were already under lock and key.

"Well, now we can go and have lunch in peace," said Thomas Lieven, in Paris, to Colonel Werthe. They were standing over a teleprinter through which the admiral kept his colonel hourly informed of the situation.

"It seems you're in luck, you damned rascal," said Werthe with a grin.

"Touch wood," Thomas remarked, touching it. "When did the avenging angels take off who are to pass sentence in this affair?"

"Half an hour ago. There's an SS judge and two courts-martial counsel. They ought to touch down between half-past four and five this afternoon."

At half-past four Thomas was being helped into his camel-hair overcoat by the extremely pretty Nanette. As he emerged into the street he said to himself: Now let's just hope that there really isn't going to be any fog. For if there is my three angels won't be able to land. And then good-bye to the vengeance of my own that I've been hoping for on those bloodhounds in the Avenue Foch, who once nearly beat me to death.

The Security Service chiefs in the Avenue Foch received Thomas with solemn and severe expressions. He realized at once that they had no idea what was in store for them. "Reichsheini" hadn't warned them.

The red-faced Sturmbannführer Eicher and his pallid adjutant, Fritz Winter, addressed Thomas in calm and emphatic tones. They behaved like many generals, courts-martial counsel and officers who sentenced German soldiers to death, often on the most trifling grounds, during the last years of the war. They used to make an appearance, before the execution of their victims, in order to explain to the guilty parties, with stern solemnity, why it was so absolutely necessary for them to be shot.

Such was the fashion in which Messrs. Eicher and Winter harangued Thomas Lieven, who sat in front of them wearing a gray tweed suit, with a white shirt, a black tie, black socks and shoes, and crossed legs.

Said Eicher: "You know, Lieven, we have nothing against you personally. On the contrary! I admire your courage in having come here. But the welfare of the nation and the community is here at stake . . ."

Winter added: "Grin away, Lieven. You won't be grinning when you face the court-martial."

Eicher continued: "It is right to do what is of advantage to the German people, wrong to do what injures them. You have injured your country. I want to make you realize that . . ."

"May I put a question?" asked Thomas with a courteous inclination of the head. "Is it really just ten minutes past five or is my watch slow?"

The look which Eicher shot at him contained both hate and admiration. "Why couldn't you remain a decent human being and join us? You might have been a Sturmbannführer today. Your watch is right."

Thomas rose and lounged over to the window. He gazed down into the autumnal garden and up into an autumnal sky. Not a sign of fog.

"I should be interested to hear how you tracked me down, gentlemen," said Thomas Lieven.

Sturmbannführer Eicher and his adjutant complacently related how they had discovered that Thomas Lieven had taken a dangerous female member of the French resistance named Yvonne Dechamps to Lisbon in the guise of a German secret agent with a Paris Intelligence pass.

Lieven listened to them politely. Then he again glanced at his watch.

Eicher grunted: "Self-control to the last, eh? I like that, my lad. I like it very much."

Winter said: "All the evidence against you is already before the Reichsführer SS. Your court-martial will be held in a very few days now."

Eicher observed: "And now no one can help you any more. Neither Colonel Werthe nor Admiral Canaris. No one!"

Thomas again glanced at his watch.

Muffled sounds reached the room from the staircase. There was a hum of voices, words of command rang out and jack-boots tramped. Thomas felt his heart beating faster. "I hope," he said, "that you gentlemen will do me the honor to attend my execution."

Eicher turned to listen to the noise outside. "What's going on out there?" he exclaimed.

The door flew open. A scared-looking orderly appeared, saluted and announced in a husky tone: "Three gentlemen from Berlin, Sturmbannführer, on most urgent business . . . Special Security Headquarters Committee . . ."

So there we are, thought Thomas. For the last time that day he glanced out of the window, up at the sky. I thank Thee, O God!

Eicher and Winter seemed to be rooted to their chairs. Eicher stammered: "Sp-spe-special committee?"

Then they were in the room. The SS judge wore the black uniform and boots of a Gruppenführer and looked very sinister. The two counsel were of slighter build, wore glasses and saluted in military style.

The SS judge raised his hand in the so-called German salute. He spoke in icy tones. "Heil Hitler! Sturmbannführer Eicher? Glad to meet you. I'll give you all the necessary explanations in a moment. And you, sir?"

"Untersturmführer Winter . . ."

"And who is this?"

Eicher began to recover his equanimity. "Merely a visitor. You may leave us now, Herr Lieven."

The SS judge pricked up his ears. "Sonderführer Thomas Lieven?"

"In person," said our friend.

"Then please stay where you are."

Eicher mumbled: "But why . . .?"

"Sturmbannführer, be good enough to summon Obersturmführer Redecker to join us. But say nothing else, do you understand?"

The brother-in-law of Heinrich Himmler entered a moment or two later, with a smile on his thin lips. The smile stiffened when he saw the visitors.

The SS judge said to Winter: "Search that man for weapons."

Winter obeyed, in utter bewilderment.

Redecker swallowed hard, staggered and dropped heavily into a chair.

The SS judge looked down at him with disgust. "Obersturmführer," he said. "You are under arrest."

"Reichsheini's" brother-in-law burst into sobs. The pallid Winter gulped violently.

Eicher suddenly cried out in a broken voice: "But what for?"

The colossus in black retorted coldly: "The Obersturmführer is involved in a fraud connected with German Treasury bills to the value of millions. In common with Untersturmführer Petersen, who was shot at Toulouse, he has inflicted injury upon his country in the basest and vilest manner. The investigation now proceeding will show what other members of the Paris Security Service have been implicated in this affair."

Eicher stared at the judge in amazement. "I don't understand a word of this . . . Who has brought this monstrous charge?"

The judge in black told him who had brought it.

Eicher's jaw dropped. With glassy eyes he gaped at Thomas Lieven and stuttered: "You . . . you . . . you . . ."

Then an incident occurred which almost deprived Sturmbannführer Eicher of his reason. The SS judge walked up to Thomas Lieven, shook him by the hand and said: "Sonderführer, in the name of the Reichsführer SS, I declare to you his gratitude and appreciation."

"Don't mention it," said Thomas modestly. "I was only too happy to be of service."

"The Reichsführer SS authorizes me to inform you that he has already consulted Admiral Canaris concerning this matter and that no steps will be taken against you in connection therewith."

"Well, how nice of Herr Himmler," said Thomas Lieven.

[10]

Altogether twenty-three arrests were made as a consequence of the German Treasury bills fraud. The guilty parties included only two Frenchmen and three Rumanians.

The case was heard in camera. The two Frenchmen, one of the Rumanians and Untersturmführer Hansmann were condemned to death. The rest of the accused were sentenced to long terms of imprisonment.

Obersturmführer Redecker got eight years. But Heinrich Himmler soon proved his sense of family solidarity. Obersturmführer Redecker was only in jail for six months. Then the Reichsführer SS personally directed that he should be released and summoned to Berlin. He worked there in a subordinate capacity until the end of the war.

He came through all this troubles not a whit the worse. Today he is a prominent member of a nationalist group in northern Germany.

[11]

During the morning of August 28, 1944, Thomas left the hotel in Marseilles where he had been staying while on a service mission and deposited a bag in the cloakroom of the main station. There had been a little fighting in the suburbs, but not much. Marseilles was liberated in the afternoon of August 29. Thomas Lieven tore up his various Security Service passes and collected a number of papers which had done him good service in the days of the Crozant resistance group.

That evening a certain Captain Robert Almond Everett, a British agent recently parachuted into France, reported to American headquarters. He stated that he required immediate repatriation to London. The American authorities entertained their gallant ally, who looked the very image of Thomas Lieven, with whisky and K rations.

French troops and partisan units which had marched in

from all the southern regions had also helped in the liberation of Marseilles. Two days after the victory a great celebration took place at the Hôtel de Noailles, occupied by the Americans. All present, including Captain Robert Almond Everett, sang the French national anthem.

He was just singing *"Le jour de gloire est arrivé"* when a heavy hand dropped on his shoulder. He swung around. Two gigantic American military policemen stood behind him. Beside them stood a man who looked like an oversize Adolphe Menjou.

"Arrest that man," said Colonel Jules Siméon, who now wore a splendid uniform. "He is one of the most dangerous German agents employed during the war. Put up your hands, Herr Lieven. You've gone too far this time and the game's up."

[12]

General de Gaulle and the Americans had entered Paris on August 25. On September 15 Thomas Lieven found himself, for the second time in his life, in the prison at Fresnes, close to the capital. First it had been the Gestapo which looked him up in Fresnes. Now it was the French.

A week went by, then two. Thomas endured this new incarceration philosophically. He often thought, with resignation, Well, it was bound to come and I suppose I deserve it. In those evil years I did make a pact with the devil. And "who eats with the devil must have a long spoon!"

On the other hand . . .

On the other hand I have so many friends here. I have helped so many French people, Yvonne Dechamps, for instance, Ferroud the banker and Mme. Page. I have saved many French lives. Now I am sure they will help me.

How long a sentence am I likely to get? Six months? Well, that would be all right. I shall survive it. And then, then at last I shall be free. Then at last I can return to England. After so many years at last I shall be living in peace. No more secret service, so more adventures! I shall live as I used to. On the capital I have in Zurich in the name of Eugen Wälterli.

Heavy footsteps approached the cell. A key was turned in the lock. The door swung open. Two French soldiers stood on the threshold.

"Get ready!" said the first soldier.

"Ah, at last," said Thomas Lieven, putting on his jacket.

"You've certainly kept me waiting a devil of a time for interrogation!"

"Interrogation be damned," said the second soldier. "You're going to be shot."

BOOK IV

CHAPTER 1

[1]

Not a single cloud appeared in the deep blue summer sky. It was hot in Baden-Baden, very hot, on that July 7, 1945. The citizens slunk about the streets looking pale, thin, ill-dressed and hopeless.

Toward midday an olive-green staff car, with a two-star general sitting in the back, approached the Leopoldsplatz crossing. A French military policeman was regulating the traffic. It was French traffic. There were no more German cars. But there were plenty of French ones. Baden-Baden was the seat of the French Military Government. The German inhabitants numbered 30,000. French troops and civilian administrative staff, with their families, numbered 32,000.

"Stop here a minute," said the general. The driver stopped beside the M.P., who saluted so negligently that he would immediately have been given a dressing-down if the general had been a German. But dressings-down were no longer being given by German generals at this period, not for the time being at any rate.

The officer with the two stars wound the window down and said: "I'm a stranger here. I expect you know the ropes. Which mess has the best food?"

"Mon général, for heaven's sake don't go to any of the messes. Go to Captain Clairmont of the War Crimes Investigation Department." The M.P. gave the necessary directions.

"Off we go, then," commanded the hungry general.

The staff car stopped at the gates of a big villa. It had been the headquarters of the Gestapo right up to the end of the so-called Thousand-Year Reich. Now it accommodated the French War Crimes Investigation Department.

The general entered the villa and asked for Captain Clairmont.

The man who went by this name appeared. He was slender

and of medium height, with a narrow head, black hair and shrewd eyes. He wore a well-fitting uniform and looked about thirty-five. But despite the uniform the impression he made was decidedly non-military.

The captain, whose real name was Thomas Lieven and who had been long, long ago a successful private banker in London, shook hands with the two-star general and said: "I shall be honored if you will join us for lunch, sir."

[2]

To be shot? thought Thomas Lieven in horror, as the soldiers led him out, handcuffed, into the gloomy prison yard. Good God! And I believed they were only going to sentence me to a few months!

The soldiers pushed him into the same windowless, evil-smelling bus which in former days he had been forced to enter by German soldiers.

The vehicle still stank of sweat and anguish. Thomas Lieven, emaciated, pallid and unshaven, crouched there in a crumpled suit. His braces, tie and shoelaces had been taken away. A wave of nausea overwhelmed him.

He did not know where he was when the vehicle stopped somewhere in Paris, in another gloomy courtyard. Apathetically he allowed the soldiers to hustle him into a room in a large building.

When the door opened he felt giddy and began gasping for breath. He heard voices and words without understanding them. He stared at a man seated in the uniform of a French colonel behind a desk. He was a tall man with tanned features, hair graying at the temples and frank, steady eye. The blood began to beat wildly in Thomas's brain as he realized that he was safe. He had recognized Josephine Baker's friend, whose life he himself had once saved in Lisbon, Colonel Débras of the Deuxième Bureau.

The colonel gave no sign, by word or gesture, that he knew Thomas Lieven. "Get over there," he snared at Thomas. "Sit down and keep your trap shut." Thomas sat down where he was told and kept his trap shut.

The soldiers made a great to-do over unfastening his handcuffs and formally handing over their prisoner. It seemed an eternity before they finally departed with their receipt, leaving Thomas alone with Débras.

Débras smiled. "Josephine sends you her regards, you infernal rascal."

"Thanks, that's very good of her. Where . . . where is madame?"

"In Casablanca. I acted as governor of the town, you know."

"How interesting."

"I had business in Paris and learned by chance that you had been arrested."

Thomas began to feel better. "Your colleague Colonel Siméon was responsible. I was just singing the 'Marseillaise.' At a national liberation ceremony. I ought to have stayed in the hotel and kept my mouth shut. Then I should long ago have been in London. But national anthems never did bring anyone good luck."

Débras said: "I know a lot about you and everything you have done against us. But I also know what you have done for us. When I arrived in Paris the other day I heard about the jam you were in. I don't belong to the Deuxième Bureau any longer. I'm a member of the War Crimes Investigation Department. So I could only get hold of you by putting you on my list of war criminals and stating that you would be shot. It was the only way of getting you out of jail at Fresnes. Not a bad dodge, eh?"

Thomas wiped the sweat from his forehead. "Yes," said he. "It was a good dodge. Perhaps a bit of a strain on the nerves."

Débras shrugged his shoulders. "Our whole lives are that, Lieven. I hope that you are not laboring under any illusions, by the way, as to your future. I hope you realize for what purpose I had you brought here from Fresnes."

"I'm afraid I do," Thomas answered resignedly. "I take it you mean that I shall now have to start working for you again, Colonel."

"That's it, yes."

"Just one more question. Who told you, when you came to Paris, that I had been arrested?"

"Ferroud, the banker."

Good old Ferroud, thought Thomas. Many thanks! Aloud he asked: "What are your plans for me, Colonel?"

The friend of Josephine Baker gave Thomas a shrewd, affable glance. "Do you speak Italian? Or not?"

"Yes."

"You may remember that when the Germans invaded France in 1940 the Italians also, at the last moment, as soon as they could be assured it was quite safe, poked in their noses and declared war on us. One of the most mischievous scoundrels who then terrorized the South of France was General Luigi Contanelli. After the liberation he got into mufti just in time . . ."

"Like most of the other Axis generals . . ."

". . . and went to ground. So far as we know, he's somewhere near Naples."

Forty-eight hours later Thomas Lieven was in Naples.

Some eleven days later, in the village of Caivano, northeast of Naples, he arrested General Contanelli, who was at that time, in obedience to necessity rather than virtue, trying himself out as shepherd.

After returning with his illustrious prisoner to Paris, Thomas explained to Colonel Débras during an evening hour of agreeable relaxation in an agreeable bar: "It was really all quite simple. The American counter-intelligence corps helped me a lot. They were charming young fellows. Nor can I complain about the Italian authorities. They had no time at all for generals. But it also seems, unfortunately, that they have no time for the Americans either. Circumstances must be blamed for that." He went on to describe his adventures in Italy.

While he was still searching for the shepherd general, he returned on one occasion to the headquarters of the counter-intelligence corps to make some further inquiries and witnessed an extraordinary scene there.

The American secret agents were dashing about in a state of hysterical fury, all shouting at once. They gave orders only to cancel them in the same breath, made frantic telephone calls and wrote out warrants for arrest on conveyor belts, so to speak.

Thomas soon discovered what had happened. Three days previously another big American freighter had cast anchor in the port. It was the *Victory*, with a cargo of provisions for the American fighting forces in Italy. But since Sunday the *Victory* had been missing. No one knew where she had gone. Both the Italian and the American authorities concerned passed the blame from one to another of their own offices.

What on earth had happened to the *Victory*? She couldn't have simply vanished into thin air! Thomas Lieven's curiosity was aroused. He went down to the harbor, visited various taverns and seamen's dives and at last came to one known as Luigi's.

Luigi looked like the actor Orson Welles, ran a dirty little eating house and in addition exercised the trades of receiver of stolen property, forger and gang boss.

Luigi took to Thomas, that smartly dressed civilian with the knowing, ironic smile, at their very first meeting. This fraternal feeling grew even warmer when Luigi learned that Thomas was a German.

It sounds incredible. But the mystery which had baffled the counter-intelligence corps was solved by Thomas in a few hours. He even met at Luigi's the very men who had engineered the disappearance of the *Victory.*

The sequence of events had been as follows. On the previous Sunday the freighter's crew had been given shore leave. Only one man remained aboard to watch. Luigi's friend arranged for a sham fight on the jetty between three pretty girls right in front of the gangway. One of the girls uttered a piercing scream for help. The watchman dashed gallantly to her assistance. Dark-skinned Neapolitans joined in the fray, which became fast and furious.

Meanwhile Luigi's friends, disguised as seamen, rowed alongside the *Victory,* to port, and took possession of her. Working fast, they slipped her moorings, weighed anchor and steamed her out of the harbor, around a projecting tongue of land and on to Pozzuoli.

Here they cast anchor again and loaded the cargo on to waiting trucks. Aboard the ship they had found tinned food, frozen poultry, sugar, rice, flour, all kinds of alcoholic liquor, a ton or so of cigarettes, and some thousands of tins of *pâté de foie gras.*

The pirates had deliberately chosen Pozzuoli as their unloading point. Extensive shipyards were avilable there. Demolition gangs were paid overtime to break up the stolen vessel immediately.

Even its separate components were sold to buyers who had already gathered on the spot. They stood around the ship and stated their requirements. They got anything they wanted, from engines and crankshafts to steel plates and bulkheads. It was as though industrious butchers were cutting steak after steak from the carcass of an ox.

In Naples at this period some use could be found for everything. Consequently, not even a rivet was left of the *Victory.* In fact it is to be feared that Luigi's friends were even in a position to make something of the rats they discovered aboard.

[3]

Such was the story with which Thomas entertained Colonel Débras on a certain pleasant evening in a pleasant bar in Paris. Débras then became serious. He said: "You are a German, Lieven. We need you now in Germany. No one knows better than yourself how to distinguish between the true big villains and the harmless little fellow travellers. You could prevent innocent people from being punished in the steps now being taken. Would that sort of work suit you?"

"Yes," said Thomas Lieven.

"But in Germany it will be absolutely necessary for you to wear a uniform."

"No!"

"Sorry, but that's indispensable. We shall also have to give you a French name and military rank. I suggest that of captain."

"But, good Lord, what sort of a uniform shall I have to wear, then?"

"Please yourself, Lieven. Order what you like."

Accordingly, Thomas went to the best military tailor in Paris and ordered what he liked. He chose dove-gray air force trousers and a jacket to match, with large pockets, a long pleat down the back and a narrow waistband. It had a strap over the shoulder, a chip, and three chevrons on the sleeve.

This uniform, invented by Thomas, was so generally approved that a month later, it was laid down officially for all members of the War Crimes Investigation Service.

Thomas returned as Captain René Clairmont, with the advancing Allied troops, to his native land. The end of the war found him at Baden-Baden, where he set up his office in the former Gestapo headquarters in the Kaiser Wilhelm Strasse.

Seventeen men worked at No. 1 Kaiser Wilhelm Strasse. They lived in the villa opposite. Their work was hard and far from enjoyable. Some of them, moreover, did not get on too well together, for political or other reasons. Thomas Lieven, for example, immediately fell out with Lieutenant Pierre Valentine, a good-looking young fellow with ice-cold eyes and thin lips, who might equally well have been taken, from his appearance, for an SS man.

Valentine fairly reveled in the reckless issue of warrants for arrest and confiscation. The more prudent officers of the French War Crimes Investigation Service kept as closely as their prudent American and British colleagues to the Military

Government's wanted-persons lists. But Valentine used his power arbitrarily and unscrupulously.

Thomas Lieven protested against this stupid generalization. Valentine retorted negligently: "My views are based on figures. In our section alone, during the past month, we registered over six thousand denunciations of Germans by Germans. That's what they're like. When they invade weaker nations they consider themselves a master race. When they get hit on the nose themselves they play Beethoven and denounce one another. Am I to respect people like that?"

Lieutenant Valentine, repulsive character as he might be, was quite right there. After the war, an appalling wave of informing activities. Meanness and baseness of every kind, flooded Germany from end to end.

On August 2, 1945, Thomas had an experience that made him shudder. A haggard, white-haired man, looking half starved and wearing old, ragged clothing, entered the office, removed his hat and said: "Good morning, sir. My name is Werner Hellbricht. You are looking for me. I was district peasants' leader in—" He named the Black Forest village in which he lived. "I have been in hiding up to now. But I have decided to give myself up."

Thomas stared at him. "Why?"

"Because I have discovered that frightful crimes have been committed in my country. I am ready to do penance, work on the roads, break stones, anything you like. I sincerely regret having served so criminal a government. I believed in it. I was wrong. I ought to have believed less and thought more."

Thomas rose. "Herr Hellbricht, it is one o'clock. Before we continue this conversation I'd like to ask you a question. Will you have lunch with me?"

"Lunch? With you? But I have just told you I was a Nazi!"

"I ignore that for the time being, as you so honestly confessed it."

"Then I have a request to make in my turn. Come with me to my farm. I've something to show you there, in a glade behind the house," said the former district peasants' leader.

[4]

Frau Hellbricht had prepared for the midday meal a pitifully thin soup flavored with sorrel, chervil, dandelions and many other common herbs. She looked as pale and drawn as her husband. The farmhouse was much dilapidated, with broken windows, the locks on the doors shot to pieces, the stables empty and the rooms stripped bare by the foreign slave laborers.

"You can hardly blame them for it," said Hellbricht with a wry smile. "We plundered them first, during the war, in their own countries . . ."

The wife of the former district peasants' leader, standing at the stove in the barely furnished kitchen, said: "After the soup there will be mashed potatoes and dried fruit, as rationed. I'm sorry we have nothing else."

Thomas went out into the yard and opened the boot of his car. He returned with half a pound of butter, a tin of cream, another of meat extract and another of corned beef.

"Now let me get at that kitchen table of yours, Frau Hellbricht," he said. He immediately set to work at it, strengthening the thin soup with meat extract, opening the tin of corned beef and spreading out its contents. Then he found a basin with some skimmed milk curds in it.

"Put that through a sieve, please, Frau Hellbricht," said he. "With our united efforts we shall soon have a first-rate lunch ready."

"Oh dear," murmured Frau Hellbricht, beginning to cry. "Corned beef! I used to dream of it. But I never saw any of it."

"And there are people even today," said Hellbricht, "who look on contemptuously while others starve. They are the very people who are responsible for our plight. Captain, I am not an informer. But I feel it my duty to report that in the glade behind the house an enormous dump of provisions had been buried under the moss."

"Who buried it? And when?"

"It was in the autumn of 1944. The adjutant of Darré, the president of the National Farmers' Union, came to see me. He brought with him Dr. Zimmermann, head of the Karlsruhe Gestapo. They said they were to bury supplies of food for . . . for the Führer's own staff . . . for the highest in the land . . ."

The faded, careworn and melancholy Frau Hellbricht added, as she sieved the skimmed milk: "That was why we wanted you to come here. The food must be dug up. So many are starving . . . We at least still have our own roof over our heads. We'll get by somehow. But what about those who have been bombed out and the refugees and the children?"

MENU

Herb Soup
Bewitched Corned Beef
Curds Dessert

BADEN-BADEN, 2 AUGUST 1945

This meal can be eaten even today. At that time it put Thomas Lieven on the track of Nazi bosses.

Herb Soup

Clean and chop fine a portion of herbs such as sorrel, nettle tops, chives, parsley, chervil, dill, celery leaves and leeks. Then take a small portion and mix it into a light butter and flour *roux,* add water or stock, bring to a boil and season with pepper, salt and a little muscat. Simmer. Add the rest of the herbs just before serving. Egg yolk and cream can be added, or a poached egg dropped into it for each person. The soup is served with croutons.

Bewitched Corned Beef

Take plenty of onion rings and braise them in butter till glazed. Add the chopped contents of one tin of corned beef. Leave to braise a little longer but do not brown. Add some potato purée, not too thick, mix all together, season well with salt and pepper and leave over a low flame till well cooked and hot.

Curds Dessert

Put some curds through a sieve, mix to taste with fine sugar, add double cream and whip to a medium thick consistency. Add a few sultanas and some drops of lemon juice. Pour into a dish, garnish with whipped cream and chill.

Starting on that August 2, 1945, two very different trains of events were set in motion. First an enormous dump of provisions was dug up in secret, consisting of several thousand tins of food containing suet, meat, jam, synthetic honey, coffee, tea, aviation chocolate, grape sugar, flour, vegetables and fruit. These treasures were handed over to charitable organizations for distribution to invalids, the aged and children.

Then all traces of the excavation were removed from the glade as quickly as possible and the moss was replaced. Thereafter the woods behind the Hellbrichts' farm were patroled day and night by picked members of the War Crimes Investigation Service.

At dusk on August 11, while Thomas was on duty, a man came creeping into the glade, keeping a keen lookout on all sides. He started at every sound. He had an empty rucksack hanging from his belt and a small spade in his hand. Thomas recognized the man's cruel, pallid features from the photograph on the warrant for his arrest.

The man started digging, faster and faster, more and more anxiously. He did not notice until it was too late that three men had suddenly come to stand behind him. Then he swung around, got to his feet with an effort and staggered back, panic in his face.

"Zimmermann of the Gestapo," said Thomas, who had suddenly drawn a revolver, "you are under arrest."

One after another of the Nazi bosses who knew of the buried dump of provisions came to dig them up.

Thomas Lieven had told his men: "Anyone who starts digging in this glade is a Nazi boss and is to be instantly arrested."

Seventeen high-ranking Nazis were captured in this simple way between August and October 1945.

Thomas contrived to have the former district peasants' leader Hellbricht classified as a fellow traveler and let off with a fine. He was allowed to keep his farm.

[5]

Although Thomas Lieven was sent for, complimented and thanked by General König, the French Military Governor, on December 3, 1945, he received the following letter on the seventh.

WAR MINISTRY OF THE FRENCH REPUBLIC

Paris

5th December 1945

Captain René Clairmont
Army Serial Number S 324,213
War Crimes Investigation Service
Baden-Baden
Ref. CS Hr. Zt. 324/1945

In connection with the preliminary investigation of evidence relative to the court-martial of Lieutenant Pierre Valentine and others the Deuxième Bureau was requested to forward your personal file.

It appears from this file, to which further material has been added by a leading official of the Deuxième Bureau, that you served as an agent of German Intelligence, Paris, during the war. You will appreciate that anyone with your record cannot in any circumstances be tolerated as a member of the French War Crimes Investigation Service. Colonel Maurice Débras, who originally transferred you to this organization, ceased to be a member of it four months ago.

You are hereby requested to vacate your offices in Baden-Baden by 12 noon on the 15th December 1945 and submit to your superior officer all documents, files, stamps and records in your possession, together with your Army papers and passes. You are forthwith to relinquish your duties on suspension. Further instructions will follow by next post.

The signature was illegible. Below it was typed the word: "Brigadier General."

Thomas Lieven sat at his desk humming gently to himself. He read the letter again, went on humming and thought: Well, well. So there we go again. My life does nothing but repeat itself with paralyzing monotony. I play a crooked trick and everyone loves me. I'm snowed under with decorations, money and kisses. I'm the darling of all the belligerents. Then I do a decent action and—wham! There I am in the mud again.

"A leading official of the Deuxième Bureau" has apparently added something to my personal file for the benefit of the gentlemen at the War Ministry. A leading official, eh? So

Colonel Jules Siméon must be still alive and still hating me as much as ever . . .

An hour later the man who still called himself Captain Clairmont handed over his office and all his records to the head of his department. By noon on December 7, 1945, Captain Clairmont had vanished. Vanished without a trace.

[6]

On February 22, 1946, two gentlemen inquired at the porter's office in the Paris luxury hotel called the Crillon in the Place de la Concorde for a certain M. Hauser.

The beaming smile of the porter seemed to indicate that M. Hauser was a favorite resident.

The porter called up M. Hauser's room. "Two gentlemen wish to speak to you, sir. Their names are M. Fabre and M. le Baron Kutusov."

"Ask them to come up, please."

A page conducted the gentlemen up to the second floor. Bastian Fabre's fiery bush of hair stood up even more fiercely than ever from his skull. His companion, bearer of the name of a famous Russian general, seemed about forty-five years old. He was broad-shouldered and very soberly dressed.

In the drawing room of Suite 213 the two visitors were warmly received by M. Hauser, who wore a suit cut by a first-rate tailor.

Bastian waited until the page had left the room. Then he fell around his old friend's neck. "Boy, am I glad to see you again!"

"Same to you, Bastian, and how!" said Thomas Lieven. Extricating himself from Bastian's embrace, he shook the Russian's hand. "It's a pleasure to meet you, Baron Kutusov. But from now on I propose to stop calling you Baron. I shall call you, instead, Comrade Commissar."

"But why?" the Russian demanded, blinking nervously.

"Patience, my dear sir! One thing at a time! I've so much to tell you both, little brothers! I've ordered lunch to be served here. It'll arrive in ten minutes. Borsch among other things, Comrade Commissar. Do please sit down . . ."

Thomas Lieven was behaving with amazing coolness and self-assurance considering that the French military authorities had been looking for him for weeks and that here in Paris he was actually, so to speak, in the lion's mouth. But he consoled himself with the reflection that lions seek their prey anywhere but in their own mouths.

When he left Baden-Baden surreptitiously on December 11, he was carrying an excellently forged French passport in the name of Maurice Hauser, prepared for him by a specialist who had at one time worked for Paris Intelligence. He had also written to Bastian Fabre in Marseilles to inform him that he, Thomas, was absolutely broke.

Bastian's answer came by return of post.

"Now you see, Pierre, how right we were in those days not to let you have all the swag you collared from de Lesseps. Now you can have the bit we kept back. I've picked up a pal here, son of a Russian baron. Name's Kutusov. His old man used to be a taxi driver in Paris. Now he's popped off and the boy drives. A Pontiac . . ."

Thomas sent the following telegram to Bastian:

EXPECTING YOU AND BARON WITH CAR 22 FEBRUARY HOTEL CRILLON.

As soon as his guests arrived he checked up. "Where's the car?"

"Outside the hotel."

"That's good. They'd better see it. But it's you, my dear Bastian, who will have to drive it during the next few days, while Comrade Commissar Kutusov sits at the back. Did you bring the louis d'or?"

"Yes. In my suitcase."

Three waiters entered with the luncheon trolley. Then Thomas, Bastian and Kutusov sat down to table and added fresh cream to the appetizing borsch soup. The Russian taxi-nobleman exclaimed in astonishment: "Just like home! Cream on the table!"

MENU

Russian Borsch
Beef Stroganoff
Lemon Soufflé

PARIS, 22 FEBRUARY 1946

Thomas Lieven's first postwar millions were made in the Russian style.

Russian Borsch

Boil together one pound each of lean beef and pork. Add half a pound of streaky smoked bacon. Boil to a strong stock, then remove the meat and cut it into small pieces. Cut two pounds of cabbage into thin strips. Pepper and salt. Fry in lard, adding some spice and bay leaf. In another pot braise a chipped beetroot. Add vegetables as used for stock, with pepper, salt, bay leaf and a whole pepper. Add a little vinegar to the beetroot, so that it keeps its color. The lightly boiled vegetables, but not the bay leaf, are placed in the stock. Then the cut meat is added and the whole left to boil together. Before serving, a grated beetroot is added. At table one large tablespoonful of sour cream is poured into each plate of the soup.

Beef Stroganoff

Cut a well-hung fillet of beef into thin strips. Fry chopped onions in butter until tender, but do not brown them. Then add the meat and leave the whole to fry for one minute on each side. Add pepper, salt and plenty of thick sour cream. Stir well. Bring to a boil and serve.

Lemon Soufflé

Cream three egg yolks together with three tablespoonfuls of sugar until foamy. Add all the juice and the grated rind of half a lemon, half a teaspoon of corn flour and the white of an egg beaten stiff. Place this mixture in a buttered soufflé baking tin and bake in medium heat until risen and golden-brown. Serve immediately in tin, with biscuits.

"Might I ask you to eat in a rather more mass-produced style, Comrade Commissar? Elbows on the table, for example. And in the future could you be a little less particular about your fingernails?"

"But why? What are you bothering about all that for?"

"Gentlemen, I have some big business to propose to you. It's an undertaking in which you, Baron, would pose as a commissar, Bastian as his driver and I as a wholesale dealer in spirituous liquors."

"Spiri—what?" demanded Bastian in bewilderment.

"Don't speak with your mouth full. Let's say a wholesale

dealer in schnapps. I've been most bitterly disappointed by my treatment in the French Army, gentlemen. I intend to take a pretty drastic revenge on it."

"With schnapps?"

"Yes, with schnapps."

"But there isn't any schnapps about now, my dear sir! Everything's rationed!" cried Kutusov.

"You've no idea how much schnapps there'll be about all of a sudden if you and Bastian play your parts decently as commissar and chauffeur," said Thomas. "Now come on, let's each have another helping. Then after lunch we'll go shopping."

"What are we going to buy?"

"Black leather overcoats. Fur caps. Heavy socks." Thomas lowered his voice. "A Soviet delegation has been living in this hotel ever since the end of the war. There are five of them. Their job is to look after all the Soviet citizens in France. Do you know how many there are?"

"No idea."

"Over five thousand. And they're all suffering from the same thing . . ." While two guests listened intently over their spoonfuls of borsch, the best soup in the world, Thomas told them what was wrong with all the Soviet citizens in France . . .

[7]

Two days later a black Pontiac stopped in front of the French Ministry of Food, which controlled, among other things, the distribution of alcohol. A chauffeur in black leather, with a fur cap perched on his spiky red hair, opened the door of the car. A gentleman similarly clothed alighted and entered the great gray building. He took the elevator to the third floor, where he was received with open arms in the office of a certain Hippolyte Lassandre.

"My dear, my most honored M. Kutusov! It was I with whom you spoke on the telephone yesterday. Let me take your coat. Pray be seated."

M. Kutusov was wearing under his black leather overcoat a rather crumpled, blue suit of ready-made manufacture. His shoes were big and clumsy. He seemed to be in a great rage. "I consider the attitude of your Ministry a hostile act, which I shall report to Moscow . . ."

"I beg you, I entreat you, my dear M. Kutusov . . . I mean dear Commissar Kutusov . . . please do nothing of the kind. I shall get into the most terrible trouble with the Central Committee if you do!"

"What Committee are you talking about?"

"That of the Communist Party of France, Comrade Commissar, of which I am a member. I assure you that it was a pure oversight."

"A pure oversight to ignore five thousand Soviet citizens for months in the distribution of alcohol?" The bogus commissar laughed scornfully. "Oversight, indeed! I find it very peculiar that while the British and American citizens in your country duly received their alcohol my own brave compatriots who beat the Fascists before any other nation did . . ."

"Say no more, Comrade Commissar, I beg of you! Of course you are right. It was unpardonable. But the error will be made good forthwith."

The commissar proclaimed: "I demand in the name of the Soviet Union, naturally, deliveries retroactive to cover all the months when none was made."

"Naturally, Comrade Commissar, naturally."

The fact that the Soviet citizens living in France did not receive any alcohol rations had been learned by Thomas Lieven from Zizi, a slender young woman with auburn hair, who was employed by a prosperous house of assignation in Paris. Thomas had met her during the war and she was very fond of him. He had saved her lover, at the time, from deportation to Germany. Zizi told Thomas she was now getting on very well, especially since the Russians had come to Paris. Certain Russians were, so to speak, permanent guests in her establishment.

"What sort of Russians?" Thomas asked her.

"Oh, they're members of a delegation living at the Crillon. Five of 'em. Great big hefty chaps, I can tell you. Strong as bears! Talk about the male animal!"

Zizi went on to say that the five Soviet citizens were positively enraptured by the decadent phenomena of the capitalist West and for that reason were sadly neglecting their duties. They were supposed to be doing their best to encourage their five thousand compatriots living in France to return to Russia. But the delegates hardly ever applied themselves to this task. They preferred Zizi's place, and a few others, too . . .

"Just imagine, they don't even bother about the schnapps rationing," Zizi told Thomas.

"What should they be doing about that?" he asked. He soon found out what the position was.

The bogus commissar, Kutusov, adequately equipped, with

forged papers, as a Soviet official, took delivery of the supplementary distribution of alcohol. No less than three hundred thousand quarts were conveyed in trucks to a gloomy, partially demolished brewery near the airport at Orly.

It had been discovered by Thomas while he was waiting for Bastian. The place had belonged to a collaborator now in exile. In February 1946—the reader should always bear in mind—much confusion still existed in most of the European countries, including France.

Eight men now resumed work in the abandoned brewery. Production went on day and night. Under M. Hauser's directions the well-known and deservedly popular aniseed brandy known as pastis was distilled according to the following family recipe which was supplied to Thomas by a lady in Zizi's establishment.

To one quart of chemically pure ninety-per-cent alcohol add:

8 grams or 1 tablespoon of fennel seed
12 grams or 4 tablespoons of balm-mint leaves
5 grams or 2½ teaspoons of star anise
2 grams or 1 teaspoon of coriander
5 grams or 5 teaspoons of sage
8 grams or 1 tablespoon of green anise seeds

The mixture is left to draw, in darkness, for eight days. Shortly before filtering ten drops of anise oil are added. Finally the alcohol content is reduced to forty-four per cent by dilution.

Kutusov paid for the alcohol with the proceeds of the sale of the gold coins which Bastian had brought with him. Labels ordered by Thomas from a small printing shop were attached by Bastian's friends to the filled bottles.

While wholesale production was still going on Thomas went to see a French military official on the commissariat staff who lived in the Parisian quarter of Latour-Maubourg. This part of the city was entirely occupied by the Army and constituted a small township within the capital.

"M. Hauser" asked the commissariat officer Villard if he would be interested in a private bargain involving schnapps. "I am in possession of raw materials which would enable me to produce pastis. I know that your officers' club is short of schnapps. I could sell it to you cheap."

"What do you call cheap?"

Thomas's offer was of course cheap at that period of appalling scarcity of alcohol. Today his price would be considered a bit high. He demanded in modern terms something like four dollars for a bottle of pastis.

The commissariat officer clinched the deal as if it were the bargain of his life. And so it was from his point of view, considering that in those days a bottle of pastis on the black market would cost around about fourteen in currency of the present time.

Business prospered at lightning speed. The commissariat officer didn't confine himself to supplying his own officers' club with Hauser's Pastis. He also passed on the glad news to his friends. Soon army trucks were transporting Hauser's Pastis to every officers' club in the country.

In fact, Thomas Lieven could well be said to be supplying the whole French Army. And the French Army paid on the nail. And all went well until May 7, 1946. Then there was a bit of a hitch.

On that day, just before seven P.M., the permanent head of the Soviet delegation, M. Andreyev S. Shenkov, turned up at the suite of the bogus commissar Kutusov in the Hôtel Crillon and demanded, very red in the face, an explanation of his conduct.

For M. Shenkov, a few days before, had decided to pay a little more attention to his duties. He, too, therefore, proposed to supply his five thousand compatriots with alcohol. But he learned from the Ministry in charge of the rationing system that the alcohol due had long since been delivered to a certain Commissar Kutusov, in residence at the Hôtel Crillon.

"I demand an explanation!" roared Shenkov in French, with a strong Russian accent. "Who are you, monsieur? I don't know you! I never saw you before in my life! I'll have you arrested! I'll . . ."

"Shut your trap!" Kutusov yelled back at him, but in the purest Russian. Then for half an hour he addressed Comrade Shenkov in Russian in exactly the fashion and on exactly the subjects imparted to him by Thomas Lieven. For Thomas had naturally allowed, from the start, for some such little hitch in his plans.

Half an hour later Comrade Andreyev S. Shenkov returned to his room pale and agitated, his forehead damp with sweat. His friends Tushin, Bolkonsky, Balashev and Alpalych were waiting for him there.

"Comrades," groaned Shenkov, dropping into a chair, "we are lost!"

"Lost?"

"We're practically already in Siberia. It's ghastly. It's horrible. Do you know who Kutusov is? He is the commissar they've sent to spy on us. He has all the necessary powers and he knows all about us."

"All?" cried Bolkonsky in horror.

Shenkov answered in a depressed tone: "Everything. How we've neglected our work here and what we've been doing instead." His four friends looked terror-stricken. "There's only one thing we can do, comrades. We must try to make a friend of him. And we must work like dogs, day and night. No more Zizi! No more nylons and American canned food and cigarettes! Then it's just possible that Kutusov will condescend to be merciful . . ."

Such was the way in which, thanks to Lieven's prophetic insight, the little hitch was surmounted and the great pastis undertaking could go on developing without the slightest interruption.

On May 29 a very happy, because relatively wealthy, ex-comrade, commissar and taxi-nobleman, Kutusov, drove his two friends in his old Pontiac to Strasbourg. In that city Thomas had got to know, during the carefree days of his work for the War Crimes Investigation Service, a few friendly French and a few friendly German frontier guards. With their help it was not too difficult to transport the two trunks of Messrs. Lieven and Fabre, without examination, from the one country to the other. The trunks contained the profits of the pastis enterprise.

On the back seat of the Pontiac, Thomas was talking excitedly. "Next move England, Bastian! The land of the free! Oh, my club, my lovely flat, my little bank! You'll love England, old chap . . ."

"But look here, didn't the English chuck you out in 1939?"

"Yes," said Thomas. "So we shall just have to make a detour first, to Munich. A friend of my youth who lives there will help me to get back into England."

"Who's this friend of your youth, then?"

"He's a Berliner. But at present he's an American major, editing a newspaper. Name's Kurt Westenhoff." Thomas smiled blissfully. "Oh, Bastian, I'm so happy. All our troubles are over now. A new life is beginning—a new era."

[8]

Thomas Lieven, together with many other callers, sat in the anteroom of the office of the American major, Kurt Westenhoff, at Munich, situated in the Schelling Strasse, in the enormous building formerly occupied by the publishing firm of Eher.

In the days of the Thousand-Year Reich the Nazis had printed the *Völkische Beobachter* there. Now a different newspaper was being printed on the same premises by the Americans.

It was very hot in Munich on that May 30, 1946. Many of the lean, pallid men seated in Westenhoff's anteroom had sweat standing on their brows. Thomas Lieven watched then pensively. There you sit, he was thinking, in your old suits, which have grown too big for you, with your shirt collars now too loose, and your haggard, undernourished and bloodless features. Beggars and jetsam of this first postwar period, coming here for help, for a job, for Persil tickets . . . you don't look to me now as if you could have held your own out at the front or in any genuine resistance movement against the Nazis. You kept pretty quiet during those "Thousand Years." You stopped your ears, covered your eyes and shut your mouths. But now at last you mean to get somewhere. You'll soon be pushing your way to the national manager and extracting your share from the big sausage vat. You'll soon find places upstairs, in the government, in commerce and industry, everywhere. For the Americans will help you . . .

But are you the right people on the right road? Will you use this unique opportunity to shift Germany and the Germans a bit out of the limelight of history, for a time at any rate?

We have started and lost two world wars in the course of thirty-two years. A tough performance! How would it be if we now withdrew from the arena and cultivated neutrality, gave in a bit both to the Amis and the Russians, traded with both West and East? We've been shooting such a lot! Suppose—now don't start losing your temper right away, it's only a suggestion—suppose we decided never to do any more shooting at all? God in heaven, that would be something to be proud of!

An extremely pretty girl secretary appeared. "Herr Lieven, Major Westenhoff is waiting for you," said the young lady, who was later to become Mrs. Westenhoff. Thomas walked past her into the editor's office. The latter rose to meet him with outstretched hand.

"Morning, Thomas," said Kurt Westenhoff, who was short and chubby. He had thin fair hair, a fine forehead and shrewd blue eyes which always expressed both amiability and melancholy. His father, Dr. Hans Westenhoff, had been editor in chief in the Berlin publishing firm of Ullstein and had also been on the staff of *BZ am Mittag* and *Tempo*. Then the family had to emigrate. Now the war was over and Kurt Westenhoff had returned to the land which had driven him out.

"Morning, Kurt," said Thomas. He had last seen the man in 1933, in Berlin. Thirteen years had passed. Yet Westenhoff had immediately recognized him.

"Fancy your remembering me," said Thomas hoarsely.

"Why shouldn't I, man? We've known each other since we were schoolboys. I knew your father. I don't need to put any questions to you except—how can I help you?"

Thomas said: "As you know, before the war I was a banker in London. Marlock and Lieven, Dominion Agency, in Lombard Street."

"Ah, yes, Dominion Agency. I remember."

"I've been living a wild life since then. Your counter-intelligence corps no doubt has a big file about me. But it's the plain truth that I only got into all that mess owing to my partner Marlock. He arranged to have me deported from England and thus tricked me out of my share in the bank. Ever since 1939 my one idea has been to get my hands on that swine."

"I understand," said Westenhoff. "You'd like to go to England."

"Yes. To settle accounts with Marlock. Can you help me to do that?"

"Sure, boy, sure," said the Americanized Berliner. But he was wrong there.

Two weeks later, on June 14, Westenhoff invited Thomas to come and see him in his villa that evening.

"I'm sorry, Thomas," said his friend, as they sat on the terrace behind the house, gazing into the dusk of the garden. "I'm really most awfully sorry. Have another big whisky straight before I tell you about it."

Thomas took his advice.

"That Robert E. Marlock of yours has disappeared. I alerted my friends in the counter-intelligence corps and they got in touch with the British. Looks like a bad show, Thomas, very bad. Your little bank has gone, too. Another whisky?"

"You might just as well pass me the whole bottle right away. I'm gradually beginning to feel like Job." Thomas smiled wryly. "Job plus Johnnie Walker. When did my little bank vanish?"

"In 1942." Westenhoff drew a sheet of paper from his pocket. "The precise date was August 14. On that day Marlock ceased payment. Drafts were not being met. Depositors wanted to withdraw their accounts. On that day Marlock disappeared and hasn't been seen since. That was all my friends in the counter-intelligence corps could tell me. They're very anxious to make your acquaintance, by the way."

"But I'm not anxious to make theirs."

Thomas sighed. He stared out into the blossoming garden, where the trees and bushes were losing their contours more and more and turning to smoky shadows in the deepening evening dusk. He fiddled with his glass for a long time. At last he said: "I'll stay here, then. I've earned enough money in France to keep me. But I'll work, though never again—you hear me, Kurt?—never again for a secret service. Not as long as I live!"

He was mistaken. As mistaken as Kurt Westenhoff when he assumed that Thomas Lieven would never meet his criminal ex-partner Robert E. Marlock again.

[9]

One fine day in July 1946 a gentleman wearing only a sports shirt and trousers was strolling on a lawn of the English type belonging to a comfortable villa in Grünwald, a suburb on the outskirts of Munich. The gentleman looked pale and bore a resigned expression. He was accompanied by a muscular giant in similar clothing who bore a contented expression under the spiky bush of his red hair.

"Nice little place we've bought for ourselves, Bastian, old lad, eh?" Thomas Lieven remarked.

"And all out of French army funds too," grunted the former Marseilles gangster, who had been trying himself out for some weeks as Lieven's valet.

They returned to the house. Thomas said: "Last night I worked out how much we owe the French Treasury for our turnover."

"And how much was it?"

"About thirty million francs," said Thomas quietly.

Bastian's face expressed the utmost delight. *"Vive la grande armée!"* he exclaimed.

CHAPTER 2

[1]

Some months later Thomas sat with Bastian in the lounge of his villa, watching the flames leaping on the hearth and drinking pastis, the liquor with which they had earned so much money in France.

"I'm getting bored and restless," said Bastian. "Let's think of something new. What'll we do now?"

"I think I have an idea," said Thomas, stretching himself. "We're now going to go and look for uranium cubes."

"Look for *what*?"

"You heard me, old lad."

"And where are we going to look?" asked Bastian.

"Probably somewhere in South Germany, not far from the Austrian frontier," replied Thomas. "That was where they were last seen, in the so-called disengagement trains."

The trains in question were running south at the end of April 1945. They were overcrowded with top-ranking functionaries of the SA and SS, diplomats and heads of government departments. The passengers carried gold and jewels, plans of still secret, hiterto unused weapons, enormous quantities of morphine, cocaine and other narcotics from army stocks and finally uranium cubes from the Kaiser Wilhelm Institute in Berlin.

Just before they reached the frontier the Nazi bosses began to get a bit worried, at any rate so far as the uranium was concerned. They threw the precious cubes out of the windows of the train.

"They've never been found," said Thomas, who was soon going to change his name again. "Nor have the plans of those miracle weapons. They may very well be still lying about somewhere in the woods, under the snow. Or of course they may have been found by peasants. Lord only knows."

[2]

Thomas's new forged papers, of first-rate quality, which he had himself produced, represented him as Peter Scheuner and Bastian as Jean Lequoc.

The little town near the Austrian border, which Thomas had mentioned to Bastian, was crammed with soldiers, refugees and displaced persons. There simply wasn't enough room for all of them. All the hotels and boardinghouses were packed to the brim.

But Thomas and Bastian found two quiet rooms in a farmhouse not far from the town. They rented this accommodation under their false names, from the evening of February 20, 1947, and stayed there three months. That was a long time, during which they were both extremely busy.

To begin with they spent a few days and nights investigating the Bristol Hotel. Sometimes there was quite a lot going on there. Dancing and drinking, flirting and shady dealings, whispered conferences, business decisions and telephone calls took up the time. There were swarms of ladies of easy virtue, soldiers spending their pay, mysterious Poles, sinister Czechs, a few Hungarian aristocrats, a few Russian adherents of Vlassov and, naturally, also some Germans.

After Thomas and Bastian had observed conditions in the little town for a week they held a council of war in a snowed-up country inn. Said Thomas: "We've seen lots of girls, soldiers and displaced persons, my boy. But we've seen, above all, Nazis! Nazis from elsewhere and Nazis who were born here. I realize that now. The Amis don't seem to know it. We two, however, you and I, must never forget it. What we're after is that uranium and those plans."

"Assuming they're still here."

"There's a strong probability that they are. And I believe I've hit upon a first-class scheme to prove it."

"Well, let's hear it," said Bastian.

Thomas told him. His plan was as simple as it was ingenious. It was on February 28 that Thomas first drew it up. By April 19 he had in his possession:

28 cubes of uranium 238, each measuring 5 cm. across, weighing 2.2 kilos and without exception bearing the stamp of the Kaiser Wilhelm Institute in Berlin;

a specimen of the MKO secret sighting mechanism and

precise plans for the construction of the apparatus in question, developed in the Third Reich but only manufactured in a few models which were never used. It had been intended for fighter aircraft and would have enabled the adversary to be hit the moment he cropped up in the crosswires without the gunner having to make the usual allowance for lead.

How did Thomas Lieven manage it?

How did the alleged Peter Scheuner manage it? That was the question asked, very reasonably, in the middle of April 1947 by French, American, British and other agents, herds of whom were dashing about in South Germany at this time and had tried, just like Thomas Lieven alias Peter Scheuner, to unearth that vanished sighting mechanism and its blueprints.

The news soon spread among the agents of the various nations and they approached him with offers to buy his treasures, beginning with the uranium cubes.

In this connection Thomas Lieven favored an Argentinian businessman and personal representative of Juan Domingo Perón, who had been elected president of his country a year previously.

Thomas had remarked to Bastian: "That's our man. We want to get that stuff out of Europe and a long way out, somewhere where they won't make bombs with it."

The Argentinian paid $3,200 American for each cube of uranium, i.e. $89,600 in all. The cubes were flown off in the diplomatic bag to the Argentine.

Then the agents began to compete for Thomas Lieven's MKO sighting mechanism. Like the good pacifist he was, Thomas had naturally introduced certain modifications into the plans, to such an extent indeed that even technicians of genius would have racked their brains in vain over the blueprints so altered. And like the good salesman he was, Thomas had also of course made copies of the plans with a view to disposing of them not to one but to several purchasers.

He was just driving the hardest of bargains when Herr Gregor Marek turned up. Herr Marek came from Bohemia. Thomas had often seen him at the Bristol, where he seemed to be doing quite brilliantly. He was always smartly dressed, though he was small and squat and had the broad cheekbones and slanting eyes characteristic of the Slav. He spoke with a similarly typical accent. "Tell me, gentlemen, if you please, might I join you for a little while? I hear you've something to sell . . ."

Thomas and Bastian couldn't understand him at first.

But he finally made himself clear. "I've got good friends

over in Czechoslovakia who'll pay top prices. So let's have a look, eh, at the mechanism and the prints."

After some further talk Thomas and Bastian gave Herr Marek a look at the mechanism and the plans.

The Czech's eyes popped out of his head. "Just can't believe it! Here I've been after that bit of old iron for a year and couldn't find it. Tell me, if you please, how you got hold of it?"

"Oh, it was quite simple, Herr Marek," Thomas told him. "I took the political views of the population into consideration. There are an awful lot of Nazis here. My friend and I wandered about for a few weeks, going from one Nazi to the other. We hinted that we belonged to a Werewolf group . . ."

"Jesus, Mary and Joseph, you must have gone off your heads!"

"Not at all, my dear fellow. You'll soon see how well the idea worked. We talked as Nazis to Nazis to both local people and recent arrivals. Where was that uranium, we asked. Where were the plans of those miracle weapons? Our organization needed money and we must be in a position to sell that uranium and those plans. The Nazis saw our point immediately. One passed us on to another and . . . *voilà, monsieur!*"

"Good God Almighty! And didn't you have to pay anything for the stuff?"

"Not a cent. They were pure idealists. And now, what do your friends in the East offer?"

"I'll have to pop across there and see how the land lies." The agent disappeared for three days. He returned in the best of tempers. "I'm to give you their very best respects. Come and have lunch with me today. I hear you're fond of cooking. I've got everything at my place. Then we can have a nice quiet business chat."

Bastian and Thomas called at about eleven A.M. on May 6, 1947, at the apartment of the representative of the People's Democracy. It was luxuriously furnished. Thomas inquired in astonishment: "Are your Czech friends so generous?"

Marek grinned. "Please, please! You haven't seen anything yet! Come this way." He led his visitors into a big room next to the kitchen. He showed them hundreds of picture books from the Thousand-Year Reich, stacked yards high. *The Führer and the Children, The Nationalist Party Congress at Nuremberg, The Roads the Führer Built, Victory in the West, Victory in the East* and so on were some of the titles.

Thomas picked up one of the volumes and leafed through

it. Nothing but full page photographs of parades, Nazi bosses, generals and, again and again, the Führer.

"I've only got just a few of 'em up here," said the Czech. "My whole cellar's packed with the stuff. To say nothing of SS daggers, medals, death's-head rings—take your pick! It's amazing how fast it all sells. The Amis go perfectly mad about that sort of rubbish. They take it home with them as souvenirs!"

They went into the kitchen. Even here the profits of the sale of souvenirs were evident in the rows of canned provisions and bottles of whisky. "I've bought a fine eel, Herr Scheuner," said their host. "Can you do us eel in sage? It's my favorite dish."

"Let's get to it," said Thomas. He began to clean the eel and cut it into portions. As he did so Marek told him: "My principals would very much like to talk to one of you two personally. That can be easily arranged. You would be met at the frontier. You wouldn't bring the plans, naturally. Meanwhile I would stay here with whichever one of you remains behind."

Thomas and Bastian went into the garden and discussed the proposal briefly. Bastian said: "I'll go. You don't let Marek out of your sight. If there's any funny business, you hand him over to the Americans. Let's hope the boys over there speak French."

Marek, when questioned on this last point, replied: "Sure! They're regular chatterboxes. Fluent, gentlemen, fluent!"

On May 9, Bastian Fabre left his friend Thomas Lieven for Czechoslovakia. He had arranged to be back by May 15. But by that date and even later he had not returned.

Herr Marek showed more signs of uneasiness than Thomas. "Something's happened over there . . . I've never known anything like this before . . . my principals are always most punctilious . . ."

"Marek, if anything's happened to my friend, then God help you!"

On May 22, one of Marek's compatriots called on him, handed him a letter and immediately departed in a great hurry. Marek grew paler and paler as he read the letter.

Thomas watched him steadily. "What's wrong?" he demanded, out of patience.

Herrr Marek, in his excitement, could only ejaculate: "Oh God, Oh God!"

"What's the matter, man? Talk, will you?"

"Your friend's been arrested by the Russians!"

"By the *Russians?*"

"They found out that we Czechs wanted to buy that sighting mechanism. They forbade us to do so and locked your friend up. They say they want the thing themselves. Oh God, Oh God!"

"Where did they lock my friend up?"

"In Zwickau. Your friend must have crossed into the Soviet zone of occupation."

"Herr Marek," said Thomas. "Pack your bag."

"You mean . . . you want to go to Zwickau?"

"Obviously," said Thomas.

[3]

A map lay before him on the moss. Thomas was once more checking his position from the map. A flowery meadow stretched before him, beginning at the edge of the wood. Through the middle of the meadow a cheerful little brook babbled.

At that brook one Germany ended and another began. This situation was indicated on the map by hatching of a brown tint. Let us hope, thought Thomas, that the color was chosen in order to remind one of the people who were to blame for splitting Germany into two.

Midday on May 27 was the agreed time. The group of three trees on the other side of the brook marked the agreed place. There ought to be a Red Army soldier standing there ready to escort Thomas. But there was no such person in sight.

Dear, dear, thought Thomas Lieven, how very careless of them! First I send my friend Bastian to Zwickau to confer with the Czechs about the handing over to them of certain plans—falsified of course—of a miraculous sighting mechanism. Then the Soviet authorities run him in. Obviously I have to get him out. Obviously, therefore, I lie here at midday on May 27, all ready to do so, with the falsified plans in my brief case. Here I lie waiting for the Red Army man who is to get me out of one Germany into the other. But the fellow just isn't there. I wonder if anything in this life ever does run smooth, without undue irritation?

Thomas Lieven lay there at the edge of the wood until 12:28 P.M. Just as his stomach rumbled for the first time a Soviet soldier appeared on the other side of the brook. He was carrying a tommy-gun at the ready. When he reached the three trees he stood still and looked about him. Ah, there he is, thought Thomas. He stood up and walked out into the meadow. The Red Army man, who was quite young, stared at him in amazement.

"Hello!" Thomas called out in a friendly tone, waving his hand as he marched on as far as the brook. There he stopped, took off his shoes and socks, rolled his trousers above the knee and waded through the ice-cold water to the other bank. He was about halfway across when he heard a hoarse shout and looked up in surprise.

"Stoi!" yelled the young Red Army man, adding a number of other words in Russian. Thomas, having no idea what he meant, nodded affably and waded on till he reached the other bank. The young soldier came to meet him. Then Thomas realized with a sudden shock that this could not be the man who was to escort him. He must be quite a different soldier, who had no knowledge of the meeting that had been arranged.

The Red Army man shouted at him in a guttural voice.

"My dear young friend, please listen to me," Thomas began. Then he found the barrel of the tommy-gun against his ribs. He dropped his shoes, socks and brief case and put up his hands. This is really disgusting, he thought. Now I've got the Red Army after me too.

Remembering the excellent judo training he had received in France all those years ago Thomas immediately resorted to the so-called double-butterfly hold. Less than a second later the Red Army man whirled shrieking through the air and dropped into the brook, tommy-gun and all. Thomas picked up his shoes, socks and brief case and turned to make a dash into the Soviet zone.

Then a trampling and rumbling shook the ground. Thomas looked up in a fright. From the woods on the Soviet side of the meadow at least fifty people, men, women and children, came racing toward the brook as if they had gone crazy. They splashed through the water and went charging on into the American zone.

Thomas stared after them in amazement. He had actually helped all those people to escape into the West! They had all been lying in wait here in the East, just as he had in the West. He burst into a wild fit of laughter. Then he saw the Russian scrambling to his feet in the water, gasping for breath and rushing after him. He heard the young soldier yelling behind him. Then shots rang out. Bullets whistled past him. He noted mechanically that Soviet tommy-guns fired even after a ducking.

Up the road came a Russian jeep, with a captain sitting next to the driver. The officer jumped up, seized the windshield in both hands and yelled frantically in Russian at the frantically firing Red Army soldier on the rising ground ahead of the jeep. The shooting ceased. The jeep braked beside Thomas Lieven.

"*Gospodin* Scheuner," said the Captain in guttural German. "Sorry for the delay. Tires no good, went *kaput*. But you're welcome, *gospodin*, most welcome!"

[4]

The Palace Café at Zwickau looked as shabby as everything else in the little town of 120,000 inhabitants. Six hours after Thomas had shown quite a considerable number of refugees the way into freedom he sat in a corner of the aforesaid establishment and drank substitute lemonade.

He had nothing else to do on that May 27. The captain who had met him at the frontier had driven him to the Russian military headquarters in Zwickau. The commandant, a certain Colonel Melanin, had apologized through an interpreter for being obliged to keep him watiing until nine o'clock next morning for an appointment.

So Thomas had first gone to a dull hotel and then turned in to the Palace. Everone seemed very gloomy, both the men in their ancient double-breasted suits and tattered shirts and the woman without cosmetics, wearing woolen stockings and bark shoes, their hair hanging in wisps. Good Lord, thought Thomas. And where I've just come from the wheels seem to be going around quite nicely again. People are profiteering, toiling, grabbing what they can. But you poor devils look as though you were the only ones who had lost the war!

At the table opposite sat a rather imposing couple, the only one of its kind that Thomas had hitherto seen in Zwickau. The woman had a taut, well-developed figure, glorious corn-colored hair, sensual Slavonic features and piercing blue eyes. She wore a close-fitting green summer frock. A leopard-skin jacket hung on the back of a chair.

Her companion was a muscular giant with gray hair cut very short. He wore the typical blue, standarized suit of the Russian civilian, with exaggeratedly wide trouser legs, and had his back to Thomas as he talked to the lady. The pair could not have been anything but Soviet citizens.

Suddenly Thomas gave a start. The lady with the corn-colored hair was flirting with him. She smiled, showed her little teeth, and winked at him, half closing one of her eyes.

Good Lord, thought Thomas. Surely I'm not going crazy? He turned away and ordered another bottle of substitute lemonade. After his third sip of it he looked across at the opposite table again.

The lady smiled at him. So he smiled too. After that things happened fast. The lady's companion swung around. He looked like a version of Tarzan made in the U.S.S.R. Leaping to his feet, he reached Thomas in four strides and seized him by the lapels. Shrieks resounded among the tables, infurating Thomas. He was still more infuriated when he caught sight of the blonde with the corn-colored hair behind the jealous giant. She had risen and seemed to be enjoying the scene tremendously. You slut, thought Thomas. So that was a trick, was it? You get a bit of a thrill when . . .

This train of thought was interrupted by a blow in the stomach from the giant's fist. This was too much for Thomas. He dived for the Russian Tarzan's legs. Judo for the second time that day. On this occasion the "glider" hold.

As the Russian Othello happened to be standing in front of the cloakroom counter, he sailed over it and dropped down on the other side. Thomas saw out of the corner of his eye that a Soviet non-commissioned officer had drawn his revolver.

Courage must be accompanied by intelligence. One has to know when one has had enough. Thomas ducked, raced to the exit and out into the street. Luckily there were no Red Army men about. The Germans he met took little notice of him. In those days, when a German ran, other Germans immediately felt sorry for him.

Thomas ran on until he reached the Swannery. In the beautiful old park he dropped, panting, onto a bench. After a while he felt better. Then he made his way cautiously back to his hotel.

The next morning, punctually at nine o'clock, the interpreter ushered Thomas Lieven, duly shaved, smartly dressed and self-assured, into the office of the military governor of Zwickau. Thereupon, however, our friend almost had a stroke. For the Zwickau commandant, rising from behind his desk to greet the visitor, was none other than the jealous Soviet Tarzan whom Thomas had transported, by means of the "glider" hold, to the other side of the cloakroom counter, the previous afternoon, at the Palace Café.

Today the giant was wearing a uniform. Many decorations could be admired upon his bosom. He scrutinized Thomas in silence.

The latter was meanwhile reflecting. This office is on the third floor. No point in jumping out of the window. Farewell, Europe. Some people say that Siberia can be quite delightful.

At last Colonel Vassili L. Melanin spoke, in guttural accented German. "Gospodin Scheuner, I beg your pardon for yesterday's behavior."

Thomas could only stare at him.

"I'm sorry about it. It was Dunya's fault." Melanin suddenly roared, as if he had gone out of his mind: "That accursed she-devil!"

"Do I understand you, Colonel, to be speaking of your revered consort?"

Melanin hissed through his teeth: "That infamous wretch! I might have been a brigadier by this time. Twice they've demoted me . . . on her account . . . for brawling."

"Colonel, you should compose yourself," Thomas said soothingly.

Melanin struck the desk with his fist. "For all that, I love my little pigeon Dunya. But enough, let's get to business. A drink first, though, my dear Scheuner."

Accordingly, they shared a bottle of vodka. An hour later Thomas Lieven was hopelessly tight, Colonel Melanin was stone-cold sober and they were both discussing the business in hand fluently and wittily. But they didn't make the slightest progress.

Colonel Melanin saw the situation as follows. "You wanted to sell the Czechs that MKO sighting mechanism. So you sent your friend here. You can return to the West with him if you hand us over the plans."

"Sell them to you, you mean," Thomas corrected him severely.

"I mean hand over. We shan't pay anything," the colonel said. He added with a cryptic grin: "I don't think you're quite a fool, Thomas Lieven."

Sometimes one's knees seem to turn into jelly, thought Thomas. He murmured faintly: "What was that you said just now, Colonel?"

"I said Lieven. Thomas Lieven. That's your name, isn't it? D'you think we're complete idiots? D'you think our secret service doesn't know what's in Allied files? Our people in Moscow have been laughing themselves sick over your doings."

Thomas pulled himself together. "If you . . . if you already know who I am . . . why haven't you locked me up long ago?"

"What could we have done with you? You're such a—forgive me—such a ludicrously bad agent!"

"Thanks very much."

"We need first-rate agents, not comic characters like you."

"You're very polite."

"I hear you're fond of cooking. Well, I'm fond of eating. Come to my place. Dunyasha will be delighted. We'll have pancakes. I've plenty of caviar. Then we can have a further little chat. What do you say?"

"That's an excellent idea," said Thomas Lieven. At the same time he thought remorsefully, A thoroughly bad agent? A comic character? Well, perhaps I am. So what?

Accordingly, he set about preparing a Côtelette Maréchale in the kitchen of a requisitioned villa. He felt extremely uneasy meanwhile. Colonel Melanin kept out of the way. But just as Thomas was cutting off a big leg of chicken for the cutlet the colonel's wife came in. She was in fact, so to speak, entering Thomas Lieven's life, though he didn't yet know that.

She was a most beautiful woman. Hair, eyes, lips and figure were all magnificent. She had a skin the color of ground almonds and looked so fresh, healthy and strong, positively unique! It was instantly evident that Dunya had no need of corset, brassière or any other vital accessories required by normal women.

After entering she closed the door and gazed at Thomas in silence, with a brooding expression, parted lips and half-closed eyes.

Exquisite but mad, was the thought that flashed through Thomas's mind. Heaven help me! If I don't kiss her, I believe she'll strangle me with her bare hands. Or else she'll call a National Security police officer and accuse me of sabotage.

Elsewhere in the villa footsteps resounded. The couple parted. About time too, Thomas thought.

Dunya absently prodded the leg of chicken. "Save me," she whispered. "Fly with me. My husband doesn't love me any more. He'll kill me or I'll kill him."

"Bu-but—madame—what makes you think that your husband doesn't love you?"

Dunya uttered a fiendish laugh. "You won your fight with

him yesterday in the café. The other men he used to half kill. He used to half kill me too. But now he never hits me, never! I don't call that love . . . Don't you think I speak good German?"

"Yes, very good."

"I had a German mother. I liked you from the start. I'll make you happy. Take me over there with you . . ."

The footsteps were coming nearer.

Dunya was still prodding the leg of chicken when the colonel entered the kitchen. He smiled enigmatically. "Ah, there you are, my little pigeon. Are you learning to cook as they do in the capitalist West, where the workers are so oppressed? What's the matter, Herr Lieven? Don't you feel well?"

"Just a momentary faintness, Colonel. Might I . . . might I ask you for a glass of vodka?"

MENU

Caviar Pancakes
Côtelette Maréchale with Peas and Potatoes
Caramel Pudding

ZWICKAU, 28 MAY 1947

Dunya the Russian enters Lieven's life with a leg of chicken.

Caviar Pancakes

For each person two very thin pancakes, about the size of one's hand, are cooked in butter, then immediately placed on preheated plates. Spread one pancake with caviar and place the other on top of it. Pour hot melted butter over the two pancakes and cover them thickly with sour cream. (The true Russian *blini* [pancake] is made of buckwheat flour, difficult to obtain in the West.)

Côtelette Maréchale

Bone the legs of a tender capon without breaking the skin. Prepare a stuffing from the chopped breast, with one tablespoonful of butter, a quarter of a teaspoonful each of chopped shallots, parsley and tarragon, a quarter of a cup of fresh bread crumbs soaked in wine, one tablespoonful of chopped mushrooms, pepper and salt. Put this mixture twice through the mincer. Then leave it to cook very slowly, stirring continuously. Add one tablespoonful of butter and one of double cream. The mixture must not harden. After cooling, this stuffing is inserted in the boned capon legs, which are then sewed together, rolled in fine bread crumbs and fried in butter till golden-brown. The breast may be stuffed in the same way, the two halves being sewed together after boning and some veal added to the stuffing.

Caramel Pudding

Put one quart of milk on to boil with half a cup of sugar and a little vanilla pod. After the milk has boiled allow it to cool slightly and then pour into it five eggs beaten up with a little salt. Prepare a caramel from one cup of sugar, not too dark, add a little water and pour the mixture into a warmed pudding basin. Tilt the basin to all sides so as to spread the caramel around before it hardens. Then add the milk mixture, close the basin tightly and boil the contents for three quarters of an hour in a pan of water. Chill for a few hours. When the pudding is turned out the caramel will cover it as a sauce.

One thing was quite clear to Thomas. He would have to take care to get back as fast as possible into the West. He didn't feel capable of dealing with this couple. So the Soviet Union would get those falsified plans for nothing. It was lucky, at any rate, that they were worthless.

Over the meal he still put up a show of stubborn resistance but only because he knew that Russians enjoy that sort of tug of war. The colonel, indeed, was obviously delighted as he heatedly pursued the argument. Dunya sat between them, watching both gentlemen with her brooding expression. Everyone ate and drank a tremendous lot. But after those rich pancakes Thomas managed this time to keep a clear head.

"Very well, Colonel. I'll make you a different proposal. You get the plans for nothing and in return you let my friend and another gentleman go back to the West."

"Another gentleman?"

"Herr Reuben Achazian. I don't know whether you are acquainted with him. A little more leg, madame?"

"Yes, I should like a lot more, Herr Lieven."

"I should say I am acquainted with that scamp," said the colonel scornfully. "Damned profiteer. What do you want with him?"

"Profits," said Thomas modestly. "You'll pardon me for saying so, Colonel. But as the Red Army has just deprived me of all my expectations, I shall really have to see how I can recoup."

"Where did you get to know that American swine?"

"Here in Zwickau, Colonel."

In fact, Reuben Achazian, a stout little fellow with sharklike eyes and a small mustache, had turned up at the Stag Hotel that morning while Thomas sat at breakfast. Herr Achazian had come straight to the point without more ado. "Wait, let me talk, don't interrupt me, I'm in a hurry and so are you. I know who you are—"

"Who told you?"

"Reuben Achazian knows everything. Don't interrupt. I've run into trouble here. With the Russians. To be quite frank, I've been taking part in a very big trade organization racket and they won't let me work here."

"Now look here, Herr Achazian . . ."

"S'sh. Help me to get across to the West and I'll make you a rich man. Did you ever hear of the ZVG?"

"Yes, of course."

The ZVG (*Zentrale Verwertungs Gesellschaft* or Central Disposals Company) had its headquarters in Wiesbaden and had been organized by the Americans. The company collected in vast dumps the aftermath of war, worth millions of dollars. There were weapons and ammunition, railway engines and trucks, bandages, scrap metal, wood, steel, entire bridges, medicaments, aircraft and textiles. The managers were Germans. But the Americans allowed them to sell only to foreigners.

"Only to foreigners," Reuben Achazian, looking as sharp as a weasel, told Thomas Lieven. "Not to Germans. But I'm a foreigner and the company can sell to me. I have a cousin in London who will advance us, you and me, funds to found a trading firm. I can make you a millionaire within a year if you help me to escape to the West."

"I'll think it over, Herr Achazian," Thomas Lieven replied.

He had thought it over. Accordingly, as he sat over that magnificent luncheon in the confiscated villa of a Zwickau Nazi he said to the Russian military governor of the town,

Vassili Melanin: "If you'll allow Herr Achazian to leave with me you can have the plans."

"Herr Achazian stays here. And I'll have those plans just the same."

"Listen, sir. I've left Herr Marek, the Czech agent, whom of course you know, in the custody of the American counter-intelligence corps at Hof. He'll stay in prison unless I come back and release him."

"Well, if he does it'll break my heart, naturally. You give me those plans or you stay here yourself."

"Very well then, I'll stay here," said Thomas.

[6]

On June 1, 1947, Thomas Lieven, Bastian Fabre and Reuben Achazian reached Munich. They were tired but in good shape. They drove out at once to Thomas's villa in Grünwald. He had been obliged to eat several more meals with Colonel Melanin and to participate in even more drinking sessions with him before he could persuade that officer to change his mind. At last they actually parted as friends. But the plans, of course, had to stay in Zwickau.

The three travelers only remained a few days in the Bavarian capital. Thomas explained to Bastian: "We've passed on those plans to the British, the French and the Russians. They'll soon find out that we've altered them. We shall have to assume different names and go for a while to Wiesbaden."

"That's all right with me, boy. I can't stand that character Achazian, though. He's a real racketeer, that chap, wanting to sell weapons and ammunition even today!"

"He won't," said Thomas. "Wait till we get to Wiesbaden. He'll find a surprise waiting for him."

Talking of surprises, the night before the three travelers left Munich they were just finishing a bottle of wine—it was about 7:30 P.M.—when the front doorbell rang. Bastian went to answer it. He returned white to the lips. He could only stammer: "C-c-come, please—"

Thomas accompanied him back to the hall. When he saw who was standing there he shut his eyes and reeled, clutching at the doorknob.

"No," he murmured. "Oh, no—"

"Yes," said she of the corn-colored hair, the beautiful consort of Colonel Melanin of Zwickau. "Yes, yes, it's me!"

It was. There she stood, with a huge trunk, looking as youthful and healthy as ever.

"How . . . how did you . . . I mean, madame . . . how did you get across the frontier?"

"By air. There were a whole lot of us. I'm a political refugee. I've been given political asylum. And I want to stay with you and go wherever you're going."

"No."

"Yes. And if you won't let met stay with you I shall go straight to the police and tell them you took plans to my husband . . . and everything else I know about you . . ."

"But why? Why should you want to give me away?"

"Because I love you," she calmly declared.

Well, man is a creature of habit.

Two months later, in August 1947, Thomas Lieven remarked, in a large apartment which he, Bastian Fabre and Reuben Achazian had rented as working and living accommodation in the Parkstrasse at Wiesbaden:

"I really can't imagine what you have against Dunya. She is charming. She cooks for you. She works hard. I find her delightful."

"But she makes too many demands on you," said Bastian. "Just look at your hands shaking!"

"Nonsense," Thomas retorted. But he spoke without conviction, for he did find his new mistress a bit of a strain. Dunya lived in a furnished room close by. She didn't come every evening. But when she did—

In Thomas's few moments of leisure he often thought of Colonel Melanin. He could well understand why the colonel had never been made a general.

At Wiesbaden Thomas Lieven was known as Ernst Heller, with forged papers to match, of course. He had founded a private firm in the name of his foreign colleague, Achazian. The undertaking bought up large quantities of the most various kinds of merchandise and stacked them in the dumps of the Central Disposals Company adjoining the devastated city.

The vast depots contained for sale not only former property of the German Army but also jeeps, trucks and supplies belonging to the American troops which had become obsolete or would not be worth sending back to the United States.

Thomas explained to his friends: "We can't do any business with America because we all have too dubious a past. We shall have to stick to other countries. And they'll have to be countries at war, which are not allowed to buy from the Disposals Company."

"I can put you in touch with a certain Aristoteles Pangalos, representing Greek partisans, and with one Ho Irawadi of Indo-China," said Reuben Achazian.

"But you can't sell those fellows weapons!" Bastian cried angrily.

Thomas Lieven gave them a ruling. "If we don't sell them weapons somebody else will. So we will sell them weapons. But they won't like them."

"What do you mean?"

"Listen. I've rented an empty factory near Mainz. We'll take the powder out of the ammunition and replace it with sawdust. As for tommy-guns, they're packed in chests with certain letters branded on the wood, which is also nailed down and sealed with lead. I've found a carpenter's shop which will supply us with exactly the same sort of chests with exactly the same sort of lettering. Even the lead seals can be imitated. And soft soap will give the chests the proper weight."

"Then what are we going to do with the powder and the tommy-guns themselves?"

"They'll be shipped from Hamburg," said Thomas. "And off Hamburg the water's deep. Need I say more?"

In that August of 1947 the supply situation at Wiesbaden touched rock-bottom. The calorie figure dropped to 800. The shortage of potatoes grew worse and worse. They were distributed only to hospitals and camps. The population lived almost entirely on maize products, unpopular on account of their bitter taste. The fat ration had to be reduced from 200 to 150 grams. Sugar was doled out at the rate of half a pound of white and half a pound of yellow per head. Four additional eggs were allowed in compensation for "the worse imaginable yield of fruit and vegetables owing to the great drought." Milk supplies broke down altogether. Two thirds of the Wiesbaden adults received no milk at all.

It may be observed that a terrible war is never anything like finished after it has been lost.

[7]

The firm of Achazian began by selling to Pangalos and Ho Irawadi two thousand kilos each of the malaria specific atebrin taking from stocks of the German Army. The packages were still stamped with the German eagle and swastika. That object had to be removed! Thomas and his partners took the atebrin to a pharmaceutical goods factory where the stuff was repacked. Then it could be shipped.

This was comparative child's play. But in another case the problem appeared at first sight absolutely insoluble. Pangalos and Ho Irawadi wanted to buy tropical helmets. Each customer required thirty thousand. They were available. But the swastikas on the helmets were so deeply engraved that they couldn't be removed. In these circumstances the firm naturally felt obliged to renounce the idea of selling the helmets abroad.

What on earth are we to do with the blasted things? Thomas wondered. He wondered for days on end. Then he had a brilliant inspiration. There were splendid sweat-absorber bands in the helmets, brand-new and of first-rate quality. Not a single scrap of hatband leather remained throughout the whole German hat industry.

Thomas contacted its leading representatives. Suddenly the helmets began to sell like hot cakes.

The firm of Achazian made a far greater profit from the sale of those hatbands than it would have made by selling the helmets themselves. Moreover, Thomas had succeeded in gingering up the German postwar hat industry.

But he had his worries, though they were not business ones. Thomas felt that Dunya was steadily encroaching upon his energies. She made scenes arising from her love or jealousy. She was both exciting and exhausting. Thomas quarreled with her and made it up again. It was the craziest period of his life.

Bastian was also worried. "You can't go on like this, boy. You're ruining yourself with that lady."

"What am I to do? I can't chuck her out. And she won't go."

"She'll go one of these days."

"Yes, but to the police."

"Damn it all," said Bastian. "You've got to consider the future a bit."

"That's just what I keep on doing. In any case our business here won't prosper much longer. Then we shall have to get out, and quite suddenly, as you can imagine—too suddenly for Dunya . . ."

"Well, I don't know," said Bastian.

Next they sold ball bearings to Greeks and Indo-Chinese, then trucks, jeeps, plows and other agricultural implements. "So that they can't start any trouble," said Thomas Lieven, staring out of the windows of his office at the desolate heaps of rubbish and ruins representing Wiesbaden.

The town looked as if it never wanted to rise again. Before the war only rich people lived there. Now there were simply persons of scanty private means dwelling in piles of rubble. The entire rubble area was later officially stated to comprise six hundred thousand cubic meters. Until the currency reform the removal of rubbish and rubble had cost Wiesbaden 3.36 million marks. Laborers and "rubble women" toiled shoulder to shoulder with other citizens, working in shifts. Thomas Lieven, Bastian Fabre and Reuben Achazian also dug for days on end in the muck. They regarded it as a kind of sport to counter-balance their other activities.

In the autumn of 1947 they suddenly realized that a pair of trousers could be made out of every American sleeping bag. They had forty thousand such bags. Clothing factories in South Germany still remember the flood of materials and orders which overwhelmed them in November 1947.

In the spring of 1948 they began, as a last undertaking, to do business in munitions. Hitherto they had given munitions the "preliminary treatment." Now they shipped the stuff in the same way as the chests filled with soft soap which were supposed to contain tommy-guns.

The vessels carrying such cargoes for Greece and Indo-China put to sea. They would be a good while on the way, thought Thomas. He could proceed at his leisure to close his offices in Wiesbaden, at just about the same time as several film companies opened theirs in the city.

The films shot in Wiesbaden all had the naïvely trivial, sadly gay or guaranteed harmless themes and titles of the German re-education period, such as *When a Woman Loves, Wedding Night in Paradise, Akbar the Tiger* or *Fatal Dreams.*

"The time's gradually coming when we shall have to clear out, old lad," said Thomas to Bastian on May 14, 1948.

"What do you think the Greeks and Indo-Chinese are likely to do when they find out what's happened?"

"Kill us if they can catch us," said Thomas Lieven.

But the purchasers of weapons did not catch Thomas and Bastian. Instead, foreign agents caught a few "genuine" dealers in armaments, as may be remembered, in the Federal Republic between the years 1948 and 1956. Time-bombs were placed in their cars or they were shot down in the open street.

Thomas Lieven remarked philosophically on one of these

macabre occasions: "He who delivers violence perishes by violence. We delivered soft soap. So we live."

But this occasion, as stated above, came later. On May 14, 1948, Thomas believed for a short time, quite suddenly, that he might come to a violent end. Toward midday the front doorbell rang. Bastian answered it. He returned waxen-faced. "Two gentlemen from the Soviet Military Mission."

"God Almighty," murmured Thomas. Then they were in the room, stern-featured and heavily built. In spite of the heat they still wore their leather overcoats. All of a sudden Thomas felt very hot, then, equally suddenly, very cold.

It's all over, he was thinking. Finish. They've found me.

"Good morning," said one of the Russians throatily.

"Kherrr Khelllerrr?"

"Yes."

"We are looking for Frau Dunya Melanin. We are told she's with you."

"Well—er—" Thomas pulled himself together. "The lady *may* be here."

"Would you permit us, please, to speak with her? Alone?"

"Certainly," said Thomas. He took the two men to another room, where Dunya was giving herself a manicure.

Ten minutes later the gentlemen in the leather overcoats left as they had come, stern-featured and taciturn.

Bastian and Thomas rushed at Dunya. "What was it about?"

With a shriek of delight the blond beauty flung her arms around Thomas's neck, almost knocking him down. "This is the happiest day of my life!" She kissed him. "My beloved!" Another kiss. "My only one!" A third kiss. "We can marry!"

Bastian's jaw dropped.

Thomas stammered: "We . . . can . . . what?"

"Marry!"

"But you're married already, Dunya!"

"Not now! Not for the last two minutes! Those men requested me to return home at once, to comply with the order of a Soviet divorce court petitioned by my husband, I refused. Then the men said: 'In that case your marriage is dissolved from this moment.' Look, here's the decree!"

"I can't read Russian," Thomas murmured. The room seemed to be whirling around him. He stared first at the beaming Dunya, then at Bastian's waxen features.

Well, let's hope we all enjoy ourselves, he was thinking.

Those ships with the sawdust ammunition and the soft soap are on the high seas and—

Help!

[8]

The best thing I can do is to take a rope and shoot myself with it, Thomas reflected sadly. How shall I ever get out of this ghastly mess? For the next few days he crept about feeling thoroughly miserable. On the night of May 18, returning from a visit to Dunya's furnished room, he shuffled, groaning, into the bathroom and in his nervousness tore the little medicine cupboard off the wall. It fell to the floor with a thunderous crash.

Bastian Fabre blundered out of his room half asleep. "What on earth's the matter, man?"

"Bromide," wailed our friend. "I need bromide, I must calm myself . . ."

"Have you been to see Dunya?"

"Yes. Just imagine, she's already arranged for publication of the banns. You're to be one of the witnesses. The show is to come off in a month's time. And she wants children! Five! And as soon as possible! Bastian, I shall be done for if something doesn't happen at once—at once, do you hear?"

"I heard you. Well, take a sip of that stuff first. I've got an idea which may work. But you'll have to give me two or three days' leave to see about it."

"Take your time, old lad," said Thomas Lieven. Bastian took it. When he returned six days later he was unusually silent.

"For goodness sake say something!" the desperate future bridegroom urged him. "Did you get anywhere?"

"We shall see," Bastian replied.

That was on May 25. That day Thomas heard nothing from Dunya. Nor did he on the next. When he called on her in the evening she was not at home.

On May 27, at a quarter past six in the evening, the telephone bell rang in his apartment. When he lifted the receiver all he could hear at first was a deafening uproar of voices and combustion engines.

Then suddenly he heard Dunya's despairing accents, choked by tears. "My beloved—my darling . . ."

"Dunya!" he cried. "Where are you?"

"At the airport in Frankfurt—at the military police station . . ."

"The military police station?"

A fresh outburst of sobbing reached him in Frankfurt. Then he heard her gasp: "I'm flying to America, dearest . . ."

Thomas dropped into a chair. "You—*what*?"

"We start in ten minutes . . . oh, I'm so terribly unhappy . . . but my life's in danger. I shall be killed if I stay here . . ."

"Killed—" Thomas repeated idiotically. Bastian entered the room humming to himself, went to a wall cabinet and helped himself to a small whisky. Meanwhile Thomas heard Dunya's voice say: "I received threatening letters—I was assaulted, almost strangled. They said they were going to kill me because I wouldn't go home—the Americans said that too—"

"The Americans—too?"

"Oh, not the way you mean!" cried the hysterical voice in Frankfurt. "The State Department has ordered me to be flown to America—for my own safety . . . after all my husband was a Russian general, don't forget . . ."

"Dunya, why didn't you tell me all this before?"

"I didn't want to endanger you. And they told me I wasn't to speak to anybody . . ." She was talking very fast. Thomas felt giddy. Dunya spoke of love and a future meeting, of eternal fidelity and indissoluble bonds of union across the oceans. She ended: "I must stop, beloved. The aircraft's waiting . . . good-bye . . ."

"Good-bye," said Thomas. Then he was cut off. He replaced the receiver.

He stared at Bastian, moistening his lips. "Give me one too. And hurry up with it. I suppose you're responsible for this?"

Bastian nodded. "Actually, it wasn't so very difficult," said he.

It really hadn't been, after his discovery of a huge camp for foreigners, called the Valka, outside Nuremberg. The loyal Bastian paid it a visit.

There were a great many drinking shops in the cheerless surroundings of that cheerless camp. On his third evening Bastian ran across two gentlemen who were willing, for a very reasonable fee, to compose certain threatening letters in Russian. They also agreed to come to Wiesbaden, break into a certain furnished room there, take a lady by the throat and give her a devil of a fright.

"Reaction was immediate," Bastian reported to his friend, rubbing his hands gleefully.

"Bastian!" Thomas shouted at him in a fury.

"The strangling was guaranteed harmless. I warned that Ivan johnny that she mustn't be seriously hurt."

"Get me another whisky, quick, and make it straight," groaned Thomas.

"With pleasure. I admit it was rather a rough and ready scheme."

"It was barbarous!"

"But I was getting very worried about you, old lad. I kept on seeing you going about with five children . . . can you forgive me?"

Later that evening they discussed their future. Thomas mentioned a new project. "We've made quite a bit of money here. We ought to invest it now—and quickly."

"Why so quickly?"

"I've been hearing things . . . Believe me, we'll have to work fast. We're going to buy cars. American Pontiacs, Cadillacs and so on."

Thomas warmed to his theme. A dollar, he explained, was worth at the moment about two hundred marks. Well, they had the money. But of course no German could obtain an import license for American cars. Never mind! Thomas knew a minor clerk in the Military Government who was just on the point of retirement. This man, Jackson Taylor, could obtain an import license.

"He'll start a showroom in Hamburg where he'll sell the cars. But for us."

"Who's he going to sell 'em to? No one has a bean in this country."

"They soon will have."

"Now many cars will you be buying, then?"

"Oh, about a hundred."

"Jesus! And have them brought over right away?"

"Yes. No. I'll buy 'em and have 'em brought over. But perhaps not right away."

"When, then?"

"That depends on when my little show comes off."

"What little show?"

Thomas told him.

[9]

On June 10, 1948, the *Olivia* left New York harbor. On May 17 the vessel, which carried a cargo of one hundred American cars, had reached the point 10 degrees 15 minutes longitude North and 48 degrees 30 minutes latitude West off the west coast of France. That day the captain received the following wireless message in code.

> north german radio—17 june 48—1543 hours—from schwertmann shipping office hamburg to captain hannes droge in name of cargo owner request you retain your present position till further notice and refrain from entering german territorial waters for the time being—maintain contact with us—further instructions follow—end

The *Olivia* cruised for three days and nights within the area mentioned. The crew kept skeleton watches, played poker and tippled. They toasted the unknown cargo owner over and over again.

On June 20 the following cable in code was taken down by a merry first wireless officer.

> north german radio—20 june 48—1123 hours—from schwertmann shipping office hamburg to captain hannes droge—in name of cargo owner request you now proceed hamburg harbor immediately—end

While the first wireless officer decoded the cable for his merry captain, the merry second wireless officer listened to the news from London. He removed his headphones and said: "A drastic currency reform has been announced today by our people in Germany. The old money is worthless. You only get forty marks to the dollar now."

"Always bad news," grumbled the second wireless officer.

"Good Lord, my savings," exclaimed the captain.

"The man with goods is well off today," said the first wireless officer.

The second wireless officer's jaw dropped. "That cargo owner of ours with his hundred cars!"

The captain nodded gloomily. "Just like our people to do a thing like that. What a sly devil! I'd like to know who he is . . ."

Well, Captain Hannes Dröge, if by any chance you're reading these lines, now you know.

In the spring of 1949 Thomas and Bastian were doing well in Zurich. Their favorite daily reading was the financial section of the *Neue Zürcher Zeitung*.

Thomas had bought up large quantities of pre-reform German shares with the proceeds of his recent operations. These shares were negotiated after the war at extremely low prices, since no one knew at that time how completely the victorious powers would destroy the centers of German economic life.

The most valuable plants were demolished. The biggest concerns were dissolved. In 1946–47 the shares of the United Steel Works were only negotiated to the extent of about fifteen per cent, General Electric thirty per cent and I. G. Farben not at all.

People who had nevertheless bought these and other shares were now richly rewarded for their optimism. After the currency reform, when the German mark was substituted for the reichsmark, prices rose month by month. At least one gentleman who occupied a Zurich flat could not complain of the situation.

But it changed on April 14, 1949. That day Thomas and Bastian visited the Scala Cinema at Zurich. They wanted to see the famous Italian film *The Bicycle Thief*. They saw the advertisements and the news pictures, including one of the Spring Derby at Hamburg.

Fine horses, gentlemen in morning dress and fascinating women could be admired. The camera indulged in some large close-ups of eminent spectators, a stout gentleman, a bewitching lady, another bewitching lady and then another. The Economic Miracle had begun. Another illustrious gentleman appeared.

Suddenly, in Box 5, a man yelled at the top of his voice: "*Marlock!*"

Thomas Lieven gasped. For there on the screen, over life-size, stood his rascally partner, whom he had believed dead, the criminal who had annihilated his peaceable career and hurled him into the grinding mills of international secret service. There he stood, faultlessly clad, in morning dress, with binoculars dangling on his chest.

"It's him . . . I'll kill him, the bastard!" Thomas raged. "I thought he was stewing in hell ages ago—but he's alive . . . now I'll settle accounts with him!"

[10]

"Excuse me, sir, I don't think I understood you quite rightly just now," said the owner of the Scala Cinema. "*What* exactly was it you wanted?"

"You understood me quite correctly, my dear sir," Thomas rejoined, with a polite bow. "I should like to borrow today's newsreel after its last showing."

"To borrow it? But why?"

"Because I should like to see it again in private. I saw an acquaintance of mine in it, whom I lost sight of when the war broke out."

Some hours later Thomas was racing, with the film under his arm, through the nocturnal streets of Zurich, out to the Praesens Studios, where he had engaged a cutting room and the appropriate technician. The cutter ran the newsreel copy through his apparatus until Thomas called out "Stop!"

The tiny section of screen now showed a still of the Hamburg Spring Derby. A few stout gentlemen and a few smart ladies appeared on the stand. In the foreground the banker Robert E. Marlock could be clearly recognized.

Thomas clenched his fists. He could feel the sweat coming out on his forehead in his excitement. Keep calm, he told himself. Quite calm now. You're going to take your revenge.

"Can you copy that picture and let me have a few specimens early tomorrow morning, as much enlarged as possible?"

"Certainly, sir," said the cutter.

Next day Thomas caught the 11:45 A.M. express to Frankfurt-am-Main. There he looked up two leading officials in the German Bank Inspectorate Building. He showed them photographs of Robert E. Marlock. Half an hour later Thomas was handed a staff card of the kind kept by the Inspectorate for everyone in Germany engaged in banking.

On the evening of April 15, 1949, Thomas, back in his Zurich flat, said to his friend Bastian Fabre: "That accursed scoundrel lives in Hamburg under the name of Walter Pretorius. And he owns a little bank again. The monstrous impudence of that arch-ruffian!"

Bastian played with his bulbing brandy glass. "I expect he feels pretty sure you're dead," he remarked. "Or have you been to see him?"

"Are you crazy? No, no. I intend that he shall go on quietly believing me dead."

"I suppose you mean to take your revenge?"

"I am *going* to do so. But consider this. Marlock has obtained a German banker's license. He thinks he's nothing to fear in Hamburg. Am I to go before a German court there and say that Pretorius' real name is Marlock and that he cheated me in 1939? If I do that I shall have to sue as

Thomas Lieven, the name I had when I was a banker in London. And that name will be printed in every newspaper."

"Oh Lord!"

"Just so, Oh Lord. D'you suppose I want to be rubbed out for certain by some Red, Green, Blue or Black Hand club? A man with my past must take the greatest possible pains to avoid any kind of publicity."

"Well then, how are you going to get hold of Marlock?"

"I have a plan. But I need a stooge. And I've got one. It'll be Reuben Achazian, with whom we worked the Disposals Company racket. I've written to him and he's coming here."

"And I? Where do I come in?"

"You'll just have to leave me for a while, old lad," said Thomas, laying a hand on his friend's shoulder. "Don't look so miserable about it. We've simply got to separate. Otherwise we run too great a risk. You take all the money I don't need and go to Germany. Düsseldorf, preferably. You buy a villa for us there in the best quarter, plus a car and so on. If I'm unlucky in this affair and lose everything, I shall need credit. And confidence. And must be able to command it. Get me?"

"I get you."

"The Cecilien Allee," murmured Thomas dreamily. "That would be the right place for us. Have a look around there. That's where we ought to settle. All the *really* best people live there."

"Well, well," said Bastian. "Then it's naturally as clear as daylight that we shall have to go there too."

[11]

Thomas Lieven's biggest and most risky financial deal is now to be related. We shall try to describe it in such a way that anyone can see how subtly he planned his vengeance.

We must first take a look at Stuttgart. The Excelsior Works Company used to own territory outside the gates of that fair city. During the war the company employed over 5,000 people on the production of fittings and instruments for Goering's Air Force. In 1945 production ceased. For a very brief period practically no military aircraft were manufactured in Germany.

Accordingly, the Excelsior Works turned to the making of technical instruments on a very small scale. But after the currency reform of the summer of 1948 bankruptcy seemed unavoidable. Excelsior shares were negotiated at far below their nominal value. Quotations varied from 18 to 25. By the early summer of 1949 experts considered that collapse would ensue within a matter of weeks.

Matters were in this desperate state when the directors of the company made the acquaintance, on May 9, 1949, of an Armenian named Reuben Achazian, who came to see them in Stuttgart.

Herr Achazian, immaculately dressed and the possessor of a brand new 1949 Cadillac, informed the board as follows. "Gentlemen, I represent a Swiss undertaking which, however, desires to remain anonymous. It is most anxious to transfer part of its production plant to Germany."

The board asked why.

"Because in Germany the production costs of technical instruments are substantially lower. I am empowered to offer you a long-term agreement. My principals are prepared to collaborate on advantageous conditions in the reorganization of your factory. You will see that they are in earnest when I tell you that their group will be ready to guarantee payment of your drafts as they fall due up to a total amount of one million German marks."

A million marks constituted a silver lining to the cloud of competition threatening the works. It was understandable enough that the directors didn't hesitate long.

Punctually on May 25, 1949, a sum of 900,000 marks was paid over to the company. This was the amount Thomas Lieven was investing in his revenge. He worked hard these days. After he had talked to a number of city editors and journalists, articles appeared in Swiss newspapers according to which industrial circles in Switzerland were experimenting with the establishment of branches of their undertakings in the German Federal Republic. These reports and the fact that all bills drawn on the Excelsior Works were met without delay as they fell due caused a sensation on West German stock exchanges. A lively demand for Excelsior shares arose. Quotations improved considerably, standing at between 40 and 50.

Stooges engaged by Thomas Lieven proceeded to inquire of the Pretorius Bank in Hamburg whether it had any information about the position of the Excelsior Works. In this way the interest of the extraordinary avaricious Pretorius himself was aroused.

A few days later a certain Herr Reuben Achazian called on Walter Pretorius, whom from now on we may as well designate by his correct name of Marlock, at the latter's bank in Hamburg.

"My Swiss friends," said the Armenian, who had brought his magnificent Cadillac to the Free City of the Hanseatic League, "would be interested to hear whether you would collaborate with them in an extensive reorganization of the Excelsior Works." In view of the rapidly rising quotations of the company's shares Marlock at once declared himself ready to participate in principle. Immediately afterward he bought up, through representatives, large quantities of Excelsior shares, thus causing their prices to rise still higher. But he went on purchasing them at these excessive quotations in the firm conviction that he was about to bring off the financial killing of a lifetime.

On September 19, Thomas Lieven said to Reuben Achazian in Zurich: "I've now trapped that scoundrel into investing his whole fortune in that bankrupt Excelsior firm. The next step is for me to arrange to get back those nine hundred thousand marks, and if possible a bit more, which I sank in meeting Excelsior bills."

"And how do you propose to do that?" inquired the gentleman with the moist, almond-shaped eyes.

"By blocked marks, my friend," replied Thomas Lieven quietly.

The expression "blocked marks" at that time meant the financial resources of foreigners in Germany which their owners could only disburse by special permission. For otherwise such expenditure would prejudice the stability of the currency.

Before 1951 such marks could only be sold abroad surreptitiously. One hundred blocked marks as a rule brought from eight to ten dollars, in other words, a very low price. Thomas Lieven found certain industrial undertakings in Switzerland which still held blocked mark credits dating back to 1931–36. The owners readily sold our friend such balances even at the miserable figure just mentioned. They didn't care so long as at last they saw something of their money back.

Thomas accordingly now possessed blocked-mark credits in Germany. He proceeded to dispatch Herr Achazian once more to Hamburg. The little Armenian told Marlock: "The reorganization of the Excelsior Works will be largely financed by my Swiss principals' holdings of blocked marks. Under existing regulations that can be done with the assent of the German Territories Bank. I am empowered to transfer to your bank the blocked-mark holdings in question to the amount of 2.3 millions."

Marlock rubbed his hands. He'd always known he was about to bring off the best business deal of his life! He went to Frankfurt and negotiated stubbornly for several days with the German Territories Bank. He engaged on oath to use the 2.3 millions exclusively for the reorganization of the Excelsior Works at Stuttgart. The blocked marks were then placed freely at his dispoal.

That same day Thomas Lieven, in his Zurich flat, was telling Herr Achazian: "Now you go off to him again. I shall supply you with full powers of attorney, first-rate forgeries ostensibly emanating from Swiss firms participating in the reorganization project. That rascally scoundrel in Hamburg will hand you over those millions without hesitation. After all, they don't belong to him. You cash the lot and bring the money back here."

The little Armenian gazed upon Thomas with deep admiration. "Wish I had your head. How much did you really pay for those 2.3 million blocked marks?"

"About a hundred and sixty thousand dollars." Thomas smiled modestly. But he couldn't prevent himself from rubbing his hands. It happened, so to speak, automatically. "And as soon as you have brought the cash back to Zurich in that splendid Cadillac of yours, my friend, the blocked marks will have turned into genuine German marks. You will have to make the journey more than once. The money will be stored in the spare tires and chassis. And then we'll let the Excelsior Works crash. We shan't reorganize them. And that blackguard in Hamburg will be ruined."

On December 7, 1949, Herr Reuben Achazian set out for Hamburg. He was to be back on the sixteenth. That was the day on which the Federal Republic received a credit of one milliard German marks from the United States.

Herr Reuben Achazian did not return on that historic day of German reconstruction. Herr Reuben Achazian did not return at all.

On December 28, the banker Walter Pretorius was arrested in Hamburg by German Criminal police. At the same hour Swiss Federal police arrested Thomas Lieven in his rented apartment at Zurich. They were acting on urgent instructions issued by Interpol and the German Federal Criminal police office in Wiesbaden. Both men were accused of having perpetrated a vast fraud in connection with blocked marks.

"Who accuses me of such a thing?" Thomas asked the Swiss officers.

"A certain Reuben Achazian laid information against you. He put a quantity of supporting documentary evidence at the disposal of the German authorities. Incidentally, he cannot now be found."

And my 2.3 million German marks have gone down the drain, thought Thomas Lieven. Heigh-ho! So I did in the end make a mistake, after all. But really that Reuben Achazian was an awfully nice sort of Armenian . . .

[12]

Thomas Lieven remained in prison on remand for nearly twelve months. It was a bewildering year, notable for the hottest summer for a hundred years, the cessation of food rationing and on June 28, the outbreak of the Korean war, which plunged all Europe into a hoarding psychosis for months on end.

On November 19, 1950, High Criminal Court No. 2 of the Frankfurt Petty Sessions sentenced Thomas Lieven to three and a half years imprisonment. The judge in his verbal summing up stressed the frankness and straightforward attitude of the defendant Lieven. The Court had the impression, the judge continued, that certain obscure, probably entirely personal motives had impelled the accused to his reprehensible behavior. For "this highly intelligent, extremely cultured man is not the usual type of criminal . . ."

The other defendant, the Hamburg banker Walter Pretorius, was not characterized by the judge in any such favorable manner. Pretorius was given a four-year sentence. His bank had to go into liquidation. The German Bank Inspectorate prohibited him from any further practice of his profession and struck his name off their index of reputable bankers.

There were two intriguing features of the Frankfurt trial. Although the two defendants, as we know, were intimately acquainted, this state of affairs was not revealed by a single word or gesture from either of them in court.

In the second place the judge excluded the public from the court on the very first day of the trial. This step was taken after the defendant Lieven had indicated his willingness to explain in detail the trick by which he had caused the blocked marks to be placed freely at his disposal. No exhaustive account could therefore be given in the press of the trial of

Lieven and Pretorius. Accordingly, the publicity which Thomas had feared, on account of his activities in various secret services, was spared him.

In a certain sense he had attained his objective. Walter Pretorius, alias Robert E. Marlock, was ruined for life. It was as a pale, trembling, nervous wreck that he confronted the court.

Neither defendant exchanged a single word with the other throughout the trial. Neither made any reply when sentence was passed. But Thomas Lieven, after hearing it, smiled across the court at his former partner. Robert E. Marlock turned his head away from that smile. He couldn't bear to meet it.

[13]

On May 14, 1954, Thomas Lieven was released from prison. His friend Bastian met him outside the gates of the jail. They traveled together immediately to the Riviera, where Thomas was completely restored to health at Cap Ferrat.

It was not until the summer of 1955 that Thomas returned to his fine house in the Cecilien Allee at Düsseldorf. He still had a certain amount of money in his account at the Rhine Main Bank. His neighbors considered him a substantial businessman of the Federal Republic, though they felt slightly uneasy at not being able to obtain more definite information about him.

For months Thomas gave up his whole time to reflection and rest.

"We really must start doing something," said Bastian Fabre. "Our money won't last forever. What do you suggest?"

Thomas answered modestly: "I suggest something big in the share line. But I don't want anybody injured by it."

He worked with great enjoyment on the project for several months. It was not until April 11, 1957, that he took the first step by inviting to dinner the stout Herr Direktor Schallenberg, who possessed, in addition to his dueling scars, a paper mill.

Thomas had found out that during the war Schallenberg, under the name of Mack, had been in charge of "Organization for Total War" in the so-called Warthegau and was still on the Polish Government's extradition list. In these circumstances Schallenberg could do nothing but grind his teeth and comply with Thomas's request. He put at Thomas's disposal fifty large sheets of specially watermarked paper used in the printing of share certificates.

We already know what Thomas Lieven did with this paper and how he put through his big business deal in Zurich with forged German Steel Union share certificates. As stated in detail at the beginning of this narrative he made a profit of 717,850 Swiss franks and went to the Riviera with the beautiful young Hélène de Couville, whom he had met in Zurich.

During the night in which the charming Hélène became his mistress in the luxury hotel at Cannes, the Carlton, Thomas, as again we already know, had a dreadful surprise. With alarming recklessness Hélène suddenly sobbed out: "I've lied to you! Oh, my beloved Thomas, I must tell you that I work for the American secret service . . . I . . . was forced to pursue you . . . the FBI mean to hire you at any cost . . . and if you won't work for us they'll have you arrested . . ."

Thomas left his despairing companion alone. In his own bedroom he sat at the open window and looked up at the stars shining over the Mediterranean. He reflected on his wild, chaotic past and the crazy adventure that had now come full circle, after starting on a certain warm day in May 1939.

CHAPTER 3

[1]

Thomas did not see the beautiful Hélène again until they met at breakfast. She looked pale and nervous, with deep shadows under her fine eyes. "Can you ever forgive me?"

"I'll try, my dear," he said gently.

"And . . . and . . . and will you work for us?"

"I'll try to do that, too."

She uttered a little shriek of pleasure. In flinging her arms around his neck she knocked over the cup of soft-boiled eggs. Said he: "I shall of course impose my own conditions. I am not going to take my orders from either you or your chief, Colonel Herrick, but only from the man in charge of the whole FBI."

She burst out laughing. "From J. Edgar Hoover? That's funny! Because it's he who insists on talking to you personally. We were ordered to bring you to Washington at any cost."

Well, well! How extraordinary life is!

On May 23, 1957, Thomas Lieven was sitting in the restaurant of the Rhine Main Airport. He felt extremely uneasy. It was twenty minutes past six by his repeater. At a quarter to seven the Super-constellation in which he was to fly to New York would take off. And that damned agent Faber had still not turned up!

The damned agent Faber had been mentioned to him by Colonel Herrick when they parted in Zurich. "Faber will take you to Hoover." But Faber hadn't yet arrived. Thomas glared angrily at the entrance to the restaurant.

At that moment a young woman came through it. Thomas let out a low moan. A wave of warmth surged up in him. His whole body tingled.

The young woman walked straight up to him. She had on a red coat, red shoes and a red cap, with blue-black hair straying from under it. The mouth was big and red, the eyes big and black. The girl's complexion was very white. Thomas's heart was beating at lightning speed. He was thinking, No, no, no! For pity's sake! That can't be, there isn't such a thing! Chantal walking up to me, my dear, dead Chantal, the only woman I ever loved. Here she comes, smiling at me. Oh God, but she is dead, she was shot in Marseilles . . .

The young woman came right up to his table. Thomas felt the sweat running down his back as he staggered to his feet. There she stood, near enough to be touched. "Chantal . . ." he groaned.

"Well, Thomas Lieven," said the girl in a rather husky voice. "How are you?"

"Chantal . . " he stammered again.

"I beg your pardon?"

He drew a deep breath. No, it wasn't her. Of course it wasn't. What madness. She was smaller, more graceful, younger by quite a few years. But what a fantastic resemblance!

"Who are you?" he asked with an effort.

"My name is Pamela Faber. I'm traveling with you. Sorry I'm late. My car broke down."

"You . . . your name is Faber?" Thomas was feeling giddy again. "But Colonel Herrick mentioned a man."

"Colonel Herrick doesn't know me. He was told something about an agent. So he naturally assumed it would be a man." She smiled broadly. "Come along, Herr Lieven. Our plane will be taking off soon."

He stared at her as though she were a ghost. And that was just what Pamela Faber was. A sweet, sad memory, a distant greeting from the realm of the dead.

Flying at 18,000 feet across the Atlantic, they talked almost all through the night in a quiet, friendly fashion.

She made him feel sentimental. He wondered why he was so affected by her. Was it simply because she looked so much like Chantal? Why did it seem to him that he had known her well for years, for whole ages?

Pamela told him that she had been born in America of German parents. Since 1950 she had been working for the American secret service. He asked what made her adopt that profession. She shrugged her shoulders, answering frankly; I suppose it was chiefly a longing for adventure. My parents are dead. I wanted to travel, see foreign countries and get experience . . ."

Experience, Thomas thought. Foreign countries. The parents dead. Chantal might have answered the same if she had been asked why she became an adventuress. Chantal, oh Chantal! Why on earth should this young woman resemble her so closely?

"But I've had enough of it now, you know. It's not my sort of life. I was wrong. Or else I'm already too old for it."

"How old are you, then?"

"Thirty-two."

"Good Lord," he murmured, remembering his own age of forty-eight.

"I'd like to stop now. Marry, have children and a little home where I could cook nice meals for my family."

Thomas asked hoarsely: "You . . . you're fond of cooking?"

"It's a perfect passion with me. But why do you look at me like that, Herr Lieven?"

"Oh . . . nothing . . . nothing."

"But a secret service is a sort of fiendish trap that never lets anyone go. As for stopping, who can ever do that? Can you? No one can. No one's allowed to . . ."

[2]

The enchantment that took possession of Thomas Lieven that night kept its hold on him. It increased steadily. He sank into it as into a sea of sweetness or a cloud of bewildering fragrance.

From New York he flew on to Washington with Pamela Faber. He was now observing her closely, with positively clinical interest. She had Chantal's frankness, good humor and courage. She had the same feline wildness and energy. But she was better educated and shrewder. Thomas wondered why he always felt so distressed when he looked at her.

J. Edgar Hoover, at sixty-two the head of the United States Federal Bureau of Investigation, received Thomas Lieven in his Washington office. Their first meeting lasted only a few minutes. After a cordial greeting the thick-set man, whose keen eyes always seemed a little melancholy, observed: "We can't talk in peace here. Do you know what? The three of us are going to the country for the weekend."

The house was in Maryland, among ranges of low, wooded hills. There were many such comfortable houses scattered about. The retreat owned by J. Edgar Hoover, the top criminologist of the United States, was full of fine old furniture.

On Saturday morning, at breakfast, the FBI boss remarked, rubbing his hands: "I think we'll have turkey today. It's a bit early in the season. But I've seen some splendid young birds down in the village. I'll go and get them presently. And cranberries too."

"Cranberries?" Thomas wrinkled his forehead. Pamela, who was looking more stimulating than ever in a lumber-jacket and blue jeans, explained smiling: "In the States we always have turkey with cranberries, Mr. Lieven."

"How ghastly! Well, personally I always—"

"Stuff them, don't you?" Pamela nodded. "So did my mother. She made the stuffing from minced turkey and goose liver and—"

"Veal, bacon and yolk of egg—" Thomas interrupted her excitedly.

"Then you add truffles, rub off the husks, chop the truffles up, then two rolls—"

"And the bacon must be fat—" They suddenly both stopped speaking, looked at each other and blushed.

J. Edgar Hoover laughed. "Well, what an extraordinary thing! The way you two top each other! It's fantastic! What do you think, Mr. Lieven?"

"It certainly is," said Thomas. "I've been thinking so for a long time now."

Two hours later they stood in the kitchen together. Pamela helped Thomas to clean the bird and draw it. She also helped him to prepare the stuffing. When he looked for the pepper she handed it to him. When it seemed to him that the stuffing needed thickening, she was already putting a soaked roll through the mincer.

Good God, thought Thomas. Good God Almighty!

Pamela said: "Let's wrap the breast in bacon. That's what my mother always used to do."

"Ah, your mother wrapped the breast in fresh, fat bacon?" Thomas repeated, beaming. "So did mine! She used to put it on one side for half an hour before she began roasting."

"Yes, of course, to prevent it getting too dry."

Thomas held up the turkey's backside while Pamela dexterously sewed up the natural aperture through which the stuffing had been inserted in the fowl's interior.

Hoover, who was watching them, said slowly: "Mr. Lieven, I'm sure you must be aware that we didn't bring you to America simply because you're such a good cook."

"But because?" Thomas turned the turkey's backside this way and that.

"But because you know Mme. Dunya Melanin."

Thomas dropped the turkey on the table.

"Oh!" cried Pamela.

"Pardon," Thomas picked the bird up again. "Where . . . where is the lady at present?"

"In New York. She was your mistress, I believe?"

"Well, yes . . . I mean . . ." Thomas knew Pamela was looking at him. He stared desperately at the turkey's backside. "She imagined she was in love with me . . ."

Hoover stood up. He had now adopted a very serious tone. "We know that a powerful Russian espionage ring has been operating in New York for a long time. We don't know how it operates. We don't know who's in it. But three weeks ago a member of the ring turned up at our embassy in Paris. His name is Morris and he was the last lover of Mme. Melanin."

Thomas laid the turkey carefully down on the table again. "You need say no more, Mr. Hoover," he said pleasantly. "I'll do my best. Under one condition."

"And that is?"

Thomas glanced at the sad-eyed authority on criminal law, at that delicious turkey and at Pamela with her stained, wet hands and her flushed cheeks. How beautiful and desirable she was! He said cheerfully to Hoover: "That I shall be allowed to die as soon as my mission is completed."

MENU

Clear Soup with Toast
Turkey with Truffle Stuffing
Lemon Sponge Cake

MARYLAND, 25 MAY 1957

Thomas cooks for America and decides to die.

Turkey with Truffle Stuffing

Prepare a stuffing from a third of a pound of lean pork, a quarter of a pound of veal, half a pound of fresh pork fat, the turkey liver, a quarter of a pound of raw goose liver. Put the mixture through the mincer and add two soaked and squeezed bread rolls and two yolks of egg. Add the finely chopped husks of two truffles and the sliced truffles themselves. Add a further quarter of a pound of goose liver fried in butter and chopped, with salt, mixed spices and a dash of madeira. Stuff the turkey with this mixture, sprinkle the fowl with salt and wrap the breast in slices, not too thin, of fresh bacon. Remove the bacon half an hour before the turkey is fully cooked, so as to allow the skin to brown. To roast the bird place it in a large pan with plenty of butter and some boiling water. The fowl should be laid sideways, turned frequently and basted. Only in the last half-hour should it be turned on its back. The cooking time depends on the size of the turkey. It is also possible to use the above mentioned stuffing for the crop only, using a simpler stuffing for the inside of the bird. In that case the goose liver should be replaced by calf's liver. Serve with buttered tinned corn, cranberry sauce and a special salad made from cubed raw apples, oranges and boiled celeriac, mixed with mayonnaise and sprinkled with grated coconut.

Lemon Sponge Cake

Take two cups of sugar, six eggs, half a cup of hot water, two tablespoonfuls of lemon juice, the grated rind of one lemon and two cups of flour. Cream the eggs, add the sugar, the hot water, the lemon juice and peel, the flour and lastly the whites of the eggs, whisked until stiff. Pour the mixture into a cake tin and bake at medium heat for forty-five to fifty minutes. The cake can be served hot or cold, with fruit juice.

[3]

In the early morning of November 21, 1957, children playing on the white beach of the fishing village of Cascais near Lisbon found a number of different shells, starfish, fish that were half dead and a gentleman who was quite dead.

The corpse lay on its back. The face bore an astonished expression. The body was clothed in a gray worsted suit of extremely fashionable cut, though soaked through and through with sea water. On the feet were black shoes and socks. The dead man had on a white shirt and a black tie. There was a circular hole in the shirt over the heart and a great bloodstain, which had also spread to the jacket.

The children ran away screaming. Five minutes later fishermen and their wives came running to the spot and gathered around the corpse in great excitement.

An old man said to his son: "See whether the gentleman has a passport on him, José." The younger man knelt and searched the corpse. He found four passports on the body.

Another old man exclaimed: "I know that fellow!" He declared that in September 1940, seventeen years before, he had been well paid by German agents to assist in the kidnapping of an elegantly dressed gentleman. The speaker had at that time been the mate of a fishing boat. "They'd knocked him out somewhere in the city and brought him down here unconscious. Then we stowed him aboard and put out to sea. The Germans told me that a German submarine would be waiting outside the three-mile limit to take him over. But the submarine never got him. Something else happened instead." The old man told them what it was. The attentive reader knows already.

"He was referred to several times as a merchant named Jonas," the old seaman added.

"José," said the other old fisherman. "Look and see whether one of his passports is in that name."

José confirmed that one of the documents had been made out in the name of Emil Jonas of Rüdesheim, a merchant.

"We'd better tell the police at once," he said.

[4]

The police inspector Manuel Vayda of the Lisbon Murder Department dictated the following report to his secretary. "The corpse found on the beach at Cascais was of male sex and aged between 45 and 50. The enclosed Police Surgeon's report—um—um—certifies the cause of death as shooting with a 9mm. American Army pistol . . . paragraph.

"In the pockets of the clothing there were found 891 dollars 45 cents, two accounts from New York restaurants, one from the Waldorf-Astoria Hotel, a German driving license made out in the name of Thomas Lieven, an old-fashioned gold repeater watch and four passports, of which two were German in the names of Thomas Lieven and Emil Jonas and two French in the names of Maurice Hauser and Jean Leblanc . . . paragraph.

"Photographs of Jean Leblanc and Emil Jonas in police archives correspond, both with each other and with the photographs in the other two passports of the dead man. From all this evidence the conclusion can reasonably be drawn that the murdered man was the agent Thomas Lieven, who has been the cause of so much talk during the last few years. No doubt the murderer was another agent. The case is being investigated with the utmost vigor . . . what awful rot! As if anybody ever bothered to investigate the murder of an agent! The murderer must have got clear long ago . . . good heavens, senhorita, have you gone quite mad? What possessed you to type out those last three sentences?"

[5]

"The life of man born of woman is short and full of trouble," intoned the priest at the open grave. It was half-past four in the afternoon of November 24, 1957. Rather more time than usual had elapsed before permission was given for burial.

It was raining in Lisbon that day and quite cold. The few mourners were shivering. They were all men, with the exception of one young woman. The men looked what they were, professional colleagues of the deceased. Ex-Major Fritz Loos, formerly of the Cologne Army Recruiting Office, stood with bent head. The British agent, Lovejoy, yellow as a quince, sneezed at his elbow. The Czech spy, Gregor Marek, remained motionless, with hunched shoulders. Colonel Siméon and Débras of the French secret service looked thoughtful. Colonel Erich Werthe, once of German Military Intelligence in Paris, and little Major Brenner, bore melancholy expressions. Nearest to the priest stood the American agent, Pamela Faber, who had so much reminded Thomas Lieven of his dead mistress, Chantal Tessier.

"May the earth rest lightly upon thee, Thomas Lieven. Amen," said the priest.

"Amen," responded the unusual group of mourners. They had all known Thomas Lieven. He had fooled them all in his time. They had been sent by their chiefs to make sure that the accursed rascal was really dead. Well, thank God, he really is, they thought.

The grave was filled in. Thomas Lieven's former colleagues each threw a small shovelful of earth into it. Workmen brought up the plain marble stone that was to mark the spot.

The agents climbed into taxis outside the cemetery. They might just as well have hired a small coach, for they all lived in the same hotel, the best, naturally. Their respective countries paid expenses. They proceeded to send telephone messages to England, France, Germany and even beyond the Iron Curtain, from their rooms in the magnificent luxury hotel Palacio do Estoril-Parque.

As soon as they got their connections they uttered incomprehensible sentences such as: "The yellow shark was served up this afternoon."

That meant: "I've inspected the corpse in the mortuary. It was Lieven."

On that afternoon of November 24, 1957, therefore, certain more or less thick files were closed and shelved in various secret service centers. They were all labeled THOMAS LIEVEN, with a cross underneath the name.

Pamela Faber, while the other agents, her colleagues, remained glued to their telephones, sat in her room resting. She had ordered iced whisky and soda. She had kicked off her high-heeled shoes and put her admirable legs up on a stool. She sat relaxed in an armchair and played with a big glass of whisky.

Her black eyes were shining like stars. Her wide mouth seemed forever on the point of bursting into a laugh at some prodigious secret joke. She sat there smoking, drinking and chuckling while the dusk of a wet autumn evening closed over the city of Lisbon. Suddenly she raised her glass and said aloud: "Here's luck, Thomas, my beloved! Long life to you—for my sake!"

When we last saw Thomas Lieven, he was in a country house among the rolling hills of Maryland, as a guest of the highest authority on American criminal law. He had just expressed the surprising wish to die as soon as his mission was completed.

"Aha," said Hoover coolly. "And what sort of death do you propose to die?"

Thomas Lieven told him and also Pamela what he had in view. He closed with the words: "It is absolutely essential for me to die in order that I may at last—*at last*—be able to live in peace."

Hoover and Pamela laughed heartily at this remark and the projected end of Thomas Lieven.

"We can discuss the details later," Thomas said. "For the time being perhaps you can tell me a little more about my friend Dunya and your Mr. Morris. Where is he?"

"In Paris," said J. Edgar Hoover.

"Oh, I thought he was in New York?"

"He was, up to a few weeks ago. Then he went to Europe.

In Paris he put up at the Crillon. But then he must have lost his nerve. For on the afternoon of May 4 he left his hotel and crossed the Place de la Concorde to the American Embassy. He asked for the ambassador and said: 'I am a Soviet spy.' "

[6]

"I am a Soviet spy," said Victor Morris to the American ambassador in Paris. "I can give you information about the biggest Soviet spy ring in the United States."

That was at a quarter to six P.M. on May 4, 1957.

"And why do you wish to do that, Mr. Morris?" asked the ambassador.

"Because I need your help," Morris replied. His broad, bloated features were adorned with heavy black horn rims. "I received orders to leave the United States and return to Moscow through Paris. I knew what that meant. They were going to liquidate me."

"Why?"

"Well, I . . . I think I was a failure," answered Morris in faultless American English. "Women. Liquor. Too much hot air. And then Dunya as a chaser . . ."

"Who is Dunya?"

"Dunya Melanin, the former wife of a Russian officer. Employed as a doctor's receptionist. I got friendly with her. But we were always quarreling. People noticed it. Mark told me I'd have to make myself scarce at once."

"Who is Mark?"

"Head of the biggest spy ring in America for the last ten years."

It soon came out that Victor Morris was a man of many aliases. His real name was Hayhanem. He was a lieutenant colonel in the Russian secret service. From 1946 to 1952 he was trained in Russia for espionage work in the United States as a colleague of the legendary, the fabulous "Mr. Mark."

It is worth while considering what that six years' training meant. Hayhanem, alias Morris, had to forget his old personality completely and enter upon a new one. He had to learn to read, speak, eat, walk, think and argue like a man with a New York background. He had to drive his car like an American. And dance, write, smoke and get drunk like one.

Colonel Hayhanem became a new man. The task had been tremendous. And yet someone else had already succeeded in it.

This was "Mr. Mark," the best spy the Kremlin had ever had in the States. It was ten years before anyone suspected him.

Hayhanem, alias Morris, passed all the tests. On April 14, 1952, he reported, armed with an excellently forged American passport, to Michael Svirin, secretary of the Soviet Delegation to the United Nations in New York. Svirin met him after taking every conceivable precautionary measure, gave him money and instructed him as follows. "Contact Mr. Mark. You and I will never see each other again. From this moment on you exist for me as little as Mr. Mark does officially. You can never count on any help from me. I am a diplomat and must not have anything to do with you."

"And how do I recognize Mark?"

"He will call you up. At your hotel. Here is a little carved pipe. Keep it in your mouth as a recognition signal when you go to meet Mark after he has made an appointment with you."

Three days later Mark telephoned. "Five-thirty P.M. precisely in the men's room at the RKO movie theater, Flushing."

The men's room! Probably no secret service in the world could get along without such places! Morris entered the retreat mentioned punctually at half-past five. A man about forty-five emerged from one of the closets. He was tall and nearly bald, had skeptical, intelligent features, large ears, thin lips and rimless spectacles. He wore a flannel suit with a blue, open-necked shirt, such as artists sometimes wear. He glanced at Morris and at the queerly shaped little pipe hanging from the corner of Morris's mouth. He nodded briefly and said: "You're on the dot, Morris."

[7]

"Mark nodded briefly and said: 'You're on the dot, Morris.'" The FBI chief, J. Edgar Hoover, was talking to the intently listening Thomas Lieven. Pamela Faber sat next him, looking serious. All three were smoking, as they drank black coffee and French brandy. The big turkey luncheon was over.

Hoover lit a long, thick cigar and blew out a cloud of fragrant smoke. "Let me tell you what came next. Morris and Mark couldn't stand each other. But they had to get along together."

That certainly was so. That afternoon Mark gave Morris money and a code book. He then told him he was to open a photographer's studio, by way of camouflage, so as to prevent the authorities from wondering how he lived. Mark also instructed Morris where and how he was to deposit his secret intelligence and receive orders.

Microfilms no bigger than a pin's head were to be hidden in coins, old paper handkerchiefs or orange peel. They could also be stuck, by means of small magnetic discs, on benches, public telephones, or letter boxes.

"The work went on quite smoothly," said Hoover. "Although Morris couldn't endure Mark, he carried out his orders to the letter."

"What orders, for instance?"

"Some had serious consequences, unfortunately," Hoover answered with a sigh. "According to what Morris told the ambassador in Paris, there's no denying that. An enormous amount of data was supplied to the Soviet Union by Mark's organization. On Morris's own confession, for example, he had been spying on a new, top-secret rocket installation."

"No hitches or breakdowns, then?" asked Thomas.

"Yes, once. And it at least proved that Morris's later admissions were true. Look at this." Hoover laid a worn five-cent piece on the table in front of Thomas. "Pick it up and let it drop."

Thomas did so. The coin broke in two. The inside was hollow. A tiny section of film adhered to one of the inner surfaces.

"That section of microfilm," said Hoover, "contains information from Mark in code. Our best men in the FBI have been trying to decipher it for four years."

How did you get hold of that coin?" Thomas asked.

"By pure chance. A boy called James Bozart, who sold newspapers, found it in 1953 . . ."

He went on to say that on a hot summer evening in that year the freckled lad in question was tearing down the stairs of a large block of flats in Brooklyn. He fell flat on his face and all the money rolled out of his pocket. Rotten luck! James started picking up the coins, swearing softly to himself. Suddenly he found a five cent piece in his hand which felt funny—damned funny.

He turned it in his fingers, examining it. Then it broke in two. On the inner side of one part of the coin he caught sight of a dark spot. Good Lord! Only a few days before, the boy had seen a film about espionage. Messages on microfilm were there said to have been concealed in cigarette cases. James wondered if the dark dot in the coin could be a microfilm.

The United States has cause to be eternally grateful to James Bozart. For he took his find straight to the nearest police station. The officer on duty laughed in the boy's face. But Sergeant Levon said: "No, Joe. Let's send it to the FBI. Maybe we'll all see our names in the paper."

Their names weren't printed at that time. But two FBI agents called on James at his home and interrogated him closely. Where had he fallen down, they asked.

Two-fifty-two Fulton Street, he answered. It was a huge block in which the ground floors were occupied as shops. The first and second floors were used as offices. Higher up still lived commercial travelers, artists and junior clerks. And the FBI itself had an office in the vast building.

The two agents thoroughly investigated everyone who lived there but couldn't pin anything on any of them.

Years passed. The message on the microfilm remained undeciphered and its author undiscovered. The men responsible for the national security of the United States became more and more convinced, between the years of 1953 and 1957, of the existence of a spy ring in their midst, operating more and more dangerously.

"During those years," J. Edgar Hoover told Thomas Lieven, "Morris must have been degenerating steadily. After meeting Dunya Melanin he got into quite a bad way. They beat each other regularly. Mark must have reported this state of affairs to Moscow, for Morris was suddenly recalled. He went to the American Embassy in Paris, asked for political asylum and told all he knew."

"Well, after all, it doesn't seem to have been very much," said Thomas.

"It wasn't enough," said Hoover. "But it was quite a lot to go on. For although the mysterious Mark did all he could to keep Morris in ignorance of his address, Morris declared that he was able to follow him to it on one occasion without his knowledge. Guess where it was."

"I'll play. Wasn't it 252 Fulton Street?"

"Correct. It was in the very block in which little James Bozart had fallen down four years previously and found that coin."

For a while no one spoke. Then Thomas rose and walked over to the window. He stood there gazing out over the wide, pleasant landscape.

J. Edgar Hoover said: "A squad of my people, including Miss Faber, has been putting every inhabitant of the block under the microscope again during the last few weeks. The description of Mark given by Morris exactly fits the most popular occupant of the building, a painter who lives on the very top floor. Name of Goldfuss. Emil Robert Goldfuss, an American citizen in residence at 252 Fulton Street ever since 1948. Miss Faber, you can now take over."

Pamela said: "We've been shadowing Goldfuss for weeks. A dozen FBI cars carrying radar, wireless and television equipment are on the job. Goldfuss can't take a single step now without being followed by us. Result—negative."

"But I don't understand that," said Thomas. "If you so strongly suspect him of being a spy why don't you arrest him?"

Pamela shook her head. "We're not in Europe, Herr Lieven."

"In the United States," J. Edgar Hoover explained, "a man can only be arrested if it is quite certain that he has committed an illegal act. Only in such a case will a warrant be issued. We suspect Goldfuss of being a spy. But we can't prove it. And so long as we have no irrefutable proof of his being a spy no judge in the country will permit his arrest."

"What about Morris's evidence?"

"It was all submitted to us in confidence. He would never endanger his family in Russia by testifying against Goldfuss in public."

"I see. Well, in that case how on earth are we ever to lay our hands on him?"

Hoover smiled quietly. "We are addressing that question to you, Herr Lieven. That is why we sent for you, after finding that you were an old friend of Mme. Dunya Melanin."

[8]

"In Russia shashlik is prepared with onions!" shouted the fat Boris Roganoff.

"In Russia shashlik is not prepared with onions," shouted Thomas Lieven.

The two men stood opposite each other, trembling with rage. Blows were in the offing. The date was June 19, 1957, the hour was one thirty P.M. and it was fearfully hot in New York. The quarrel about shashlik was taking place in the kitchen of a Russian restaurant for connoisseurs on Forty-first

Street. The stout Roganoff owned the place. Thomas had been frequenting it for some days. Dunya Melanin was in the habit of lunching there. She worked in the consulting rooms of a certain Dr. Mason close by.

It had been a melancholy reunion. Dunya, still passionate and attractive, was forever lamenting Morris's departure. She burst into tears whenever she mentioned him. And she mentioned him continually, partly of her own accord and partly because Thomas kept encouraging her to do so.

Nothing useful came to light at these interviews. Dunya told Thomas a lot. But it didn't get him any further. When he left her he went to see Pamela, through whom he was to report to Hoover. Pamela had a small apartment in Manhattan. Thomas lived at the Waldorf-Astoria.

Day after day went by. Nothing happened. Goldfuss wasn't taking any chances. Thomas noticed a growing irritation on Pamela's part which he found inexplicable. He met Dunya repeatedly, trying to find out something which might incriminate Goldfuss or at least bring him into the conversation. But Dunya didn't seem ever to have even seen the man. She only went on and on moaning about her dear Morris.

Yesterday she had wanted shashlik. Thomas had promptly pickled some lamb chops and kept them steeped for twelve hours. The meat was just about right now and Thomas had been in the act of placing it on the spit, with some bacon, when that fat Boris Roganoff had actually begun to cut onions into thick slices. A fierce quarrel broke out. Then they made it up again. Yet nothing but trouble was in store that day.

MENU

Spring Salad

Shashlik with Risotto

Fried Bananas

NEW YORK, 19 JUNE 1957

This meal helped Thomas to catch the biggest Soviet spy.

Spring Salad

Cut into slices a peeled young cucumber, some tender radishes and hard-boiled eggs. Place the slices on a dish. Sprinkle with pepper, salt and plenty of finely chopped dill, chives and parsley. Mix with plenty of sour cream. Serve immediately, as otherwise the cucumber slices will get dry.

Shashlik

Cut a fillet of mutton into inch-thick slices. Soak for at least twelve hours in a solution of olive oil, lemon juice, salt, chopped onion, parsley, crushed peppercorns and juniper berries. Add one crushed clove of garlic and a dash of wine. Place meat on skewers, alternating it with pieces of bacon. Grill, taking care that meat remains pink inside.

Risotto

Braise a large sliced onion in butter or olive oil in a casserole till golden-brown. Add dry rice and leave to fry for about ten minutes. Stir continuously, as the rice must not turn brown. Add to the rice one and a half times the quantity of boiling water, salt sparingly and leave to cook under a tight lid. It is best to cook over an asbestos mat, on the lowest possible flame, for thirty minutes.

Fried Bananas

Fry on each side, in butter, ripe but not too soft peeled bananas. Add some liquid honey and a dash of rum. Turn the bananas carefully in the liquid and then place immediately on warm plates. Sprinkle with ground almonds or pistachio nuts.

When Dunya—who was of course late—at last appeared and began to have lunch with Thomas, she too revealed a shocking state of irritation. She kept seizing her aching head in both hands and found fault with everything Thomas said or did. Finally she seemed to calm down a bit. "Excuse me! We're working at such a crazy rate I think I shall collapse!"

"What's the matter then?"

"Well, half New York seems to be getting vaccinated."

"Why?"

"With the new serum against infantile paralysis. Dr. Salk's. You must have heard of it. The vaccination itself wouldn't be so bad if it weren't for all that writing."

"What writing?"

"Every patient has to bring his or her birth certificate. No passports or registration forms. Just the birth certificate."

"What for?"

"It's the law. I have to write out the number of every birth certificate and the name of the authority that issued it. And they come in by hundreds! I shall go raving mad! Nothing but vaccinate, vaccinate, vaccinate!"

"Vaccinate, eh—" he repeated mechanically, catching his breath. For a pretty young woman in a yellow summer frock had just entered the restaurant. He couldn't believe his eyes. She must have gone out of her mind! For FBI regulations strictly forbade two agents who were working together to meet in public. Pamela Faber didn't seem to care a nickel about that rule. She sat down right opposite Thomas, crossed her legs, leaned back and stared at Dunya.

Naturally, Dunya soon noticed this proceeding. "Who is that?"

"I—I beg your pardon?"

"That person over there. She's staring at me. Do you know her?"

"I? Whom do you mean?"

"That painted thing in yellow. Don't pretend!"

"Good Lord! I never saw her before in my life!"

"Liar! You do know her. And you know her well, too!"

That was how it started. And that was how it went on all through lunch. By the time coffee was served Thomas's shirt was damp with perspiration. And Pamela Faber was still staring across at them.

Nor was it the end of the fun that day.

When Thomas Lieven returned to the Waldorf-Astoria he found a certain William Ackroyd waiting for him. Mr. Ackroyd was known in the hotel as an export merchant who often collaborated with European businessmen.

Herr Peter Scheuner—Thomas's alias at this time—was known in the hotel as one of the European businessmen in question. The two merchants—who were nothing of the sort—sat down together in the empty bar. Mr. Ackroyd said quietly: "The matter's getting more and more urgent for us, Lieven. Have you made any progress?"

"Not an inch."

"Pity," said Mr. Ackroyd. "There are several indications that Goldfuss is just about to run for it. We don't know where he'll be off to."

"We shall have to watch the frontiers, the airfields and the ports. Et cetera."

"It's not practicable. We simply haven't got enough officers. Goldfuss will obviously be traveling with an absolutely 'genuine' false passport." Thomas had long known that a "genuine" false passport was one that would survive comparison with the official registers.

"Do you think he'll have reliable 'genuine' forged papers too?"

"Don't know. Hardly probable if he's in such a hurry. But he's certain to have a passport and that will be enough. It'll be a miracle if the fellow doesn't slip through our fingers."

Thomas sighed deeply. And on top of all this there's that wonderful colleague of mine, Miss Faber, he thought bitterly. I'll give her hell for behaving like that.

[9]

"You deserve a damned good thrashing!" Thomas shouted. He stood breathing heavily, that evening, in Pamela's little apartment, facing its occupant, who was wearing a black dressing gown and obviously very little else. "What on earth did you come to Roganoff's for?"

"I suppose I've got a perfect right to go to Roganoff's?"

"But not when I'm there!"

"I didn't know you were there!" she cried, as loudly as he had.

He roared back: "You knew perfectly well I was!"

"Well, what if I did?"

"What did you come for, then?"

"Because I wanted to see that Dunya of yours, the sweet little pigeon—"

His jaw dropped. "And it was for that reason you endangered everything—the whole assignment?"

"Don't shout at me! Fallen for her in a big way, haven't you?"

"Hold your tongue or I'll tan the hide off you!"

"Try it!"

"Right, I will!" He rushed at her. But the girl knew her stuff. With a dexterous judo hold she sent him crashing, on his back, to the carpet. She laughed and dodged away. He scrambled to his feet and dashed after her into her bedroom, where a short wrestling bout ensued. They both dropped on the bed.

Then he had her across his knee, kicking and panting. "Let me go—let me go—or I'll kill you—"

The dressing gown fell open. Pamela was wearing little underneath it. Thomas, unmoved, gave her a smacking. She shrieked, struck out right and left and bit him.

Like Chantal, he thought confusedly, as the blood began to beat in his temples. She's just like Chantal—Oh God! He suddenly bent over her. His lips met hers. She bit, then her mouth opened and softened. She flung her arms around him and both lost themselves in the numbing delight of their first kiss. The room swam before Thomas Lieven's eyes. Time ceased to make sense.

When he recovered control of himself he was looking into eyes full of love. Pamela whispered: "I was so jealous—so frightfully jealous of that Russian woman of yours . . ."

He suddenly noticed on her upper arm the bright, circular patch left by a vaccination. Turning pale, he stammered the word. "Vaccination . . ."

Pamela, who was about to kiss him, stared. "What's wrong?"

"Vaccination," he repeated stupidly.

"Have you gone crazy?"

He looked at her as though lost in thought. "Goldfuss knows he is in danger. He will try to leave America and return to Russia. Every traveler to Europe has to be vaccinated against certain diseases. That's the law. And when he is vaccinated he must bring the doctor his birth certificate, so that the number may be noted . . ." He suddenly began stuttering with excitement. "His birth certificate, not his passport . . . his false passport is a 'genuine' false one?"

Pamela went white in her turn. "He's gone mad—absolutely mad."

"No, I haven't. For if Goldfuss handed in a 'false' false birth certificate, then we can at last charge him with a punishable offense—arrest him—and search his apartment—"

"Thomas!"

"Don't bother me now. How many doctors are there in New York?"

"How on earth should I know? At least ten thousand."

"It doesn't matter," said Thomas Lieven, while she stared at him in utter bewilderment. He struck the bed with his fist. "I don't care if every agent in the FBI has to be put on the job. And I don't care if it sends them all crazy. We'll have to try it out!"

[10]

That evening, June 19, 1957, 277 FBI agents were alerted in the city of New York. They were ordered to visit, as a matter of great urgency, a total of 13,810 doctors working in the area, among a population of ten million.

Each one of the 277 carried the photograph of a man about forty-five, with skeptical, intelligent features, large ears and thin lips. He wore spectacles.

That evening the 277 men with their 277 photographs put the same question a countless number of times. "Doctor, do you know this man? Is he one of your patients? Have you by any chance vaccinated him recently?"

The question was put all through the following day also.

Meanwhile a certain German export merchant named Peter Scheuner sat in the Waldorf-Astoria on tenterhooks. From time to time his telephone bell rang. The callers were FBI agents who informed Thomas by code words that the operation was still continuing without success. Each time Thomas replaced the receiver with a sigh.

This situation changed abruptly on June 21 at 4:35 P.M. Once again the telephone bell rang. A deep voice said: "Zero."

Thomas, electrified, sprang to his feet. "Where?" was all he said.

The voice answered: "3145 Riverside Drive. Dr. Willcox."

Twenty minutes later Thomas Lieven stood in Dr. Ted Willcox's little consulting room. The doctor was an elderly man who had set up practice in a poor quarter of New York.

He held a photograph in his hand and said: "Of course I remember this man, if only because well-dressed people so seldom come to see me."

Well, there at last you made a mistake, you super-agent of the Soviet Union, thought Thomas. You visited a doctor living as far away as possible from your own place. I understand why. And yet it was wrong. Dr. Willcox continued: "He came to see me in the afternoon of June 16, and I vaccinated him. Then I handed him a so-called International Epidemics Pass, such as is required by travelers to Europe, for instance." The old doctor limped across to his card index cabinet and turned up his notes for June 16. He drew out a card. "The man's name was Martin Collins. According to his birth certificate he was born an American citizen on July 7, 1910, in Manhattan. The number of the certificate was: 32027/7/71897."

At a quarter-past Thomas Lieven and a permanent member of the FBI staff obliged two officials in the Manhattan registry of births to work overtime. After a long time one of them came shuffling back, blew the dust off a yellowed registration card and growled: "Martin Collins . . . Collins, Martin—what's the meaning of that twaddle? Didn't you say 32027/7/71897?"

"I did," Thomas nodded.

The official looked up at him. "Then listen to me. Birth Certificate 32027/7/71897 was issued on January 4, 1898, for a certain Emilie Woermann, who died on January 6, 1902, at the age of four. Of pneumonia."

Thomas glanced at the FBI agent, saying quietly: "Now we have the fellow."

[11]

A brass plate on the door read:

EMIL ROBERT GOLDFUSS

Outside the door in question, on the top floor of the huge apartment block at 252 Fulton Street, stood two men. It was 7:06 P.M. on June 21, 1957. One of the men drew a pistol from his shoulder holster and released the safety catch. The other drew an old-fashioned gold repeater out of his pocket. "That's funny," said Thomas Lieven. "It's only just seven and I'm terribly hungry." The FBI man banged on the door, stepped aside and leveled his revolver.

The door opened. A lean man in a blue painter's smock, holding a palette in his hand, stood on the threshold. His winning smile radiated sympathy and intelligence. With a glance at the agent's pistol he inquired: "What's this for, sir? Is it a joke? An ad? Or a gift?"

"Mr. Goldfuss or Mark or Collins," said the FBI man, "or whatever you like to call yourself, you're under arrest."

"Who's arresting me?"

"The FBI."

"My dear sir," said the other in a friendly tone, "you can't arrest me. I haven't committed any punishable offense and you haven't a warrant."

"Oh, yes, we have, Mr. Goldfuss," said Thomas, taking a step toward him. Thomas's features also bore a winning smile.

"Who are you?"

"A friend of the family," replied Thomas. "I mean the FBI family. I must tell you, Mr. Goldfuss, that a warrant for your arrest was drawn up several days ago. We only needed a decent excuse to fill in on the form. Yesterday we found a very nice one. A false birth certificate."

Two men suddenly appeared from the floor below and two others from the attic.

Thomas said: "We brought these dear friends with us because we know, of course, that you're not only a charming forger of birth certificates."

"Oh? What else am I, then?"

"Probably the best agent the Soviet Union ever had," Thomas Lieven rejoined with a smile. "And I never pay undeserved compliments."

Goldfuss smiled back at him. The two men looked at each other in silence for a long moment.

The studio apartment was immediately searched. The FBI men found the birth certificate in the name of Martin Collins, papers in the name of Goldfuss, $3545 in cash, a steamer ticket to Europe in the name of Collins, booked for July 1, 1957, and a powerful short-wave transmitter of the Hallicrafter type, standing quite unconcealed between two pictures.

The FBI men helped Mr. Goldfuss to pack a small bag. Thomas noticed that in the process he threw away a few obviously used paper handkerchiefs. When Thomas retrieved these crumpled flimsies from the wastepaper basket, Goldfuss turned as pale as a corpse. Thomas smoothed out the handkerchiefs carefully. A few dark spots, no more noticeable than fly specks, were visible.

"H'm," grunted Thomas. Twenty years of secret service in the most various countries at the constant risk of his life had left him extremely observant.

Two days later sensational news broke in the United States. The most dangerous Russian agent of all time had been apprehended. Microfilms which he had hidden in used paper handkerchiefs revealed the complicated code he used, his true name and his true history.

He held the rank of colonel in the Russian secret service and had been able to work as a spy in the States, undisturbed and unsuspected, for ten years. His name was Rudolf Ivanovich Abel.

By the evening of June 23, 1957, teleprinters were tapping out information of his arrest and its importance to the newspaper offices of five continents, all over the world. Even during the following days and weeks the exploits of Colonel Rudolf Ivanovich Abel continued to reach the headlines. The world learned a lot about him, but by no means all.

The world never learned, for instance, of the luncheon to which one cheerful gentleman and two solemn gentlemen sat down on August 17, 1957, in a luxurious log cabin situated among the idyllic wooden slopes of the state of Maryland.

MENU

Calf Kidneys in Champagne
Larded Pike
Pineapple Dessert

MARYLAND, 17 AUGUST 1957

Lieven's kidneys in champagne
Made even big shots think again.

Calf Kidneys in Champagne

Remove the fat and skin from two calf kidneys, cut them into cubes, fry them for three minutes in very hot butter. Season with pepper and salt. Bring them to the table in a chafing dish over a spirit lamp. Pour a small glass of cognac over the kidneys. Light the flame. Put it out with champagne. Add one cup of sliced mushrooms, braised in butter, and a tablespoonful of chopped parsley. Reheat the whole but do not boil. Fill into individual tart shells made of unsweetened puff or short pastry.

Larded Pike

Rub the cleaned fish with pepper and salt, sprinkle it with lemon juice and leave it to stand one hour. Dry well. Lard on both sides with strips of fat bacon. Place in a fireproof dish with the back of the fish toward the top. Baste with brown butter and place in a preheated oven. Bake the fish, without turning it, for about half an hour, basting frequently and adding slowly sour cream mixed with a little cornstarch. Serve in the same dish.

Pineapple Dessert

Line a large, flat glass dish with sponge fingers. Pour pineapple juice over them. Cover with a layer of slightly sweetened whipped cream. Fill to the top with pieces of chopped pineapple and preserved morella cherries. Serve very cold.

"Gentlemen," cried Thomas Lieven cheerfully, "why so solemn?" He was looking at J. Edgar Hoover, chief of the United States FBI, and the deeply bronzed, forty-year-old James B. Donovan, whose hair was already a dazzling white. Donovan was to defend the master spy Abel in the forthcoming trial.

Thomas had just emerged from the kitchen. He was carrying a tray with a big saucepan and all sorts of utensils on it. As he put down the tray and lit a spirit lamp standing on a side table near the laid luncheon table itself, he answered his own question. "Well, you're probably both so solemn because you're remembering your wartime experiences when you were always getting in each other's hair as the chiefs of two competing espionage outfits. Isn't that it?"

It looked as though he had scored a bull's-eye. Hoover grunted and Donovan cleared his throat irritably. The latter had in fact been in charge during the war of the famous Office of Strategic Services. He and his men had on several occasions been in conflict with Hoover's FBI.

Thomas placed the saucepan on the spirit lamp. He announced as cheerfully as ever: "Please be seated, gentlemen. In prudent anticipation of your mood I have ventured to dream up and prepare a first course calculated to calm nerves, elevate minds and raise spirits."

He moved the saucepan to and fro over the flame of the lamp. The saucepan contained little cubes of veal kidney, lightly grilled. "I hope this dish will bring us nearer to our objective."

"What objective are you talking about?" Donovan growled suspiciously.

Thomas answered with circumspection, as he poured cognac over the kidneys: "The interests of both your client and the United States of America."

Hoover glanced at Donovan. "Abel will go to the electric chair, that's certain. We've more than enough evidence against him."

Donovan shrugged his shoulders. "I shall be interested to hear, just the same, how you're going to prove that my client is a Russian spy."

Thomas shook his head. "Such a pity. Such a waste of a unique talent. Lamentable, really lamentable."

"What do you mean by that?"

"I mean it's lamentable to think of a man like Abel being grilled on the chair."

"I should be obliged if you'd be a little more tactful just before lunch, Mr. Scheuner."

"I beg your pardon. But really my heart bleeds. Abel is not only gifted. He is a genius."

"Oh, come now!"

"It's true, Mr. Donovan. Might I remind you that during the war you tried to operate in Switzerland on behalf of the Office of Strategic Services? Within six months the Swiss tracked you down and deported you. But Abel worked for ten years in the States without being spotted."

"Never mind the hot air." Donovan glanced at Hoover. "I know you people are after something. You can't suggest it to me officially. So come around to the back door. Now then, out with it!"

"And now the champagne," said Thomas Lieven, pouring the wine in question into the heated saucepan. Immediately an extraordinarily stimulating and most promising odor of well-being began to circulate.

"Aaaahhh!" murmured Hoover, leaning back in his chair. Even Donovan's nervous features relaxed in a brief smile.

"You see," said Thomas. "It's working already." Busy at the side table, he went on casually: "The FBI is holding back the weightiest pieces of evidence against Abel. He won't be sentenced to death."

"To what then?"

"I beg your pardon?" Thomas wrinkled his forehead censoriously. "Mr. Donovan, I'm surprised at you! Surely you wouldn't begrudge your client a few years more of life?"

"Don't twist my words about! It was Mr. Hoover who said Abel would have to go to the electric chair."

"According to the law, yes," Thomas replied, as he handed around portions of his delicate first course. "But suppose the FBI had its own plans for the future of your client?"

"What would happen then?"

"Well, then of course there would be alternatives to the death sentence. Penal servitude for life for thirty years perhaps or for twenty or for ten . . ."

"What about the evidence for the prosecution which Mr. Hoover mentioned?"

"Evidence can be held back, in part at least. The most damaging part. But for heaven's sake start eating, Mr. Donovan. Your kidneys will really be getting cold."

Abel's white-haired defense counsel began to eat mechanically. Then he glanced up at Thomas with narrowed eyes, still chewing. "And what good would it do you if you . . ." Something went down the wrong way and he had to cough. Thomas clapped him on the back solicitously.

"There you are, you see. I wanted to tell you a moment ago, but I hadn't got the courage. I thought it would be impertinent to draw the attention of a man of your standing to such a thing."

"To what thing?" Donovan groaned, red in the face and gasping for breath.

"To the inadvisability of speaking with one's mouth full," rejoined our friend modestly. "But I think you're all right again now."

James B. Donovan laid down his knife and fork, compressing his lips. His voice sounded as would that of an icicle, if an icicle could speak. "Let's drop this cat and mouse business. Give me a straight answer. What would the the FBI get out of holding back the most damaging evidence against Abel and so saving his life?"

Thomas looked at Hoover. "Won't you answer that question, sir?"

Hoover muttered something incomprehensible and bent low over his plate.

"Well done," said Thomas. "I'm always left to answer the most awkward questions and I enjoy it. I can tell you then, Mr. Donovan, that in all probability the FBI would then have the chance, sooner or later, to save the life of an American agent."

"An American agent?"

"Mr. Donovan, I'm really most awfully reluctant to poke about in the internal organs of the American secret service, but after all you yourself were at one time a member of the club, weren't you? And in those days, toward the end of the war, you did help to build up a counter-intelligence service against the Soviet Union—or didn't you?"

James B. Donovan did not reply.

"I don't blame you for doing it," said Thomas with a wink. "After all, it was your job. That's true enough . . . no one could consider it paradoxical for you of all people to defend a Russian spy today."

"I felt it my duty to do so. The law might as well prove its objectivity."

"Oh, no blame should be attributed to you at all," Thomas declared indulgently.

"I presume that every country has its news service," Donovan went on in a slightly vexed tone.

"It must never be caught, that's all," Hoover mumbled, still bending over his plate.

"Just so," said Thomas. "All the same I can already foresee the day—simply on the theory of probabilities—when the Russians will catch an American agent. It might really happen, don't you think? Do take some more kidneys, gentlemen." He served them with elegant gestures. "For example I have heard that the secret service has for some years been sending out special aircraft which don't only photograph the clouds over foreign countries."

"That's a mere rumor, utterly without foundation, of course," said J. Edgar Hoover, still without lifting his head.

"Of course, of course," said Thomas quietly. Donovan had suddenly begun to listen very intently. "The Soviet protests against violations of Russian air space are also of course entirely without foundation."

Hoover looked up, winking one eye. "The aircraft concerned are always on meteorological duty and deviate from their lines of flight by chance."

"Obviously. But what would happen if one of those—ahem—meteorological pilots were shot down by chance?" Thomas inquired.

Donovan said slowly: "I know those meteorological aircraft. They could never be shot down by anti-aircraft guns. They fly much too high."

"The non-existent may come to exist. Apart from that I hear that there have now been for some time rockets which can be very accurately aimed. If such a rocket shoots down such an American meteorological pilot in Russian skies and he survives and is tried and is a meteorological pilot whom Mr. Hoover would be happy to see again, wouldn't it then be a pity if Mr. Abel had already departed this life? A corpse is no use as a bargaining counter, gentlemen."

"Really, Mr. Scheuner," said J. Edgar Hoover in a strangled tone. "Your cynicism goes too far."

"Your pardon, gentlemen. I was really only speaking of a possibility, a pure hypothesis."

The lawyer said with great deliberation: "And suppose none of our meteorological pilots ever gets shot down?"

"There now," said Thomas affably. "I see that at last we understand each other, Mr. Donovan. I could well imagine that Mr. Abel, out of sheer gratitude, might decide to change fronts and work for the American secret service."

James B. Donovan gave J. Edgar Hoover a steady look. "Is that also your opinion?"

"You heard what Mr. Scheuner said. I have nothing to add."

The lawyer turned a deep crimson. "Who on earth do you think I am, Mr. Scheuner? Who do you think my client is? You're dropping pretty broad hints, aren't you?"

"Oh," said Thomas modestly. "I'm only building castles in the air, Mr. Donovan. That's all."

"My client will never agree to any such arrangement," James B. Donovan exclaimed.

[12]

On August 24, 1957, a certain Peter Scheuner visited the warden of the prison where Abel was being held. He had obtained permission from the highest quarters to talk to Rudolf Ivanovich Abel alone. The warden himself conducted this obviously Very Important Person through endless corridors to the interview room.

When they entered, they saw Abel standing in a smart civilian suit behind a barrier of finely meshed wire netting. He eyed Thomas gravely. The warden waved his hand at the guards in the room. They followed him out. The heavy iron doors closed.

Thomas Lieven and the Russian spy stood watching each other in silence, through the wire netting, for quite a time. It was very still in the room. Then Thomas began to speak.

We do not know what he said and we do not know what Abel answered. Abel never talked about it. Nor did Thomas. Their interview lasted forty-nine minutes.

The trial of Rudolf Ivanovich Abel began on September 26,

1957. His honor Judge Mortimer Byers presided. The hearing was for the most part public.

Abel had made sure, by a trick, of securing the services of one of the best lawyers in the United States. When he was requested to name his defense counsel, he explained: "I have no money. The $3545 found in my apartment are not mine. And I can't expect anyone to defend me for nothing. I therefore request the Court to provide me with an attorney."

The trial had unprecedented features. The accused was permitted to move freely about the building, to take his meals with the jury in the canteen and to talk to reporters. On the other hand Judge Byers ordered: "None of the thirty-eight witnesses is to enter the court for the purpose of hearing the whole course of the trial until he has given his evidence."

Most of the thirty-eight would not in fact have found it necessary to attend the court from the beginning, since from the afternoon of the first day onward they could read the most detailed descriptions of the proceedings in the newspapers.

For security reasons the FBI agents and other endangered persons giving evidence had to appear on the witness stand with their faces covered. They wore hoods provided with small apertures for mouth and eyes.

Thomas Lieven also appeared with a head covering of this description. There was a card affixed to his chest with a number on it, as in all the other cases of masked witnesses.

Extracts from his examination in court by Judge Byers, taken down in shorthand, read as follows.

Q. Number seventeen, you were present when Mr. Abel was arrested. Describe his behavior.

A. Mr. Abel was very calm. He only became upset during the search of his premises.

Q. Why?

A. Because a radio was turned on full blast in the apartment next door. Elvis Presley was singing. Mr. Abel pressed both fists against his ears. He exclaimed—and I report his exact words—"That is sheer poison to the nerves. This chap is the main reason why I want to return to Russia." (Laughter.)

Q. I must insist on absolute quiet in court. Number seventeen, you interviewed some of the tenants of the block. What were their impressions of Mr. Abel?

A. The best conceivable. They all thought him a most admirable human being. He had painted many portraits of them and also of officials of the branch of the FBI which was situated in the building. (Sensation in court.)

Q. He painted officials of the FBI?

A. Half a dozen of them, your honor. And very good portraits they were, too.

Q. According to the papers submitted in this case Abel kept the short-wave transmitter he was in the habit of using quite openly in his studio.

A. That is so, your honor.

Q. Did it not attract the attention of the FBI agents whom he painted?

A. It did. Many asked to have the apparatus explained to them. They supposed Abel to be an amateur wireless expert. Once the transmitter began to function while Abel was painting one of the agents. He sent a brief reply. Transmission then ceased. The agent asked: "Who was transmitting then?" Abel replied: "Who do you think it was? Moscow, of course!" (Loud laughter.)

Q. If that occurs again I shall have the court cleared. Number seventeen, it was you who picked up a quantity of old paper handkerchiefs in which Abel had concealed tiny rolls of microfilm. One of them contained the key to a complicated cipher. Did you succeed in decoding the message which the defendant had written out immediately before his arrest, in the form of several four-figure groups of numbers?

A. I did so succeed, your honor.

Q. What was the message?

A. (read out from a card) "We congratulate you on your lovely rabbit. Don't forget to practice your Beethoven score. Smoke your pipe, but hold the red book in your right hand."

Q. That cannot possibly be the text in clear.

A. Of course not, your honor. It is the deciphered numerical code. Abel seems to have double-coded all his messages.

Q. What about the key to the second code?

A. I'm afraid it never came to light, your honor. (Loud laughter. Sensation in court. Judge Byers adjourned the hearing at 11:34 A.M.)

The trial lasted nearly a month. The jury then retired to consider their verdict. They debated for hours, while the spectators and the reporters grew more and more restless. They wondered what could be keeping the jury so long.

It was not until a quarter to eight on the evening of October 23 that the jury returned. A deep silence fell in court. All present rose. Judge Byers asked: "Well, Mr. Foreman, have you decided upon your verdict?"

"Yes, your honor."

"Then how say you?"

"Our unanimous verdict is that the accused is guilty in the sense of the indictment."

Not a muscle twitched in the features of Rudolf Ivanovich Abel.

On November 15 judgment was pronounced. The accused was sentenced to thirty years' imprisonment and ordered to pay a fine of two thousand dollars.

Such a sentence on the greatest Russian spy of all time was found incomprehensible. The entire country was bewildered by it. But only for a few days. Then the Abel case, like everything else in life, was forgotten.

By a strange coincidence, in the summer of 1960, as these lines were going to press, history, so to speak, overhauled us and made the forecast of our friend Thomas Lieven a reality. We hope that the kindly-disposed reader will pardon a short leap forward into the present. We must attempt it, for otherwise the story of the Abel case would remain incomplete.

On May 1, 1960, an American reconnaissance aircraft of the U2 type fell into the hands of the Soviets near the Russian city of Sverdlovsk. All newspapers carried the headline: AMERICAN AIRCRAFT SHOT DOWN BY RUSSIAN ROCKET. The pilot answered to the name of Francis G. Powers. He was thirty years old, married and a citizen of the state of Virginia in North America. The event occurred at a time of great political tension, immediately before the so-called Paris summit conference, at which Eisenhower, Khrushchev, Macmillan and De Gaulle were to discuss the prospects of world peace. The Sverdlovsk incident served the Soviet Union as a pretext for cancellation of the conference before it had even started.

The pilot was brought before a military court in Moscow. The Soviets made the occasion one of a great stroke of propaganda. Rudenko, the public prosecutor, who had acted as such on behalf of Russia at the Nurenberg trials, declared in his opening speech: "In this court not only the pilot Powers but also the Government of the United States, the true instigator and organizer of this outrageous crime, stands on trial."

Although the public prosecutor had characterized the crime as "outrageous," he showed a more reasonable spirit at the conclusion of his speech. "I take the remorse of the defendant into consideration and do not insist upon the death penalty." He asked for a sentence of fifteen years' imprisonment. The Court reduced this period to ten years.

The Soviet spy Abel, sentenced to thirty years' incarceration, had a wife, a married daughter and a small son in Russia. They had not been allowed to testify at his trial. On the other hand the wife of Powers, his parents and his mother-in-law received entry permits to the Soviet Union and were given special seats at his trial.

Oliver Powers, the defendant's father, a respectable shoemaker, told journalists: "I hope that Khrushchev will pardon my poor boy. After all, the Russian leader lost a son in the war against the Germans, in which our soldiers fought side by side with the Russians. But if Khrushchev cannot pardon my son perhaps he could be exchanged for a soviet spy who has been imprisoned in the United States. I mean the secret agent Abel."

So what will happen now?

Hard to say.

[13]

Now let us return with all speed to the autumn of 1957. And once more we have to apologize, this time to the Federal Bureau of Investigation itself, for speaking of the "Harper Clinic," which of course, since we wish to oblige the FBI in this matter, is not called by any such name. Nor do we intend to state where it is situated. But it exists, we know where it is and we also know its right name.

It was on October 23, 1957, that the Soviet spy Abel was found guilty. On October 25 two persons visited J. Edgar Hoover's office in Washington. They were Thomas Lieven and Pamela Faber.

The beautiful young woman with blue-black hair and wide, glowing red lips repeatedly glanced sideways, with great affection, at Thomas Lieven.

Hoover was in good temper. He greeted the pair heartily.

"What can I do for you?" he asked.

"You can redeem your promise," said Thomas amiably. "You remember that I once asked you the favor of allowing me to die once my mission was fulfilled?"

"Yes, I remember," answered Hoover slowly.

"Well," exclaimed Pamela cheerfully. "Now the time has come. We want to be married as soon as possible afterward."

Hoover bit his underlip. "Naturally I'll keep my word," he said. "But you mustn't suppose that it will be a pleasant job, Mr. Lieven. Things like that hurt. They hurt like hell."

"Well, one should be ready to do anything to ensure one's death," Thomas remarked. "Apart from that, I hear you have some really first-class men at the Harper Clinic."

He didn't call it the Harper.

"Very well, then. I'll fix it up with them. Have a good death and be very, very happy with Pamela. All the same, it may be weeks before you're dead. We shall have to wait until we can find a corpse that looks like you. They don't crop up every day."

"Really, Mr. Hoover, in a big country like the United States you ought soon to be able to hunt up something suitable," said Thomas Lieven.

On October 27, Thomas Lieven, accompanied by Pamela Faber, entered the Harper Clinic, a secluded building surrounded by high walls and guarded day and night by FBI agents. It lies somewhere in the United States.

Thomas was given a comfortable room with a window overlooking a great park. Pamela was accommodated next door. As soon as they had settled in she came to see him. They took two hours to say hello to each other.

At last Pamela murmured, with a tired, happy sigh: "Oh, how wonderful it is to be alone with you after all this time!"

"When they give us the chance," he said, caressing her affectionately. "It's really a funny sort of situation. Just think, I'm going to have a new face, new papers, a new name and a new nationality—everything will be new! Not many people are so lucky." He kissed her. "How would you like me to look then, my sweet?"

"What do you mean?"

"Well, you know, when they begin cutting up my face, I shall undoubtedly be allowed to make certain suggestions. Regarding my ears or nose, for instance."

Pamela had to laugh. "As a matter of fact, when I was a child I was mad about the Greeks. I used to think, the man I marry must have a Grecian profile. Do you suppose . . . er . . ." She blushed. "Oh, it's too silly," she murmured.

"You mean you'd like a Grecian nose?" he inquired indulgently. "Well, if that's all! My ears all right?"

"Absolutely, darling. Everything else is quite in order."

"Are you sure? Now's the time, you know! The operation will be like washing up dishes. The doctors here can unquestionably make everything about me nicer—bigger or smaller—just as you wish . . ."

"No," she cried passionately. "No! Otherwise everything ought to remain exactly as it is!"

[14]

During the next few days three doctors had their hands full dealing with Thomas. They photographed him, measured his skull and left no part of him unexamined. Then he was forbidden to smoke. Then he was forbidden to drink. Then Pamela had to— Then Thomas had to drop everything.

They operated on him on November 7. When he recovered consciousness he was lying in his room with his head bandaged and painful.

On the fourth day after the operation he began slowly to feel better. The doctors changed his bandages. Pamela sat all day at his bedside and talked to him. But she could only tell him serious stories. For whenever he tried to laugh under his bandages it still hurt.

One day an impatiently awaited telegram arrived for Mr. Grey, as he was known at the Clinic. He read:

AUNT VERA ARRIVED SAFELY STOP BEST LOVE EDGAR

Pamela read the telegram with him. She uttered a happy little cry and squeezed his hand. "They've found the corpse, darling! They've found the right corpse!"

"Nothing can go wrong now," Thomas commented, with satisfaction. But he was mistaken. Something did go wrong unfortunately, most unfortunately. On November 13 a worried gentleman with melancholy eyes and a heavy cold arrived at the clinic. He asked to see Mr. Grey alone and then introduced himself as John Misaras, FBI agent. He brought bad news.

"An annoying thing happened to that body. We're most distressed about it, Mr. Grey, believe me."

"What happened to it then?" Thomas asked anxiously.

"It's gone."

"Where is it now then?"

"In Ankara."
"Aha," Thomas murmured, disconcerted.
"It's been buried."
"Aha," Thomas murmured for the second time.
"There were five bodies available that day, you know. And two were mixed up. Ours and another. We still have the other, a Turkish diplomat. But unfortunately he doesn't look like you. It's a pity."
"Aha," murmured Thomas for the third time.
"You don't understand?"
"Sorry. Not a word."
"We found a corpse without relatives in Detroit. Might have been your twin brother. Died of a heart attack. We gave the body suitable treatment—"
"Treatment?"
"Yes. And then we packed it in a special coffin to be flown to Europe. My boss wanted to ensure its safety. So as not to attract the attention of other agents, he had our corpse flown to Europe in an aircraft which had four other coffins on board. It was a charter plane hired by the Turkish Embassy. One of their diplomats had been killed in a car accident together with his wife and their two grown-up children. The affair was reported in all the newspapers at the time and also the fact that an aircraft had been hired to transport the bodies. Consequently no one took any notice when we brought another coffin on board. Didn't strike anyone as peculiar."
"I understand."
"Unfortunately a mistake was made in Paris, where our coffin was to be unloaded. The other four were to be flown on to Ankara. We had of course specially marked the coffin with our own body. But a transmission error had crept into the coded telegram and our people in Paris accordingly unloaded the wrong coffin."
"Oh God."
"Yes, it's most embarrassing. We found the Turkish diplomat himself in the coffin."
"And . . . and . . . and what about the corpse that looked like me?"
"It was buried yesterday in Ankara. In the family vault. I'm really sorry, Mr. Grey, but we can't do anything more about it. We must wait till we find another one for you."

So Thomas and Pamela waited. On November 19, another telegram arrived for Mr. Grey.

UNCLE FRED SAFE STOP BEST LOVE EDGAR

"So they've found another suitable body," Pamela whispered.

"We'd better keep our fingers crossed in case anything else goes wrong," Thomas said. But this time all went well. The second suitable body lay, while Thomas and Pamela clenched their fingers over their thumbs, on the operating table of a trusted doctor on the staff of the FBI in Chicago. The dead man looked extraordinarily like Thomas Lieven. The doctor, working from photographs of Thomas, used hydrogen peroxide and paraffin injections and other ingenious methods to ensure that the corpse came to resemble Thomas Lieven more and more. Meanwhile collaborators of the FBI held in readiness articles of clothing and other objects which had belonged to Thomas, including his gold repeater and four passports in different names.

One of the FBI agents watched with particular interest the cosmetic surgeon as he injected a little liquid paraffin into the dead man's nose. "Who was this fellow, by the way?" asked the surgeon.

"Lucky Campanello," said the agent. "Narcotics, blackmail and white slave traffic. Couple of hours ago some of my pals shot it out with him. They were lucky. He wasn't."

"So I see," said the doctor, looking at the place where a revolver bullet had penetrated the heart of Lucky Campanello.

In his forty-seven years of life on this earth Campanello had always done evil and lived from evil. He had never given pleasure to anyone. No one had loved him. Many had hated him. He had no relatives. And that circumstance enabled him to play for the first time an important positive part in life—after his death.

As soon as the doctor in Chicago had finished with him, Lucky was flown to Malta in a special receptacle. An American ship lay at anchor in the harbor. The special receptacle was rushed at high speed from the airfield to the ship. A few minutes later the vessel put to sea.

At midnight on November 20, she was rocking gently off Lisbon, outside Portuguese territorial waters. A boat was lowered. Three living men and one who had ceased to live found accommodation in it. The boat made for the coast.

On the early morning of November 21, 1957, accordingly, children playing on the white beach of the fishing village of Cascais near Lisbon found all sorts of shells, starfish, half dead fish and a dead man.

EPILOGUE

[1]

Well, and what is the rest of the story? How does it end? What else happened to Thomas Lieven and his Pamela? Who told us the tale of all his wild adventures? How on earth did we come to be in a position to describe contemporary events hitherto kept secret and top secret?

Many questions! We can answer all of them. But for that purpose it will be necessary, unfortunately, for someone to emerge from the shadows where his profession obliges and always will oblige him to remain.

That man is myself. I, the author who has written down for you the adventures and the recipes of the secret agent Thomas Lieven.

In August 1958 I flew to the United States on behalf of my publishers. It was understood that I should stay a month. I stayed four. I was supposed to collect material for a novel. The novel was never written.

But the story you are reading was. I came on the scent of it over there. And the scent originated—how else could it?—in the company of an enchantingly beautiful woman.

I have good reasons for not mentioning the name of the city where I first saw the lady. It was a mild September afternoon. I was hungry. A journalist friend had recommended a connoisseurs' restaurant. I was on my way to it. Then I saw her.

She was walking ahead of me on high heels. She wore a beige costume, had blue-black hair and a lovely figure. She was of medium height and built like a racing yacht.

Suddenly my hunger was forgotten.

I hope my beloved Lulu will forgive me. She knows men. She knows that they are all alike and a worthless lot when they are allowed to go traveling alone.

For just over half a mile of pavement I played my wicked

tricks. Sometimes I walked in front of her, sometimes behind. The longer I looked at her the better I liked her. Forgive me, dearest Lulu, forgive me! You know I love only you!

The lady, naturally, noticed what I was up to. Once she smiled briefly. She was not annoyed. Nice ladies are never annoyed. She only walked rather faster. So did I.

Then I saw the restaurant my friend had recommended to me. And then something unexpected happened. That interesting lady did not pass the restaurant. On the contrary, she entered it.

Well, all I can do is the same, I thought. I followed her. I had no idea what was in store for me on the other side of the door.

In the little check room I caught up with that beautiful lady. She was standing in front of the mirror fixing her hair.

"Hello," I said in English.

She smiled into the mirror and also said "Hallo!"

I bowed and mentioned my name. Then I said: "Madame, I must tell you that from birth I have suffered from pathological shyness. I have never in my life even dreamed of speaking to someone I did not know."

"Is that so?" she said, turning around.

"That is so. But today, when I saw you, I just couldn't help it. Madame, you have helped me to conquer my inferiority complex. I thank you. That calls for a celebration. I believe they serve a wonderfully good breast of pheasant with vegetables here."

She looked at me gravely.

"Yes, the breast of pheasant here is excellent."

"In that case may I precede you?" I stepped forward. She followed me.

The restaurant was of only medium size. It was furnished in an uncommonly ageeeable antique style and absolutely crammed. There was only one table free, in a corner. But a small card on it bore the word RESERVED.

A waiter hurried up to us. I gave him five dollars and said: "How nice of you to have kept that table so long for us."

I helped the charming lady to take her seat. Said she: "We'll have breast of pheasant with vegetables for two, Henry. Crayfish soup first. But before that an apéritif. What would you say to a dry martini, Mr. Simmel?"

Lucky I have such a generous publisher, I thought. My word, this will have to be another item on the expense account!

"I should prefer a small whisky if that's all right with you," I replied.

"So should I," said the lady. "Two doubles then, Henry."

"Right, boss," said the waiter and hurried away.

"What was that?" I asked. "Did he call you boss?"

"He did."

"But why?"

"Because I'm the boss here." She laughed. "You might have saved yourself those five dollars."

"Oh, my publisher pays that, you know."

"Your publisher? Are you an author?"

"Some people consider me one, others don't, Miss—er—"

"Thompson, Pamela Thompson," said she, suddenly glancing at me with real interest. I wondered why.

"You are suddenly looking at me with real interest, Miss Thompson," I said. "Why?"

"Because you are an author, Mr. Simmel. I have a special liking for authors."

"How wonderful, Miss Thompson!"

To cut a long story short, ladies and gentlemen, the crayfish soup was excellent, the breast of pheasant enchanting. I talked without stopping. And with prodigious brilliance, that goes without saying. By the coffee stage she had consented to visit a cinema with me. "Okay, Mr. Simmel. I'll arrange for our tickets. I know the manager. The show begins at half-past eight. Perhaps you could call for me?"

"Most willingly, Miss Thompson."

"Shall we say half-past seven, then? That will give us time for a drink at my place before leaving."

"Half-past seven will be fine."

Heavens, I thought, my influence over women is positively uncanny! Damn it all, I should have been a movie star!

[2]

That afternoon I visited a barber. Then I bought a couple of fine orchids. I put on my best suit, the dark blue one. Punctually at half-past seven, a cellophane carton in my hand, I rang the bell of an apartment with a brass plate on the door bearing the name THOMPSON.

I didn't have to wait long. The door opened. A man stood on the threshold. He seemed about fifty and was tall and slender, with a narrow face, shrewd eyes, a high forehead and graying temples. He had an aristocratic Greek nose and a small mustache of the kind ladies are so fond of.

"I take it you're Mr. Simmel," said he. "Come along in. I'm very glad to know you. My wife has been telling me about you."

"Your . . . ahem . . . your wife?"

"Yes, my wife. My name's Thompson. Roger Thompson."

There was a movement behind him. Pamela, my charming Pamela, entered the little hall. She wore a green cocktail dress adorned with gold arabesques and cut very low. She was smiling radiantly, with a great air of innocence. "So there you are! Oh, what wonderful orchids! Isn't he charming, Roger? I hope you won't mind, by the way, if my husband comes with us to the movies?"

My beloved Lulu, who knows me inside out, went into fits of laughter when I told her this story later on. "Splendid!" she cried. "You deserved that!"

I felt very sorry for myself that evening at the movies. My seat was uncomfortably hard. And it was hot. I also had a bit of a headache. And when I saw that Mr. and Mrs. Thompson were holding hands, once the newsreel was over, I said to myself, There's a typical case of a wasted evening!

But I was making another mistake, quite a huge one, in saying that.

For that evening, after we came out of the theater, proved to be the pleasantest I had ever spent in America. We had supper, naturally, in the Thompsons' restaurant. And what a supper that was. My goodness! Mr. Thompson did the ordering. He went into the kitchen himself, leaving me alone for a while with Pamela.

"Are you angry with me?" she asked.

"Oh, no."

"I liked you so much earlier today, you know . . . you were so nice . . . I enjoyed everything you said . . ."

"What in particular?"

"That you were fond of good meals and the company of good-looking women, that you didn't ever want to wear a uniform again, that you felt at home anywhere in the world where you had friends . . ."

"There's something else I should like to say, dear lady."

"Yes?"

"I . . . I . . . I think your husband's also very nice . . . I like him very much . . ."

She beamed. "Yes, he is nice, isn't he? But you don't really know him. You don't know what I've been through with him. You don't know his ideas. In my case the head always ruled the heart. Men whom I couldn't admire for what they said and thought I could never really love. In Roger's case I loved him at first sight and he became the great love of my life . . ."

"But . . . but why, then, did you invite me to call on you, Mrs. Thompson?"

"Pamela."

"Why did you, Pamela?"

"Because you are an author . . . perhaps you'll understand what I mean later. Or perhaps you won't. It all depends on him."

"Do you do everything he tells you?"

"Yes." She gave me a radiant smile. "And he does everything I tell him. Always. He's always asking my advice. Sometimes, of course, he seems a bit queer, like all men. But he always comes back to me. I know I'm the only woman he would ever care to live with. That gives a woman a lot of strength, don't you think so?"

Life's funny.

What I expected didn't happen. I didn't get what I wanted from Pamela. I got something better. Her friendship and that of her husband.

We met almost daily during the next three weeks. We got on like a house on fire. It seemed as though we really agreed about everything.

It often struck me that Thompson was watching me in a thoughtful, intent sort of way. Then it struck me that he was asking me a lot of questions. About my past, my views and my experiences. Especially about my views. He himself gave me no personal information at all.

I collected materials for the new novel, as I had been instructed. For that purpose I occasionally had to leave the city. I was always glad to come back, for the Thompsons met me every time, at the railway station or the airfield. As soon as I considered I had collected enough material I booked my flight to Frankfurt-am-Main. My aircraft was due to start on October 29, 1958, at 8:45 P.M.

On the twenty-eighth Roger Thompson called me up at my hotel. "I hear you're leaving us," he said. "And I should like to invite you to a last little meal."

"That would be marvelous, Roger."

"Shall we say this evening at half-past seven, then?"

"Half-past seven is okay by me."

"One more thing. Call up your airline and cancel your reservation for tomorrow evening."

"Why?"

"Well, because I think you might want to stay a bit longer."

"I don't understand."

I heard him laugh. "Tomorrow evening," he said, "you'll understand everything. And for goodness' sake don't bring another couple of orchids with you!"

So I brought three. And Pamela was more enchantingly beautiful than ever, Roger more charming than ever and the meal, which he had cooked himself, better than ever. The first course consisted of boiled turbot served with fried oysters in a fine Dutch sauce containing caviar.

MENU

Turbot and Oysters in Dutch Sauce with Caviar

Wellington Steak with Madeira Sauce

Salzburg Dumplings

SOMEWHERE IN THE UNITED STATES, 28 OCTOBER 1958

At this meal this book was born.

Turbot

A lightly poached turbot is laid, white side up, on a previously warmed dish and surrounded with fried oysters.

Fried Oysters

The oysters should be opened by the fishmonger and kept on ice till needed. The shells are then removed. Next the oysters are dried with a cloth and turned in flour, beaten egg and bread crumbs. The mixture is fried in brown butter and served immediately.

Dutch Sauce with Caviar

Beat two egg yolks in a bowl with a dash of vinegar and a dessertspoonful of hot water. Place the bowl in a saucepan of hot water over a low flame and add half a cup of butter. Whip continuously, without boiling, until the sauce thickens. Season with salt and lemon juice. In the last minute before serving add four tablespoons of caviar to the hot sauce.

Wellington Steak with Madeira Sauce

The central portion of a fillet of beef is fried lightly, cooled and placed on puff pastry over a layer of braised shallots, mushrooms, parsley and tarragon. Place on top of the fillet some goose liver cooked in madeira and some slices of truffles. Fold the other half of the puff pastry over these ingredients, fastening the edges with egg yolk, and bake to a golden color. Prepare sauce in the frying pan used for cooking the fillet and braising the shallots, adding plenty of madeira.

Salzburg Dumplings

Whip six egg whites in a large bowl till stiff, stir in six yolks, with two tablespoonfuls each of flour and sugar, a quarter of a cup of melted butter and a quarter of a cup of warm sweetened milk, flavored with vanilla. Heat a quarter of a cup of butter in a deep iron frying pan, add the mixture from the bowl, cover and bake till bottom is browned. Cut into large dumplings with a slicer, cover, and cook again till bottom is browned. Add another quarter of a cup of the above mentioned vanilla-flavored milk and leave for a short time to stand off heat. The dumplings will absorb the milk and become loose. They must be served, sprinkled with castor sugar, before they disintegrate.

"I've never eaten anything so good as this," I admitted. "I must jot down the recipe for my wife . . ."

"There might be a lot more to jot down than my recipes," murmured the master of the house dreamily.

I glanced at him, then at his beautiful wife. Both were smiling benevolently and affectionately.

Said Roger Thompson: "My dear fellow, I have unlimited confidence in Pamela's judgment. She considered you reliable as soon as she laid eyes on you. I am the sort of man who has to be very careful . . ."

"Indeed? Why so?"

"You may well ask!" Thompson poked at his fish. Then he smiled. "Mario, I didn't always run a restaurant for gourmets. My name wasn't always Roger Thompson. I've lived a very wild life. A little more caviar?"

"Let's be serious," said Pamela. She glanced at me. "My husband has really been through a good deal. Some of it was funny. Some of it was sad. Much was exciting. I've always said someone ought to write it down one day. A lot of people should know what happened to him. They might find it very useful."

"Useful?"

"My husband is a convicted pacifist."

"The only question is," said the man who called himself Roger Thompson, "whether you can promise me that no one will ever know my real name and address if I tell you my story."

"I can promise you that," I said.

[3]

28 october 1958 stop 2348 hours stop schweizer druck and verlagshaus zurich stop return flight canceled stop on track of new story stop air express letter with details follows stop request earliest possible reaction and immediate remittance 1000 dollars stop cordially simmel

[4]

1 november 1958 0945 hours stop schweizer druck and verlagshaus authorises you having read letter with information to arrange option for acquisition of copyright and investigate possibility of soundtrack recording stop stay as long as necessary stop 1000 dollars allotted stop meyer schweizer druck and verlagshaus

I remained in the United States until January 2, 1959. When I left I had in my luggage sixteen double-sized sound recordings. I was taking the story of an exemplary life back to Europe, viz., the adventures and recipes of the secret agent, Thomas Lieven.

I shall now be understood and forgiven if I say that the

man who told me the story of his life was not named Roger Thompson or Thomas Lieven. I shall be understood if I do not mention the name of the city in which he lives and works today with his beautiful wife. Incidentally, he bought his restaurant with the money he earned by his dealings with the German Steel Union share certificates, as reported at the outset of this narrative. The loan advanced to him by the Swiss broker Pierre Muerrli had brought Thomas luck. He had speculated with it successfully and become a wealthy man. As early as the summer of 1958 Pamela flew to Zurich on his instructions and with full powers from him. She handed back Herr Muerrli his 717,850 francs, retrieved the forged certificates from the numbered safe at the bank, tore them up and washed them down the drain of the bath in her hotel suite. So everyone had now made a profit and no one was any the worse, just as Thomas Lieven had foreseen. Moreover, no one had even noticed the kind of fraud he had perpetrated.

Roger Thompson and his wife stood on the balcony of the airport building as my plane taxied faster and faster along the runway on to far horizons, the Atlantic and the Old World. My heart suddenly felt very heavy. Farewell, Pamela. Farewell, Roger. Farewell, you two. I have written down what you told me between you. I hope you'll approve of it. The last yards of the last tape are on the recorder. Thomas Lieven is speaking. I end my story with his words.

"All my life I have distrusted grand phrases and grand heroes. Nor did I ever care for national anthems, uniforms and so-called strong men.

"My old friend Bastian is back in Marseilles. He's getting on well. He works as a cargo superintendent in the harbor. He has to deal with all sorts of people, Chinese and Germans, Frenchmen, Corsicans and Arabs. He likes them all and they all like him. They say: 'First-rate fellow, that. You can talk sense to him.'

"I, too, in my little restaurant, have to deal with all sorts of people. Of the white, the yellow and the black races. Many of my customers are Jews, many Christians. A few Mohammedans also come, and a few Buddhists.

"I like to think that a time will come in which all mankind will live together on this earth as amicably as Bastian's friends and my customers. If a few hundred people get on so splendidly together, why shouldn't two milliards?

"My friend Bastian is called 'sensible' by his fellow workers. I believe that with common sense we can all get by. We are all endowed by nature with the ability to think. If only we could believe less and think more for just a little while! The consequences would be marvelous. There wouldn't even be any wars then. For since it is only human beings who make war, only human beings can have it in their power to prevent it.

"I raise my glass, then, to human reason. May it protect us all, black, yellow and white. May it lead us out of the shadowy valley of fear and into a paradise of peace and good cheer."